MW01273790

The Missing Years

Part III

The Hunt for Matt Crawford

A Tyrell Sloan western-adventure

Author: Brian T. Seifrit

Fan Email: tbseifrit@gmail.com

Website: www.booksbybriant.com

i

The Missing Years Part III
The Hunt for Matt Crawford

The Missing Years Part III
The Hunt for Matt Crawford

Published by

William Jenkins
2503-4288 Grange Street
Burnaby BC V5H 1P2 Canada

williamhenryjenkins@gmail.com
http://www.williamjenkins.ca
Telephone: 1-604-685-4136
Cell: 1-778-953-6139

Edition 1
ISBN: 978-1542788762 and 1542788765
Copyright Brian T. Seifrit © 2017

The Missing Years Part III
The Hunt for Matt Crawford

Foreword

Red Rock Canyon

It all started in the summer of 1890. Tyrell Sloan, being the only living heir to his grandfather's estate in Red Rock Canyon, began his journey to the property. Meeting up with Wilson Wesley, an old trapper from his grandfather's past, Tyrell and Wilson's friendship grows as Wilson relates a few stories about his Grandfather. Tyrell continues on his way to Red Rock Canyon. By coincidence, he meets Fry, an old prospector also known by his deceased Grandfather. The more Tyrell learns about his Grandfather, the greater is his desire to make Red Rock Canyon his home.

Discovering that three of the richest gold claims in all of Kootenay west lie on his land, Tyrell gives his best effort in working the three claims, but soon learns that panning gold isn't something he would like to do for the rest of his life. A mystery unfolds when he finds on a map where a hidden chest of gold that his Grandfather stowed away could be found. He spends some time searching for it and in the end finds pouches of gold worth an estimated value of twenty thousand dollars. Richer now than he ever thought he could be, he hires a mining outfit called The Wake-Up Jake to take over developing the gold claims, keeping the secret about the gold he found. In September of that year, he leaves Red Rock and bequeaths the entire property to a woman he met on his way to his grandfather's site; Marissa McDowell. To the lady who healed him after he was tossed from his horse, Grandma Heddy, he leaves her the sacks of gold he packed to have tested and weighed by her as well as his percentage of all the gold that the Wake-Up Jake mines during their two year contract. Then like a summer breeze, Tyrell slips into history, not telling anyone where he is going.

Return to Red Rock

This story describes what happens when Tyrell returns to Red Rock six years later.

The Missing Years Part I

This is the first story about what happened to Tyrell in the years he was away from Red Rock.

Weeks of tormented dreams about how his Grandfather died leads Tyrell to the town of Willow Gate, west of his hometown of Hells Bottom. There he meets up with the two villainous men of his dreams; Heath Roy and Ollie Johnson while playing cards in local saloon. It is in Willow Gate where a new chapter in Tyrell Sloan's life begins. Killing the two men in a fair gun-fight, he is soon pursued by the local law corrupted by Heath Roy's father, a rich and shrewd businessman, Gabe Roy. Gabe wants to see Tyrell hang and he will do anything and pay any price to see to it. Emma, the woman who Tyrell had defended in the gun fight that took the lives of Heath and Ollie, does not give up Tyrell's true identity. Being the only witness to the killing, she gives the law of Willow Gate a bad description of Tyrell which gives Tyrell time to leave and head into obscurity.

Heading north towards his hometown of Hells Bottom, Tyrell runs across Ed McCoy, a bounty hunter out of Fort Macleod who had just turned in a cattle rustler. Tyrell introduces himself as Travis Sweet. Ed noting that Tyrell was unprepared to be travelling through the unforgiving Rocky Mountains offers Tyrell a meal, which he accepts. Their friendship is secured when Tyrell offers Ed the use of his packing horse after Ed's horse breaks his leg. In turn, Ed offers Tyrell a job if he is ever in need. Parting ways, Tyrell continues north while Ed heads back to Fort Macleod.

Following close behind Tyrell is Riley Scott another bounty hunter known to be one of the best. He was hired by Gabe Roy to track down the killer of his son, Heath. Tyrell, though, outwits Riley and manages to escape.

Finally making his way to Hells Bottom, Tyrell returns home. He spends a few days there with his old friend Bannock who Tyrell had left in charge of the Sloan homestead. The two friends devise a plan to start a rumour that Tyrell Sloan was killed, leaving Tyrell the freedom to travel under the assumed name of Travis Sweet. After writing a fake note that allowed Bannock to be the sole owner of the Sloan homestead in Hells Bottom, Tyrell packs up a few belongings and once more heads north, destination unknown. After travelling for a few days, he meets up with Mac Rider a homesteader married to a Blackfoot Indian named Rose. Mac offers Tyrell a job doing some horse logging and land clearing so that Mac and Rose could build their dream home. Tyrell accepts the offer of the work as well as the accommodations of living in a tepee. Throughout the late summer and long winter Mac and Tyrell work side by side. News about the murder of Rose's father is brought to them by Rose's brother, Half Moon. It is decided that Mac and Tyrell would help track down the perpetrators. Finding the killers some time later, Tyrell and Mac are both taken back by the justice served to the killers. Finally accepting the Blackfoot's way of justice, they head back to Mac's to continue their work in logging.

Only days of being back and while Mac was not at home, a hired gunman named Earl Brubaker, a ruthless and serious gunfighter said to be the quickest draw in the land, confronts Rose and beats her up. He said that the man he was tracking led him there and that the fellow he was tracking went by the name of Tyrell a wanted murderer. Rose denies she even knows anyone named Tyrell, but admits that a man by the name of Travis Sweet works for them. The confrontation between Tyrell and Earl lasts only briefly and once more Tyrell is forced to draw his gun, this time killing the legendary Earl Brubaker. The tale of this deed spreads like wildfire and reaches the ears of Gabe Roy who then sends two more men, Tanner McBride and Buck Ainsworth to offer Travis Sweet the job of tracking down the killer of his son, Heath Roy. Tyrell, of course, turns the offer down. Coincidentally, one of the sent men, Tanner McBride happens to be an associate of Tyrell's, a long lost friend from days gone by. Tanner agrees privately with Tyrell not to reveal his true identity and furthers the story that Tyrell Sloan is dead. Tanner also informs Tyrell that he was also being accused of killing two other men, Eli Ferguson and Noble Bathgate. Tyrell is taken back at this news. Although he hadn't killed Eli or Noble, he had a good idea who had. Now, being accused of two more killings, Tyrell knew that he would hang if caught.

Tanner and Buck return to Willow Gate to relay to Gabe Roy that Travis Sweet had turned down his offer. This doesn't sit well with Gabe and he has a few of his henchmen beat up Buck for whatever reason and his bounty hunting credentials revoked. Fortunately for Tanner, he wasn't at the Willow Gate saloon that day and so he wasn't treated with the same brutality. The law gives Buck one day to leave Willow Gate or face more of the same. Without even talking to Tanner, Buck decides to head to the Yukon, leaving Tanner guessing on where he headed. That was in March 1891.

The Missing Years Part II

On May 30 1891, Tyrell leaves Mac and Rose, the work he had been hired to do now completed. He heads north, deciding as he travelled that he would head into Fort Macleod to retrieve the horse he had lent to Ed

McCoy and perhaps, if the offer still stood, he'd take Ed up on his offer of employment. During his travels he comes across a bulletin board with a wanted poster pinned to it, the poster read: *Tyrell- last name unknown. Wanted for killing Heath Roy, Ollie Johnson, Eli Ferguson and Noble Bathgate. A $2500 reward is offered by the Mounted Police for his capture or information leading to his arrest.* The sketch on the poster didn't look at all like the man he saw when he looked into a mirror, and he gave silent thanks to Emma as he continued onward.

Days came and days went as he travelled the Chase Wagon Road heading northerly, under the assumed name of Travis Sweet. He met up with a few folks and chatted with them as he carried on. Meeting up with an old fellow who only introduced himself as Nick, Tyrell shared a meal with him noting Nick's lack of provisions. Nick seemed grateful and he truly was. Tyrell could only think back to the time when Ed McCoy did the same for him. With the meal finished and countless thanks from Nick, Nick continued on his way as did Tyrell. There was more he would learn about Nick, but for now Nick seemed to be a simple traveller.

On June 9, 1891 after a day of travelling without meeting up with one passerby, Tyrell is met by a young man Brady McCoy, Ed McCoy's only son. Tyrell introduced himself as Travis Sweet, saying he had met Ed a while back and in fact had lent him his packing horse. Brady knew of this and he smiled as the two shook hands. He was grateful to Tyrell for helping his old man out.

It turned out that Brady was tracking down a bounty, a fellow by the name of Nicolai Baurduer. At first Tyrell denied seeing anyone, but on a second consideration, he explained to Brady that he had indeed seen the man. The man had introduced himself as Nick. Learning how dangerous Nicolai could be, Tyrell suggested to Brady to send a telegram to a fellow by the name of Tanner McBride whom lived in Willow Gate and who would be willing to help bring in Nicolai Baurduer for a percentage of the reward. Brady agreed to this and continued on his way.

On June 13, 1891 Tyrell finally arrives at Fort Macleod and meets up with Ed. Tyrell brings up the question of employment. Ed, a man of his word tells Tyrell that he would be more than pleased to have him work for McCoy's. So Tyrell Sloan, known by Ed McCoy as Travis Sweet, became a full-fledged bounty hunter under the alias of Travis Sweet.

With the Bounty Hunter oath out of the way and new credentials baring the name Travis Sweet, Tyrell Sloan takes on the role of bounty hunter.

The Missing Years Part III
The Hunt for Matt Crawford

Chapter 1

August 27, Thursday 1891. The court appearances for B. Atalmore and the three men who rode with him were underway. The men from McCoy's Bounty Hunting Service, Ed, Brady, Riley, Tanner, and Tyrell sat in the audience watching the proceedings. They weren't the only ones in the audience; Matt Crawford sat behind them unbeknownst to either of McCoy's men. Dressed in a cheap suit and hat, he sat quietly as he listened.

"Mr. Barclay Atalmore," the judge began as he looked at him with a stern gaze. "You have been found guilty of fraudulently portraying yourself as a U.S. Federal Marshal, to obtain legal documentation and information regarding one Matt Crawford. We frown on that type of behaviour here in Canada, and so you are sentenced to six months in the provincial prison located in Calgary. This same sentence and reason for are also binding under Canadian provincial and federal law and are imposed on both Allan Webber and Spence Hamilton," the judge paused for a moment as he waited for the Mounted Police to haul them off.

"As for you, Mr. Christian," the judge said as he looked at Colby who sat there hoping to get the same sentence, so he wouldn't be separated from the crew he had been running with. Judge Larsen shook his head as he began to speak. "For the life of me, I cannot understand why a promising young man such as you would want to be mixed up with those I have sentenced and who stood before me today."

Colby was about to speak but the judge didn't give him the chance.

"Under Canadian law and since there has been no proof of any crime you have committed here in the province of Alberta, other than being stupid. Although you have played a part in this entire charade, all be it minutely, I am not going to let you walk out of here under the impression that you have gotten away with something and therefore I am sentencing you to twenty days in the Fort Macleod holding cells under guard of the Mounted Police. You will commit yourself to twelve hours of daily community work. Perhaps this will give you time enough to realise there is no light at the end of the tunnel for any man or woman who decides to walk on the wrong side of the law. For any reason," Judge Larsen made clear as he proceeded.

Before the judge finished with sentencing Atalmore and his men, Matt, stood and exited the courthouse. No one even batted an eye. Swinging onto his horse, he headed west toward the British Columbia Rockies. He didn't know what, if anything was said of him while Atalmore and his men were in custody. He was still a wanted fugitive and it was time he decided to head into deep hiding once more.

For three weeks, he had mingled with the folks of the Fort and had avoided any suspicion about his identity. With his ex-comrades on their way to a provincial prison for a short six-month stint, there was no need for him to stick around or make his way back to his cabin near Vermillion. Whatever it was Barclay Atalmore wanted, he didn't know nor did he care. He had left the Rebel Rangers on his own accord and had no desire to reinstate his position, if that was indeed, why Atalmore had been in the area. For all Matt knew, there was a darker reason. For three years, he had been a one-man army, had put to rest a number of high profile government officials, all of whom had set him up for murder. They had even tried to assassinate his sister Anne Greenwich. There were at least three men left that would meet lead from his rifle. He knew the faces and names of two, the third by name only 'Gabe Roy'.

The courthouse slowly emptied and McCoy's men stepped out into a warm August day. A Mounted Police constable met them as they headed toward McCoy's.

"Hey, Ed, hold up there a minute," the young constable said as he approached.

Ed turned and looked at him as Brady, Riley, Tanner and Tyrell continued onward.

"Good afternoon constable, what can I do for you?" Ed asked as he waited for the young man to catch up. He held in his hand a white envelope, and he handed it off to Ed as he made the distance.

"This was sent to our attention, but it is made out to you."

Ed opened it and looked at it.

"I can't believe this," Ed said as he read it over. "It's a damn legal document sent from Ottawa. Looks like some new laws regarding bounty hunting services in

Canada is going to be implemented in January. And they don't benefit us any. Damn it."

Ed was distraught and he shook his head.

"What kind of law?" the constable questioned. He hadn't heard anything regarding any new laws.

"Bounty Hunting services are being abolished throughout Canada. Seems that Canadians are no longer expected to give up their rights, therefore the bounty hunting business can no longer be supported by Canadian Law. I ain't sure exactly what it all means, but says in the letter more documents to follow. Anyway, thanks for bringing this to me."

Ed folded up the letter and tucked it into his shirt pocket. He didn't know how he was going to explain the news to those that worked for him, although he already knew a way around it. McCoy's would simply have to change their business platform to Private Security, there were a few more steps than that, but that was the basis of what he knew they would eventually have to do. The change was still some months away, and would give them time to make the decisions that would now have to be made regarding McCoy's Bounty Hunting service in the whole.

By the time Ed made it to the office, his men were all seated behind their desks, going through paper work and whatnot. It was Brady who spoke first.

"What did constable Bash want, old man?"

"A letter was delivered to the Mounted Police office in care of us, so he gave it to me," Ed said with some apprehension.

"What is it in regard to?" Brady asked as he stood from his desk and made his way over to Ed, who was leaning on the counter.

"Changes to Canadian law and the abolishing of bounty hunting practises."

"What?" Brady asked as he took the letter and read it. "That is totally stupid; I haven't heard of anything like this my entire life. How are folks that are in this business going to be able to put bread and butter onto our tables? I can't believe this crap."

"Well, it is still some months away. We can still operate as we are until January."

Ed shrugged. He wasn't impressed with the letter either.

By now Tanner, Riley and Tyrell were standing next to Ed and were taking turns reading the letter.

"At least there are some options as stated in the letter," Tyrell mentioned as he looked at the glum faces surrounding him. "It says you can change your services, Ed, to Private Security or Investigations."

"True as that might be, Travis, I 'm not sure what all that would entail."

Ed scratched his chin as he contemplated.

"For now, I say we get down and dirty and bring in as many wanted fugitives that we can between now and January. Until, I get further documentation, I honestly don't know where to end or to start. McCoy's isn't going to cease to operate. If we have to make some changes to our operating practises, so be it. The only thing it really means is that we ain't going to be able to bring in bounties the way used to. Our rights as bounty officers will no longer be upheld by federal and provincial law. It doesn't mean we can't bring them in. Anyone can bring in a bounty. The only difference between the civilian way and the way we've been allowed to do it is that we had the law backing us, and so were given different rules and regulations. As of January, those benefits will no longer be available to bounty hunting services all across Canada. That is really all it means. We can change with the times."

Ed smiled as he took the letter back from Riley who had finished reading it and was holding it in his hand as they conversed.

"Going into the private sector of this type of business, really ain't much different than what we all had to go through in becoming registered bounty hunters. Probably quite simple, actually," Riley mentioned.

He knew this because he had once considered the possibility of working for a private investigator out of Calgary, years earlier. All that was involved in the switch over back then was a bit of reading, writing, and a couple of tests, and then the acceptance from the Police Commissioner Board. After that, it was all up to the individual to make a go of it. The longest part of the whole process was probably the time it took to be accepted. Riley also knew that since they were already registered as certified bounty hunters, that there was a real possibility that they may only need to get the Police Commissioner Boards permission to operate as private investigators. No test, no writing just the reading of another oath and the licensing.

"You know a bit about that process, Riley?" Ed asked.

"I do," Riley responded as he explained the process and the possibility of simply getting a license.

"I don't know, Riley, I'm not sure it'll be that simple. Back in the day when you were thinking about it, it may have been. Things may have changed by now," Brady pointed out.

"Whether it has or not, I ain't sure but that is how it was back then. Can't see it changing too much."

"The best thing to do I guess is to carry on as we are. I'll be getting more documentation in the coming weeks," Ed responded.

"Yeah, that probably is best. I'm not too worried. Hell, we could all be dead by then," Tanner said as he chuckled and made his way back to his desk and sat down. "I agree with what Ed said we should get down and dirty and bring in as many bounties that we can while we still have federal and provincial law on our side," Tanner added.

"I reckon I agree with that," Tyrell mentioned as he looked over to Tanner. "Since we lost Matt, maybe we should try again. His bounty is well worth our effort. There are enough of us here that we could all work on his apprehension. I know it has been over a month and he could be anywhere, but we know where Riley tracked him to."

"That we do," Riley stated as he nodded. "That was a month ago as you say, and he could be anywhere. It could be tough to figure out where exactly he is now. I'd certainly be up for the task. Bringing him in before the new law and regulations take place would be at the top of my list of bounties to bring in, since I've been tracking him for a couple of years already. Just like all those times before, he out-classed me," Riley half chuckled, "so, to bring a fellow of his stature in before it is no longer legal, would certainly make me feel better."

"All right, if that is what you fellows want to do, or at least give it another try, I'm not going to say 'no'," Ed responded.

"We should come up with a plan, then," Brady replied.

"We all know how plans sometimes work out. But, we could certainly make one, not that it will matter much. Matt will be a tough bounty to apprehend. He's good at dodging us and the law," Riley pointed out as he leaned on the counter and looked out the window. "I'll say this much, if we get lucky with bringing him in, I'll buy the whiskey to celebrate."

Riley really had doubts that they'd actually succeed, but he also knew that he had never been bested by a wanted felon who had a bounty on his head. He had even tracked down Tyrell, but that was only by luck. Now he worked with him under Tyrell's alias Travis Sweet. What a coincidence that was. He chuckled to himself as he thought about that. Life certainly took some funny turns.

"You buy the whiskey, Riley and I'll have the wife throw together a meal fit for kings. We'll get him exonerated and maybe convince him to join up with us," Ed joked as he chuckled. The truth was, with Matt Crawford on the payroll, Ed knew there was nothing they wouldn't be able to do with regard to Private Security. With Matt's training alone, it would be enough to be licensed for whatever McCoy's decided to do once the new laws were instated. It was a dream, but he could dream.

Ten miles west of the Fort, Matt Crawford reached into his shirt pocket to remove his pocket notebook. He wanted to check the last location he had heard where Gabe Roy now resided. He was surprised to discover his notebook was not where he usually kept it.

"Damn, where the hell did I put that damn thing?" he questioned himself as he continued to search. Not finding it he slowed his horse down and swung off the saddle to search through his saddlebags, he didn't find it there either. *That is quite disconcerting,* he thought. The last place he remembered looking at it was at the Snakebite Hotel. He wasn't so concerned about the book that he'd risk turning back east and look for it. If it was lost, then it was lost. There really wasn't anything in the book that he didn't already know, nor was his name in the book, although he did recall scribbling his alias Ron Reginal in it. He looked east and then back the way he was travelling. He remembered that Gabe Roy was said to be living in the town of Willow Gate. Opening up a map he carried with him, he looked for Willow Gate, but it wasn't listed on his map. He knew it was west and so he'd continue in that direction.

First things first though. He was tired of the cheap suit he was wearing and finding a bit of a clearing, he slid behind a clump of bushes and changed back into his usual garb. Dressed now in appropriate attire he continued westerly.

How Gabe Roy fit into the equation only Matt knew, and because of what he knew he had every reason in his mind to file Gabe Roy under *'dead by lead'*. Three years earlier during his sister Anne's campaign to run for a U.S. Governmental position, where she was taking the U.S.A by storm and gaining popularity as a left wing opposing U.S. government appointive, Gabe Roy helped in the conspiracy to try and assassinate her, but slipped into Canada, along with $100,000.00 dollars that he swindled from Anne and her husband during a shoddy land deal, weeks before Matt managed an escape from false imprisonment.

Matt wanted and was going to get retribution and all the money back that Gabe had stolen. There were other reasons too, for now making the distance to Willow Gate without being taken in himself by bounty hunters and Mounted Police was his biggest concern. So far, using cheap disguises and quick appearance changes were working in his favor; so far, it had been easy. The only thing that put him at one time in one place recently was the small pocket notebook. He hoped it had been lost where it could not be found easily. It was an unfavorable blunder; that much he knew. There was nothing that could be done about it, except to do what it was he had been trained to do while enlisted with the U.S. Safety Board and U.S. Marshals and that was to carry on to the current objective. Willow Gate.

Back at McCoy's the men were getting ready to stop for the day. They hadn't accomplished much, but Atalmore and his men were now on their way to Calgary, that is all except Colby who was now sitting in the cell of Fort Macleod's local jail. He wasn't impressed about being there. He would have much rather been with Atalmore, Webber and Hamilton and on his way to prison. This twenty day community service work stuff, as far as he was concerned, was a joke. He wouldn't fight it though; he'd play along for now. In twenty days, he'd be walking free one way or the other. It would be then, he knew, that he'd have to head south back into the U.S., and wait for Atalmore and the others.

What he was going to do for six months until then he didn't know. Had Atalmore, Webber, and Hamilton been given a lengthier sentence, then it was obvious that it would be up to him to break them out. For a simple six-month sentence though, it wasn't worth the effort nor would it be expected of him. In six months, he would meet up with them in Big Muddy. That had always been the U.S. Rebel Rangers plan whenever one of their own had been imprisoned. Their plan was to always meet there. In February after the others were released, that is where he would meet them.

11

Colby sighed as he looked out the barred window. He wondered what it was he'd be doing in the morning as he worked off the twenty day community service sentence he had been handed. Chances were he'd be cleaning manure from the Mounted Police stables or picking up garbage, none of which would impress him any. *Twenty days ain't that bad, I'll manage,* he thought as he sat down on the bunk his head in his hands.

The men from McCoy's all headed over to the Snakebite for an after-work whiskey. The early evening sun was warm as the five of them walked along the boardwalk. Something caught Tyrell's eye and he fished through the cracks in the wooden plank walkway. The others stopped and looked at him as though he were off his rocker.

"What the heck you doing there, Travis?" Tanner asked.

"Found some kind of notebook or something. I just can't get my fingers on it."

The men walked over to him and looked on.

"Forget about it, Travis. Come on, it's just garbage," Brady commented.

"Yeah, I reckon you're right. Let's get to that whiskey," Tyrell said as he stood up and the men continued on.

They sat at Ed's favorite table and ordered a round of drafts and a couple of whiskeys for Riley and Ed. The others opted out of the rotgut, choosing to have a cold draft instead.

"We all talked about what is going to happen with businesses such as ours in the coming months," Ed started. "I've thought about it most of the day."

He took a swing from the short glass of whiskey.

"I've come to the conclusion that we're simply going to avoid all the hassle and start from scratch. Come Monday morning we're going to be reclassifying McCoy's into a Private Security operation. I read that document Bash gave me earlier today, read the fine print and found out that if we switch over to Private Security and Investigations before January, like Riley said, the five of us can simply read another oath and write a simple test. Essentially, because of the type of business we're in and the fact that we've been in business for so long already, we are grandfathered in to the Private Security sector. To be honest it really won't be any different than what we already do anyway. There are a few more benefits, that is all. So, what do you guys figure?" Ed asked as he looked at each of them.

"You mean we'll be like the Pinkertons?" Brady questioned.

"I suppose something like that, yep."

"McCoy's Private Security and Investigations has a ring to it. I don't care either way, as long as we'll still be able to do what it is we do," Brady added as he slurped from his draft beer.

"We should be able to do all that we do now as well as a few other things, too," Ed responded.

"You are the boss, Ed. Whatever you say works for me," Tyrell said as he looked over to Ed. "I just hope it is an easy transformation from Bounty Hunting Services to Private Security and Investigations. I ain't been in the business long enough to know the difference, but I can oblige to whatever you decide."

"Riley, Tanner, you have anything to add?" Ed asked as he now looked at them.

"Not really, I'm okay with whatever you folks decide."

"Me too, Ed. Like Travis said, you are the boss."

Riley smiled and took a long swallow from his whiskey. Setting his glass down on the table, he stood up.

"I got an appointment today at the land titles office. I have my eye on a piece of land not far from here. So, I have to get. I'll talk with you all in the morning."

"Where is this homestead you're talking about?" Tanner asked out of curiosity.

"No homestead, Tanner, just a piece of land. It's not far from Ed's place, about a mile west actually. One hundred acres of raw land. If I buy it, I'll toss together a shack to get me through whilst I build a house," Riley answered.

"Oh, so you are thinking about buying Miller's place. That piece has been for sale for a few years. Folks haven't shown much interest due to the lack of water nearby. Most don't want to dig wells these days," Ed mentioned.

"Yeah, I've been told that. It sure is a nice piece though, with or without water. I figure some digging and a bit of luck, one could find water. I'm just contemplating at the moment anyway. We'll see what the land titles office has to say, maybe I can get it cheaper then what is being asked. I dunno," Riley shrugged. "There has to be water on that land somewhere, so I have to dig a well. A few blisters and hard work, no big deal."

"You say that now. Wait until you have to dig," Brady chuckled.

Riley waved his hand through the air.

"Ah, a little hard work Brady that is all it is."

"Sure."

Brady took a swig from his draft beer and raised his hand to the server to get another.

"Anyone else want a refill?" he asked as the server approached. "I'm buying this round."

"Well, if you're buying, I'll sit back down."

Riley pulled his chair out and sat.

"So, it's a round for all I take it?"

"Yep. I'll take another draft and a shot of whiskey," Tanner replied.

"All right make it a five draft and three whiskeys, 'less of course you want a whiskey too, Travis."

"Nope. No whiskey for me, Brady, but I will take another draft."

The server skirted away and returned a short while later.

"Here you go, guys," she said as she handed off the drinks.

"Thanks, Kitty. That'll be all for now," Brady said as he took his stein of beer.

It didn't take long for the drinks to run dry and the men left. Tanner and Travis headed to his room above McCoy's office, Ed and Brady both headed home and Riley headed over to the land titles office. The day had come to an end.

Chapter 2

Friday August 28 1891. It was 7:00 a.m. when the constable on duty that morning brought Colby his breakfast.

"Here you go, Colby, some hotcakes, a coffee, and a couple pieces of smoked pork. You are going to have a busy day today."

"Yeah. What do you have planned for me?" Colby asked as he took the plate of food and sat back down.

"Manure and lots of it. Enjoy your breakfast, Colby; I'll gather you around 8:00."

The constable turned and walked away.

I knew I was going to have shitty day today, Colby thought as he began to eat.

The meal, although a bit cold, wasn't as bad as it could have been. He had always heard stories that the meals consisted of bread and water when one was in the clink. This meal though certainly wasn't. Finishing he slurped his coffee as he waited for the constable to return and get him started on the day's work that lay ahead.

Hearing the clinking of keys, Colby rose from his bed and waited.

"Ready Colby?" the constable asked as he approached.

"Ready as I'll ever be," he replied as constable Bash unlocked the cell door.

"Good. You have a lot of work ahead of you. The stables haven't been cleaned in a while."

"Whatever," Colby shrugged, as Bash handed him his boots.

"It is warm out today. You'll work up a good sweat."

"Look, ahh, Constable Bash, I'm not your friend, so don't talk to me like I am."

"Only being cordial, Colby, and you are right you aren't my friend nor am I yours. But, we're going to be seeing a lot of each other over the next couple of weeks, so you best get used to it."

"Not going to happen, Bash. This twenty day community service crap is just that. Crap."

"Call it what you will, Colby, but for twenty days you'll be doing community service work, and with an attitude like you have, I'm going to make certain that you work."

Bash was already fed up with Colby's attitude. He was only trying to be nice and the punk kid was having nothing to do with it. That was okay though. By the time the day was over Colby would have a new outlook and perhaps smarten up a bit. It was Bash's hope at least. Colby, he knew, wasn't all that bad. He'd slipped into the company of bad apples; that was all. He was young enough that he could turn his wayward self around. Judge Larsen saw that in Colby as well, otherwise he would have been riding alongside Atalmore and the others on his way to the Calgary provincial prison. That wasn't the case though, and the judge was giving him a break, a chance to turn around. Whether he would or not was up to Colby. One thing was for certain if he continued down the road he was following, he'd never get another break like the one Larsen had handed to him.

Back at McCoy's office the day was just starting. The men sat in the staff room pondering Ed's plan in becoming a private security and investigation business.

"A thought came to me last night after Tanner and I made our way back upstairs. If McCoy's changes to private investigations and whatnot, could we then do an investigation under police law regarding that Gabe Roy fellow?" Tyrell asked as he took a swig from his morning coffee.

"Why, would we want to do a thing like that?" Ed asked.

"Simple. You know it; Buck knew it and the rest of us know it as well, that Gabe Roy has corrupted the law of Willow Gate with all his money. I think someone should expose him and the Willow Gate law," Tyrell pointed out.

"I think that is jumping the gun a bit."

"Why do you say that, Riley?" Tyrell questioned.

"Well, we don't have the paperwork or licenses yet that could give us the right to do so."

"I realise that. I'm talking about once we do, if Ed decides to go that route."

"I've already decided Travis; we all did last night at the Snakebite. I do agree that Gabe should be exposed for what he really is, and I reckon once McCoy's changes to private investigation and security, it is something we can talk about. I'd certainly consider it once it is all said and done. We could make that our first official investigation, could make a new name for ourselves if we can prove it one way or the other. I like the idea in fact. I'll stew on it for a bit. In the meantime we could certainly begin making a case."

"So then, once we have all the paperwork updated, it is something, that we could actually look into?" Tyrell wanted to be clear.

"It is, indeed."

"That is all I wanted to know," Tyrell slurped on his coffee, his mind racing with the possibility. Exposing Gabe Roy and the corrupt law of Willow Gate could in the long run clear his name. *What a relief that would be,* he thought as he finished his coffee.

"To build a case against Gabe we'd need to know a few things about him, I reckon. Does anything come to your mind, Riley?" Ed asked.

"Other than I once worked for him in trying to track down that Tyrell fellow that was supposed to have killed his son Heath, I really haven't got much to add except that I wouldn't want to work for him ever again. He's a prick, Ed, simple as that. I have no doubt in my mind that he is crooked as a bean vine."

"Well, he did send us that wire requesting personal protection. Why would a fellow like Gabe want that if he isn't trying to hide from one thing or another?"

"Maybe that is where we could start. The only one he don't know is Travis."

Brady looked over to where Tyrell sat.

"No, don't look at me like that Brady. I don't want to have anything to do with his personal protection," Tyrell pointed out.

"All you'd need to do is hang around with him. Learn a few things about him, maybe delve a bit deeper into his past. It could be our first undercover investigation, and you Travis could lead that investigation," Brady chuckled, "I don't know; it was just a thought."

"It isn't such a bad idea at all. I know Gabe knows Tanner; Riley told him to take off and I don't see eye to eye with him. If we wanted to do something about the way he throws around his weight, and how he has bullied so many out of land and money, Travis would be our best hope in finding anything out about all that," Ed added.

"Brady would do just as well. Gabe doesn't know him," Tyrell pointed out.

"That is true. But, Gabe did once ask for your assistance, Travis. It may have been a year or so ago, but I bet he still knows your name. I wouldn't say no at tagging along. We could both go undercover."

"I don't know, Brady. That is a long trail ride to Willow Gate. How far would it be Tanner?" Tyrell looked over to Tanner and waited for him to answer.

"Took me and Buck a few weeks to meet up with you when you were living in that teepee. From here to Willow Gate, I suspect it would take at least that long, a few weeks that is. Could take less time too considering when Buck and I tracked you down it was late fall early winter. It took me a few days of steady riding to meet up with Tanner at Hells Bottom when he and I were tracking Nicolai."

"Still, I don't know if I'd want to be Gabe's personal bodyguard. I need to think on it some, besides we aren't even licensed as private security yet," Tyrell said as he sucked on an eyetooth.

"Not yet. We will be, though. It is only a matter of time. I'll fill out the paperwork today and wire it off before the day ends. Then it depends on how quickly the Police Commissioner, Blake Stevens gets back to us. Might only take a week, might take less time. I don't know, but it is certainly, where McCoy's is heading. Anyway fellows, let's get some work done today. There is a bounty to be got in bringing in a local cattle rustler. Any takers?" Ed asked as he downed the last of his coffee.

"You mean that fellow Burton?" Brady asked. He had received a wire from a woman that lived in Weesley and whom had claimed to have seen him.

"That's right. Roger Burton. Last seen near Weesley a few weeks back. The Albert Ranch south of here claims to have lost twenty head of cattle. Could be Roger's handiwork."

"Could just be simply lost, too," Riley added.

"True as that is, how about couple of you head over to the Albert Ranch and check it out? If it was Burton, he'd be long gone by now, but at least we'd know whether or not it was his doing. In which case, he'll be back. He always comes back."

"Sure, I'll volunteer," Tyrell commented.

"Yeah, I'll go along too," Tanner suggested.

"All right then, you and Travis go ahead. It'll take you until noon to make the distance. Brady and Riley, you two can head over to the Mounted Police station and find out anything that might be new regarding Emery. Maybe they have some new information on that Pinkerton fellow Miles Ranthorp that our friend Matt put to rest after he shot your horses."

"I reckon by now they should have something regarding him. Sure. Come on, Riley, let's get."

Brady and Riley rose from the table and headed out the door. Tanner and Travis followed suit and Ed went into his office and started filling out the paperwork that needed to be sent to the Commissioner. It was a good start to a good day.

Colby Christian however wasn't having such a good day. He already had blisters on the palms of his hands from shoveling manure and he was not happy about it.

"This is crap. I quit," he said as he tossed the shovel to the ground and looked at constable Bash.

"I'll allow you to rest for a couple of minutes, but you are far from done, Colby."

"I've been at it for a few hours already and I ain't so much as made a difference to the amount of horse shit in these stalls."

"Like I said, take a few minutes to rest. I'll bring you some water."

"What, you just going to leave me here alone while you do that?"

"Am so."

"Well, I might take that opportunity to split."

"You wouldn't get far, Colby, and the judge wouldn't take too kindly to you doing something like that. He'd likely add a few more days to your community service. Do you want that?"

"Hell no, but how can you trust me?"

"I don't. I do think you know better, though."

Constable Bash exited the corral and made his way over to the town pump and filled up a canteen of water for Colby. He was actually quite surprised that Colby did stick around when he made his way back.

"Here you go, Colby, a fresh canteen of water."

He handed the canteen over and Colby took a long swallow and poured some over the palms of his hands to wash the manure and blood away from the blisters.

"God damn, that hurts a bit," he said as he squinted. "I get this shit finished up today, what is in store for me tomorrow?"

"There is an old widow lady down the way some, needs her garden plowed and weeded. I think that is where we'll be going tomorrow. Depends I guess on whether or not you get this manure cleaned up. If you don't get it done today, you'll be back at it tomorrow."

"Garden, weeding, Jesus Christ. I don't want to do that either."

"It doesn't matter what you want, Colby. These are things that you are going to do."

Colby shook his head and went back to work cleaning the stalls.

It was around this time that Riley and Brady tracked Bash down and asked if the Mounties had any news to share on Emery's death and Miles Ranthorp.

"No, we haven't heard anything back from the Pinkerton Office yet."

"How long does it take to get a straight answer from that lot?" Brady questioned.

"I hope by mid-week next that we at least get a response. I do have some information on the pistol used to kill your man Emery. Ballistics proved it was a .45 Colt Ranger that was used, and yes, it is the same type of pistol the Pinkerton's use along with about everyone else in these parts. So, no definitive answer regarding that. Sorry I didn't have better news, Brady."

Brady looked over to Colby.

"How is the kid liking community service so far?"

"Why don't you just ask me?" Colby responded as he heard the question.

"All right, so how are you liking it?"

"I'd rather stick sewing needles in my eyes. The eye burn would be about the same. Does that answer your question?"

Brady and Riley started to chuckle at Colby's response.

"Yeah, I'd say that answers my question," Brady replied between breaths.

He looked again at Bash and smiled.

"Well, Rick, I guess if you haven't got any news then we'll leave you two alone. Make sure you do a good job in cleaning this manure up, Colby," Brady said with a smile adding salt to the situation.

"Why don't you and your friend there get lost? I ain't in a mood for remarks from the likes of your kind," Colby replied with anger.

"All right. We'll get. Come on, Riley, let's leave the kid and Bash to their work. Have a good day, Colby. You too, Rick. Let us know the minute you hear anything regarding Ranthorp."

"I will, Brady. You fellows have a good day too."

"I assure you we'll have a better day than Colby," Riley chuckled as he and Brady left.

Tanner and Tyrell were making their way slowly to the Albert Ranch. The day was warm and the gentle summer breeze felt good as they proceeded.

"So, I was thinking, Tanner. You've lived in Willow Gate for a couple years. What, if anything, do you know about Gabe Roy, other than the fact that he is an ass?" Tyrell wanted to know.

"Everything that has already been said about Gabe Roy is all true. He's a swindler and likes to take advantage of the less fortunate. From what I know about his deceased son Heath is that he too was going down the same road. To be honest, when you put him to rest you removed a stain. Gabe, well, he's the biggest stain of all. I like what we talked about earlier today, you know, investigating his criminality. I'd love to be the one actually to see to it that he gets what is coming to him. Only thing is, he wouldn't want me on his payroll. Like the others said, you, Travis Sweet, would be a shoe in. He'd put you on his payroll without hesitation, Brady too, probably."

"I don't know, Tanner. I like what it is I do now, tracking down bad guys. Not sure I'd have the same desire to be his personal protection, I know it would help the cause in exposing him, but I have to ask myself if it is something I'd like to do. My gut tells me *'no'*, but my heart tells me *'yes'*."

Tyrell inhaled deeply as he contemplated and they continued onward.

"You could look at it two ways. One is that if we could expose him and the corrupt law that he pays, *'you'* Tyrell Sloan, may get your name back. The other way to look at it is that McCoy's would certainly benefit the rewards as the ones who exposed him, and you could carry on as Travis Sweet, no one would be the wiser."

"I've thought about that, you know getting my name back. In a sense though, I kind of like Travis Sweet."

"A man can be named anything Tyrell. It is what he chooses to do with his life that makes a difference. You and I alike have both chose to be on the right side of the law, although there was a time we could have cared less. I personally like the good side. The bad, well, sometimes that gets a tiring. I know if Buck were here, he'd tell you the same. Either way, in time, Gabe Roy will meet his reaper; men like him always do."

"You are right, of course. He will meet his reaper, either from the right side of the law or by a vindictive victim of his who has been robbed of his life," Tyrell agreed.

"The problem with that is if someone simply kills him they won't be exposing the corrupt law, in which case it will continue to be corrupt. No, the best thing to squash a bug such as Gabe is to bring down the entire nest."

They rode in silence for a few minutes each of them in self-contemplation. Everything they had spoken about was true. Gabe Roy would meet his reaper, and if they couldn't stop the reaper who went by the name of Matt Crawford then as they had discussed the corrupt law would remain corrupt. No one knew then that Matt was heading to Willow Gate or that his reason for it was to simply kill the man named Gabe Roy. In time, though they would all learn.

Brady and Riley met up with Ed as they made their way back to the office. He was on his way to send off the paperwork that would eventually authorise McCoy's the rights and privilege of being in the Private Investigation sector. They would be regulated under the police laws of Canada and would have to honor a new oath, but in the long run, it would all be worth it.

"Hey fellows," Ed began as they met up. "Got the paperwork finished, I'm off to wire it to the Police Commission office. How did it go with the Mounties? Did they have any news on who killed Emery?"

"Nope. The Pinkerton office hasn't responded yet. Bash says though that the gun that killed Emery was a .45 Colt Ranger, which really means nothing at all, since there are many in use. I don't know," Brady shrugged.

"On the lighter side of things though, once McCoy's gets through the red tape in becoming an official Private Investigation and Security firm, we can do our own investigation," Riley added.

"True enough. It is exactly what we'll do," Ed nodded.

"Geez, we haven't even got the license yet and we've already decided on two cases that we'd like to undertake," Brady half chuckled. "Yous don't suppose that we might be getting a bit ahead of ourselves? What happens if we get denied?"

"If it turns out that way, I guess we'll all be screwed, and without jobs,' Ed responded. "Personally though, I have every confidence that won't be the case, Brady. McCoy's has been around for a long while, we've brought to justice a lot of bad men, and our performance speaks for itself."

"That is a good point, old man. I sure hope you are right. Hate the thought of having to plow fields to make a living. I've been doing this for too many years to all of a sudden be forced to stop. The whole thing still doesn't make much sense to me on why our federal government would want to abolish bounty-hunting services. I just can't wrap my head around it."

"There is nothing we can do about it. Except what it is we're trying to do now," Riley said as he looked around.

"Yeah, I know. In the meantime, though we're still bounty hunters, at least for a few more months. I'll tell you one thing, 1892 is going to bring with it a whole lot of unemployed bounty hunters. It is a shame actually. Hell, we provide the provinces with a service that is much needed."

"That same service though can be provided under the new regulations that are about to hit us all."

"True enough I suppose. I just don't like change I guess. As Travis would say, 'it is what it is.'" Brady shrugged. "Anyway, old man, you have to get that paperwork wired off and Riley and I need to get busy doing something also. Come on, Riley; let's get back to the office."

"I'll meet up with you two once I get this wired off. Make some fresh coffee would you, Brady."

"Will so," Brady responded as he and Riley headed back to the office.

Ed was surprised as he made his way to the telegraph office and saw that walking toward him was Alex Brubaker. He was the last person he would have expected to run across. Meeting up with him on the boardwalk as he proceeded onward, the two men stopped and had not so unfriendly conversation.

"Hey, Alex, how are you doing today?" Ed asked. "Wasn't expecting to see you. How is the hand holding up?" Ed asked, as he looked at the buckskin glove that now covered Alex's disfigured hand.

"As good as can be expected, Ed. And yourself, how are you?"

"On a nice summer day like this, I couldn't be better."

"Uhuh, it is a beauty today," Alex responded as he looked into Ed's eyes, not so villainous, but with definite trepidation.

"Knowing our past, Alex, can I ask what brings you to the Fort?"

Ed wasn't sure if he was there for revenge or to simply cause grief.

"No worries, Ed, I ain't here seeking retribution. I'm past that. I've done a lot of contemplating over the last while. What went on between your man Travis and I, as far as I'm concerned, is forgotten. He was quicker on the draw is all, simple as that. I should have realised my chance in beating him was damn slim. After all, he did kill my brother Earl and beat him at the draw as well and Earl could always beat me. Nope, I'm here on other family business."

"You have family in the Fort?" Ed asked with surprise.

"Yep, in a roundabout way. Only thing is, he ain't a resident but a prisoner of the Mounted Police."

Ed knew then exactly who Alex was talking about.

"Colby?" he asked.

"That's right. He and I are cousins. I'm here to take him home once he's done his time."

"I see. You have a few weeks to wait. He was sentenced to twenty days."

"Was so, and he'll finish his time too," Alex responded.

He could tell that Ed was thinking the worst and he wanted to be clear that he wasn't there for any other reason than to wait for Colby. He had a plan there was no doubt about that, but it had nothing to do with Travis, Ed or anyone else. With Colby's help he was hoping to bring in Matt Crawford for the bounty. He knew McCoy's men had failed to do it. That wasn't the only reason though. In fact, that wasn't a reason at all. The ten thousand dollar bounty was. Plus, he knew a few things more about Matt Crawford than what Ed and his men knew. *For now at least.*

He knew that Gabe Roy and Matt Crawford had a history and not a pretty one at that. He knew if the Rebel Rangers were or had been in the area their only reason he knew was to find Matt Crawford. If they were taken in, and Matt wasn't, then he knew chances were Matt was heading in whichever direction Gabe Roy's name would lead him and that was to Willow Gate.

When he had heard that Colby had been arrested and detained on minor charges and the fact that it was McCoy's that brought him in along with Barclay Atalmore, Allan Webber and Spence Hamilton of the Rebel Rangers, a group of folks he really didn't care for and had always told Colby to stay away from. But Colby was Colby and he cared less about any advice anyone would give him. He made up his own mind. That was just the way Colby was. Alex knew with Colby's help, he had a real chance at bringing Matt Crawford in. After all, Colby was as deadly with a rifle as Matt. With Colby in his pocket riding alongside him there was no one the two of them couldn't face.

"Look Ed, I hold no grudges, I ain't here to tear up this one horse town and break my cousin from the grasps of the local law. Colby will do his time. Hell, as far as I'm concerned he deserves it. I ain't a bad man or crazed hired gun most folks make my type out to be. Earl on the other hand may have fit that category. He and I were different, always were. But as you know blood is thicker than water and I chose to stick with family and will forever bear family scars that Earl carved into us Brubaker's. That's life, ain't nothing I can do about it. Earl is dead now and he ain't ever coming back. Again that is life. I accept it. So don't think my visit here is for anything more than to take my cousin home."

Ed was dumbfounded almost in awe. He never would have thought Alex to be anything more than what Earl had been. Now though, he thought better. He scratched the top of his head as he fumbled for a few words. Alex noticing this smiled and waved his hand through the air.

"You ain't got to say anything, Ed. Just take my word that once Colby finishes off his time, he and I will be gone," Alex turned, heeled and began to walk away.

"All right, Alex, rest assured that McCoy's won't be hounding you whilst you are here."

Alex stopped, turned and looked back at him.

"Never make promises that you can't keep, Ed."

With that, Alex continued onward toward the Snakebite Hotel. He knew the men from McCoy's would be watching him like a hawk and so would the Mounted Police once he announced himself to them so that he could speak with Colby. That wouldn't be today though.

Ed watched as Alex crossed the street. He had a sense that Alex was there for a lot more than waiting for Colby's release. In his experience men like Earl and Alex Brubaker weren't stained as bad men without reason. They were stained that way because they were. Perhaps he had been wrong. *Humph, not sure what to expect or think, knowing he is here,* Ed thought as he carried on. With the paperwork sent off and now back at the office, Ed refreshed Brady and Riley on who Alex Brubaker was and the conversation he and Alex had.

"Could be it is the way he says it is, Ed," Riley pointed out.

"Well, he hasn't broken any law being here or for that matter broke any law being Colby's cousin," Brady threw in. "I ain't sure how Travis will feel about it, but what is done is done. We can all keep our eyes open. I honestly don't think we have much to worry about, leastwise not a face to face encounter between Alex and Travis. Travis beat him once and I'm sure he could beat him again if it ever came down to it."

"You're leaving out other possibilities, Brady."

"Like what?" Brady questioned.

"A bullet in the back is one example. Alex might not have the speed of his pistol hand, but it only takes a trigger finger to send lead down the bore."

Brady nodded.

"Point taken."

"It is a good point too, Riley," Ed agreed with a nod. "That is what I'm talking about. And it isn't only Alex we need to worry about, but once Colby gets released we might have twice the trouble if we are to expect any trouble at all."

"It boils down to one thing only," Brady mentioned.

"And what might that be?"

"The type of business we are in."

Brady shrugged his shoulders. It was that part of the business that he liked the most, the thrill of it all.

"Look we know Alex is here; we know he and Travis had a tiff; we'll just have to keep our wits until he and Colby blow town."

Both Riley and Ed were nodding, it was true. The only thing they could do was to remain alert and hope that it was as Alex said it was, and that in twenty days both he and Colby would be on their way. However, being prepared for things to go awry between now and then was always a good thing.

"So, alert and ready we will stay," Ed said as he stood up and poured out his cold coffee. "I got some more paperwork to get out of the way. If anyone needs me, I'll be in my office."

"Yeah, okay, old man. I reckon Riley and I could spray down the horses. I hate days like this when there is nothing exciting going on."

"What, it's not enough excitement knowing Alex Brubaker is in town?" Riley smirked. "Come on; let's get them horses sprayed down."

"Right behind you, Riley," Brady said as they exited into the late afternoon sun.

By now, Tyrell and Tanner were making their way back to the Fort. The information and evidence they had gathered regarding the twenty head of cattle that went missing from the Albert Ranch did seem to point at Roger Burton and coincided with the time he had been spotted in the area. They also had a general idea on what direction he headed, and of course that was south into Montana. He was weeks ahead and likely the cattle were already auctioned off. This didn't mean, however, that he wouldn't be back. With only twenty head of cattle, he wouldn't have made more than two hundred dollars for the lot. Chances were Burton would strike again. In fact, he could already be back in the area scouting out his next heist of cattle. But until that time or until he was spotted again, it was a two thousand dollar bounty that they would have to let slide.

"We should've moved on this when Brady was first notified," Tyrell mentioned as they carried on.

"We wouldn't have been able to a damn thing about it even then. We were too busy healing up or tracking down Matt Crawford and Atalmore and his men," Tanner responded.

"Yeah, I guess you are right. One thing though, knowing there is this type of activity going on around here we can assume if we hear of anymore that it'll be Burton. We'll have to try again then."

"Yep, that is how I look at it."

There was a short pause.

"On a different note," Tanner began, "I guess I best quit calling you Tyrell now before we get back to the Fort, eh Travis?" Tanner chuckled.

"You already know my answer to that, Tanner," Tyrell said with a return smile. Heeling their horse's flanks the two of them sped up hoping to make the distance to the Fort before day's end.

Finally arriving back at the office by 6:00 that evening, they were surprised to see that Ed was still there. He filled both Tyrell and Tanner in on the fact that Alex Brubaker was in town and that he intended on staying there until Colby's release and why.

"I would have never thought I'd have heard that name so soon," Tyrell said as he sighed and sat down. "I sure hope it is the way he has said it is. I won't be shooting to wound the next time."

"I'm pretty sure he means to cause no harm here, but we're all going to stay alert, Travis. No worries there," Ed made clear.

"I can't believe he and Colby are cousins," Tanner mentioned. "I've met both Alex and Earl a time or three. To be honest, Alex isn't anything like Earl. Earl was always the one to start trouble. Of course, Alex usually followed suit. But, if he's said he's only waiting for Colby's release that is exactly how it is, would be my guess."

"That is how the rest of us feel as well, but we aren't letting our guard down until he and Colby have both vacated. He seemed pretty forthright when we were conversing. Made it a point actually to meet up with me," Ed added.

"I'll keep my fingers crossed in the meantime," Tyrell said as he poured a coffee. "Either of you want one?" he asked as he offered to pour them a cup.

"Nope, not for me, Travis. I have to get home. I'm sure the wife is waiting to serve supper. On another note, however, what did you fellows find out at the Albert Ranch?" Ed asked as he stood up and slid his chair in.

"Well, it was undoubtedly Burton. We managed to figure that out, but of course as you know, Ed, he's long gone by now," Tyrell pointed out.

"Yeah, I figured as much. We'll have to keep on the lookout for him. He always comes back. Good job, now we know," Ed mentioned as he began to leave. "I'll see you folks in the morning. We're going to take a ride out to Riley's property tomorrow. He wants to show it to us. It'll be a slack day tomorrow. See you then."

"Yep, we'll see you, Ed," Tanner and Tyrell replied in unison.

Colby by now was washing up after his long day of shovelling manure. His blistered hands stung as the cold soapy water washed away the dried blood and dirt from his palms.

"With blisters like these I should be getting a wage," Colby blurted out as he squinted and let his hands soak.

"You don't get paid for community service, Colby. You pay back to the community with your labor. That is just the way that it is, Colby."

"Yeah, well I don't like it."

"And we're supposed to care about what you don't like? You obviously did something to deserve the twenty days, in the judges eyes. Be grateful that you aren't on your way to Calgary and six months of hard labor."

"At least I'd be with my crew and not in a one-horse town."

Colby turned and sat down on his bunk.

"When will I get some food? I'm starving."

"You'll get fed soon enough," Bash said as he exited the holding cell area, closed the big iron door and locked it.

Chapter 3

It was early Saturday morning when the men from McCoy's headed over to the old Miller place that Riley was considering to buy.

"You haven't bought the place yet then?" Ed asked as they trotted along.

"Nope. I'm likely going to though. That old backroom cot in the office isn't the same as my own place to lay down my head."

"You'll be stuck on that cot a while longer, Riley. There isn't no building on that land."

"Not yet, nope. I buy the place, though, it won't take long to throw a shelter up. Hell, I'll use some wagon canvas and toss together a lean-to. It'll all be good, Ed. Only problem is the water. I was thinking I'd see if I can borrow Colby to help dig the well," Riley chuckled.

Brady too started to chuckle.

"The way he was fighting cleaning up that manure yesterday will make that job look easy once he starts breaking ground with a pick and shovel."

"You know what, Riley? Why couldn't you use that old stagecoach that I picked up when we brought in Atalmore as a shelter to get you started?" Tyrell suggested.

It was big enough and would keep the weather off.

"Never even thought about that. I reckon it would work too, might get me through the winter. You wouldn't mind if I built onto it would you?"

"Go right ahead, I don't see why you couldn't. A cabin on wheels is what it would be. Only thing is, Riley, you'll have to get clearance from Ed. He paid me for it, so it is rightfully his."

"Sure, you can have it for two hundred dollars, Riley," Ed joked. "I'm only kidding, of course. If you think you could make it into a shack, feel free. We won't have much use for it with all the new changes to our business coming."

"Well, then. See, Ed told you it'll all be good. I'll make use of it, and I thank you kindly," Riley responded as they finally made the distance to the Miller property.

"There it is all one hundred acres. Goes on for quite the stretch, don't it?"

"That it does," Tanner said as the men swung off their horses. "You could run a few head of cattle in your retirement," he teased. "What is an old folk like you going to do with this much land?"

Riley looked over to him with a smile and shook his head.

"Live and die for the most part. I'm in no rush to make the land into anything specific. I kind of like it left alone, but that all might change in time. Come on, let's take a ride," Riley said as he swung back onto his horse and gave a gesture for the men to follow.

They rode from one end to the other, stopping every now and again to talk and speculate about the land and the possibilities it held.

By midday they were back at the office and Riley was filling out the paperwork as the buyer of the Miller land. That done, he harnessed his horse to the stagecoach he was going to use for shelter, filled up a few buckets of water and headed back to the land he would own come Monday morning. He felt good about the purchase he was going to make. Finally, a place he could call home. All was good.

Constable Bash sat on the widow Donale's porch watching Colby pulling weeds and swatting at bees. The sun was hot and he could see from where he sat that Colby's shirt was soaked with sweat. He chuckled to himself as he looked on. The widow Donale stepped out onto the porch and offered both Bash and Colby a pitcher of lemonade.

"I thought the two of you could use something cool on this hot day," she said as she set the tray down. "Young man," she called out. Colby squinted from the sunlight as he looked up to her.

"What is it you want, old woman?" Colby questioned as he sighed.

"I thought perhaps you wanted something cool to drink. You've been doing a wonderful job and I know it is hot out. Come on up and help yourself."

"I ain't so sure I'd be allowed, ma'am."

Colby looked at Bash.

"I reckon you could take a break, Colby," Bash said as he thanked the widow for the cool drink, while she stepped back inside.

Colby tossed the hoe onto the ground and made his way up to the porch. Pouring himself a glass of the cold yellow liquid, he took a long swallow and wiped the back of his hand across his mouth.

"Damn hot today," he said as he took another drink and sat down next to Bash.

"Yep, it has been a hot summer," Bash commented as he too poured another lemonade. "Quite nice of the widow to offer us a cold drink, eh, Colby?"

"I suppose."

He looked down at the garden.

"Not much left to do. Any chance I can have an early day today?"

"Finish up what you have going on down there and we'll see."

Bash noted a rider approaching who stopped and looked at them on the porch.

"Something I can help you with?" Bash questioned as he stood up, recognising that the man was Alex Brubaker.

Colby thought for a minute that the rider looked familiar. Looking closer, he smiled.

"Alex? Alex Brubaker?" he questioned with surprise as he began to stand up.

Bash pushed him back down into the chair.

"Stay put, Colby. What do you want here, Alex?"

"Was passing by and thought that fellow sitting up there with you was my cousin, Colby Christian."

"Yeah, it is Colby all right. He's a prisoner for the time being. Alex, you want to see him, come by the station. For now though, turn your horse and ride off."

"I ain't here to get your feathers ruffled," Alex said as he looked at Bash and smiled.

"Colby, I'll swing by the station later. I want to have words with you."

"Well, you know where I'll be, Alex. Looking forward to seeing you. Been a long time," Colby commented.

"I'll see you later, Colby."

Alex turned his horse and headed back the way he came.

"You're related to the Brubakers?" Bash questioned as he watched Alex leave.

"I am so. Been a lot of years since I last saw him. Odd seeing him without that brother of his."

"You haven't heard what happened to Earl Brubaker."

"Like I said, Bash, I ain't saw the Brubakers in a long while. What about Earl?"

"He was gunned down a year or so ago by Travis Sweet."

"The same Travis Sweet that brought us in?" Colby asked with surprise.

"Yep. The one and only. Took a few fingers off Alex's gun slinging hand, too, a few months back."

"Well, now. That is quite interesting. I never did like Earl much, Alex and I we were pretty close back in the day."

"You have any idea why he might be here?" Bash asked with authority.

"Nope. Not a clue."

Colby shrugged. He was hoping Alex was there to bust him out. Bash too was thinking the same thing.

"I suggest you get back at it, Colby. The weeds aren't going to pick themselves," Bash said as he contemplated.

"Yeah, I guess so."

Colby rose from where he was sitting and made his way back to the garden and continued weeding it. His mind filled with what he hoped would be his escape. Until he spoke with Alex, though, he wasn't clear on why he had shown up at all. It had been years since the two of them had even spoken. Colby shrugged his shoulders as he continued with his work while Bash sat in the shade and watched. An hour later, at 3:00, Colby was tucked away once more in the holding cells at the Mounted Police station. There was more work Bash knew that he could have Colby do, but under the circumstances and knowing what he knew about Colby and Alex being cousins, he thought better and instead allowed Colby an early day.

Alex had watched from his room window at the Snakebite as Bash and Colby made their way back to the station. He waited a few minutes before he headed that way himself. Entering the building he walked up to the counter and waited for either Bash or another constable to greet him. It was Bash who approached.

"Hello, Alex. Here to see Colby?" Bash asked already knowing the answer.

"Yep, said I'd be here. I need to talk to my cousin, Rick."

"Firstly you'll have to remove that gun-belt; visitors aren't allowed to pass while packing a pistol."

"Of course," Alex said as he removed his holster and set it on the counter.

"I'm going to also ask you to remove your boots, Alex."

"My boots?" Alex questioned with dismay.

"Want my hat too, Rick?"

Alex removed his boots and tossed his hat on the counter.

"Can I see my cousin now?"

"I'll give the two of you ten minutes. After that you'll be asked to leave."

"Lead the way, Rick," Alex said as he followed behind.

Constable Bash unlocked the heavy iron door that separated the holding cells from the station's front offices. He stepped aside and gestured for Alex to go on in. Then he closed and locked the door again.

"Ten minutes, Alex," Bash said as he turned and walked away.

Alex walked down to the furthest cell and looked in at Colby, who was sitting on his bunk smiling from ear to ear. Standing he walked up to the bars and reached out his hand to shake Alex's.

"Glad to see you, Alex. How have you been?"

"Better than you, I reckon. Eighteen more days to go, eh?"

"Unless, of course, you're here to get me out," Colby mentioned, now not sure that was the case.

"Nope. I ain't going to bust you out, Colby. I'm here to ask for your help once you get this over with. Could be big money for both of us."

"Shit, you ain't going to bust me out, but you have the balls to ask for my help?" Colby was a bit perturbed; he wanted answers.

"You want to listen to what I have to say? Or are you going to stand there like a crying baby because you are behind them bars? You did that to yourself, Colby. We've been warning you for years to stay away from that lot you was running with," Alex pointed out.

"Get on with it then, Alex. What kind of help you want from me?"

"Well, I ain't sure you've heard about Earl, but he's dead now. The same man that sent him to his grave took off a couple of my fingers."

Alex brought his right hand up and showed Colby.

"Yeah, I did hear about Earl, but only today. Heard about that hand of yours, too. That Travis fellow and another is who brought us in. You planning on killing him?"

Alex shook his head.

"Not at all."

47

"What do you want from me then?"

Alex smirked as he told Colby about Matt Crawford, that he had a good idea on where Crawford was heading and that with Colby's help, the two of them could bring Matt in and reap the reward.

"Ain't that a coincidence," Colby began. "Atalmore, me, and the others were up this way to track him down too. We wasn't going to claim no reward for him; Atalmore just wanted to talk with him about one thing or the other. I really didn't understand his reasoning to be honest. I didn't pry though neither. Ten thousand dollars, eh?" Colby questioned to be sure.

"Yep. So, what do you say, Colby? You want in?"

Colby didn't have time to reply though before Bash opened the big iron door and told Alex his time was up.

"You sleep on it, Colby. I'll try to get back and see you in a day or two," Alex said as he turned heel and met up with Bash, who closed and locked the door again.

"You sure that was even ten minutes, Rick?" Alex questioned as he made his way to the front of the station, gathered his gun-belt and slipped on his boots.

"According to the time on the wall," Bash commented.

"All right, I'll give you the benefit of the doubt," Alex smiled. "Thanks for allowing me to see Colby. I'll pop by again in a day or two."

"You staying in town then, Alex?"

"Is there a law against that?"

"Nope, not that I know of. Keep your nose clean while you are here though. We don't want any trouble."

"I ain't here to cause grief to you or the town folk. Once Colby has done his time, we'll be gone," Alex said as he walked away and exited into the street.

Matt Crawford was three days ride southwest of the Fort. He had been taking it slow, not in any real rush to get to Willow Gate. The town he knew would always be there and Gabe Roy would always reside there. Gabe had nowhere else to go and most who knew him as Matt knew him, knew that. He had burned too many bridges over the past and there really wasn't anywhere safer than in the British Columbia interior. Close enough to the United States yet far enough away that not many cared as long as Gabe Roy didn't show back up in the United States, that is. Down there and only a few knew it, Gabe Roy was wanted for countless infringements, mostly bad land deals. He had left a sour taste in everyone's mouth who had met him or had dealings with him. Hence, Gabe's need for hired security and his reasons for sending a wire to the McCoy's all those months back.

He was feeling the heat from those he had taken advantage of. He knew it was only a matter of time before somebody sent lead his way. Gabe, though, couldn't know then that the only person he should fear at the present time was Matt Crawford. Full of revenge, anger, and with both the law and bounty hunters on his trail, Matt really had nowhere else to go. As far as he was concerned, if the last thing he ever did before he was captured or shot dead himself was to kill Gabe Roy then he'd die a happy man.

Matt slowed his horse to a standstill as he swung off the saddle and led him through some bramble to a slow flowing creek he had heard. Letting the horse drink, he cupped his hands and splashed water on his face to cool himself down. It had been a hot day. Soon that would change as fall approached. Filling his canteen he drank from it as he stood up and looked around.

Calculating the days since he had been at the Fort's courthouse listening to the sentencing of Barclay Atalmore along with the men that rode with him, Matt figured the day to be August 29th, Saturday. *Easily a few more weeks ride before I'll make the distance to Willow Gate,* Matt thought as he looked westerly toward the Rocky Mountains. Knowing the sun would be going down soon, he swung onto his horse's back and continued southwest toward the town of Willow Gate and the mountains he needed to cross to get there.

Rarely using the more populated trails, he chose his route in a more direct way; straight. He was quite adept in survival techniques and as far as he was concerned the only way to avoid encounters with those trying for the monetary gain in bringing him in alive was to simply avoid wagon trails and little towns. He had a good horse and enough gear to survive the trek; anything else he needed he'd take from the land. Matt now turned his horse into the thick bush that encircled the first mountain he needed to cross. At dusk he'd settle at the foot of it and in the morning carry on.

Ed McCoy walked to the front of the office and put the 'Closed' sign in place as he lowered the blinds. Making his way back to the staff room where the others were seated, except for Riley Scott who had already left for the day. He poured his last coffee and sat down.

"I don't think Riley will be coming in tomorrow, he'll be all caught up in whatever it is he's going to do to that coach," Ed mentioned as he took a swing of his coffee.

"It's going to be kind of odd around here, knowing he isn't sleeping in that backroom anymore," Tyrell commented as he looked over to Tanner and smiled. Now was the perfect opportunity for him to finally get rid of Tanner and get his room back to himself.

"So, I volunteer Tanner to take up that space," Tyrell said with a smirk and wink.

"Yeah, yeah. I'm getting tired of your snoring too," Tanner replied. "If it is all right with you, Ed, can I take up that backroom?"

"That'll put you on twenty-four hour duty," Brady teased.

"I'll take it," Tanner replied as he shook his head.

"Yeah, by all means, you are welcome to take up that space. You might want to give it a cleanup though. Old Riley isn't one of the neater folk," Ed chuckled. "I'm kind of interested in seeing what he comes up with once he starts adding onto that coach."

"Riley is quite the creative man. I'm sure he'll come up with something that'll get him through. It is a lot better than starting out without a damn thing, I reckon."

"Says the man that once lived in a teepee."

"I most certainly did, and I'd do it again too. There isn't anything wrong with a teepee, Ed."

"I suppose not. I'm sure Riley will make that coach into a home. Anyway, fellow's I'm heading to mine now," Ed stood up and set his coffee cup down. "Before I forget, Tanner, I have Riley's old backdoor key, if you're going be staying down here, you'll likely need it."

Reaching into his vest pocket he handed the key to Tanner.

"Thanks, Ed. I'll do some cleaning tonight and likely get settled."

"All right, well, I'm off," Ed said as he exited the staff room and headed out.

"Anyone want to head over to the Snakebite and have a steak?" Brady asked as he too now stood and got ready to leave.

"I'll tag along with you. You are, of course, buying, right?" Tyrell replied with a smile.

"Sure. You coming, Tanner?"

"Nah, I'll get that backroom up to snuff so I can shift my gear. Might finally get a full night's sleep."

"Trust me, Tanner; I'll be looking forward to that too. Finally."

Tyrell slid his chair in and knocked off Tanner's hat as he walked by.

"Hey! What do you have against my hat?" Tanner joked as he grabbed it and set it back on his head.

"I just couldn't resist."

"Well, be on the lookout for a rattler in that room upstairs."

"Ah, a rattler ain't nothing to frown upon. Horse scat in your boots on the other hand might be," Tyrell replied as he and Brady exited into the warm evening.

"You know what, Brady? We're likely to run into Alex over there at the Snakebite."

"There is a good chance in that, Travis, but there are two of us. I don't suppose Alex is keen on starting trouble when the odds are stacked against him."

"Good point. He's going to be here for a while too. Colby still has eighteen or so days to go. I only hope he doesn't cross me again."

"If he does, kill him. Simple," Brady said as they walked the distance and entered.

The Snakebite that evening was quiet. The two of them made their way to the table they always sat at. Sitting, they looked around. Alex was nowhere to be seen and so they relaxed.

"It doesn't look as though he is about," Brady said as he raised his hand and signalled for the server.

"Evening, Brady, Travis. How are you guys tonight?" Kitty asked as she waited to take their orders.

"Beautiful day today wasn't it?" Tyrell said as he looked at her and smiled. "I'll have the usual, steak and spuds, Kitty."

"Sure and you, Brady?"

"Yeah, a round of steaks and can you bring us a draft as well?"

"I certainly will."

Kitty turned and pranced over to the counter to place the order, then filled up two beer glasses and returned to their table.

"Here are the drafts. The steak will be ready shortly."

She set the drafts down.

"I see that Alex Brubaker is in town. Are you guys aware of that?"

"Yep. He's here waiting for a prisoner to be released, his cousin Colby."

"Oh, that is who that young man is. I saw him weeding the widow Donale's garden earlier with constable Bash on guard."

"Yeah, that's him. He was sentenced to twenty days of community service."

"Was he one of the men you guys brought in a while ago, Travis?"

"The youngest of the bunch. The others got sent to Calgary. I guess the judge figured Colby has a chance of turning himself around," Tyrell responded.

"Only time will tell though," Brady added as he took a long swallow of the cold draft.

"Who decides what he does for community service?" Kitty questioned.

"The law I reckon. Why? What are you thinking?"

"Well, the boardwalk outside of the Snakebite could use some work. There is a ton of garbage under it. It would be nice to have it cleaned up."

"Have Jim go talk to the law. Maybe it is work that kid could do," Tyrell suggested with a shrug.

"I think I will see if Jim will do that. You know how he feels about keeping this place in tip-top condition," Kitty rolled her eyes.

Everyone knew Jim didn't care and was too cheap to fix most things. Getting something done for free though that he couldn't do himself was always appealing. Kitty was about to turn and walk away when Brady noticed Constable Rick Bash coming through the front door.

"Hey, look, there is Bash now. Let's get him over here and see what he has to say about it," Brady said as he waved him over.

"Be there in a minute, Brady, just going to grab a coffee," Bash responded as he waited for his coffee.

Finally, making his way over to their table he sat down.

"What can I do for you folks?" he asked as he added sweetener to his coffee and took a swallow.

"How's the kid doing," Brady questioned as he took a bite of steak and began to chew.

"Colby you mean?"

Brady nodded as he swallowed and picked up another piece with his fork.

"All right I reckon. Still has an attitude that won't wash off. Why do you ask?"

"He's too busy chewing there, Rick, to answer. So I will," Tyrell began. "Who decides on the kid's work?"

"Anybody can make a request. Then we decide if the work is fit. You got something you folks need done?"

"Not us particularly."

It was Tyrell's turn to start chewing so he gestured for Brady to answer.

Brady took another swig from his draft to wash the steak down.

"Kitty was wondering if her and Jim could have Colby clean up the boardwalk, replace boards and such; pick up the garbage that sort of thing."

"You want us to arm that hoodwink with a hammer and crow-bar?"

"With a fellow like yourself watching over him, what is there to fear?" Tyrell questioned with a slight frown.

"Likely nothing. We aren't allowed though to pay for materials, nails, boards and such. Who is going to pay for that?"

"I'm sure Kitty would," Brady shrugged, "hell, I'll pay. This community could use some touching up here and there. Why not get it done when the labor is free? The boards and nails won't cost much. Paying someone to do it does."

"Besides, that is the point of community service, ain't it?" Tyrell asked as he finished up his steak and swallowed.

"It is. Sure, I suppose we could get Colby working on that, as long as the materials are supplied. I'll see if I can't get an extra set of eyes, with Alex Brubaker in town and the fact that Colby and he are cousins, we can't be sure what might take place. You folks knew he was in town, didn't you?"

"We've known for a couple of days. We don't think he's here to cause trouble though, and yeah, I'll supply the material to get the boardwalk fixed up to Kitty's liking," Brady made clear.

"I'll throw in a couple of bucks too, if you can get Colby to clean the stalls back at the McCoy's," Tyrell said with a chuckle. "I heard he doesn't like that kind of work."

The three men chuckled in unison.

"You got that right. The whole time he cleaned the police stables he did nothing but bellow. We'll get to yours too," Bash said as he stood up. "Best time I would think to work on the boardwalk would be tomorrow being it'll be Sunday and all. We'll start by pulling up the old boards and taking count on how many we'll need. You'll get the boards we'll need by Monday, Brady?"

"First thing, as soon as Jefferies is opened, 7:00 a.m., or there about. Will that work?"

"Yep, that'll be fine. Well, I guess I'm going to shove off. Got to get back to the station. Lucky me I'm on all week. The cook, the guard and the law," Constable Bash said as he bid them good night and left.

"There we have it. The work will get done. It'll cost us a couple of bucks, but having that kid pull up those old weathered boards will be good for entertainment. The only reason Jim don't do it is because of the back breaking work to pull the boards up and the nails out," Brady smirked at his devious ploy.

"Once Colby gets that out of the way and our stalls cleaned, I guess we'll see if we can't get him digging a well."

"You mean on Riley's land?"

"Do so. I reckon that'll be a nice way for the kid to end his services to our fine community. That is of course if the law will allow it."

"And I thought my ploy to have him pull up that boardwalk was good punishment. Digging on Riley's land for a well tops that," Brady smiled as he finished the last of his draft. "Do you want another, Travis?"

"Nah. I'm filled up on that steak and spuds. I think I'll head back to my room and make it my own again. Thanks for the steak, Brady and I'll see you in the morning."

Tyrell rose from the table while Brady ordered another draft for himself.

"Yeah, see you in the morning. I'll let Kitty know about that work Colby is going to do."

"You bet."

Tyrell walked across the room and exited onto the street to a face to face encounter with Alex Brubaker.

"Evening, Travis. How was your dinner?" Alex asked as he approached.

"Hello, Alex. How is the hand healing?" Tyrell was a little nervous, but knew he could beat Alex anytime of the week. He just didn't want to have to.

"As best as it'll ever get, I suppose. I'm getting used to using my left. Shouldn't be too much longer now and she'll be as good as what my right used to be," Alex responded as he looked at his left hand and the pistol that now draped off his left hip.

Tyrell inhaled deeply.

"You're not thinking on pulling that six shooter are you Alex?"

"Not on you and certainly not today."

"What is that supposed to mean?"

"Meaning I ain't going to pull my pistol on you, not today leastwise."

"You have intent on doing it sooner or later, then?"

"Never said that either. Look, Travis, like I told Ed, I ain't here to put holes in you or anyone else for that matter. I'm waiting to take Colby home; that is it; that is all. There is no other reason why I'm here. I do sleep better at night though, knowing you all feel threatened."

"I never said I felt threatened, Alex. Nor does anyone else as far as I know," Tyrell said with conviction. "I am getting sick and tired of this charade though, it is getting old."

Alex shook his head.

"There ain't no charade going on. I ain't holding any grudges whatsoever about what went on between you and I. In fact, it took me a day or two to realise how lucky I might have been that you and Ed didn't bury me out on the prairie all those weeks ago. But, I did realise it. If you never cross me, Travis, I'll never cross you. I deal out respect to men that I feel deserve it. You're one of the lucky ones."

"I don't know if you are talking horse scat to me or not. And frankly I don't care either way. Respect is a two way street Alex and you have a long way to go," Tyrell replied.

"I get it Travis and I ain't sore at the fact that you feel that way," Alex tilted his hat. "I'll be seeing you," he said as he walked away and entered the Snakebite.

Tyrell sighed as he watched Alex leave. He was glad in a sense that they had their encounter. It put his mind at ease. He wasn't sure Alex had been feeding him a line of crap or not, but he did believe Alex was only there to meet up with Colby.

"You'll live another day, Alex Brubaker. You'll live another day," Tyrell said quietly to himself as he continue on.

For now he would keep their encounter to himself. By the time he made it back to the McCoy's office, Tanner was all packed up and heading to the backroom.

"How was the steak?" Tanner asked as he met Tyrell on the stairs that led to his room.

"As good as always. You should have joined us."

"Wouldn't have got that backroom all cozy if I had. I'll tell you what, Ed was right. Riley ain't a very neat and tidy fellow. It took two buckets of water just to clean up the floor. I got the room to my liking now though," Tanner said with a big smile glad to have his own space.

"The only problem is bringing women there."

Tyrell began to chuckle. "Yeah, I can see how that might be an inconvenience. That cot ain't quite big enough for two is it?"

Tanner waved his hand through the air.

"Ah, it don't matter. There is always a room available at the Snakebite should the need arise. I'm going to finish up now. Maybe I'll pop upstairs and see you later."

"Sure, we can play a couple of hands. I got a fresh deck of cards."

"What do you have to offer, in a game of stud?"

"Umm, I don't know. How about a ten dollar donation."

"A donation?" Tanner asked with confusion.

"Yeah, a ten dollar donation to the Mounted Police to have our boy Colby clean our stalls."

"Now that I would like to see. Sure, a ten dollar donation."

"All right then. Maybe I'll see you later," Tyrell said as he continued up the stairs and entered his room.

He was shocked to see that everything in the room including his bed was turned upside down. All his clothes were turned inside out. The list went on. Things were in disarray. There was no doubt about it.

"Tanner, you son-of-a-bitch!" he hollered as he made his way down the stairs to give Tanner a whisterpoop.

Tanner though had locked the door. Tyrell reached for his key to unlock it realising that he no longer had it.

"You have my key too, you son-of-a-bitch?" Tyrell questioned loud enough for Tanner to hear him on the other side of the door.

"Yep. See you in the morning."

He could hear Tanner laughing.

"You'll get yours, Tanner, rest assured."

Tyrell shook his head as he chuckled at the fun Tanner was having with him.

"Cockroach," he mumbled as he headed back up the stairs to straighten his room. Black Dog lay at the door laughing, it would seem, as Tyrell wrestled with putting things back in order.

"You couldn't have at least put a stop to him before tipping this damn bed over?"

Tyrell shook his head as Black Dog looked at him and continued to pant and laugh.

"The two of you were in on this together I reckon. No jerky for you tonight," Tyrell teased as he continued with the tasks in front of him.

Chapter 4

Sundays were always lazy at McCoy's and the men usually called it a day at noon. Today would be no different. Tyrell had to wait for Ed or Brady to let him in since Tanner had pocketed his key the night before. It was Brady who showed up first and he questioned why Tyrell was sitting on the stairs. Explaining what took place the night before, Brady began to chuckle.

"He turned everything upside down?"

"Yep. Turned all my clothes inside out, dumped out all my bullets and hid the damn water bucket to fill the toilet cistern."

Brady continued to chuckle as he unlocked the door. "I can't believe that, damn that is funny."

"From the outside maybe. It wasn't so fun cleaning things up," Tyrell said as he followed Brady inside. He knew it was all in fun and he would get his revenge in time. Pouring himself a coffee he sat down across from Tanner who began to chuckle.

"Did you have a good night, Travis?" Tanner asked with a smirk as he tossed Tyrell his key.

"I think you know what kind of night I had. No thanks to you," Tyrell took a swig from his coffee and smiled. "You know, Tanner, revenge can be a real kick in the pants."

"Oh, come on now, admit it. It was funny. You never expected that did you? I owed you at least that for knocking off my hat all those times."

"Well, don't be surprised to find a wasp nest in your bedroll one time or another," Tyrell said as he slurped again from his coffee.

"Ouch. That could be nasty," Brady said as he too now sat. "Fun and games aside, I ran across Alex last night, said you and he had words."

"We did," Tyrell confirmed.

"What did he say to you?"

"Nothing that makes any difference. I don't think he is here to cause problems though. He seemed sincere that he was only waiting for Colby to be released."

"Same impression I got. Nonetheless, makes me wonder why?" Brady replied as he took a drink from his own steaming hot cup of coffee.

"I don't reckon anyone can know why, except for what he says that he's here to gather Colby. What might take place after that is anyone's guess. He ain't broke any law and he ain't threatened any of us. That is about all we can say about that," Tyrell pointed out.

"True enough. But, I have a hunch there is more to it than simply that."

"That is likely true, but as I said we can't know what that might be 'less we start prying into his business. Which, I really have no desire to do. I say let him be."

"One thing I can say about Alex," Tanner began as he stood up and poured a second coffee. "Like I told Ed, Alex ain't nothing like Earl had been. He took orders from his brother, did most things under his influence. With Earl pushing up daisies Alex will now be running on his own steam, making his own decisions and whatnot. Even while Earl was alive neither one really tore up the law. Sure, they have a reputation but so do most men. Remember they brought to justice worse men.

Although, I know Earl was likely turned away at the pearly gates, and he bullied most, may have even killed a few men in cold blood, he's dead now. His influence on Alex has ended, and just like the dirt that covers his carcass, Alex will always bear the scars that Earl carved into him. I mean that in the literal sense not a physical sense," Tanner sat down.

"I think we know what you mean, Tanner, and I would agree, but there is something going on. I feel it in my bones." Brady was certain of it.

"Speculation and assumptions, Brady. That is all that is."

"I suppose you are right, Travis. We'll just have to wait and see what comes about once Colby is released. As long as the two of them leave here I won't care much about what happens after that."

Tyrell inhaled deeply then sighed.

"Yeah, truth be known I'll feel better once the both of them are gone too."

A few minutes later both Riley and Ed showed up. They met the others in the staff room and poured themselves a coffee.

"How was your first night sleeping in that stagecoach, Riley?" Brady asked as Riley pulled up a chair and sat down.

"Compared to the cot, I slept like a lamb. Sure had a symphony of coyotes howling. They got a bit annoying after a while. That aside though it was exactly what I expected. I'm going to like living there if that is what you mean. Came up with a few ideas of things I'm going to do to that coach too, to make it more home like."

"Such as?" Ed asked as he leaned on the small counter and slurped his coffee.

"To start I got to rip out the seats and build a bunk; they just ain't quite long enough to stretch out on. Next I'll put a wood stove in the coach section and another in the room I'm going to build off of it. I reckon I'll use the coach section for sleep. The other room will be for sitting and entertaining. It won't take long I don't think. Any volunteers to give me a hand?" Riley tossed out.

"I figure we can give you hand. There ain't much else we're doing at the present time," Ed responded. "What are you going to do about water?"

"I'll get a well dug. You know of any water-dowsers in these parts?"

"Water-witchery? You don't believe in that mumbo-jumbo do you, Riley?" Tanner questioned.

"Sure do. Saw folks finding water first hand that way a number of times. What, you don't believe in it Tanner?"

"I guess not. I've never saw it done only heard about it. Thought it was a dime story. Still do as a matter-of-fact."

"Nope, there are folks that have the knack. They use a willow branch and somehow when they get close to water, the damn stick actually points to the ground. A good dowser gets it right every time. So, back to the question, Ed, you know of anyone like that around here?" Riley questioned a second time.

"I'm thinking on it, Riley. I do recall that the widow Donale's brother may have dabbled in that. It was him, wasn't it, Brady, that found the water here in town all those years back, wasn't it?"

"How many years back are we talking old man? We dug our own well at the house, didn't use no water witch then. As for this place, it already had water plumbed in case in your old age you've forgotten that."

Brady shook his head.

"Yeah, that's right. You were still suckling your ma's breast when the town found water. You wouldn't remember such a thing," Ed said with a chuckle, as Brady's face turned three shades of red. He was speechless; not often did his old man get a dig in like that.

"Yep, that there was a good one old man, it certainly was," Brady responded with discomfort.

The others laughed softly until Riley spoke.

"How did this conversation go from water witching to Brady's ma's tits?" Riley asked as though it were nothing offensive at all.

That is when the entire crew burst out into peals of loud table slapping laughter. It took Riley a second to clue in at what he said and when he did his laughter was the loudest heard.

"Aw Jesus, I didn't mean nothing disrespectful, Ed, Brady. It kind of just jumped out of my mouth is all."

"No disrespect taken, Riley. It was quite fitting," Ed said as he continued to snicker.

"Geez, what a hell of a start to the day," Tanner mentioned as he wiped away the tears from laughing so hard.

"I'll second that," Tyrell said as he slowly caught his breath. "That was damn witty, Ed, but I don't think the beautiful woman standing at the counter thinks it was."

Ed swallowed deeply and his eyes got big.

"Is she there?" he whispered, thinking that it was his wife that Tyrell was referring to.

How he hoped that wasn't the case.

Tyrell smiled and shrugged his shoulders.

"I ain't sure, Ed, it might be her."

He stood up and greeted the lady.

"Hello there," he began as he stepped out of the staff room and walked toward the front counter.

"Is there something, I can help you with, ma'am?"

"Perhaps. You must be Travis."

The lady reached out her hand.

"I'm Mrs. McCoy; you can call me Beth," she responded as Travis shook her hand.

Ed and Brady hearing the voice grew nervous with dread. If she had heard what they were laughing at earlier, she would be having words with them once she got them alone.

"Damn," Brady said in a quiet voice. "What a time for her to show up. You didn't know anything about this old man?"

Ed shook his head as he slowly rose and slid his chair back under the table. Making his way to the front counter, he put on a smile and hoped for the best.

"Hello, hon, what a nice surprise to see you here today. What brings you?" he asked with apprehension.

"Well, it certainly isn't for the jokes," she commented. "But now isn't the time or place for me to get into that, and on a Sabbath, Ed, really."

She rolled her eyes at him.

"My visit is to meet Travis and to see how Tanner is getting along and to say hello to Riley. I haven't seen him or Tanner since the shootings and I only recently met this wonderful man," she said referring to Travis.

"Thank you, ma'am," Tyrell said as he nodded his respect. "It was nice meeting you too for the first time. I guess I'll leave the two of you alone."

He began to walk away.

"Before you go, Travis, I would like to invite you and the others to dinner next Sunday. Can you pass that invitation onto both Riley and Tanner for me?"

"Sure will, ma'am, yes indeed. And thank you for the invite. I will certainly look forward to it," Tyrell tilted his hat and returned to the staff room leaving Ed and his Misses alone.

A brief squabble took place and a few choice words were tossed around. The four men sitting in the staff room, Brady included, chuckled softly and shook their heads.

"There is no need for you to be chuckling in there, Brady McCoy! I'll be having words with you soon enough," they heard Beth say. "Come on Ed, take me home. You have chores to do."

She was dead set in ruining his day; there was no doubt about it.

"Give me a minute to gather my stuff," Ed said with misgivings as he turned and walked back into the staff room to let the fellows know he was headed to Hell in a hand basket.

"Yeah, we heard old man; you best get," Brady said with a grin from ear to ear.

"Keep grinning, son, 'cause I'm sure your ma ain't done with you yet. The rest of you are safe I reckon. I'll see you all in the morning, if I live that long."

"Yep, we'll see you then, Ed. Have a great rest of the day," Tyrell gibed as Ed turned and walked to his awaiting fate.

"Damn, I still didn't get the answer about that water dowser," Riley commented as he stood up and poured another coffee.

"Ed said that he thought it was the widow Donale's brother who found the water for the town. We could take a ride down to her place and inquire about it," Tyrell suggested.

"Ah, no need to do it today; I don't own the land yet."

Riley took a drink from his coffee.

"With the boss gone for the rest of the day, should we get a hand of stud going?"

"Kind of early for a game of stud, Riley."

"No takers then, eh? All right, well, I'm going to head back over to the Miller place. Come morning I'll be owning that chunk," Riley said as he downed his last coffee.

"I reckon there isn't much else going on today. With Ed gone and all my paperwork caught up, I think I'll join you if you don't mind, Riley?" Tyrell questioned.

"Sure, we can grab us a bottle and hang out in the shade. Got the coach sitting nicely under a big ol' tree. It's probably the only one that big that exists on that land," Riley chuckled.

"Anyone else want to tag along is welcome," Tyrell and Riley slid their chairs in.

"Sure," Tanner said as he too stood up and slid his chair in.

"You going to come along, Brady?"

"Nah, you fellows go ahead, I'll stick close to here. Never know what might go on with Colby fixing the boardwalk and Alex nearby. I'll likely head over that way and see how things are going. An extra set of eyes and pistol can't hurt."

"Think there is a need for that, Brady?" Tyrell asked in mid-stride.

"Not sure, who knows, maybe."

"Well, maybe we all ought to consider that. Heck, we only have a few more hours 'til the day ends anyway. I'll take you up on that bottle another time, Riley. I think Brady might have a point."

Tyrell leaned up on the counter.

"Humph, here I thought I could have a nice relaxing day in the shade, but on reconsideration, we'll get a bottle another time. Might be as relaxing to watch that Colby kid pull up that boardwalk."

"So no bottle and no shade. All right I guess we'll tag along with you, Brady," Tanner shrugged, "like Riley said, could be as relaxing to watch that kid work his fingers to the bone. Think he is learning anything yet?"

"I figure he's going to be no different than he was beforehand. Smart mouths like that Colby kid don't change much overnight. It is going to take a lot longer than twenty days of hard labor for him to see the light."

"I don't know, Brady. People do change. Could be Colby might too."

"You might be right, Riley, but I'd put no stock into that," Brady added.

An hour later, the four men were sitting on a boardwalk bench on the other side of the street where Colby was working. Every now and again, he would cuss at the next board he was tearing up and so on. It was quite the spectacle and surprisingly Alex never even showed up. Brady and the others though had a few good laughs as they taunted Colby. At it now for a couple of hours, Bash let him rest and gave him a canteen of water.

"Only a few more boards to go, Colby. I figure since it is Sunday, once you get those last four boards up, I'll take you back," Bash said as he waited for Colby to finish his cold drink.

Colby wiped his mouth.

"The boards might be a pain in the backside to rip up, Bash, but I'd rather do something else once I'm done here, than have to sit in a cell."

"We can get you started on cleaning the McCoy's stable if you are that dead set on doing something. We can't replace any of these boards yet until we get the lumber. It should be here tomorrow morning."

"Anything is better than sitting in a damn cell. Let me get these boards up," Colby said as he handed Bash the canteen and went back at it.

"I'm going to walk over to where Brady and the others are sitting, Colby and a have a few words. Don't try anything stupid. I'm sure they'd be on you like flies on scat."

"I ain't going to do anything Bash, 'cept get these damn boards up. I ain't stupid," Colby said as he turned and grabbed the crowbar to rip up the next board. He struggled with it and the board broke in half, the crowbar danced out of his hand and he slammed his knuckles hard and fast into the rotting board.

"Goddamn!" he shouted as he looked at his bloodied, bruised and skinned knuckles.

Bash stopped in the middle of the street and looked back; Colby was standing and shaking his hand.

"You okay, Colby?" he asked with slight concern as he looked on.

"Yeah, I'll be fine. The damn bar slipped and I slammed my fist into the board is all, a little bruised and bloodied, but I'll live," Colby replied as he looked down and saw a notebook.

He made sure Bash wasn't looking and he scooped it up and flipped through a couple of pages. He knew he had found something of importance when he read the name 'Ron Reginal'. It was the name that Matt Crawford was using as an alias. It meant that he had stumbled onto Matt Crawford's notebook. He would have not known this had he not been riding with Atalmore and his Rebel Rangers. Colby smiled as he tucked it away in his pocket. He'd have to ditch it somewhere and when he and Alex finally got together they could read it more thoroughly. The first few pages he glanced at had a few names listed that weren't new to him; he had heard those names spoken before. Gabe Roy, Talbot Hunter and Riley Scott were three amongst a dozen or so that he recognized. His mind filled with the unknown and what it all meant. He hoped Alex would have the answers.

By now Bash was on the other side of the street talking with Brady and the others.

"I appreciate you folks being here. I know you're probably here to help keep an eye on things while Colby rips up the boardwalk, but is it necessary to taunt him?" Bash asked as he smiled and shook his head, knowing they meant no harm.

"I suppose you are right. How is the kid doing anyway?"

"Same as he was the first day. He might come around, I don't know," Bash sighed as he squinted and looked across to where Colby continued to work.

"He doesn't want to go back to his cell once he is done there. If you folks want we can get him started on your stables."

"Well as you know, Rick, we shut down at noon on Sundays. Not much longer and that is what time it'll be."

"None of you need to be there, Brady, as long as you give me the go ahead. Otherwise, I'll be dragging him back to the cell. It doesn't matter either way to me," Constable Bash shrugged his shoulders.

"Tanner and I would be around, Brady. The stable could use a cleaning. None of us have done that in a while," Tyrell pointed out.

He understood Colby's desire to avoid being sent back to a cell, probably the most boring place on earth. It was a warm day and there was a lot of it left before it ended.

"There you have it, Rick. If you want Colby to start that, go ahead I guess. Travis and Tanner will be around."

"Good enough, Brady. We'll get started as soon he gets those last couple of boards tore up," Bash said as he began to walk away.

75

"Hold up a minute, Rick. You have an estimate on how many boards you need over there?" Brady asked, reaffirming that he'd be buying them.

"If you can give me a number now, I'll make sure you get them in the morning."

"Sure, he's tore up a dozen give or take; each is about three foot long. To be on the safe side, say forty feet plus or minus."

"All right. I'll make sure you have that in the morning. A couple pounds of four inch nails too, I reckon."

"Yep, that ought to do it, Brady."

"Good enough," Brady called after him as Bash continued across the street.

"Well, Colby," Bash began as he made the distance to where Colby worked, "Brady says it is all right to start on their stables if you want to do that."

"I might want to get this hand tended to before that."

Colby showed the wound to Bash.

"Damn, that must've stung some. Yeah, we best get that looked at. Might have broke a knuckle or two."

"Nope, I don't think anything is broke, but I don't want to be digging in horse shit without it being bandaged."

"No, no, we'd never expect you to do that, Colby. An infection is all we'd need to have to deal with. Nope we'll get you bandaged," Bash said as he gestured for Colby to continue.

"Pop up that last board and we'll see to it."

Colby nodded as he went about tearing up the next board which surprisingly came up a lot easier than any other.

"I guess I found the technique in popping these damn boards up. That came up easy."

"Hey, you learned something," Bash teased with a smile.

"Now come on, let's get that last piece of garbage cleaned up and gather the tools. We'll get you over to the Doc's once we've done that."

Constable Bash watched as Colby finished up.

"You find anything interesting while you tore up those boards, coins or anything like that?" Bash asked out of curiosity.

He was surprised at Colby's honesty when he responded.

"Found about six dollars' worth of coins. Does the law want them?"

He'd hand them over if that were the case. The notebook though, he wouldn't say a thing about. The information it might contain was worth more than six dollars.

"Not at all. You found them, you keep them. I'll put them in with your belongings once we get back to the station later today."

Not often could a boardwalk be tore up without something being found and Bash knew that. By asking he was testing Colby. The kid had passed the test as far as he knew.

With the work now done, Bash and Colby made their way over to the Doc's house and had Colby's hand tended to. No breaks were found, but he did have a nasty bruise. With Colby cleaned and bandaged, the two headed over to the McCoy's stable. Bash opened the big back sliding door and they entered the barn.

"There is a wheelbarrow over there and a scoop shovel beside it. I guess it all gets piled over there," Bash pointed at a pile of manure. "You know what to do. I'll be outside if you have any questions. Travis or Tanner should be by soon."

Bash stepped into the horse corral, climbed to the top railing and sat down. He could see Colby from there and he watched as the kid went about the task of scooping up manure. Colby, knowing that Bash had his eye on him, waited for the right time to hide the notebook he found. It wasn't until Tyrell showed up an hour later that Colby was able to hide the book. He stuck it behind a few old feed barrels and kicked straw over it. He and Alex would have to sneak into the barn to retrieve it, but that wouldn't be a problem. Satisfied, he continued with the task at hand.

"Looks like Colby is doing a heck of a job, Rick," Tyrell pointed out as he leaned on the railed fence.

Bash hopped down from where he was sitting.

"A couple more hours and he'll have it all cleaned up."

"Yeah, he's doing a fine job. We appreciate Colby doing it, so here is a few bucks for him once he gets released."

Tyrell reached into his pocket and pulled out some coins and a couple of dollar bills that added up to ten dollars.

"I reckon he deserves this," he said as he handed the money to Constable Bash.

"Thank you, Travis. I'll be sure he gets it."

Bash slipped the money into his own pocket.

"He found six dollars tearing up the boardwalk. He had about twenty on him when the judge sent him our way. At least he'll have a bit of cash to get by once we set him loose."

"He didn't happen to find an old notebook, did he?" Tyrell questioned as he remembered that he had tried fishing one out from the same boardwalk that Colby was repairing. He didn't care; he was only curious.

"Notebook?" Bash questioned, "Nope, he didn't say nothing about that. Did you lose one?"

"No, no, saw one under the boardwalk a while ago, tried grabbing it, but I couldn't," Tyrell shrugged. "It was probably garbage."

"Well, he did clean up a lot of that. Never mentioned anything about a notebook, though. Like you said, it was probably garbage."

"More than likely, yep," Tyrell nodded in agreement.

"You folks want anything to drink? I can gather some water or if you like, it won't take long to bring you fellows a couple of coffees."

"I figure Colby is almost done. It shouldn't be much longer, so, no thanks, Travis."

"All right," Tyrell nodded and thanked Bash again for Colby's service. Then he turned and walked away with Black Dog trailing close behind.

A short while later, Colby dumped the last load of manure onto the pile.

"That is the end of it, Bash. All done," Colby said as he approached.

"Let's have a look at how clean you got it."

Bash followed Colby into the barn and looked around.

"Good job, Colby. I guess that'll be it for the day. Tomorrow, we'll have the lumber to finish the boardwalk. You feel like getting cleaned up?"

"That is a dumb question, Bash. I just spent four or five hours cleaning up scat. Of course I'd like to clean up."

"It is early enough. I'm sure that the widow Donale has a tub of water available. You want to dip into a bath or clean up at the station?"

"A bath sounds good to me. I ain't had one of those in a while."

"You are allowed one a week while in custody. I'll take you over to her place. You best make it a quick bath too. And don't try anything stupid because I'll be right outside the door."

"Yeah, I wouldn't imagine you being anywhere else but outside the damn door," Colby said as they walked the distance.

The widow Donale was sitting on her porch and watched as Bash and Colby came up to her stoop.

"Afternoon, Constable Bash and Mr. Colby. I bet you are here for a bath."

"I am, ma'am. Is there a tub available?" Colby asked politely.

"There is. Come on, follow me," she said as she lead them to the bath.

"I have fresh water heating up, so go ahead and get started. I'll bring it along shortly."

"Thank you, ma'am. It has been a long while since I last had a bath."

Colby stripped down to his birthday suit and stepped into the cooling water. Bash remained outside the door and entered only when the widow brought a tub of fresh clean water.

"Here you go, Colby. This should make your bath more enjoyable," she said as she poured the tub of water into his bath.

Colby thanked her as he continued to scrub for a few more minutes. Finished, he stood up and dried off, then slipped his dirty clothes on. Bash met him outside the door and after paying for Colby's bath, the two of them made their way back to the Mounted Police station.

"Feel a little better, Colby?"

"Best as I can feel under the circumstances. I'm hungry now, though," he said as he sat down on his bunk.

"I'll put some beans and bread on for you. How does that sound?"

"Beans is better than nothing, I suppose," Colby responded as Bash left, locked the big door and headed into the small kitchen.

Returning a few minutes later, he handed Colby his plate of beans and a few pieces of bread.

"Thank you, Bash," Colby said as he took the plate and sat back down.

"After I'm done with that boardwalk, what else do you have planned for me?" he asked as he took a spoonful of beans and began to eat.

"I'll come up with something. I'm not sure what yet," Bash responded as he watched Colby for a few minutes. "When you are done with that plate, give me a shout."

Bash turned and walked away to fill out the day's reports on Colby and the work he had done. He put the money Tyrell had given him for Colby and the money Colby had found into an envelope and stuck it in the drawer with Colby's other belongings. Colby finally hollered that he was done and Bash poured him a coffee and brought it to him as he gathered the plate and spoon.

"How were the beans?" Bash asked as he handed him a coffee and took the plate and spoon from him.

"What could ever be different with beans?" Colby half chuckled as he took the coffee and sat back down.

"Ah, they was good enough. Thanks for the coffee, Bash. Much appreciated."

"You did good work today, Colby. Keep it up and the days will go by fast."

"Nope, I don't think the days will go any faster, Bash. I still have a long way to go."

"True as that might be, I'd think not doing anything at all would make the time drag on. At least you get out on a daily basis."

Colby shrugged.

"You might be right there, but time is still time and twenty days of community service ain't something I look forward to."

Colby took a drink from his coffee and sighed.

"I can't wait 'til it is over and the law opens that door and sends me on my way."

The two of them conversed for a few minutes longer and then Bash closed the door for the last time that night.

"I'll see you in the morning," he said as he exited.

"I reckon so."

Colby watched Bash leave.

Alone now, he reminisced and contemplated on what he and Alex would do once he was released. The notebook he had hidden, he knew, would come in handy as the two of them pursued Matt Crawford or so he hoped. He didn't have enough time to read much of what was in it. He was certain though that it contained useful information that pertained to Matt. Soon his eyes got heavy and he curled up on his bunk and wrapped the one blanket over his shoulders. Closing his eyes he fell asleep as the evening grew dark.

Chapter 5

On Monday, August 31 1891, Constable Bash opened the big iron door and made his way down the corridor to Colby's cell. In his hands he had a plate of eggs and coffee.

"Rise and shine, Colby. Got your breakfast and coffee," Bash said as he waited for Colby to approach.

Colby rolled over and looked toward Bash. "Eggs again this morning?" he asked as he pulled the woolen blanket off and stood up.

"Nothing wrong with eggs, Colby; they are a good start to the day. I got you a coffee too."

Bash handed the meal and drink to Colby.

"Never said there was anything wrong with eggs, Bash."

Colby took the plate and coffee and sat back down on the bunk.

"Figure I'll get that boardwalk finished today?"

"It shouldn't take long to nail a dozen boards down. It all depends on how hard you want to work, I guess."

"I hope to get it done today. Did you come up with anything for me to do afterwards?"

Colby took a drink from his coffee.

"That is decent coffee today, Bash. Did your Ma make it?" Colby teased with a smile.

It was then Bash heard the bell up front being rung.

"Sounds like someone is looking for a lawman. I'll come back after I deal with whatever it is I need to deal with now."

"I'll be here, Bash. I'll be here," Colby repeated.

Constable Bash made his way to the front counter and was greeted by Riley Scott.

"Morning, Rick," Riley started.

"What brings you, Riley? And how are you today?"

"Pretty good, today. Just got back from the land titles office."

"So, you're the new owner of the Miller place, then?"

"Am so. Well worth the fifteen hundred dollar price tag. I'm here to ask a question, Bash. Any chance I could use Colby to do some work on the land? I'll pay a fee if that is required."

"What kind of work are we talking about?"

"Labor intense I'm sure. I'll be looking into finding a water-dowser in the next couple of days. Could use a young whippersnapper like that kid to help dig a well."

"That ought to take up a few days. I'll have to run it by Lieutenant Cannon first, though. Community service usually means those sentenced to it do community work. I'm not so sure digging a well on private land is community service. The work he did for the widow Donale was a type of community service since she's the one that keeps our prisoners fed most times. I will run your offer by Cannon. He is in tomorrow."

Riley rapped his knuckles on the counter.

"Okay, it'll probably take a day or two to find a dowser in these parts anyway. Which brings me to my next question. You know anyone that does dowsing?"

"There is an old fellow I can't remember his name off hand, but I think he is the widow Donale's brother," Bash shrugged. "He is the only one I've ever heard about that might be able to help you."

"Yeah, Ed mentioned that the other day. I guess I'll pay the widow a visit. Thanks, Rick."

Riley tilted his hat and exited. Making his way over to the widow Donale's place he gently knocked on the door. He heard the widow approach and standing back he removed his hat to show respect.

"Mr. Scott, how nice of you to stop by. Are you here for a bath or a laundry wash?" she asked as he gestured for him to come in.

"No ma'am, neither. I've heard tale that you have a brother that dabbles in water dowsing."

"Yes. You must have bought the old Miller place."

"How did you know that ma'am?"

"It is the only place around here that doesn't have a well of sorts."

"Really, every other place has water?" Riley asked with curiosity.

"Most do, or they at least have a creek nearby. The Miller place though, I know, has not. That is why they were having so much trouble selling that place. One could always put a cistern in I suppose and haul water in from town. With all the new fancy hand pumps and whatnot that shouldn't be too hard to do."

Riley nodded his head. It was something he hadn't even thought about.

"I guess that is another option if all else fails. So, about your brother, does he live nearby?"

"He now lives in Pincher Station. You could send him a wire, but I have to warn you he is a bit of a codger. Downright miserable at the best of times. But that aside, he could maybe find water for you. I won't make any promises though. His name is Thomas Matchery. Does that help?"

"I think so. Thank you very much, ma'am. I'll send him a wire and wait to see what he has to say. You say his name is Thomas Matchery?" Riley wanted to be clear.

"Yes. Tell him that I sent you. I haven't seen him in a year or so and it would be nice to see him, before he and I both get too old and die," she chuckled. She wasn't as old as most folks thought.

"I will, ma'am. I'll tell him you sent me."

Riley thanked her and was about to leave when she offered him a cup of coffee.

"Mr. Scott, before you leave would you like to join me for a hot cup of coffee? I have a fresh pot brewing."

"Thank you. Yes indeed, I'll join you."

Riley followed her to the kitchen. She directed him to the table and poured them each a cup.

"Will you take cream and sugar?" she asked from the counter.

"Yes, please," Riley said as he looked around the quaint room and waited. The smell of fresh coffee and pie wafted up his nostrils, it made his mouth water slightly.

"Sure smells good in here."

"I'm baking pies for the Snakebite today and fresh bread for the Mounted Police station so they can keep that young fellow Colby fed. Would you like a piece and some jam to go with your coffee?"

"I wouldn't want to feel like I'm intruding, ma'am. I'm quite content with a coffee."

"Oh, don't be silly, Mr. Scott. I'll cut you up some bread," she said as she went about the task.

Riley didn't argue. Fresh bread and jam with coffee sounded good. A few minutes later the widow brought the tray of bread and coffee and set it down on the table. It was a nice visit and they each learned one thing or another about the other. Two cups of coffee later and a few more pieces of the widow Donale's bread, Riley stood up, thanked her again and told her he'd be by later in the week to have a bath and laundry done.

"That'll be fine, Mr. Scott. I'm always open," she said as she walked him to the door.

Riley waved at her as he headed down the street toward McCoy's. It didn't take him long to get there and he was met by Ed.

"Hey, Riley running a little late today?" he asked.

Usually, Riley was one of the first to show up at the office.

"Stopped off at the widow Donale's place to see if her brother is, as you and Bash have both said, a water dowser. He is. Lives in Pincher Station. I'll probably send off a wire today or tomorrow. Also asked Bash if that kid Colby could help dig a well. He's going to talk it over with Cannon, I guess in the next day or so."

"I knew it was the widow's brother. His name escapes me, though. What is it?" Ed asked.

"Thomas. I guess he's a bit of an ol' codger, according to the widow. Still, if he can help me find water, I ain't going to complain."

Riley looked around.

"Where's the others?"

"Sent them out to pick up old Whiskey Tooth George. Reportedly, he's been in the area again, bootlegging whiskey to those that don't need it," Ed replied as he shook his head.

"That ol' son-of-a-bitch just don't want to learn, does he?"

"Nope. Was slow around here so figured, Brady and the others could use some excitement. He's still only worth the five hundred dollars offered, but it'll be worth the chuckle when they finally track him down. If they even manage."

Old Whiskey Tooth was a hard man to take in and both Riley and Ed knew that.

"Excitement they'll get," Riley snickered. "I brought him in once a few years back, took me all day to find him and another two to bring him in. He'll skip on them every chance he gets," Riley pointed out as he poured a coffee.

"Yep, I know. A good learning experience for them I reckon," Ed smiled back as the two of them sat down and quietly conversed.

The others had been pointed in the direction of where old Whiskey Tooth was heading and they finally came across his trail.

"That'd be our man, Whiskey Tooth, I reckon. The witnesses did say they saw him head this way and was leading two mules," Brady pointed out.

"Yep, I'd agree. One horse and two mules. Looks like they're weighed down heavily," Tyrell mentioned as he looked closer.

"Likely weighed down with a couple kegs of whiskey," Tanner snickered. "We best get back on the saddle and keep following. Those tracks look to be a few hours old already," he added as they swung back on their horses.

"We'll carry on westerly I guess. Looks to be the way he's heading," Tyrell said as he heeled Pony's flank and the three riders carried on.

It was mid-afternoon when they lost the trail. It was as though the horse and mules grew wings and headed to the stars. The three of them looked around, but couldn't decipher any tracks anywhere. It was confusing to say the least.

"Guess we head back the way we came, maybe we'll pick up the trail again. If not we'll have to set up for the evening. Looks like a late summer storm is coming our way," Tanner said as he looked to the greying sky.

"Whiskey Tooth's trail has to be around here somewhere. We know it led this way. Could be he headed up into the rocks rather than go back since that storm is approaching fast. I say we travel a bit further into the Rockies. We're bound to find his trail again."

"If we don't pick it up soon, Travis, the rain will wash his trail away. I tend to agree with you though. We should continue this way a while longer."

Brady looked up to the rock bluffs ahead.

"We get up there before the rain comes, we'll have a view of the area; likely see any smoke rising if he's camped somewhere."

"All right, well, let's get," Tanner said as the three continued on.

Old Whiskey Tooth George wasn't too far away. In fact, he was watching the three horsemen from some undergrowth, chuckling silently to himself.

"The three of yous ain't gonna take me in, no sir," he said beneath his breath.

He knew who they were. They were bounty hunters. It was obvious to ol' George. The only problem was that he hadn't seen Black Dog, not yet at least, but Black Dog had picked up his scent. He meandered into the undergrowth walked right up to George and sniffed him. George wasn't afraid and he shooed the dog off. Black Dog realising that ol' George was no more a threat than the squirrel jumping from branch to branch, simply walked away, unaware that George was the one that the others were looking for. Usually, Black Dog could sense certain things, such as who his master was tracking. This time, though, his senses escaped him. Making his way back to the others, he strolled alongside as the three men continued westerly.

"Where the heck did you take off to, Black Dog? Chasing rabbits again?" Tyrell asked as he looked down to his companion.

Black Dog simply looked up and wagged his tail.

George continued to watch as the horsemen slipped into the bush and vanished from his sight. He waited a few minutes then headed north. His plan to go west into British Columbia he now put on hold. It didn't bother him terribly. Hell, British Columbia could be accessed from the north too. He'd get there.

It was the thunder that rolled across the sky and the crack of lightning that warned all that the storm was about to hit.

"Here it comes," Tanner began as he looked up to the sky. "We ought to head into them cedars. Their branches will at least keep us dry for the time being. The damn rain though is going to clear away any tracks we might have been able to find."

"Yeah, well we already lost his trail a while back. We'll have to start fresh in the morn. We know he headed this way. We might get lucky," Brady said as he and Tyrell followed in behind Tanner to a stand of big cedars.

They made it to cover as the first raindrops began to spill from the sky. In only a few short minutes they could barely hear themselves talking. The downpour was unrelenting, and the fog that followed was thick as smoke.

"I say we set up here beneath these trees for the night. We'll stay dry leastwise," Tyrell pointed out as he looked at the others.

"Well, let's get settled then. I ain't going to argue."

Brady gathered his gear and the others followed suit. They tethered their horses, grabbed their saddles and headed to the cover of the drooping cedar bows of the big cedar tree. The rain continued to make mud out of the forest floor and the fog remained well into the evening. They were dry though and the fire snapped and crackled as they added more sticks.

"I'm up for another round of coffee. How about you?" Brady asked as he went about the task.

"No need to not say no. And don't make no woman coffee again, Brady. That last stuff was as weak as tea," Tyrell mentioned as he patted Black Dog who sat near.

"Yeah, I'll second that. Shit, the stuff back at the office, no matter how old it gets to be, is better than that last batch of coffee that you made," Tanner added.

"Was only trying to go easy, but I'd agree it wasn't that good. Is why I want a second pot myself."

Brady added the grounds and set the pot to perk.

"Any guess on what time it might be. I seemed to have left my time piece back at the office."

"It was daylight when we got under this tree, we've only been here I bet an hour tops. Hard to tell though with the damn fog so thick, but I'd guess it'd be near

6:00 p.m. That would be my guess. That be your guess too, Travis?"

"Probably close enough, Tanner. Might be 7:00 p.m., but I don't reckon it'll be any later. Hopefully the fog will be gone soon and then we can make a fair judgement."

Tyrell stirred the coals of the fire and added another stick as he contemplated.

"What do you know, if anything, about this fellow Whiskey George, Brady? First I ever heard of him was today when Ed sent us off."

Brady poured a coffee.

"Not any more than what you know. I heard the old man speak his name a couple of times; that is about it. Kind of makes me wonder why he insisted all three of us would be needed to bring him in. Hell, his bounty is only five hundred bucks."

Brady shook his head. Now that they were stopped for the evening it struck him as odd on why Ed sent the three of them.

Whiskey George by now had already emptied the kegs of whiskey his mules were packing. Now as he sat near his own fire, he slowly broke the wooden casks and burned them. The metal bands that held the oak slabs together, well, they were worth a handful of gold dust to the Blackfoot. There was nothing illegal about picking up a few pieces of scrap metal, and as far as anybody might question, that is exactly what he'd tell them. He had learned long ago that without evidence of wrong doing; he couldn't be arrested. He didn't believe he was wrong at all in bootlegging whiskey. Regardless of that, the law did, and so he knew getting rid of the evidence meant then that the only thing the law or anybody else had to go on if he were caught with his hand in the whiskey barrel was pure speculation. He chuckled softly to himself as he thought about the men trailing him.

"Greenhorns, the three of them," he said to himself in a muffled voice.

Tanner inhaled a deep breath. He swore he had smelled whiskey in the air. He inhaled again and looked over to Tyrell and Brady sitting on their saddles and sipping coffee. He could tell they hadn't smelled anything yet.

"Hey, Travis, Brady you two smell whiskey?" he asked as he stood up and whiffed again at the air.

"Whiskey? What the hell you going on about Tanner? I don't smell no whiskey. What about you, Brady? You smell whiskey?"

Brady inhaled deeply.

"Come to think about it, I think I do, Travis. Thought I'd smelled it earlier too. Thought only it was wishful thinking that I was back at the Snakebite having a shot or two instead of sitting under this tree waiting for the rain to stop and waiting to chase down a fellow worth only five hundred dollars."

Brady stood and looked out from under the drooping cedar bows of the tree they sought to keep dry while the rain pelted down.

"You know what that means?" Brady stated, "means we're near Whiskey Tooth. He must've dumped out the whiskey he was hauling. Can't be far from where we stand. I don't see no smoke, though, to clarify. Damn, would have been nice to catch up with him whilst the casks had remnants. Makes it a lot easier to prove he's been doing exactly what folks have said."

Brady shrugged.

"It don't mean we can't get his bounty though."

"Well, I ain't spending a day tracking him not to bring him in. Nope, we'll keep on him. With the way the two of you can smell whiskey, that means come daylight or break in this rain, he should be easy to find," Tyrell chuckled.

"By the time this rain lets up, there ain't going to be no scent for us two hound dogs to follow," Brady joked back. "Makes me wonder though, why Black Dog there ain't raised a fuss. I reckon if me and Tanner can smell whiskey, your dog must smell it too. He don't seem too anxious though."

"He never gets anxious, Brady, unless he senses a threat or is commanded. Likely old George don't come across to him as much of a threat as some other hoodwinks might. Could be too, he ain't so inclined on traipsing out in that rain," Tyrell shrugged with a smile as he looked across to where Black Dog lay next to the small fire.

His mind drifted back to how he and Black Dog met. It was while he travelled to Red Rock to claim his grandfather's homestead. It seemed like a long time ago, but really it hadn't been. It had been only a couple of years. He wondered now as he thought about that time, if Marissa did move onto the homestead. He had given her full rights to the place back when he left, albeit in a simple letter. Still, he hoped she had taken him up on his offer. He would not know until he returned, if he ever did. He sighed in self contemplation, stood up and poured another coffee.

Back at the Fort, Colby managed to get the boardwalk finished before the rain came and now he sat on his bunk, his eyes pointed to the barred window as he watched the weather. Now more than ever he longed to be free. It had been only a few days since he started his sentence and already he was missing his freedom. Perhaps he wasn't cut out to be an outlaw after all.

It was then that Bash showed up and offered him a coffee and a couple of oatmeal cookies that the widow Donale had baked.

"The widow lady you did work for the other day baked you some cookies, Colby. Also, I brought you a coffee. Interested?" Bash asked as he pulled up a chair outside the cell and sat down.

"Cookies? Sure, I wouldn't say no to that. A coffee sounds good too. Thanks, Bash," Colby responded as he made his way near and took the coffee and cookies that Bash offered up.

"Quite the downpour going on out there, ain't it?" Colby mentioned as he sat back down on his bunk.

"I think it is going to let up soon. But, yeah, it was quite the storm at the brunt of it. It'll do the farmlands good, and keep the farmers happy. By the way, Colby, I wanted to let you know that you did good work today. You didn't even complain once," Bash chuckled.

"I learned earlier on complaining don't get the work done."

"True as that might be, I hope you are learning more than that alone. You know, Colby, in life the decisions we make can improve our lives or make them hell."

"Yeah, well, sometimes we haven't got any other choices except the ones that make it hell. I know what you are referring to Bash and to be honest I care little on what you might think. I ran with Atalmore simply because he offered me a type of living, more than what most folks could offer me."

Colby looked into his cup of coffee, and shrugged.

"Once I'm done with this community service, my life ain't going to change. I'll still be me."

"There is always room for change, remember that," Bash said as he stood and exited the cell corridor.

He liked Colby. He was a good man as far as he was concerned, perhaps a bit arrogant, but there was definitely some good in him. Bash was certain of that and so was the judge who sentenced him. With a bit more guidance and direction he could change. There was no doubt about it.

Bash sat down at his desk and filled out that day's reports. He made a quick note reminding himself to question Lieutenant Bob Cannon about Riley Scott's request to have Colby help him dig a well on the old Miller land that Riley now owned. The more he thought about it the more he thought it was a good learning experience and undoubtedly one that Colby wouldn't forget. It would be unlike all the other mediocre bits and pieces of work that Colby had already done. Digging a well into the dry earth of the prairie would be hard work and since Riley already said he'd pay a fee for the help, it wasn't a bad idea at all. Colby would get a percentage on his release and that could only be helpful. Bash scribbled a star next to the reminder. He'd do his best to convince Cannon. Standing now, he made his way to the on residence quarters. A bit tired and bored, he lay out on the small single bed and dozed.

Chapter 6

It wasn't until early morning Tuesday that the rain let up in the mountains. Brady, Tanner and Tyrell worked together in rounding up their gear and made early morning coffee. Their horses were still soaking wet from the unrelenting downpour and they decided to give them a few more minutes to shake themselves dry before saddling up and looking for Whiskey George's lost trail, a feat they knew was next to impossible. The rain would have washed it away completely by now. Their best hope was to find old George's overnight camp. Not even an old mountain man like him would have continued onward when the rain hit the night before.

The same thick fog that enveloped them the previous evening when the rain came remained for a few hours until the sun finally broke out and dried everything up. They had been scouting for old George's camp for close to an hour, and so far they had empty hands.

"Damn, I knew this wasn't going to be easy; tracking someone after a downpour like we had last night. I'm beginning to wonder if the old codger did carry on once the rain pelted down. Can't see it, but I have to say that might be the case."

Brady swung off his horse to rest. The three of them were soaked to the bone from all the undergrowth and brush they had traipsed through.

"Right here is a good place to rest. The sun beats down nice. It will help dry us some. I'm soaked through to the skin."

"Me too," Tyrell said as he pulled up next to Brady's horse, Tanner following behind him.

"I sure hate that wet cold feeling of soaked clothing sticking to my skin. Couldn't have picked a brighter spot there, Brady. Nice. Like you said the sun will dry us in no time."

Tanner swung off his horse and tethered him with the others.

"If this is what we can expect for September weather, we're gonna have a cold winter coming up."

"That's right. We're into September now, ain't we? Time sure flies, eh?" Tyrell commented back as Tanner made his way over to where Tyrell and Brady stood, soaking up the sun and trying to dry off.

"Yep, sure does. Jus' like ol' Whiskey Tooth and his mules," Brady spit to the ground.

It was going to be a long day.

They had been soaking up the sun for only a few minutes when they heard laughter coming from high up in the mountains.

"You greenhorns might as well jus' git. You ain't bringing me in, no sir. So, turn your rides around."

"Damn, he's right above us. Can't see a thing, though," Tyrell said as he squinted and looked up toward the rocky crags.

"Taunting us like that, I'd say he's got some nerve. C'mon lets saddle up and head up that way. Might get lucky enough to find his trail," Brady said as he swung onto his horse.

Tanner and Tyrell did the same and the three of them headed toward the calls. It took another hour before they found a few slight track impressions.

"He must've stopped here. Can't be too far ahead," Tyrell suggested and he looked again in the direction the trail seemed to be heading.

"You don't suppose he went that way up into those bluffs do you?" he questioned with little enthusiasm.

"Ain't sure. The tracks say so. Could be he's fooling with us too. I don't know. Not so sure I want to head up that way. Looks quite perilous to me," Tanner interjected.

"Well, he either went up that way or he headed back down. I don't see no other tracks except these that we're looking at now," Brady said as he shook his head.

"You'd have to be a mad man to head up that way. Could be George is that. C'mon, we ain't going to know until we find another track or two."

The three men turned their steeds and followed the direction in which the tracks seemed to be going. It wasn't long before they heard the laughter again, coming now from below.

"Told ya's to turn around. Didn't want to listen, though, did ya's."

That was the last they heard from George. They spent another two days trying to track him, but he was lost to them.

Stopping their horses now they looked around.

"How the hell did that old codger outwit us? We've been fooled by him over and over again. I've had enough. Time to head back to the Fort, I reckon," Brady said as he swung off his horse and cupped his hands to have a drink from the cold glacial-fed creek that crossed their trail.

He looked upstream into the mountains. Something caught his eye and he stood up.

"There is something up over yonder," he pointed in the direction.

All eyes were now looking at the pile of rubble.

"Yep, sure is something there. We best go have a look see," Tanner said as he walked the short distance, Brady and Tyrell following close behind.

"Looks like we have found old George," Tanner said as he got close.

Sure enough there he lay, a half dozen arrows sticking out of his back.

"Damn, the Indians must've been having target practice. Not much point in sticking a man with that many arrows. What do you fellows make of that?"

Brady shook his head as he knelt next to George's limp body.

"Goddamn! He's still alive," Brady jumped up shocked and surprised.

"What are we going to do with him now? I can't believe he lived through that."

Brady turned him over onto his side to get a better look at the old codger.

"Can you hear me?" he asked as he put his ear close to George's face to be sure that he was indeed still breathing. He was.

"I can hear you fine, youngin'. Now if the three of yous would be so kind to pull a few of them arrows out, I'd feel a lot more comfortable. The damn renegades took my mules and my horse," George said as though it were nothing at all that he'd been used as a pin cushion.

Black Dog even began licking George's face which in turn caused George to laugh a bit.

"That your dog?"

"Is so," Tyrell said as he too knelt next to George.

"He seems to like you some. How long have you been in this predicament, George?"

"Late yesterday. Now about them damn pins in my back, you wanna pull a few out. I'll be able to stand then."

The three of them shook their heads. It was inconceivable that a man could live through what George had obviously been through, but he had and he was even talking.

"You sure you want us to do that?" Brady asked. "It is going to hurt like no tomorrow."

"Damn it, greenhorn, if yous don't, I ain't likely gonna see tomorrow. So, quit your lollygagging and get on with it."

"Go ahead, Brady, yank a few of them arrows out," Tyrell said with encouragement.

"I knew you was Ed's boy. You were the young whippersnapper that used to kick me in the shins," George said with a half snicker. "Now get on with it. I reckon Ed wants to see me to try and get that damn five hundred dollar reward. He won't get it if I'm dead."

Brady was shocked to hear that from old George. He couldn't remember ever kicking him in the shins. Hell, as far as he knew, he had never met the man.

"All right, here it goes."

Brady pulled out the arrows while Tanner and Tyrell sat waiting for him to finish so they could remove his bearskin coat to staunch the bleeding. It took a few minutes to finish and finally old George sat up on his own. Gritting his teeth, he stood up.

"There that feels a bit better."

He stretched and yawned as though he'd been through worse.

"Now introductions, please."

He looked at the three men that had been tailing him. Looking at Brady he smiled and kicked him so hard in the shins that Brady fell over.

"There. We're even now," he said with a loud chuckle.

"Jesus Christ! What was that for?" Brady asked as he rubbed his shin and stood up.

"Oh, I owed that one to you," George chuckled. "So, who are these two?"

"I'm Travis Sweet and this here is Tanner McBride," Tyrell said as he looked at George and back to Brady who was still rubbing his shin.

"You seem to know Brady, so he don't need no introduction."

"Travis, Tanner and Brady. Nice to meet yous. You already know who I am so I don't need no introduction either. And your dog, what does he go by?"

"That there is Black Dog."

George reached down and scratched the dog behind the ears.

"Hello, Black Dog. We met a few days ago, he and I," George smiled.

"What?" Tyrell asked as he raised an eyebrow. "You two met?"

"That is right. He came right up to me. Gave me a sniff and left. It was while I was watching the three of you traipse by where I held up. He's a nice looking dog."

George looked over to Tyrell.

"And I'd put a wager on it that you are the same Travis Sweet that put to rest Earl Brubaker some time ago. Would I be right?"

"I might be him, I might not be too."

"Nope, you are him. No use denying it," George said as he sat back down on a log.

"I often wondered when Brubaker would meet his demise. He and that brother of his, I think his name is

Alex, tracked me some years ago. They was easier to fool than the three of yous. Anyway, that was a long time ago. What is next?"

"As soon as you are able to travel, we'll head back to the Fort. We'll get a doctor to have a look at them wounds of yours and then we'll turn you in," Brady said nonchalantly.

"Five hundred dollars is worth that much to you, eh? I'm ready as I'll ever be. Let's get then," George commented as he stood up.

"Which one of yous am I gonna be doubling with?"

"Take your pick I guess."

Tanner looked at Brady and Tyrell. The three of them were in awe that the old codger was alive, ready and willing to travel.

"All right, then. I'll double behind kid shin kicker," George said as he stood up. "You want to tie my hands?"

"Nope, don't see much point in that," Brady said as he helped George onto his horse and just as quickly George heeled Brady's horse and darted off.

"You should have tied my hands, greenhorn," George hollered as he disappeared into the undergrowth and out of sight with Brady's horse and gear.

Tanner and Tyrell started to laugh, seeing old George pull off that stunt although it really wasn't a laughing matter.

"I can't believe that. That son-of-a-bitch!" Brady exclaimed.

"Who you want to double with Brady?" Tanner asked with a smirk as he shook his head in disbelief. "I guess we should've tied his hands after all."

Tyrell had nothing to add and he too shook his head.

"Yep, should've tied his hands, I reckon."

Brady looked over to Tanner and back again to Tyrell.

"I would have never thought an old codger like him would pull a stunt like that, especially after taking a few arrows. He must be as tough as a railroad tie. Who wants to double?"

"Take your pick, Brady. Pony can haul us both or you can hop onto Tanner's horse. It really don't matter either way. What does matter is the longer we sit contemplating what just took place, the further away George gets."

Brady nodded in agreement and swung up behind Tanner.

"Let's get," he said as he made himself comfortable.

Following the trail at that point was easy and it didn't take them long to come across Brady's saddle and gear, but not his horse.

"Look at that. Why would he drop that off? Seems kind of odd don't it?" Brady questioned befuddled as he swung down and looked his gear and saddle over.

"Damn, he left me everything 'cept my lucky can of beans."

"What? Lucky can of beans," Tyrell looked at him raising his eyebrow.

"Long story," Brady replied. "I'll tell you about it sometime. Think we can toss this saddle up behind you, Travis? I'll carry the gear on my lap."

"Sure, I reckon we could tie it down on Pony's rump, probably could haul the gear too."

It took a few minutes to get the saddle and gear secured and once more they headed off after old George.

"What do you fellows make of him leaving my gear behind like that?" Brady questioned again as he thought about *the why*.

Tanner shrugged his shoulders, "I couldn't tell ya, Brady. Does seem odd."

"Likely, didn't like that girly saddle of yours," Tyrell spoke up with a chuckle.

"Girly saddle? Shit. That saddle is one of the most damn comfortable saddles I've ever owned?"

"Did your Ma own it before you?" Tyrell teased.

Brady's saddle was an English-type saddle used in horse shows and what not. Not like the common saddles most folks had and especially not the type of saddle one would expect a bounty hunter to have. Brady though had always claimed it to be comfortable. The others always badgered him about it. It was common place. The three of them chuckled as they continued on.

By early evening they had again lost old George's trail. Stopping they decided to set up for the evening.

"It has been a few days since we have we been tracking old Whiskey Tooth," Tanner pointed out as he struck a match and lit the fire.

"How can he be so damn hard to track? I'm beginning to understand why Ed sent the three of us."

"He's got lucky in more ways than one. Most red-blooded men wouldn't have been so raring to take off on a stolen horse after being knocked down with a quiver of arrows. Like Brady says, he has to be as tough as a railroad tie. I reckon though that bearskin coat he wears helped in his not dying."

Tyrell looked into the flames of the small fire that burned as they waited for their coffee to perk.

"Yeah, I'd say it likely helped in the penetrating factor. Still, them arrows take down buffalo, bear, elk and the like. How he managed to stand up and run on us after that has me baffled."

Brady shook his head.

"I'm pissed off too that he took my beans."

"Tell us about that can of beans."

Tanner wanted to know the story.

The beans must have meant something to Brady, for one reason or the other. He couldn't make out heads or tails on why a man would have a lucky can of beans, of all things.

"When Riley and I were tracking Matt, we came across an old fire pit. We thought nothing of it and went ahead and lit a fire in the same spot. Our beans were cookin' and almost ready to eat when I noticed something glowing orange in the coals. It took me a second or two to realise what it was and not a moment too late either. Damned if it wasn't a couple of rifle rounds. We dove for cover just as the powder inside got hot enough to send a barrage of coal and shrapnel, not to mention two cans of beans lobbing through the air. Anyway, when it was all over we had a few cans of beans left. Riley seems to like them a lot. By the time we made it back to the Fort we had one can left and that is the can I've always called my lucky can of beans. I guess it is more of a reminder to myself about what could have been. Either one of us could've been wounded or killed. So in short, I don't and never will again use another man's fire pit. We never did know if it were Matt that set the booby trap or that Pinkerton fellow Ranthorp that Matt shot for killing our horses and for trying to frame him for killing Emery."

Brady sighed as he thought about that time now. It seemed so long ago.

"Interesting story, Brady. What are you gonna do now that your beans is gone?" Tanner asked.

"I guess I'll have to live without the luck."

Brady poured himself a coffee.

"Only got to remember not to use another man's fire pit, Brady. Pretty easy thing to acknowledge if you ever come upon a used pit. It is a good story, though. How do you know you ain't ate them beans by now?"

"I kept them separated from the others. Was never going to eat them."

Brady slurped from his coffee, while Tyrell and Tanner poured themselves a cup.

The three men sat and averted their gaze to the western horizon that was quickly turning grey again. It kept them silent for a time, their minds drifting to this or that. Tyrell looked out across the vast forest of evergreens and cedars, in the distance he spotted smoke rising. He stood up and gestured to the others.

"See that smoke rising? Could be George has set up for the evening; we could never make that distance though before dark. I'd say he's North West of us, a few miles distance."

"Son-of-a-bitch! Yep, I'd bet my share of his bounty that be him," Tanner wagered as the three men looked on.

"Could be Indians," Brady suggested as he took a swallow from his coffee.

"Either way, Travis is right we couldn't make that distance before dark. We'll keep our eye on the smoke as evening grows dark. First thing tomorrow we'll head that way. I reckon he's at least three maybe even five miles away. We might have him in our clutches and make it back to the Fort before Sunday dinner. Ma is planning to put on quite the spread."

"That's right we was invited to dinner this Sunday," Tyrell remembered.

"Yep, and we best get this bounty tied up in more ways than one by then or ma will spank us all," Brady joked.

Tanner nodded his head and smiled.

"I almost forgot about that. It's been a long while since I ate anything home cooked and not from a can."

"Same here. The Snakebite makes good food, but nothing beats home cooking," Tyrell added. "You have any ideas what it is she might be cooking?"

"Roast pork, spuds, biscuits, corn and probably a few other things too. I know she has been gathering berries for her huckleberry pie. Almost as good as the widow Donale's."

"The widow told me once that your ma and her use the same recipe. How can one be different than the other?"

"Don't know. Seems one is better than the other. I will admit ma's does seem sweeter. Maybe that is the difference. Ma's is too sweet."

"Difference or no difference, you two is making me hungry. All's we got for food is a couple cans of not 'lucky' beans, biscuit stuff, and a few sticks of jerky."

"We could always kill a couple of grouse, I heard a ruffling not long ago," Tyrell said as grabbed his rifle.

"Come on, let's walk some distance and see if we can't knock down a few Rocky Mountain blue grouse."

"Yeah, all right sounds like it could liven up our day. Popping them though with that rifle of yours ain't going to leave much to eat."

"I ain't going to knock them down with the rifle; we are going to throw rocks at them. The rifle is for protection."

"Rocks? Are you crazy, Travis? We can't kill them with a couple of rocks," Brady said with doubt as the three men headed into the bramble.

"Can so. I've done it," Tanner spoke up.

"Just a matter of throwing them at the right time. Best to throw at them when they're on the ground. Black Dog ain't going to ruin it for us is he?"

"Nope. He'll stay near me, 'less of course he scents a bear. I haven't saw no tracks though, so likely aren't no bears around that he could smell."

"He's a dog, Travis, should be easy for him to scent a bear even at a half mile."

"True as that might be, Brady, a bear which is a half mile away ain't no threat. He won't care."

"Maybe we should've brought that horse of yours along. He don't like grouse; he'd find them for us."

"Yeah and flatten them like a biscuit too. I have hopes of eatin' a couple. Squished like bugs ain't going to be edible, are they?"

"Good point," Tanner chuckled as he picked up a couple of rocks that he kept in his hand.

"That's all right. A nice toss by one of these rocks and we'll be eating grouse for dinner."

"Rocks work, so do sticks, though," Tyrell said as he picked up an old broken branch.

"Yep, this here is the stick which will feed us tonight."

"You making a wager, Travis?" Tanner asked with jubilance.

"How about this: whoever knocks a couple down don't have to clean them," Brady suggested.

Tyrell shook his head and smiled.

"Shit, cleaning them is easier than tossing sticks and rocks at them. All you have to do is stand on their wings, grab their legs and yank. Everything pulls out nice and easy and only a few feathers stick to the breast. You just chop the wings off afterwards. How about this:

whoever knocks them down, the others have to buy him a cold drink and steak dinner at the Snakebite."

"Okay, I'll agree to that," Tanner committed.

Brady nodded in agreement.

"So will I."

"All right then. There is our wager," Tyrell replied as they continued onward.

A few minutes later they heard the sound of a grouse or two fluttering their wings and getting ready to take flight. The three men stopped, crouched and looked around.

Tyrell pointed.

"I see it; it's right there. We can't get it from here though, too much bramble in the way," he said with a whisper as to not startle their dinner.

It was Brady who simply pulled out his single shot shoulder pistol and before another word was said, the grouse was flopping on the ground, its head completely removed from its neck.

Brady smiled.

"See, with rocks and sticks you wouldn't have been able to do that. I guess the two of you get to buy me dinner."

"Shhhh. There is another one. I can get it from here."

Tanner stood up and just as quick threw his rock hitting the grouse broadside. It flopped on the ground then fell silent.

"Told ya I could get one with a rock."

"Well, two are better than one. One more though is even better."

Tyrell crawled along the ground for a few yards and then he stood up and snapped his wrist with a flick and let his stick fly. Down went the third grouse.

"There, now we have one apiece. And would you look at that. Seems mine is the biggest of all. So, who is buying who dinner now?" Tyrell teased as he held his grouse up and smiled.

"We never said anything about size," Brady announced as he picked up his headless dinner.

"Nope, never said anything about using a shoulder pistol either. I was under the impression that we were supposed to use sticks and rocks."

Tanner shook his head.

"You did get the first one, so I'll keep up my end of the bargain I'll buy you dinner, Brady."

"Yeah, I reckon we wasn't too clear on the rules," Tyrell smiled, "mine is still bigger than either of yours."

"You are only talking about that bird in your hand, ain't ya?"

"Geeze, Tanner, of course I am."

Tyrell half chuckled to hide his embarrassment on saying such a thing in regard to size.

"Good, I was just making sure."

"Yeah, yeah, whatever Tanner."

Brady looked at both of them and shook his head.

"I wonder about you two sometimes."

"Shit, Tanner knew exactly what I was referring to. He was being cocky is all."

"Cocky, size. I dunno Travis sounds like you're speaking about your dangly parts," Tanner laughed.

"Anyway, enough of that. Let's get these feathered birds on a spit and roasting on the flames. They'll go good with some biscuits and beans."

"I think Tanner decided to make us dinner. Thanks, Tanner," Brady said as he handed his grouse over to him.

Tyrell smiled and did the same.

"Wait, I, I didn't say that."

"I think it was implied."

"The hell it was. I was jus' pointing out that they'd go good with the other."

Tanner sighed as he looked at the three birds in his hand and back to Tyrell and Brady.

"Leastwise you've both cleaned them up."

He looked at the birds again.

"All right, I'll cook them, but I ain't cleanin' up afterwards. The two of you can decide on who does that."

"Nope. I think it is traditionally up to the cook to do the clean up afterwards," Tyrell teased as they finally made it back to their evening camp.

The smoke in the horizon still rose and the three men contemplated whether or not it was George. If it was they'd be getting close to him in a day or so. If it wasn't, they'd be getting close to whoever it was whose fire burned. They drank coffee and conversed as Tanner prepared their dinner. It didn't take long and soon they were eating the best meal they had had since leaving the Fort three or four days earlier.

Tyrell picked his teeth with a small bone from his dinner and sucked on an eyetooth as he looked out over the vast forest that lay ahead and toward the rising smoke.

"You know, if we can see the smoke from that fire, makes me wonder if whoever is down there can see ours?"

"Ah, I don't reckon so, we're up high. Even if he or they could, won't make much of a difference I don't think. Besides, our fire don't seem to be puffing much smoke, leastwise not as much it would seem as that one down there."

Brady inhaled deeply as he took a drink from his coffee.

"Which brings up another question, though. Why does that one seem to be smoking more than ours?"

"Hmmm, good point. Could be they is cooking more than a few grouse."

Tanner stood up quickly.

"Hold on, I can see flames! That ain't no campfire, the damn woods is on fire."

All three now turned their eyes and looked on. Sure enough, it seemed as though there was a forest fire and it was spreading.

"Damn. We best get down low. Fire always goes up!" Brady announced as the three of them doused their fire and gathered their gear in a heated rush to get down low and away.

"Looks like the cleanup is going to have to wait. You got lucky, Tanner," Tyrell joked as he cinched up his saddle and the three men headed to lower altitudes.

Traversing the terrain as it grew dark wasn't easy, but finally they made it down to a lower plateau. They were a safe distance away, but it didn't mean they were safe.

"Must've been lightning that started that blaze," Brady looked around as he swung off Tanner's horse and stood on a boulder that gave him some height.

"Looks like the best way to go from here is west. The flames seem to be dancing South East for the time being. That'll change though once they hit the rock bluffs."

Tyrell looked toward the fire that seemed to grow with every blink of an eye. Brady was right. Their best hope to find a reprieve was west.

"I'd say so. C'mon get back up there behind Tanner. Let's make some more tracks before we are took over by the damn smoke which seems to be getting thicker."

Tyrell turned Pony westerly and took the lead. It took Brady a moment to swing back up onto Tanner's horse and he and Tanner caught up to Tyrell a short distance away.

"Quite the thing that fire is, ain't it?" Tanner commented as he pulled his horse up next to Tyrell and Pony.

"Hey! Bounty hunters, that fire weren't lit by nothin' more than the renegades that took my horse."

They heard the voice from up high in the rocks. The three of them looked up toward the echoing voice.

"Damn, he's above us again. Too dark to try and find his whereabouts now," Brady commented as he tried to discern where exactly the voice came from, but not even he could make an educated guess.

"I'll have yous know I got my horse, mules and gear back from that lot. Left one or two still alive. The others, well the buzzards can have them. Kid shin kicker, I left your horse tied about 500 yards north of where you are now standin'. He's tethered and in no harm of that fire."

They heard the voice as it faded over the rocks.

"That old codger is really getting on my nerves," Tanner mentioned as he continued to gaze up at the rock bluffs.

"He's up, he's down. Shit, he's likely going' sideways now."

"We'll worry about him later. C'mon, let's go gather my horse," Brady said as he took one last look above.

Tanner heeled his horse northerly, followed close behind by Tyrell and Pony. Sure enough, a few minutes later they could hear Brady's horse neighing and snorting.

"Well, he don't sound no worse for wear. He must be up behind that clump of trees," Brady said as he and Tanner continued onward.

Finally able to see him now, Brady swung off Tanner's horse and ambled over to his own. He gently patted him on his neck as he looked him over.

"Yep, he's fine. Now where the hell did Travis get to? Wasn't he behind us?"

Tanner looked back.

"Hey, Travis!" he yelled as he looked around.

"Yeah, yeah. I'm right here looking at a couple of dead Indians," Tyrell called back.

"They don't look like Blackfoot to me. Grab your horse, Brady and get over here, the both of you."

Tyrell was kneeling next to the corpses when Tanner and Brady finally made the distance. He pointed at the bodies.

"These ain't Blackfoot," he said as he stood up and looked around.

"Nope they sure isn't. They ain't even Indians," Brady said as he turned one of the bodies over.

"What do you mean? They look like Indians to me," Tanner said as he swung off his horse and met up with Brady and Tyrell.

"Just long hairs. Heard stories about them. They live up here in the high country. Most times don't bother a soul."

Brady stood up and looked around.

"Could be old George figured them to be Indians."

"Either way, they did have his horse and gear. Deserved what they got, I reckon. You don't steal a man's horse and leave him for dead."

"Yep, I would agree. Only thing is, I don't see no bow," Brady sighed.

"In fact, I don't see any weapon in either of their hands."

"What do you figure we're looking at then?"

"To be honest, Travis, I ain't sure. Long hairs, like I said, don't usually bring harm to anyone. Either these ain't the renegades George was telling us about and there are few dead Indians around here somewhere or these are the renegades and George has taken their weapons if they had such. Won't know much more until morning, I reckon. It's too dark now to go lookin'. Besides, these ain't our problem, George is."

Brady spit to the ground and squinted up to the dark mountains.

"No point in holding up here. Ain't nothing we can do for these men. I say we turn back the way we came now that I got my horse and set up another camp for the evening a bit closer to the mountains. The fire down below seems to have slowed," Brady pointed out as he looked toward it.

"I don't reckon we need to worry about it for now. We'll try and pick up George's trail in daylight."

"You mean to say we're gonna leave these poor bastards here for the worms?" Tanner questioned with confusion.

"Nothing else we can do, Tanner," Tyrell said with little concern.

"The kin to these long hairs will be missing them soon enough and will go looking for them. Once they find them, they'll take care of their own. If you like, Tanner, feel free to say a prayer," Brady teased as he swung back onto his horse.

Tanner shrugged his shoulder. Whether Brady was joking or not, he really didn't have any prayers for folks he didn't know.

"All right, I guess the worms can have them."

All in agreement now, they left the three bodies lying where they were and headed back in the direction of the ominous mountains. The only one that held answers was George, but they had to find him first. Tanner looked at the bodies once more and turned his steed, following behind Tyrell and Brady. The three men rode silently. None had many words to share.

When they finally stopped for the evening, the valley below remained shrouded in smoke. Every now and again they could still see flames, but the fire was dying down. There wasn't much for it to ignite once it got up into the rocks.

"I don't reckon there will be any flames left to that fire once morning comes."

Brady looked up to the sky. There were clouds swirling around and it looked like they were going to be in for another rainstorm.

"Rain is coming again tonight. I reckon we still have time to find a better place to stop. Up yonder in them rocks we'll likely find a cave of some sort."

"I ain't traipsing up no rock bluffs at this time of night. Let's get to work and toss together a lean-to. Hell of a lot safer, Brady, than crawling up rocks," Tyrell said as he looked at both Brady and Tanner.

"Yeah, I'd agree with Travis, Brady. A lean-to will be a lot quicker. Besides, I like this spot and so do our rides it appears. They got plenty of mountain grass to fill up on and enough bramble to keep them dry. Up in the rocks, they wouldn't have it so good."

"Well then, let's get some poles knocked down and gather some branches for the roof to keep the rain out."

The three went about the tasks and before the first raindrop fell they were tucked away beneath their shelter. A fire gently burned a few feet away and it kept them warm as the evening grew dark and wet.

Chapter 7

Friday, September 4 1891. Rising in the early twilight, Tyrell added a few sticks to their past evening fire and gently blew on the coals. It took a few minutes for the smouldering coals to ignite the few sticks and once the fire picked up a decent flame, he added coffee to the pot and set it next to the flames to brew. The ground was wet still from the second evening of rain that they had tolerated. Now though, the sun was showing its brilliance in the distance and he guessed the day would turn out warm and pleasant, not like the past two days that were wet and damp for the most part.

Looking down into the valley, he could see that the flames which danced through the woods the night before no longer held a spark. Obviously, the fire wasn't as big or threatening as they first thought. The darkness of the past evening sure made it look as though it were. In daylight now, he could see that it wasn't. Sitting down on his saddle, he waited for Tanner and Brady to come to life. There was no point in trying to rouse them. It wasn't even 5:00 a.m. yet, he guessed. He enjoyed the serenity as he slurped his first coffee. Pony and the other horses along with Black Dog mulled around close by. Everything was as it should be.

By midday they finally gave up on looking for George. He had managed to get away somehow, some way. None of the men cared at that point. He was gone.

It was that simple. There wasn't anything they could do about it.

"We've done our best, but that old codger has slipped into the void. Don't know how and at this point I don't care. I'm tired. Besides, we have only two days left before dinner is served at ma and pa's place. I say we head back empty handed. Five hundred dollars ain't worth the effort anymore. Damn, he's a slick son-of- a bitch, that George is," Brady said as he swung off his horse to rest.

Tanner and Tyrell followed suit.

"Yep, an old folk like him ain't so easy to catch up to. Likely knows these woods better than any red-blooded Indian, I reckon."

Tyrell sat down on a rock and looked around.

"What do you suppose Ed is going to say about us coming back empty handed?"

"Don't know and don't care," Brady said as he looked at both Tanner and Tyrell.

"I reckon the old man was betting that old George would fool us. He's probably sitting back at the office laughing. Damn him," Brady chuckled and shook his head.

"We gave it our best and we lost. Lesson learned, I guess."

"What lesson might that be, Brady? That we should've tied his hands that first time," Tanner questioned with a half-smile.

"I'd say so. But who'd have thought a fellow like him after being stuck with arrows would have the gumption to steal a ride and vacate?"

"Well, I didn't see it coming, but when I did, I have to admit it was admirable," Tyrell pointed out.

"In a way I suppose it was. Still, I can't get over it. Hell, he had a dozen arrows in his back. Incredible tenacity and wit, for sure. I'd say he deserves to get away."

Brady looked over to his horse.

"Not many men would steal a horse and then give it back. Glad he did."

The three men rested for a while longer then headed back east toward the Fort. It took a day and half to make the distance without distractions. Early Saturday evening they were sitting in the office, a pot of coffee gently perking on the woodstove. They were home at last, albeit without their bounty. Still, it was good to be home. Nothing else mattered at that moment.

"We'll make it to dinner leastwise, and that puts a smile on my face," Tanner said as he took a swallow from his coffee.

"I agree, can hardly wait."

Tyrell set his coffee down and looked at Brady.

"You reckon Ed's going to be upset that we returned empty handed?"

"Like I said a few days ago, he probably knew what the outcome would be. Nah, he won't be upset. I assume though he'll certainly have a good laugh, he and Riley both."

Brady finished his cup of coffee and set the empty cup on the counter.

"I guess I best head home. I'll be riding in before the old man tomorrow, though. We'll fill him in together once he and Riley get in. I'll see you two in the morning," he said as he turned to exit and head for home.

"Yeah, we'll see you in the morning, Brady," Travis and Tanner nodded as Brady headed for home.

"Well, Travis, what do you feel like doing? There is a few more hours left before it gets dark. Want to head over to the Snakebite and have a draft?"

"Sure, I wouldn't mind having a cold draft. Whiskey George, I'm afraid, has turned me off of whiskey," Tyrell chuckled.

"Lead the way Tanner, I'm right behind you."

The two men rose from the table and exited into the cool evening. Unbeknownst to either man, Alex Brubaker was standing outside on his veranda. The second floor veranda faced the McCoy's office. Alex watched as Tanner and Tyrell approached, then he spoke up.

"Evening, fellas," he started as Tyrell and Tanner looked up to him.

"Evening back, Alex. How are you doing?"

"Things could be worse, I reckon. I ain't seen the two of you or for that matter Brady in a few days. You guys been hidin'?"

"Jus' working Alex. What is with the questions?" Tyrell asked somewhat evasively.

"Friendly conversation is all, Travis. Why are you so uptight?"

"I ain't uptight, Alex. Curious is all on why you'd ask where we've been."

"I was only making conversation is all."

Alex turned and entered his second floor room, leaving both Tyrell and Tanner looking at each other in confusion.

"What do you suppose he meant by all that?" Tanner questioned as the two men continued to the entrance of the Snakebite.

"Ain't sure."

Tyrell shrugged his shoulders as they continued on to the Snakebite and a cold draft. Standing in the foyer as they entered was Alex. He looked at them and nodded.

"I figured you were on your way here. Can I buy you a drink?" Alex questioned with sincerity.

"Why would you want to buy us a drink? What is going on, Alex? What is your true intent?" Tanner asked.

"I ain't got any intentions but to offer buying you folk a drink is all. Hell, I was only trying to be cordial. Never mind though, I get it."

Alex tipped his hat and walked past them and into the saloon. Making his way over to the bar counter, he pulled up a stool and ordered a whiskey. Tyrell and Tanner sat down at a table near the entrance and ordered a couple of cold drafts. Each of them was a little bit uneasy at the fact that Alex was near. After three or four shots of whiskey, Alex stood up and exited, not saying a word to either Tyrell or Tanner as he left. It was a curious situation to say the least.

The truth was that Alex was only trying to be cordial. It was Tyrell and Tanner who read into Alex's friendliness more than what was needed, but they couldn't be expected to think anything else. After all, it was Tyrell who took away Alex's shooting hand and it was Tyrell who also laid Alex's brother, Earl, to rest a year earlier. Then, to learn later on that Colby Christian was Alex's cousin, it made another family member of the Brubaker clan that Tyrell had a hand in putting behind bars. There was no reason for them to think Alex was simply being cordial. They thought the worst that maybe Alex was up to something, maybe seeking retaliation for the wrong doings he believed that Tyrell committed. Either way in their minds, there was more to it than simple cordiality.

At 11:00 p.m., both Tyrell and Tanner headed back to the McCoy's office, Tanner to the back room cot and Tyrell to the upstairs apartment. Sleep found them both quite quickly. It had been a long and tiring week as they searched for and tracked Whiskey Tooth George only to be outwitted and beaten by a man twice their age. Now home at last in some kind of normalcy, their tired minds and aching bodies that had been deprived of luxuries such as sleep and relaxation were no longer deprived.

Sunday would bring good news to the men working for McCoy's. During the week they were gone, Ed got word back from the Police Commissioner saying that he had accepted Ed's application to be grandfathered in to the Private Investigation Sector. McCoy's could now become a Private Investigations and Security firm. Ed never filled his crew in though, not even Riley knew yet. He had decided he'd bring it up at dinner that night.

After hearing from Brady and the others on how old George got away, both Ed and Riley were quite amused at the tale and often laughed as it was told to them. The only thing that didn't sit well with the men around the table that morning was the fact that they had found three dead long hairs who they assumed were killed by George. There was nothing they could do about that though. They weren't even considering on telling the law about their assumption because that is all it was, a simple assumption. Without proof that indeed it was George who killed them, they had nothing to go on. It was best, they decided, that they'd leave that as it were. The longhair took care of their own, always had and always would.

"He said to me one time that I used to kick him in the shins. What did he mean by that, old man?" Brady asked. "I don't recall ever meeting him."

"It was years ago, Brady. You were just a snot-nosed kid running around the office. He wasn't known as Whiskey Tooth back then. He was a bounty I brought in. We didn't have this set up as we do now. Only had a small office with a couple of chairs. I brought him in for a minor offence, card cheating or something like that. It's been so long I can't rightly remember. Anyway, he was teasing you about one thing or the other and you were a spunky brat, much like you are today. You put up with his teasing for a bit. You stuck out your tongue at him a couple of times. Being as he was handcuffed, you eventually got up the nerve to approach him and you kicked him in his shins a few dozen times. The whole time he sat there and laughed. He kept taunting you and you kept kicking his shins. Finally you must've kicked him good because he fell off the chair. When the Mounties came to retrieve him, he limped out of here. So, I guess that is what he was mentioning. Hard to believe he even remembered that. It was years ago," Ed explained.

"So what you are saying is that you've had a run in with him before?"

"Not just that one time, Brady. Riley and I both have run across him a time or three. He wasn't any easier to bring in back then than he is today. He's a hard bounty to track and even harder to restrain. That is why I sent the three of you. I figured you all needed something to do since the three of you seemed to be getting bored."

Ed and Riley both began to chuckle.

"It is true what he says, Brady. Old Whiskey Tooth is a bastard to bring in. You either get lucky or you lose him."

Riley added with a smile, "He's fooled many a bounty hunter, not only the three of you."

"Shit, I feel like a school kid getting a lesson in class," Brady said as he poured another coffee.

"I figured there was a reason for you sending the three of us after a lone bounty of five hundred dollars. I understand why now."

Brady shook his head.

"It would have been nice to have had some background history on him before we set off, though. It may have helped us in the long run."

"Might not have too, Brady. I figure a folk like old George has a lot of tricks up his sleeve and I bet he used every one of them. We just didn't expect it. He ain't a threat to the public anyway. There are bigger bounties we could look at now. Matt Crawford comes to mind," Tanner pointed out.

"Yeah, speaking of which, have we decided if we want to pursuit him or not?" Tyrell asked.

"We only have a few more months before the law changes."

"I say we discuss that tonight at dinner," Ed put forth. "I figure we close up early, get ourselves cleaned up and meet at the house around 5:00 p.m. You still going to show up, Riley? It wouldn't be the same without you."

"I wouldn't miss a home cooked meal put on by a pretty wife like yours, Ed. Damn right I'll be there," Riley said with a smile.

"Good, the rest of you are going to be there as well, correct?"

"You can count on it, Ed. We'll all be there."

"Yeah, most definitely. I haven't had a home cooked meal in a long time and have been patiently waiting for this night," Tanner said, as they pushed in their chairs to leave.

"All right then, we'll see you folks at 5:00 p.m."

Ed wanted to be clear as he began to exit and head for home.

"Yep, we'll see you then, Ed."

"Good. Beth has gone through a lot of trouble to put this dinner together. It'd piss her off if no one showed. I'll see you fellows at dinner."

Closing the door, Ed hopped onto his horse and headed for home. He was excited to fill them in on the news that he received from the Police Commissioner. He hoped it would be as pleasing to them as it was to him. They could still operate as bounty hunters for the time being, or they could jump right on board and become McCoy's Private Investigations Co. and with that a lot more doors would open. Either way they would all still have their jobs and that in itself brought a smile to his face as he rode on.

Riley, Brady, Tanner and Tyrell remained at the office for a few more minutes, talking amongst themselves as they hung around the front counter. Riley mentioned that Colby had been helping him dig a well and that the widow Donale's brother had dowsed the area where he believed water to be.

"We've been digging in that spot for three or four days and still not a damn drop of water has shown itself. I don't know, maybe you were right, Tanner, when you said you didn't believe in that mumbo jumbo. Maybe dowsing ain't an art after all," Riley half-smiled.

"Well, since there ain't much for us to do around here, maybe we can all give you a hand in the next couple of days. There has to be water on that land somewhere, Riley."

"I don't know, Travis. I'm beginning to think there is a better way to get water. Maybe a cistern, like the widow mentioned to me a while back is more feasible. Either way, I have to keep Colby busy for a few more days. I reckon I'll just keep him digging. Who knows? Maybe we'll strike water tomorrow. We're down about ten foot maybe more. The widow's brother did say we'd need to get down near fifteen to twenty foot. If nothing comes of it, at least I'll have a big enough hole in the ground to get a cistern put in. Not to mention, I'd get my fifteen dollars' worth of labour out of Colby," Riley chuckled.

"I'll tell you one thing; that Colby kid can sure work. He don't stop, just keeps going and going. Hard worker he is. Even with his attitude, he's a pleasant fellow. I don't understand how a kid like him with as much as he has going for him, could ever get mixed up with the likes of the Rebel Rangers and that Atalmore fellow. Makes no sense to me."

Riley shrugged his shoulders.

"Then again a lot of things in life don't make sense. I reckon Atalmore and his Rebel Rangers were appealing to Colby. It gave him a sense of worth to be involved with such a group. Hopefully that will all change once the kid is set free."

135

"Being as he has Brubaker blood flowing through his veins though makes me wonder if change for him is even possible. For now though, I'd give him the benefit of doubt. Anyone can change if they so want," Tyrell pointed out.

"Yeah, like Travis says, anyone can change if they want. Colby is young enough to take those steps if he feels it is the right thing to do. If not, then he'll be who he is until the day he dies or gets gunned down. There is nothing anyone can do about that," Brady commented.

"I've known the Brubaker brothers, Earl and Alex for a time, and like I've always said, it was Earl's influence that made Alex who he is today. It doesn't mean Colby although he is a cousin is going to be anything like the Brubakers, unless of course, Alex has the same influence. I don't think he does. I think Alex has seen the light now that Earl is dead. Maybe he and Colby aren't going to be any more of a threat to the public than Whiskey Tooth George. Then again, only time will tell," Tanner threw into the mix.

"Speaking of time, I reckon we all best get cleaned up and ready for dinner," said Riley as he rapped his knuckles on the counter.

"I'm going to head over to the widow's place and get in a hot bath. Any of you care to tag along? The widow has four or five baths."

"A hot bath and shave sounds good to me. I'll tag along, Riley."

"Count me in too," Tanner said as he brought his hand up to his face and stroked his whiskered chin.

"Yep, a shave and hot bath sounds good to me. What about you, Brady?"

"I'll get cleaned up at home. I have a big wash basin heating on the woodstove. I'll see you all at dinner," he said as he turned and began to exit.

"All right. We'll catch up with you at dinner, Brady."

Riley waited for Tyrell and Tanner and then the three of them headed over to the bathhouse. Lucky for them, there were three available baths each with steaming hot water. It was as if the widow was expecting them. Cleaned and shaved now, the three men went their separate ways. Riley headed back to his place to fetch on clean clothes while Tyrell and Tanner did the same. They met up at Riley's place an hour later and he showed them the well he and Colby had been digging. Surprisingly there was a show of water, only a few inches deep, but it did mean water was there.

"Humph, well now that wasn't there yesterday. A good sign, I'd say."

"Indeed it is, Riley. Looks like you'll be hitting water soon," Tyrell said as he looked on.

"Yep, you'll get water from this well. Maybe dowsing is an art after all, eh?" Tanner remarked with positivity. "Unless of course it is only rainfall."

"Damn, I never even thought about that. It did rain yesterday."

Riley wasn't so thrilled at the possibility.

"Oh well, I guess we'll just keep digging."

"Don't listen to Tanner, Riley. Hell, if it rained yesterday that water would have seeped away by now. I think the water is coming up from the ground myself."

"Sure, it could be, but like I said, it could be rain water too," Tanner teased.

"Ah, anyway, we best get going, I'm sure Ed and Beth are expecting us," Riley said as he turned and walked over to where their horses were. Tanner and Tyrell followed and soon the three were off to Sunday dinner at the McCoy's.

They were the first to arrive. Brady hadn't shown up yet. Ed greeted them outside at the horse rail.

"I used to have three men working for me that looked a lot like you folks. They was a lot dirtier though," he joked as they swung off their horses.

The sound of a wagon pulling up made the men pause and look.

"Oh, would you look at that. There is Adele, Beth's sister. Wasn't expecting her just yet," Ed said as he now greeted her.

The others removed their hats in respect of the oncoming wagon and the pretty lady steering the horse.

"Hello, Adele," Ed started.

"Hello back to you, Ed," Adele said as she pulled her horse to a halt.

Handing the reins to Ed, she slipped off the seat and stepped down. She was wearing denim jeans and a black blouse. She was stunningly beautiful.

"These must be the men that work for you," she smiled. "I know Riley; and these two are?" she asked as she stepped closer and looked at Tanner and Tyrell.

"Yep, these are the men. This here is Tanner and this fellow is Travis," he said as he pointed each of them out.

"It is a great pleasure to meet you, Adele."

Tyrell reached out his hand and the two shook gently.

"It is a pleasure to meet you as well, Mr. Travis."

She took back her hand and moved over to Tanner.

"And you must be Tanner?"

"Yes, ma'am. Tanner McBride at your service."

Tanner shook her hand and smiled.

"It is quite the pleasure to meet the two of you," Adele said referring to both Tyrell and Tanner. "Beth has spoken highly of you, you as well, Riley. Beth always has nice things to say about you."

"I try to be as gentlemanly as possible," Riley smiled.

"All right, now that we are all acquainted with each other, I'm sure Beth would like for all of us to step into the house. We have brandy and whiskey. Any takers?" Ed asked as they made their way inside.

"You know me, Ed. I'll take a glass of brandy."

"I knew you would, Adele, anyone else?"

"Neither for me, Ed. I'd have a coffee though," Tyrell said as Ed poured Adele her brandy.

"Sure, we have that too. What about you and Tanner, Riley? Either of you want a stiff drink. I have thirteen year old whiskey."

"I might consider a whiskey; sure, pour me a glass, Ed."

"Coming right up, Riley. What about you, Tanner? You want a whiskey?"

"Presently I'd prefer a coffee, Ed. A bit early for me to be dipping into the whiskey."

"All right, two coffees and a whiskey coming right up. You folks go ahead and make yourselves comfortable. Adele, I'm sure Beth would like to see you. The two of you ain't saw each other in a while."

Ed gestured for her to follow him into the kitchen.

"Right behind you, Ed," she said as she coursed her way into the kitchen, a glass of brandy in her hand. She set her glass down on the table and gave Beth big hug.

"It sure smells good, Bethy. How have you been?" she asked as she looked over the food cooking.

"I've been well. How about you, Adele. Are things going well with you?"

"I have no complaints."

"Good. I'm so glad you came along. It has been a while since we saw each other."

"Yes. Yes it has been," Adele said as she tasted the gravy that was simmering gently on the stove.

"Yum, that tastes just like mother's."

"Thank you, Adele. I did use her recipe."

"That pie even smells scrumptious."

"Can I butt in her for a minute, ladies?" Ed asked as he tried to make his way over to the percolator.

"Tanner and Travis want a coffee. Let me get it and I'll be gone. The two of you can catch up then. Do we have sugar and cream, Beth?"

"Sure do. It is right here."

Beth handed him the condiments. He set them down and thanked her. Pouring the coffees, he set them onto a tray along with the cream and sugar and scooted off into the sitting room.

"Here are the coffees, cream and sugar."

He set the tray down on the table.

"Thank you, Ed," Tyrell said as he took a cup and added his fixings.

"Mmm, that is good coffee."

Tyrell made his way over to the chair he was sitting on.

"So that is Adele, eh? Quite the looker she is," he mentioned between mouthfuls of the hot drink.

"Yep, that is Adele. Younger and as beautiful as her older sister."

Ed smiled as he sat down.

"I have to agree that is damn fine coffee," Tanner said as he took a drink from his cup.

"When is Brady showing up?"

"Hard to say. He'll likely be here around the same time that dinner is served. A couple more hours I reckon."

Ed took a swig of the whiskey in his hand.

"You want another, Riley?"

"Sure fill me up, Ed. Thank you."

He handed Ed his empty glass.

"I have to say, dinner sure smells good. What is Beth cooking?"

"Roast pork, vegetables and a couple of pies."

Ed handed Riley another shot of whiskey.

"How is that Colby kid working out for you, Riley? How is the well digging going? Finding any water yet?"

"Hard to say. We may have or it may be rain water that has gathered in the hole. As for Colby, you already know how I feel about him. He's a hard worker, Ed."

Riley tilted his glass up to his lips and took a swallow.

"He hasn't got many days left of community service, does he?"

"Nope, I think he's finished on the sixteenth."

"I'm actually gonna miss him being around."

Riley finished his whiskey and set the empty glass on the table.

"You are welcome to more of that if you want, Riley."

"Nah, I'll wait until dinner. Thanks though, Ed."

"Travis, Tanner, how are your coffees?"

"Still have some. So, Colby is going to be done on the sixteenth, eh?"

"If my math ain't wrong. That's right, Tanner. You going to miss him too," Ed teased with a smile.

"Not really. I'm kind of interested though to know what he and Alex have planned, if anything."

"I don't think they have anything planned. What makes you think they might have something planned?" Tyrell asked as he took a drink from his coffee.

"I just think it is a long time for a relative to hang out in this two horse town, waiting for their kin to be sprung loose," Tanner shrugged. Deep down he was certain that both Alex and Colby were up to something, he didn't know what, but there was definitely something going on.

"I think your speculation that the two are up to something is without merit," Riley mentioned as he looked at Tanner. "Clearly, Alex Brubaker is only here to escort Colby home. Leastwise that is what he has said a time or two. I ain't worried that they might be up to something."

Ed waved his hand through the air.

"Ah, let's not talk about the two of them. There are more important things to talk about. Besides, once Colby does get sprung, he is a free man, Tanner. I wouldn't worry."

"I didn't say I was worried, Ed; only stated I was curious is all. And you are right; there are better things to talk about. Colby though, he is an American, ain't he?"

"What has that got to do with anything?"

"Nothing really, jus' my curiosity again."

"You ever hear the saying, Tanner, that curiosity killed the cat," Tyrell joked.

"Nothing wrong with being curious about this, that or the other thing. It is when we start making assumptions that things can go awry," Ed pointed out as he poured himself another whiskey.

"You sure you don't want another, Riley?"

"I reckon if I don't you'll keeping twisting my arm. Sure, pour me another, Ed," Riley relented.

"Travis, Tanner, you two sure you don't want one. It is damn good whiskey."

"What is with the pushing of the booze, Ed?" Tyrell asked.

"Are you being curious, Travis?" Tanner tossed into the conversation with a smile.

"I guess I am, Tanner, I guess I am. I get your point," Tyrell chuckled. "All right Ed, pour me a glass. I can see how this day is going to be."

"I'll take one too, Ed."

Tanner stood up and met Ed over at the whiskey canter.

"Better make Travis a double," he joked as Ed poured two fresh glasses and handed them to Tanner, who in turn handed one to Tyrell.

"Here you go, Travis. Not sure it is a double."

Tanner raised his glass in the air.

"Cheers," he said as he put it back in one swallow. The four men conversed back and forth as they waited for Brady to show up and dinner to be served.

Finally, at 4:00 p.m., Brady walked in.

"Shit, the four of you have been swilling whiskey all day, haven't you?"

"Here, here," they said in unison as they chuckled.

"Well, I might as well join in. When is dinner going to be ready, old man?" Brady questioned as he opened another bottle of whiskey and poured himself a glass.

"Go ask your ma, 'cause I ain't even sure what time it is," Ed said in his half drunken state.

"I think it is time for you to have some coffee, old man."

Brady sat down next to Travis.

"Has he been drinking all day?" he questioned, referring to Ed.

"Ain't sure, cause I ain't sure when we started," Tyrell slurred.

He too was half drunk and so were the others.

By the time dinner was served the four men except for Brady had managed to kick back a couple cups of coffee each and were now beginning to sober up.

"It sure smells good, Beth. You outdid yourself I figure," Ed said as he and the others made their way into the dining room and took up seats around the table. There was nothing better than a home cooked meal and the men ate in silence most of the time. Full and sober now, they drank coffee and ate pie while Beth and Adele returned to the kitchen to begin the cleanup.

"That there was some good food, Ed. Beth is a damn fine cook," Tyrell said as he poured himself another black coffee to wash down the second piece of pie he had.

"I'll say. I ain't ate that well in months," Riley added as he too poured another cup of coffee.

"There's nothing more that I can add. I don't reckon either of us have had a meal that good in a long while. I think you are spoiled, Ed," Tanner joked as he picked his teeth with a fork.

"I wouldn't deny that Tanner, no sir, I wouldn't."

Ed reached over to a box of cigars that sat on the china cabinet behind his chair. It was time he decided to fill his men in on the news he received from the Police Commissioner's office.

"What is going on, old man? You don't smoke those unless you have something to say."

"I do have something to say, Brady. Anyone want a cigar before I start."

"This ain't going to be one of your long winded speeches, is it?" Riley questioned.

"It might be. You want a cigar or not, Riley."

"I ain't one to turn down a good cigar, Ed. You know that."

Riley took the cigar.

"Should I grab us that bottle of whiskey?"

"No whiskey for me, Riley," Tyrell said as Ed handed him the box of cigars.

Taking one, he handed the box over to Tanner who then handed it to Brady.

"All right, we'll let the whiskey be for now, but I'm telling you folks, if Ed starts going on and on, we're all going to need whiskey."

Riley brought his cigar up to his lips and struck a match. Handing the lit match down the line, they all fired up their cigars.

"So, what you got to tell us, old man?" Brady asked as he inhaled a lung full of the acrid smoke and blew a smoke ring.

"This past Friday I received the letter back from the Commissioner's office," Ed started as he took a long pull on his cigar.

"McCoy's has been grandfathered in to the Private Security sector. The Commissioner has given us the go ahead to do so, all legal and binding. What do you fellows think of that?" Ed asked with enthusiasm and vigour.

"Damn, two good things in one day, first the meal and now this," Tyrell spoke up with a smile. "That is good news, but what does it all mean in the end, Ed?"

"Means we still have jobs come January," Tanner mentioned as he took a swig from his coffee, "and that there like you say, Travis, is damn good news."

"Yep, you will all keep your jobs. I guess what it means in the end, Travis, is that private folk can hire us now for an array of different tasks, everything from private protection to private investigations. Even the provincial and federal police can hire us to help with criminal cases, not just in British Columbia, but in all of Canada. We get to pick and choose what jobs we want and what jobs we don't. Protecting citizens and upholding the law is what will be expected of us. It really ain't going to be much different than what we do now except that we aren't going to have to rely on bounties we bring in anymore to make a living," Ed pointed out as he paused and waited for someone to respond.

Those around the table remained silent as they contemplated.

Tyrell was the first to speak.

"I liked that part of the job though, Ed. You know bringing in bounties."

"We can still do that, except now we don't have to. There is good money to be made on jobs that are less perilous, Travis."

"True as that might be, Ed, when we apprehend wanted men for their bounty our legal obligations when apprehending them will entail a lot more legalities. We'll have to follow police rules and regulations," Riley made clear. "It differs somewhat from what we are allowed by law to do now," he added.

"It does indeed, but in the end that money owed to us... is still owed," Ed said as he looked at each of his men with assurance.

"Yep, it is. Except you'll be waiting three to six months to see it. Due to all the legalities and such."

"I know, but there will be other things we can do, Riley. We can have a man or two working specifically on bringing in felons whilst the others focus on private security. We can switch it up once a month or every other month, or hell, even once a year. That part of the job don't change much except like you've said we'll have to follow police rules. And we'd be traveling with a Private Investigator badge instead of a Bounty Hunter's star and handbook."

"How are we going to pay wages, old man?" Brady wanted to know. "That part of this conversation I ain't getting."

"Wages will be paid the same as they are now, Brady, by the job. It might be less, but if we hustle our asses and work it could be more. I don't pretend to think that it'll all be peaches and cream 'cause I know damn well it won't be, but these are the choices we have. We can either work with what has been handed to us or we can close up shop come January."

"Don't be talking about closing up shop, old man. No one sitting at this table has even suggested that. I simply want us all to be clear on how wages will work once this all takes place and becomes our reality. Are we going to pay the men an hourly wage or like you have suggested by the job. It is something you can't just decide. It has to be thought on a while."

Riley, Tyrell and Travis sat in silence as father and son bickered back and forth. It was an uneasy feeling and the excitement of the news was now stale. There were many things that were going to change that was obvious and not one man at that table that night could know how it would affect any one of them when the transition from Bounty Hunter to Private Investigator took place. *Would it be for the better or would it be for the worse?*

Finally, Tanner spoke up.

"Hell, there ain't no point in arguing on wages or anything of the sort. We all knew this was coming and I think in the process we all forgot that as of right now we're all still bounty hunters. I ain't worried about what is to come. I'm just glad that McCoy's has been given this opportunity. Come January we would've been unemployed. Gambling and women wouldn't be so fun then," he joked as he carried on. "I'd take a monthly wage over being unemployed any day. So, if comes down to where only a wage could be paid to keep me working, I'll take it. I like what I do too much to not accept something like that. I personally don't care if I make more or less, as long as I can work."

He paused for a minute as he inhaled a lung full of smoke.

"I think you all forgot about Matt Crawford. That is a ten thousand dollar bounty that we can still bring in before January and who knows how many more bounties we could come up with between now and then. This here bickering about wages and stuff really don't mean a damn thing, does it?"

Tanner looked at each of the four men sitting at the table. He had made his point.

"Yeah, I reckon you are right, Tanner."

Brady looked over to Ed.

"I'm sorry, old man, if I seemed to have jumped on your back. Tanner has made some good points. There isn't a damn thing we can do to change what is to come. I say tomorrow morning when we all sit down at the office for coffee that we get a plan together to bring in Crawford. The weight weighing on us now on what is to come in January ain't so heavy that we can't lift it."

"I'd agree with that," Tyrell said with conviction.

Riley nodded his head and smiled. "Yep, me too."

Two hours later, Riley, Tyrell and Travis bid Ed and his family good night and headed home, full and satisfied at the evening's outcome. Tomorrow was another day and what lay ahead, lay ahead.

Chapter 8

Monday, September 7, 1891. Tyrell was the first to arrive at the office, other than Tanner who was asleep on the backroom cot. Tyrell went about getting the woodstove lit and prepping the morning coffee. The sun in the east was rising before the flat open prairie and he looked at it briefly. *Finally some sun,* he thought as he turned back to the task at hand. It was going to be a nice sunny day. He opened the small window above the counter and sink. From there he could look out to the back of the office and he watched immersed in the sight of the horses, including Pony, prancing around as though dancing with joy that a new day had started and for a change the yellow ball in the sky had returned. It had been so miserable as of late with a lot of rain and chill. Today, though, that wasn't how it was looking.

He had sat down for only a moment when Tanner rolled out of bed and met him in the staff room.

"Morning, Tyrell. Looks like we got sun coming today. About time I'd say," Tanner said as he walked over to the coffee pot and poured a cup.

"I couldn't agree more. Was quite miserable this past while."

"Well, it is early September. Come November we'll see more of that crap weather we've been having."

Tanner sat down at the table and slurped a drink from his hot coffee.

"What did you think of Adele?" he asked out of the blue.

"A nice lady, I'd say. Cute, charming and a damn good talker. Why you ask?" Tyrell was curious to know.

"I think she took a shining to you. Was curious myself why you didn't bring her back here with you last night."

"I don't think she took a shining to me. Besides, I ain't interested in any woman at the moment. Got too many things to think about other than a woman."

"Hell, you been saying that for the last couple of months since I've been working with you and the McCoy's. I think there is a bit more to it than no interest."

"Why do you care, Tanner?"

"Didn't say I cared, simply brought up a point. It don't matter any to me."

Tanner brought his coffee cup to his lips and took a drink.

"The truth be told, Tanner, I wouldn't want to bed down no woman that was my boss's wife's sister. That wouldn't sit well with me at all," Tyrell fibbed.

The truth was he was committed in his own way to Marissa. Loyalty is what stood in his way. He didn't know why he had been so loyal, but he certainly had been for the most part. He thought back to his journey to the Fort and the employment opportunity Ed had given him a year earlier. He stopped off at a town called Crab Apple and was greeted like a hero by the very beautiful stable lady, Serena Boalee. That was the only time desire got the better of him. She didn't know his real name; even then he used Travis Sweet as his name. He thought about that for a moment, and then shook his head. Serena was a lot closer to the Fort than Marissa was. He knew if he ever had a desire to bed a woman for a casual encounter and get it free, it would be Serena. For life though, it would be his Marissa. Tyrell took a drink from his coffee and smiled to himself. One day, perhaps sooner than he thought, he would once more be in Marissa's arms or so his mind and heart had always led him to believe.

"Hey, Tyrell," Tanner snapped his fingers, "are you in there?" he chuckled. "Looked like you were in some kind of dreamland."

Tyrell looked over and smiled.

"That I was, Tanner; that I was."

It was then that the front office door opened. Both Ed and Brady made their way into the staff room and their own morning coffee.

"Morning, gentleman," Ed said as he poured him and Brady a cup.

"How'd you enjoy dinner last night?" he asked as he handed Brady a steaming cup of the hot brew and sat down himself.

"No complaints from me at all, Ed. Like I said last night, Beth is a damn fine cook. I enjoyed every morsel I shovelled into my face," Tyrell smiled.

"Was nice to meet Adele too."

"I'm with Travis, Ed. Last night's meal at your place was the best damn food I've eaten, even in comparison to the Snakebite; and Adele, well she's a fine woman," Tanner nodded as he stood up and poured himself a second cup.

"Riley ain't showed up yet?" Brady asked as he took a swallow of his coffee.

"Nope. I reckon the whiskey is at fault. Plus ain't he supposed to be working that Colby kid?"

"He and Colby don't get to work on that well of his until noon. Cannon has Colby doing other crap jobs during the morning hours. We'll give Riley a few more minutes to show up and then we'll get on with the day. Brady and I talked some last night after everyone left and I think we're going to divvy up some tasks here."

"What kind of tasks?" Tyrell asked.

"Like we spoke on last night. I think we need to bring in Matt Crawford, but I'll get into the details once we're all here."

"Sure, that's fine."

Tyrell raised his cup to his lips and took the last swallow.

"Hey, Tanner, want to pour me another cup too? Thanks."

He handed Tanner his cup. The four men conversed for a few minutes and finally Riley showed up.

"Morning one and all. I must be getting ol', slept in today."

Riley sat down a coffee cup in his hands. He took a long swallow.

"So, what we going to get doing t'day?"

"For starters, there are a couple of things. I'm going to be the boss here for a minute; bear with me," Ed half chuckled.

Not often did he talk like that.

"Anyway, Brady and I did some talking last night. We decided that if McCoy's is going to make the transition from bounty hunting to private security, we might as well start now. Sometime today all of us have to head over to the Mountain Police station. There is a new oath of citizen protection that we got to adhere to. The Mounties have said copy and are authorised to hand out new badges for each of us. By today's end we're all going to be Private Investigator and Private Security personnel."

He paused for a moment to let it all sink in.

"If there is any man at this table who'd rather not succumb to the inevitable you are free to leave. McCoy's will give you a two week pay of three hundred dollars. Is there anyone here that would rather take this option?"

Again he paused as he waited to hear their response. The room remained silent.

"All right, then. I'm glad you've all decided to stay. Now I'm going to address wages. You'll all be paid the same, one hundred and fifty dollars a week, so six hundred a month. That is the allotted amount that the Provincial Government has agreed to pay fifty percent of, for commissioned personnel of private security. That is us. There will be times this amount will increase periodically whilst we're bringing in felons or being hired by private citizens for this, that, or the other thing. During those times we'll get no provincial help. That is just the way these things work I guess. Any questions?"

"Basically we'll be getting a guaranteed six hundred dollars a month, more if we hustle our asses," Brady added.

"That is right. I know it ain't much, but it is a lot more than some folk make. We won't be uncomfortable to say the least. I know we're used to those big paydays when we bring in a bounty. We're still going to be able to do that, but like Riley mentioned last night, we're going to have to do it within the bounds of the new oath, so police law."

"How does that differ?" Tanner asked.

"As it is right now, we can pretty much do bounty hunting without a lot of legalities. We track, we find, we bring in and we get paid. The only thing that changes other than legalities involved is the pay wait. As private security personnel we don't see a dime of any bounty until after the so called guilty party is proven to be guilty. We'll have to follow the 'innocent until proven guilty' mentality."

"And the legalities differ how?" Tyrell took his turn to question.

Ed smirked. He didn't exactly know how the legalities worked. This was all new to him as well.

"By day's end, we'll be well informed, I suppose."

"No point in lollygagging, we might as well get on with it then," Riley commented.

"If you are all in agreement on what it is we're about to embark, then I agree with Riley. I say let's get it done."

Ed stood from the table and set his cup in the sink. The others followed suit and donning their hats, the five men headed over to the Mounted Police station. By 10:00 a.m., they were all holding new shiny badges with two words on them "Private Investigator".

"There you go, Ed. You and your men have all been sworn in, have read and signed the oath and are now commissioned by federal and provincial law. Welcome on board."

Lieutenant Cannon reached out his hand for all to shake.

"It is good to have folks like you and your men protecting and serving the law."

"We'll do our best, Bob," Ed assured as he and his men exited and headed back to the office.

"That wasn't so bad now, was it?" Ed asked as they sauntered on.

"It don't feel no different than when I woke up this morning," Tyrell said with a smile.

"Nope. It sure don't, except that we now have these new shiny badges."

Tanner looked at the one he held in his pocket.

"Well, that and the new oath and the fact that we've agreed on taking a weekly wage. I'd say not a damn thing has changed."

"Not much has Brady. We're still employed and we're still doing what it is we like. I'm a bit leery though on these tasks, Ed has planned, though," Tyrell chuckled. "So, what about them, Ed? What are these tasks?"

"We'll discuss those shortly, Travis," Ed smiled back.

They walked in silence until finally making the distance back to the office. Inside now and sitting again in the staff room, Ed went on.

"First off, Brady and I really do appreciate you fellows for sticking around. I mean that. There ain't anyone else I feel more comfortable working with than the three of you and Brady, of course."

"Nice of you to say, Ed."

"It is the truth, Riley. Brady and I really do appreciate the three of you. I was somewhat sceptical about this morning; thought for sure I'd be losing one or two of you. Glad things turned out as they did."

"I don't think either of us had any intentions on leaving, Ed. I know I hadn't even considered it."

"Nor me," added Tanner, "my mind was made up last night at dinner. What about you, Riley, you had any reservations on what was to come?"

"Hell no. I like what I do, Tanner. I know if we put in a good effort on our future endeavours, we'll do jus' fine. We're going to have to come up with a payment policy though, for private citizens. I ain't sure what the going rate is for private security."

"I'll be working on that over the next couple of days. Going to need some advertising too. I think I'll leave that up to Brady."

"What kind of advertising are we talking about, old man?"

"We should get an ad in a few newspapers. Likely be a good idea to get Innis to put together some flyers. That sort of thing, Brady."

"All right, I reckon that seems reasonable. What about Crawford?"

"That is the next part of business. I say grab yourselves some coffee, 'cause I'm sure there is going to be a debate."

"I don't like the sound of that too much, Ed. What kind of debating do you suspect we're going to get into?" Tyrell asked as he raised an eyebrow.

"Well, Travis, remember we spoke a time ago about Gabe Roy? How you and Brady were really the only ones from this crew he didn't know? I reckon Gabe will be our first client. He'll pay us good, right through his nose."

"C'mon now, Ed, you know I don't want anything to do with that fellow."

"I know, but you're in a new line of work now, Travis," Ed smiled.

"Shit, can I give you back my badge, then?" Tyrell teased as he shook his head.

He knew what was coming. He was going to be sent to Willow Gate to protect Gabe Roy from Gabe's own ghosts. He wasn't impressed with the thought, but as Ed stated, he was in a new line of work.

"Brady, you think you can find that telegram Gabe sent us?"

"Might have thrown it out, old man."

Brady didn't really want to be sent to Willow Gate either.

"C'mon Brady, go get it. I know you didn't throw it out."

"Ah, whatever. I'm like Travis on this one, old man," Brady said as he stood up and fetched the telegram.

Returning, he handed it over to Ed.

"Here you go, old man. I ain't impressed with what it is you might be churning in the head of yours."

Ed smiled as he took the telegram and read it over.

"We all agreed some time ago that Gabe was as dirty as my socks at the end of the week. This here is an invite into his world, a chance to get justice for all those poor bastards and families he's swindled. It says here that he is looking for private protection. It just so happens that as of today, we're in that business."

"Sounds to me, Ed, that you've been planning this right from the beginning," Riley said with a smirk. He knew Ed and he knew how he thought.

"I might have been, Riley, but I didn't think on it much until last night after Brady left for home. I thought to myself if we were going to go into the private sector headfirst, then we needed a client. Gabe Roy, as we all know, is a first class asshole with plenty of money. I reckon we'll charge him five hundred a week plus expenses. During which time we'll, or should I say whoever I decide to send to his beckoning, will turn up as much dirt on him as you and Colby have dug up for

161

that well of yours. Once we've accumulated enough damning evidence to send him to the poor house or prison itself, we'll take the necessary action to do so. The law can decide on who and how much he'll have to pay back to those he cheated."

"What about Crawford?" Tanner asked. "We bring him in, that is ten thousand dollars. I'm sure McCoy's could find a use for that."

"We'll get to Crawford soon enough, Tanner. Right now I need to decide on how to play the Gabe Roy hand."

He looked over to Tyrell.

"I know you'd rather not be Gabe's protector, Travis, but in the end it'll be you and the evidence you can get on him that puts things right for the folks of Willow Gate. Gabe wanted your protection a long time ago. I know he'd even take it now after all these months. I'll make sure that he pays good. It'll put McCoy's Private Investigations on the map. We sink him and we'll certainly have a lot of folk rowing in for our services. You get it?"

"I get it all right and when I think on it, I like the idea of putting him in his shoes. I just ain't sure I like the idea of it being me that does it. I might shoot him."

He was being honest at least.

"That oath you took this morning and that new badge of yours won't allow you to simply shoot him. It don't stop you either, if you can prove a reason for doing so," Riley pointed out as he poured a coffee and leaned against the counter.

Tyrell inhaled deeply and sighed. Ed and Riley were both right. Something had to be done about Gabe.

"Okay, Ed, you go ahead and send Gabe a telegram. If he's still looking for private protection, let him know Travis Sweet is willing. But, I want you to charge him for these services like you said 'through the nose'."

A big smile crossed Ed's face and his eyes lit up.

"I will; you can bet on that. All right, now that that is settled let's move on to Crawford. With Travis being gone that only leaves the four of us to bring Matt in. I think I'd like to ride with Riley on this one."

Ed looked over to Brady.

"That leaves you and Tanner to do your part as well. I'll let you fellows decide if you're going to ride together or split up. I figure we get the details worked out on each of these tasks, Gabe Roy and Crawford by day's end, we can set off in the morning."

"Without a home base to set up logistics and messaging how the hell will this work, old man. We need someone here to do that."

"Not necessarily, Brady. The only one of us that is going to be stationary is Travis. Willow Gate has a telegraph office. Anything we need to relay to one another can be done from there. We send messages to Travis who in turn sends them to the receiver, keeps him in the loop at the same time. The four of us will have to keep him posted as to where we are that sort of thing, but that ain't nothing a telegram can't do."

"I'm going to be a messenger too?" Tyrell questioned in fun as he shook his head.

It was a good plan though and it did keep him informed.

"I can do that too, I suppose. I get it. Makes sense," he nodded his head in agreement.

"There we go, got messaging and logistics settled. What we know about Crawford is that his last known location was north of here in Vermillion. Now, since Riley and I are the aged in this group of misfits," Ed snickered, "that is where we'll head, to Vermillion and from there we'll head up to Hazelton. We got work to do up there as well. There is a chance that the young constable Travis spoke with is as dirty as Gabe, so Riley and I will look into that, as well as get information on who might have been responsible for Emery's death this past summer. It don't seem as though the Mounties are getting anywhere fast. We're still waiting on them to tell us about the Ranthorp fellow that was a Pinkerton. We ain't heard nothing in that regard, so now we go above them all. We got the badges now that will allow us to do that."

"Don't you think you are being a little bit over-energetic, old man? That there is a long haul. Old folk like you and Riley might not be able to pull that off."

Brady and the others, except for Riley, chuckled.

"As old as we might be, Brady, we can handle it. Ain't that right, Riley?"

Riley stood there smiling and nodding his head.

"I'd put a wager on it, Ed. I sure would."

"Well then wager away."

"Now, now. Let's not turn this into a gambling situation, Brady. You ain't got enough to wager anymore with the cut to your income," Ed teased.

Brady smiled and nodded his head.

"Good point, I reckon you are right there. I'll buy you two a bottle of whiskey if you make the distance and return here unscathed. That, I figure, we can all afford."

"Sure, a bottle of whiskey it'll be."

Riley sat back down at the table.

"So our plan is to bury Gabe Roy and I don't mean that in a literal sense, but who is to say. We've also decided to try and run in Matt Crawford and reap the ten thousand he's worth. At the same time we're going to do our own investigation into your man Emery's death up there in Hazelton. Sounds like we have a lot of work ahead of us. It is going to be a busy few weeks, I reckon. Guess I won't be getting my well dug after all," Riley shrugged.

"That is okay though; I was getting tired of that. I wasn't needed there anyway. I reckon Bash will keep Colby digging whether I'm there or not."

"I'm sure he will. Colby and Alex will be gone from the Fort by the time we get all this settled and make our way back, unless we run into Crawford before then; I have my doubts on that. It's been a while since we were last on his trail. He could be well out of Canada by now," Brady pointed out.

"Could be, might be, but we ain't going to be sure until we have exhausted any and all leads. We are in a different position now, Brady. We have new badges that allow us access to a lot more information and police documents than we had before. We'll bring Crawford in, we'll bring the law down on Gabe Roy and we'll get to the bottom of Emery's death. We'll have it all done before January."

Ed was certain of that. He had faith in his men. They were professional, intuitive and genuine, but most of all, they were honest. These were qualities he knew were hard to come by in most men. His men though were different. They were a brand all their own.

The journeys and tasks they cut out for themselves that day didn't seem forbidding at first glance. Things though had a way of going awry and they were aware of most problems that would arise. The one thing not expected and probably the most troublesome was the information Colby Christian had hidden away in the McCoy's stable. It was in a notebook in Matt Crawford's own handwriting detailing every name and place of the men Matt had killed as he sought vengeance on those who framed him for murder and those who attempted to assassinate his sister, Anne, as she ran for an U.S.A Government position. Last, but not least, of the names that were still on the list, Gabe Roy's was prominent. The men from McCoy's couldn't know that. Nor did they know that Matt Crawford was only one week's ride west of the Fort, heading in the direction of Willow Gate with the intention to put to rest one more name on his unforgotten list.

Chapter 9

Tuesday morning, after a night of fitful sleep, Tyrell rose from bed and gathered the gear he planned on taking with him as he travelled to Willow Gate. It was September 9, 1891. It would take, he guessed, until the end of the month to make the distance. There were a few shorter routes he could take, but they brought him closer to Red Rock and he was afraid that if he were that close, he might just carry right on through. More than a year had come and gone and he knew that by now most of his friends in and around Red Rock and Hells Bottom had assumed him to be dead.

There was no point rising from the dead yet. He had things he still needed to do and things he wanted to prove to himself before he could ever return to Red Rock. It was better, he decided, to go through Hells Bottom. Maybe he would stop in on Mac and Rose. He would certainly stop in and see Bannock and spend a night or two. From there, he would carry on to Willow Gate and the dirty job of being personal protection for the uncouth Gabe Roy until such time Gabe decided he no longer needed a shadow or until he could prove to the law how dirty and corrupt Gabe Roy was.

With his mind made up, he headed downstairs to the office and set the morning coffee to perk. Ed and the others would be rolling in soon. Tanner was likely going to wake up before then. Once they were all together they'd go over their plans one last time and then he'd head off. Pony and Black Dog, he knew, wouldn't have an issue going on another trip, nor did he. The only thing that didn't sit well with him was the fact on who he'd be protecting. It was uncanny to say the least. He thought back if only briefly to that moment in time when his whole world changed, when Heath Roy and his idiot friend drew their pistols and lost their lives. His world changed forever on that day. If it hadn't been for Emma, chances were he would have dangled from a rope by now. He would have to see her once he arrived in Willow Gate and explain to her his reason for being there and the name he was now using. *Ah, that is a few weeks from now before I have to cross that bridge,* he thought as he looked westerly through the staff room window in the direction he would be travelling.

Tanner, as expected, showed up shortly thereafter and poured himself a coffee.

"Morning, Tyrell. Are you looking forward to what lies ahead?"

"If you mean protecting Gabe, nope, I ain't looking forward to that. What I am looking forward to though is unmasking him for the ass he really is. Maybe even take down a few of those Mounted Police constables that we know are on Gabe's payroll in the process."

Tanner nodded his head in agreement.

"Yeah, that would be the icing on the cake. Buck would sure be proud."

"Yeah, he would be, wouldn't he?"

"Undoubtedly, Tyrell," Tanner said as the front door opened and they could hear the voices of Ed, Brady and Riley.

"All right, drop the 'Tyrell'. Remember in the company of others, I'm Travis."

Tanner waved his hand through the air.

"I know, I know."

"Morning Ed, Brady, Riley. Coffee is brewed," Tyrell said as the three men sauntered in.

"Morning, fellows. All ready for the big jump?"

"I'm packed and ready, Ed. No worries there."

Tyrell slurped from the coffee in his hand.

"Good, we're packed and ready too. Gabe, by the way has agreed on five hundred a week plus expenses for your wage, Travis. He's quite looking forward to meeting you."

Ed handed him the telegram he had received back from Gabe that morning. Tyrell read through it briefly.

"Yep, says he's quite looking forward to it," Tyrell smiled as he handed the telegram back.

"If only he knew our true intentions."

"In time, Travis, he will. How long do you figure it'll take for you to make the distance to Willow Gate?"

"Easily three weeks, I reckon. Maybe less. It is quite the distance, Ed. Plus I might make a few personal stops."

"Remember, when you do get there, check in at the telegraphers. I'm sure I'll have sent you something by then. There might be something there as well from either Brady or Tanner. You'll need to relay any messages.

Since the four of us will likely be on the constant move."

"Yeah, I'm aware, Ed. I know my role."

"Good. I knew you did, was just confirming."

"Confirmation confirmed," Tyrell smiled. "Well, I reckon I'm going to take off. Black Dog and Pony are in need of some action."

Tyrell rose from the table and put his coffee cup in the sink.

"By the look of the sun, I'd say today is a good day to travel."

"Yeah, Tanner and I will be heading out soon as well. I guess we'll head up with the old man and Riley to the last place we tracked Matt. From there it'll be anyone's guess on which way he went. Last time Riley and I found his trail, it looked like he was heading east from what I remember."

He looked over to Riley.

"Where was it again that you lost his trail?"

"He continued east for a ways. It was near Candora that I lost him. Chances are that he turned around before then, but until we're sure I'd say you and Tanner need to continue that way. Talk to homesteaders, farmers and such along the way. You might get lucky. Remember it has been over a month and like you have pointed out, he could be anywhere."

"I know; that is the real problem. Unless someone has seen him since then, it is going to be like finding fly shit in pepper. We likely should've headed out after him a lot sooner. Since we didn't though, we've made it tough on ourselves. I still say we can find him; it's just going to take some luck and determination. We'll get him."

Brady was confident in that regard.

"If you do head into Candora, Brady, you might want to talk to Will Anderson. He's a special constable for the northwest mountain police. He might have information on one thing or another regarding Matt. Might not too, but I'd say he'd be a good start in collecting any recent info. He's the fellow who arrested Buck for card cheating when I went looking for Matt or should I say Ron Reginal as he was known in those parts. I reckon he knows you too, Ed. Leastwise said he did," Tyrell responded as he began to head out.

"Yep, that's right. Will and I have had a few disagreements in the past, but we always came to some resolution. That is a good idea you bring up, Travis. It wouldn't hurt to ask him if he's seen or heard the name Ron Reginal up and around that area," Ed nodded in agreement.

"Can only ask, I reckon. Whether or not he's seen or heard of Ron is all speculation at this time, but won't know unless you ask."

Tyrell tilted his hat.

"I guess I'll be hearing from you folks in a couple of weeks. I'll be sure to check the telegrapher in Willow Gate upon my arrival."

"All right Travis. Be careful out there and good luck with Gabe."

"You folks stay safe too, Brady. I wish you good luck as well. I don't want to come back to an empty office," Tyrell smiled, nodded and left for the town of Willow Gate.

"All right fellows, we got one out the door, now let's get ourselves out," Ed said as he turned down the woodstove damper so the fire would go out.

"The four of us will head northerly I suppose. We'll have to split up around Fairmount. I reckon that is a few days ride from here. You sure you all have what you need?"

"Yeah, Tanner and I got all we need. C'mon, old man, let's head out," Brady said as the four closed shop and made their way over to the stable.

"We might as well grab a sack of grain for the horses as well. Go ahead Tanner and gather that, would you? I'll get the horses saddled."

"Sure thing, Brady. Ed, you and Riley want a sack too?"

"Might as well take some along. Bring us a sack too, Tanner."

Tanner turned heel and made his way inside the barn. Gathering a few small-sized grain sacks, he opened the barrel's lid and proceeded to fill the two sacks. Inadvertently, he noticed that tucked behind the barrel was a notebook. *Ain't that strange,* he thought to himself as he bent down to pick it up. He looked around thinking it may have fallen from the shelf, but there was no evidence that a notebook had ever sat on the shelf above the grain barrels. Holding it in his hand he flipped to the first page. What looked like the name of Ron Reginal was scribbled inside. Quickly he turned the page and read a list of names and places. Near the bottom were the names Riley Scott and Gabe Roy.

"Humph, what the hell," he said beneath his breath as he grabbed the two sacks of grain, closed the lid and met the others outside.

"Found some kind of notebook behind a barrel of grain. It's got Ron Reginal's name on the first page and a list of others on the next. Your name Riley and Gabe Roy's are near the bottom."

Tanner handed the notebook to Ed who flipped through the pages.

"You found this in our stable?" Ed asked with concern.

"Sure did, Ed. Thought it was grain ordering book. Was quite surprised to read it weren't. What do you make of it?" Tanner asked as he tossed the two sacks of grain over the rail fence.

Climbing to the top rail, he sat down as he waited for Ed's response.

"I ain't sure what to make of it. Take a look at this, Riley."

Ed handed the notebook over.

Riley thumbed through a few pages and shook his head.

"Seems like it is notebook full of names and such. I recognize some of the names. They were all killed by Matt Crawford. Not sure why my name is on the list or for that matter why Gabe Roy's would be. Hard to say,

Ed, what it is we've come across. I reckon it is of some importance. It might be that notebook Travis was trying to pull out from under the boardwalk that time; you remember that?" Riley questioned as he handed the notebook to Brady.

"Well now, we put two and two together and we come up with Colby. He cleaned our stalls and repaired the boardwalk. Makes sense to me that he found it under there and when cleaning up the stalls hid it," Brady said as he took the notebook and read through it himself.

"I recognize the handwriting too. This is Matt's book, fellows. How it ever ended up under the boardwalk makes no sense, 'less of course Matt himself has been to the Fort recently. Right beside Riley's name I see the date to be August 10th which adds another peculiar aspect to the whole thing. I say we pay a visit to Colby."

"You honestly think he'll say anything about this?"

"We can't be sure, Tanner. We'll have to ask to find out, I reckon. How far along do you suppose Travis has got. Maybe one of us ought to run him down before he gets too far away."

"Hang on a second. I didn't see no date beside my name. Let me see that again."

Brady handed the notebook back to Riley.

"Shit, did you see the date there, Ed?"

Riley handed it back to Ed.

Ed shook his head and scrolled down to Riley's name.

"Nope, never saw no date."

He squinted as he took a second look.

"I see it now, though; pretty small writing. No wonder I missed it. Good eye, Brady. I read it as August 10th as well. Wow, this here is something."

"We know that, old man; it sure is *'something'*. What, though, would be the hundred dollar question. Perhaps you and Riley ought to look into getting some eye spectacles," Brady chuckled.

"It don't say what year, though," Ed pointed out as though it may have a bearing on what it was they had stumbled upon.

"I don't reckon that means much. No point in pointing that out, old man. I'd say Matt was here in the Fort this past August, a couple of weeks before the Atalmore trial. We're wasting our time sitting here and scratching our heads. We need to talk to Colby, simple as that."

"I'd agree with that. I'd say our plans have now changed."

Tanner jumped off the top rail and stood beside his horse as he waited for the others to respond.

"Changed they have, Tanner," Ed nodded in agreement.

"Brady, how about you head off and try to catch up with Travis. Fill him in on what we've found here and carry on with him to Willow Gate. This here notebook don't change that part of the plan. I think it'd be best if you now tagged along with him. The three of us will stick around here and do some investigating. Maybe there is someone around here that saw Matt around the time of the Atalmore trial."

"I don't have a problem doing that, old man. Only thing is, Gabe is only expecting Travis, not me as well."

"I know; and it'll only be Travis that he gets. You'll be a passerby in the great town of Willow Gate, undercover. Gabe don't know you. He does know Tanner and Riley, though. Your role will be to keep an eye on both Gabe and Travis and at the same time be on high alert in case our friend Matt shows up there. In the meantime, like I said, the three of us," he began, referring to himself, Riley and Tanner, "we'll do some investigating around here. If we can come up with more evidence that Matt has been here recently and that he is indeed going after Gabe or Riley here, we'll follow in a couple of days or a week once we can confirm what it is we think we know now. I bet that was as clear as mud."

"No, I think we get it," Tanner commented as he looked around.

"Yeah, me too. All right. I guess then since I'm already packed, I'll see if I can't catch up to Travis before he gets to Willow Gate. It shouldn't take long for me to catch up. That horse Pony of his ain't too quick on the go."

Brady swung onto his horse.

"Send a telegraph to Willow Gate as soon as you fellows find anything out."

"We will, Brady. If you two happen to come across Matt, don't shoot him unless necessary. I'd like to bring him in alive. With his testimony and reasons why he's

176

killed so many, it will only further our cause. Hell, we could kill two birds with one stone: get Gabe put away and expose a few other not so righteous folks at the same time. Only good for all of us can come from that."

"I'd agree, Ed," Riley said as he leaned up against the corral fence and continued to chew the piece of straw he had between his teeth.

"All right, old man, Riley, Tanner, I'll be seeing you folks later," Brady said as he turned his horse westerly.

"You be careful, Brady. Anything happens to you, your ma will never forgive me."

"No worries, old man. I'll be cautious," Brady replied as he heeled his horse's flank and headed off to catch up with Tyrell.

"I guess we best get these horses unsaddled and put away. Then we can walk over to the station and see what, if anything, Colby knows about this notebook," Ed said as they went about the task.

A few minutes later the three of them were standing at the counter of the Mounted Police station.

"Morning, fellows. What brings the three of you here?" Bash asked as he walked over to the counter to address them.

"Morning, Rick. We was wondering if we could have a few words with Colby."

"What is it about, Ed?"

It took Ed a few minutes to explain and Bash listened with intent and curiosity.

"A notebook you say? Can I have a look at it?"

177

"Sure can, Rick."

Ed reached into his pocket and handed it to constable Bash.

Constable Bash flipped through it for a few minutes and then handed it back to Ed.

"Funny thing is, your man Travis asked if Colby found a notebook. Colby never said he did, so I assumed he didn't. If it is how you say it is, Ed, then I guess Colby knows as much about this book as you folks know."

"That is why we need to talk to him, Rick. If he didn't find it and stash it in our stable, then someone else did and they know about this book too. They likely had reasons on why they'd keep it."

"Uhuh, I see. I can't have all three of you in there with Colby. One of you could go and have a talk with him."

"One is better than none. It might as well be you, Riley. You seem to have a rapport going with the kid. He'll likely trust you some," Ed pointed out.

"Sure. I don't mind. Lead the way, Rick," Riley responded as Bash lead him to the holding cell.

"There you go, Riley. I can give you ten minutes."

Riley nodded his head and walked down the corridor to the last cell where Colby was being held.

"Morning, Colby."

Colby looked up from his bunk.

"Riley, what the hell?" he asked somewhat surprised. "What is up? You still need me for diggin' I hope. Otherwise the law will have me doin' other shit I don't want to do."

"Yep, I still need ya for diggin', that ain't why I'm here."

"So then, why are you here?"

Riley explained to him his reason for being there. But Colby wasn't about to admit anything. He knew that the notebook held the names and places of certain folk. Things he knew would help him and Alex in tracking down Matt Crawford. To give up the fact that he knew this would, in the long run, blow his and Alex's chances in bringing Matt in for the ten thousand dollar bounty that had been offered for his capture. No way was Colby going to admit to hiding the notebook.

"So, Tanner found a notebook. What does that have to do with me?" Colby shrugged.

Riley, though, wasn't stupid.

"Well, if you didn't find it, then I guess someone else might have and they tucked it away in the McCoy's stable. Hmm, well, thanks anyway, Colby."

Riley scratched his whiskered chin.

"By the way, we're getting close to water. Saw some evidence of that this morning."

"How deep was it?" Colby questioned as though he cared. He was glad that Riley had changed the subject more than anything.

"It weren't that deep I don't reckon; a couple six inches maybe less, but we're gettin' somewhere leastwise."

"Six inches ain't that much water. Sounds like we're going to have to dig a few more feet."

"Yep, you're probably right, Colby. I guess I'll see you this afternoon. Thanks for the chat."

"No problem, Riley. Sorry I couldn't have been more helpful," Colby lied.

"I think you helped a bit more than you suspect. I'll be seeing you, Colby," Riley said as he made his way to the first steel door and knocked to be let out.

"So, what did Colby tell you about that notebook?" Ed asked as Riley approached.

"Not a damn thing, Ed. I reckon he is the one who put it there, though. He seemed to want to cover up the fact that he knew anything about it at all. I could tell, though, by the way he was talking, he knows more than what he's led me to believe."

Ed nodded his head and looked over to constable Bash who was sitting at his desk.

"Thanks for letting us talk to Colby, Rick. He don't seem to want to admit he knows anything about this notebook."

"You are welcome, Ed. I'll keep my ears open in case he says something regarding it. I'll let you folks know if he does. And I'll be seeing you, Riley, around noon at your place."

"Does it matter if I'm there or not? Colby knows what to do."

"If you have other things to do, Riley, feel free to do them. There really is no need for you to be there, I don't think."

"Good. Thanks, Rick. Hopefully I'll get back to my place before you and Colby head back here."

"Sure. We'll see you if we see you," Bash commented as he went back to his report writing.

"Yep, we'll see you later, Bash. Thanks for everything."

"No problem fellows. We'll talk to you folks later," Constable Bash replied as the three men exited.

Colby sat in contemplation. The notebook he found was now in the hands of McCoy's men. He hadn't expected them to find it, but they had and now he was without it. It mattered little in all actuality. Alex had good information on where Matt was likely heading. The notebook Colby found only proved it. There was really nothing else in that notebook that mattered as far as Colby was concerned. Besides, he memorized a few of the names and places that he thought would benefit the two of them once he was sprung from community service. Chances were that McCoy's men would soon discover what Alex already knew, in which case they'd be onto Matt and ahead of the race to find him by at least a week.

Colby sighed as he thought about that and the fact that now he and Alex might never get their hands on the ten thousand dollars offered for Matt Crawford's apprehension. He hoped now, more than ever that Alex would stop by and visit him, so that he could relay to him what he knew. Maybe together they could somehow slow McCoy's men down and reap the reward themselves. He couldn't know then that Tyrell and

Brady were already on their way to Willow Gate. He'd learn about that soon enough. For now though, all he knew was that McCoy's had the notebook. He didn't have as much spring in his step that day when Bash came to retrieve him and put him to work.

Colby heard the big steel door open and he sat up waiting for Bash to open his cell door.

"Morning, Colby," Bash said as he opened his cell door. "We have a chicken coop to whitewash today before heading over to Riley's and some more well digging."

"Chicken coop, whitewash, three words I'd rather not have heard, Bash."

"Whitewashing doesn't take long, Colby."

"Never said it did. You know why folks whitewash chicken coops, Bash?" Colby began as Bash handed him his boots and he slipped them on.

"They do that because of chicken lice, a pesky critter I'd rather not have living on my skin."

Bash chuckled.

"No worries, Colby, I got a suit for you to wear. Plus, you'll get a nice hot lice bath later. C'mon, let's get."

Bash stood to the side as Colby walked passed him. Closing the cell door, they proceeded down the corridor to the next big steel door. Bash unlocked it and the two men stepped into the foyer of the station.

"You want a coffee before we head out?"

"I wouldn't say no to that, Bash."

"All right, grab a seat and I'll get you one."

Bash waited for Colby to be seated then he handcuffed him to the chair.

"Really, is this necessary?" Colby asked with disdain as he shook his head.

"Not sure it is necessary, but it is procedure. Sit tight and I'll get us those coffees."

"Take your time, I ain't so inclined to get all excited about what it is you're going to have me do, whitewash a chicken coop. You folks couldn't have come up with somethin' better?"

"Do I have to remind you again what community service means, Colby?" Bash questioned as he poured them each a coffee.

"Nope. I know what it means. It means I get to do shit jobs. It is the most exciting thing I get to do all day," Colby said sarcastically.

He wasn't the least bit impressed with what it was the law had him doing day in and day out. The only thing he looked forward to was digging Riley's well. The work was hard, there was no doubt about it, but it was man's work and something he felt good about doing. The rest of the work had all been stuff he'd never do if he were free, but he wasn't and so he had to put up with it. Soon it would all be over and he'd be able to walk away from all that he was subjected to do.

Community service, what a bunch of crap, he thought to himself as Bash returned and handed him his coffee.

Colby took it from him and smiled meekly.

"Thanks," he said as he brought the cup to his lips and took a swallow.

Ed, Tanner and Riley sat down at the staff room table and took turns thumbing through their find. The notebook indeed held some good information. They were able to ascertain that in all likelihood Matt was on his way to Willow Gate or, for that matter, might already be there. How Riley fit into the big picture with his name also on the list was anyone's guess. He didn't know why himself. The only thing that made sense was that he had tracked Matt on a few different occasions, a couple of times when he was on his own and the one time he and Brady tried to track him. Each time, Matt had outwitted him.

Even with Brady's help, Matt somehow managed to evade capture. Trained as he was as a U.S.A. Ranger, he likely knew every trick in the book and had probably, in his time as a Ranger, tracked worse men himself. He was no dummy. The fact that he remained on the loose proved this. There had been many a bounty hunter and Mounted Police Constable trying for years to bring him in. None so far had succeeded. Not even his own comrades, the Rebel Rangers, had been able to get close enough to him to talk.

The only thing going for the men of McCoy's was that notebook that they now had in their possession. Even that though, didn't make it easy. Tracking men like Matt Crawford was never easy. The idea of tracking him only took the edge off the plan of having to travel north to Vermilion and Hazelton. That was still something that needed to be addressed. The trip to Hazelton could in the long run prove who it was that had killed Emery Nelson. McCoy's men could perhaps, in the least, have the constable who was in charge of the investigation removed from the investigation. There were things he had lied about and things he had made assumptions on. He hadn't really investigated at all and that didn't sit well with Ed.

Now with the new badge his men carried, perhaps they alone could find the guilty party. That is, of course, if the guilty party weren't already dead. Even if he were, they needed to know who it was. The Mounted Police still hadn't heard back from the Pinkerton's office in the Montana division in regard to Miles Ranthorp, the Pinkerton man who they believed did the shooting. The 'why' wasn't clear and likely never would be, but the 'who' could certainly be proven, if Emery's death was investigated correctly, without assumptions and a dirty constable on the case.

For now though, McCoy's would concentrate their efforts in finding Matt Crawford, aka Ron Reginal, and unmasking Gabe Roy for the swindler he really was. With Matt's apprehension and Gabe Roy's convictions they would be setting the bar high for their new role in life, Private Investigation and Personal Security. Undoubtedly, they would put McCoy's Private Investigations on the map. It would be a win-win situation.

The investigation into Emery Nelson's death wasn't ending. It would be put on hold. Emery was dead and they couldn't bring him back. Once they cleaned up the slate that their hands were now tied up with, they'd once more look into it.

There was half a chance that between now and then, the Ranthorp fellow could be proven to be the killer. If that turned out to be the case, the 'why' went with him to his grave and there would be no point in trying to find out. There was a slim possibility that Matt Crawford himself might hold the answer on 'why', but they would not know until he was brought in and they had a chance to speak with him. Until then it was anybody's guess and only time would give up the answers.

Chapter 10

It was Wednesday afternoon, September 10th, when Brady finally managed to catch up with Tyrell. He spotted Tyrell from up on a ridge that overlooked the trail west. He heeled his horse and trotted up to him. Tyrell and Black Dog heard the horse approach and Tyrell sent Black Dog into hiding. He couldn't be sure who it was that was approaching so rapidly. He slowed Pony down and turned him to face the direction of the hammering hooves of the horse. He smiled and was somewhat confused when he recognised Brady.

"Hey, Brady, what the hell. What's going on?"

"Howdy, Travis. I thought I'd have caught up with you yesterday. Followed behind you shortly after you left the Fort."

Brady slowed his horse to a stop.

"For one reason or another, Pony insisted that we travel all night. I ain't rested in a long while. I reckon now is as good of a time as any."

Tyrell slid off Pony's back and whistled for Black Dog, as he removed his canteen and took a long swallow.

"So, what was your need in catching up with me? Is there something wrong back at the Fort?"

Brady too slid off his saddle and took a swig from his own canteen.

"I wouldn't say anything is wrong; something did come up though. When we was getting ready to head out yesterday, Tanner found an old notebook tucked behind a barrel of grain. It has a few names in it. Most of the folks mentioned is dead or are going to be dead. It belongs, we suspect, to Matt Crawford. Has Ron Reginal scribbled in it."

Brady took another drink from his canteen and wiped his shirt sleeve across his mouth.

"Ain't that something? How the hell did Ron's notebook get behind a barrel of grain in the McCoy's stable?"

"We assume that Colby found it when he was ripping up the Snakebite's boardwalk. It is the only thing that makes sense. It's likely the same notebook you spotted under there that time when we was heading over there for dinner. Remember that?"

"Sure do. I asked Bash if Colby found anything like that. He said he didn't."

"I don't reckon Colby would want to admit that he did. The boys were heading over to the jailhouse yesterday to see what, if anything, Colby knows about it. The old man said they'd send a telegram to Willow Gate if they find anything out. They is going to stick around the Fort for a few days and do some investigating. Could be Matt was in the Fort mid-August, jus' before Atalmore's trial."

"Humph. If he was, how come we never saw him? That don't make sense."

"A lot of things these days ain't making sense. The reason I'm standing here with you right now is that Gabe Roy's name was in the book. So was Riley's. Could be Matt is on his way to Willow Gate to put lead in Gabe. I don't know."

Brady shrugged his shoulders.

"We ain't going to know anything until we hear from the old man. I'm to travel with you to Willow Gate, goin' undercover one could say. If Matt shows up there, the two of us will be on hand to apprehend him and maybe save Gabe's life; although, I don't know why we'd want to do that."

"Well, justice handed out by the law is sometimes better than death. A man like Gabe gets unmasked for the dirty bastard he really is, will play hard on him for what will remain of his life. Makes sense to not want him dead, but rather face his accusers and let the law decide on what should come of it. As for Matt, we already know what it is McCoy's is going to try and do, and that is to get him exonerated for the crimes he has committed, was forced to commit due to a shady government, not to mention for the honour of his sister Anne. Hell, he was set up from what I understand and then he simply washed away the pricks that did it to him. He's no more of a criminal than you or I."

"I don't disagree with that at all. It is exactly what I want for Matt. The thing is, I've been stewing on a few things since leaving the Fort and I've come up with a bit of a scenario. I ask myself, what if Alex and Colby are making plans to apprehend Matt? Could be why Alex has insisted on staying in the Fort until Colby's release. We know Alex works in the business. Although not from a legal point of view, he still takes in bounties and gets paid. Could be he knows where Matt is heading and with Colby at his side, Matt himself will be up against a shooter as capable as himself."

Tyrell sucked on an eyetooth and nodded. It was a possibility that was the case or it could be nothing at all.

"Yeah, Colby you mean. He can shoot; there is no doubt about that. And the law don't care if Matt is dead or alive."

The two grew silent for a moment as they each tossed around the possibility.

"I have to say, Brady, your imagination is running away with you or you are dead on the money. You'd think smart fellows like us would've clued into that scenario. It does make sense. How though could Alex know about the Gabe Roy connection? That's the only part that don't make sense," Tyrell pointed out.

"Maybe he knew nothing at all about it until Colby found the notebook."

"That there is the key, Brady."

Tyrell thought for a moment.

"Hope Ed or Riley or even Tanner for that matter has the smarts to ask Bash if Colby has had any visitors since he tore up that boardwalk. If he hasn't, then I can't see how Alex would know of the possibility that Gabe Roy is next on Crawford's list."

"Yeah, I thought about that. Like I said, I'm only making assumptions. It was something that came to me last night around my fire. Hell, Alex works as a hired gun. Maybe he does know something that no one else does. It wouldn't surprise me as much as it seems to surprise you."

"No, no, I'm not saying that at all. It is a damn good possibility. There ain't no doubt about it. Alex could know something that we don't and if Colby did find that book then he too already knows what it is we're trying to figure out."

Tyrell shook his head at what he had just said.

"Jesus, that didn't make much sense. I'm tired is all."

"I got the gist of it. We ain't going to know nothing about nothing until we hear from the old man."

Brady looked westerly down the trail.

"Should we mount up and carry on westerly or do you prefer resting here for a spell? Like you said, you're tired and the god awful look on your face from riding all night certainly proves it," Brady chuckled.

"I'm all right to carry on a ways. There is a camping place not far from here. We'll stay there tonight. That was my goal for the day anyway."

Tyrell swung onto Pony's back.

"It is going to be nice travelling with company, rather than a damn horse who don't speak and a dog that'd rather chase rabbits. C'mon, Brady, let's get."

Brady swung back onto his saddle and the two men carried onward, Black Dog nipping at their heels. Every now and again, he'd dart off into the undergrowth and disappear for a short while, then pop up a mile or two down the road.

"I see what you mean about that dog of yours chasing rabbits. He does seem to take off quite a bit don't he?"

"Yep, I can't make heads or tails out of it. He usually sticks close. This trip though, he ain't so inclined to do so. Not sure why?"

"Near fall and all. Maybe he's scenting bears?"

"I'd much rather he scents them than the horse, so if that is the case, I guess I ain't got to worry. When I think about it, you are probably right. He's chasin' the bears off. That's got to be what it is. As for the horse not wanting to stop, well, I can't figure that part of this trip out."

"You came from the west on that horse, didn't ya? Likely knows the route and thinks he's goin' home. I don't know," Brady shrugged with a smile.

"Ah, I think he's jus' being coy. He's always been a little bit off center."

The two men chuckled as they carried on.

Three hours later they pulled up to the campsite Tyrell had mentioned earlier.

"Right here, Brady, is where we'll spend the night. There is a creek over the bank and some nice grass here for the horses."

Tyrell tethered Pony near a clump of clover and removed his saddle and gear. Brady did the same and they set their saddles near the fire pit.

"It's been quite some time since I was last here. The place ain't changed much," Tyrell said as he looked around.

"You know, I was thinking, Brady, if Matt is indeed on his way to Willow Gate, he's getting mighty close by now. If he stuck around until the Atalmore trial, he'd have been on his way by the 28th of August. That's a thirteen day head start. I reckon that'd put him a week closer than us. We might not make it by then. In fact I know we won't."

Tyrell sat down on his saddle as he contemplated.

"What I think we need to do, Travis, is find a telegrapher and send a telegram to Willow Gate to be delivered to Gabe. We let him know what our assumption is. Maybe get him to vacate the area for a week or two until we can make the distance. We'll send one to the Fort as well and let the boys back there know what we discussed and what our thoughts are. I reckon that is about all we can do. Matt still has a week's travel, by my guess, before he'll be close to Willow Gate. It gives us time to give Gabe fair warning. If he don't abide, so be it. If by the time we make it there and find out that Gabe has been killed, we can make a fair guess on who killed him. The thing about this business is that we're not always on time. It is within our powers, though, to at least inform."

"I reckon that is the best we can do, Brady. There is a telegraph office in Chase. We should be there in a day or two, depending, of course, on how hard we want to ride."

193

"We get a good night's rest tonight and I think we could push ourselves to make thirty miles tomorrow."

"Yeah, thirty miles ain't gonna be too hard to accomplish. It's twice what I would do in a day, but there is a need to do it so we'll have to do it."

Tyrell removed the map he had from his saddle bag and he studied it for a brief moment.

"I think we are here or close to it."

He pointed it out on the map.

"Chase is here," and he pointed at that as well.

"Looks to be about fifty to sixty miles. I think we can make the distance in a couple of days, three at the most."

"Hopefully, within those three days Matt, if he is even going in that direction, won't have made the distance."

"Unless he's been riding hard and steady, I reckon we'll still have a day or two to warn Gabe about Matt's pending arrival in Willow Gate. Hard to say, though. Could be Matt went cross-country. Can't see a fellow like him sticking to the trails and wagon roads. If that is the case, Matt could already be there."

"Uhuh. Could be. Wouldn't hurt my feelings none," Brady replied as though he cared.

"You don't sound too concerned."

"I ain't. We all know the type of man Gabe Roy is. If Matt puts lead in him, whether or not that is the kind of justice we want, it is still a kind of justice."

"Yeah, I suppose you are right. I wonder what Gabe did to have a fellow like Matt on his tail?"

"I ain't sure. He has to have one reason or another. My guess would be that he may have been involved with the assassination attempts on Anne, Matt's sister. Either that or Gabe swindled Matt along the way at one time."

"Could be something totally unrelated too."

"Yep, it could be."

For a moment the two men sat in silence and drank from their canteens.

"I guess we should get a fire pit set up for the evening. We'll use these rocks here," Brady said as he pointed at the rocks that were already around a fire pit.

"I ain't going to light no fire in this pit."

Of course Brady had his reasons for that.

Tyrell half chuckled.

"See, Brady, you don't need no lucky can of beans," he said as the two went about moving the rocks from one location to another.

"There, that ought to make it safe. I'll gather some wood," Tyrell said as he went about the task.

"All right, I'll head down to the creek and get us some water for coffee."

A short while later they were sitting on their saddles around a small fire that burned and their coffee was cooking.

"You ever wonder what might have come of ol' Whiskey Tooth George, Brady?"

"I imagine he hightailed it to wherever it was he came from. He ain't our problem now anyway. We have bigger fish to fry."

Brady smiled as he poured each of them a coffee.

195

"I'll never forget tracking him though. Was quite the experience."

"It was indeed," Tyrell agreed as Brady handed him his coffee. "You reckon it was he who killed those long hairs?"

"Only one that has that answer is George himself. If he did, there ain't no one who can prove it."

Brady took a swig from the tin cup in his hand.

"Could be also, that if he did, the long hairs will see to his justice. I think though, it were the renegade Indians, George mentioned that stole his horse and mules. The long hairs don't have much use for horses, most travel on foot. Makes me believe they was just caught up in one thing or another. The Indians probably killed them and then George killed the Indians. That is how I see it anyway. I could be wrong."

Brady shrugged his shoulders.

"What is your interest in all that anyway, Travis?"

"Was just thinking about it is all. I never once heard about long hairs before."

"They is a breed all their own, no doubt about it. Most folks ain't heard or seen them before, so you ain't the only one."

"How did you know about them?" Tyrell asked as he took a sip from his coffee and stared into the flames of their fire.

"Every now and again they make their way into the Fort, gather supplies and head back to the mountains. I guess one could say they are mountain men, trappers, prospectors, that type of man. They is mostly harmless, but don't get along too well with the Indians in the area. Never once have I heard about them hurting white folk though."

"So they stick to themselves, eh?"

"Sure do. Yep."

Brady finished his coffee and gazed into their fire as well.

Around this time and back at the Fort, Colby had finally hit water. Riley stood on the bank and looked on as the water filled the hole they had been digging.

"Well done, Colby; looks like we found what we was looking for."

He reached into the hole and gave Colby a hand in climbing out.

"Down quite a distance too, near fifteen feet I reckon," Riley said as he and Colby stood on the pile of dirt and rock that they had piled near the well.

"Damn, was hopin' it'd take a while longer. Now Bash will have me cleaning someone's chicken-coop," Colby said as he watched along with Riley as the water kept rising.

"I think I can help you out with that. Now that we got water, in the next day or two I could still use you. We need to make the well good and proper. The work here ain't done yet, Colby, not by a long shot. The worst part is done though, and you did helluva good job too. I'll make sure to let Bash know."

"I don't think Bash will give a rat's ass; he's a bit of scat hound," Colby said as he stepped away and off the pile of rubble.

"Now that this is done, you gonna ride me back to the station?"

"I will in time. Bash ain't around right now, how about a shot of whiskey, Colby?"

"The offer sounds good and I ain't had whiskey in a while, but I think I'll pass, Riley. I don't think the law would take kindly to me smellin' like a whiskey drum."

"How about a coffee then?"

"That I would consider and thanks for the invite."

"Not a problem, Colby. C'mon let's get back to the coach and I'll set a pot up."

Making their way over to Riley's coach they sat beneath the canvas tarp as the coffee perked.

"It is going to be nice being able to gather water from my own well rather than packing it in from the town well. Makes my life a lot more easy," Riley chuckled. "I'm getting too old to be packing it."

"I reckon a fellow like yourself would still have a lot of pecker left, Riley," Colby snickered as he averted his eyes to the road that led to Riley's place.

"Shit, here comes Bash. I guess I won't be joinin' you for a coffee after all."

"Ah, let me talk to him. I figure I can convince him to allow that. I'll tell him we still got work to do and we're only taking a short break."

"You go ahead; tell him whatever you want. I don't think he's goin' to care."

Bash, finally made the distance and swung off his horse.

"What is going on? Why isn't Colby sweating?"

"Jesus Christ, Bash, the kid was sweating. Worked his ass off, too. So, I thought we could use a break. Care to join us for a coffee?"

"You weren't given permission to invite Colby to your fire alone, Riley. He was supposed to break when I got back," Bash pointed out with authority as he stood over Colby.

"Well, you're back now, so grab a seat and have a coffee."

"Is the work done? If it is I'll be taking him back to the station."

"Nope, the work ain't done. Still got some digging to do," Riley fibbed.

"All right, I guess I'll allow him to break, but the law doesn't take to kindly to folks assuming they can let our prisoners rest without a law man near. Keep that in mind for the next time."

Bash pulled up a piece of wood and sat down close to Colby.

"You seem to have forgot that I am part of the law."

Riley flashed Bash his badge and smiled.

"You're a Private Investigator, Riley, not a Mounted Police Constable."

Bash shook his head and smiled back.

"But I respect that fact, so I'll let you get away with allowing Colby to break."

"Good," Riley replied as he poured each of them a coffee.

"I have sugar, but no cream. Either of you want sugar?" he offered as he grabbed the tin of sugar and a spoon.

"I'll take a smidge thanks, Riley," Colby said as Riley handed him the sugar and spoon.

"I'll take mine black," Bash replied as Colby stirred his own coffee and took a drink.

"You have to be pretty damn brave to drink my coffee black," Riley teased as Colby handed back the sugar and spoon.

"I'll agree with that. Damn strong coffee there, Riley, even with sugar."

Bash took a swallow and nodded in agreement.

"Yep, that is some strong coffee. It is good though. Thanks, Riley."

"You is both welcome."

Riley stirred his cup and brought it up to his lips and gently blew on the hot beverage.

"How much longer do you figure you'll be needing Colby?" Bash asked as he took a second drink.

"Until we strike water or his time comes up, whichever comes first."

"Well, he's got a week left before he'll be sprung. There was some other work I lined up for him."

"Oh, and what kind of work might that be, Bash?" Colby asked with little enthusiasm.

"Helping the Harlow family, east of here, bring in their potato crop."

"Really? Potatoes, couldn't you have found somethin' better for me to do?" Colby questioned as he finished his coffee.

He had never harvested a vegetable in his life and the work sounded like it was humdrum.

"Work is work, Colby, no matter what it is," Bash answered.

"He does have a point there, Colby."

"Whatever. Should we get back to diggin', Riley? I'm ready to get back at it."

"Yeah, I reckon we've rested long enough. Got a few more hours of daylight, I suppose."

The three made their way over to the hole in the ground. Both Colby and Riley acted surprised when they made the distance and could see that the water had almost filled the hole.

"Look at that, Colby. We got water."

"Well now, ain't that something?"

"Looks like you're going to have a well after all, Riley," Bash commented as he looked on.

Both Colby and Riley smiled and nodded.

"Yep, sure does. I guess what we have to do next is see how much water comes up. Then we'll need to make it proper," Riley pointed out, hoping Bash was going to allow Colby to continue with the work.

"You aren't going to need Colby for that are you?"

"What do you mean? Of course I am. I ain't going to be able to do the work without a young whippersnapper like him giving me a hand."

Bash shook his head.

"I don't know, Riley. You got water. The worst part is done and that be the digging. I'm not sure you'll need Colby for the rest."

"Damn right I will, Rick. C'mon let me keep Colby working on this with me. Shit, I'll even up my donation for his labour."

"I don't know. I'll have to run it by Cannon again. There is still the Harlow's that need help with their harvest."

Bash removed his hat and scratched the top of his head as he contemplated.

"I guess though, Colby has been doing good work here. We don't necessarily have to tell Cannon you found water. How long do you figure it'll take to make this hole into a well?"

"We'll need to line it with timbers and back fill it. Then there will be some building to do."

Riley grew silent for a moment as he thought about the work that still needed to be done.

"Might still need him for a few more days at the least."

"All right, I'll let you keep him for a few more days. After that though, Colby can expect to be harvesting spuds. That is the best I can do. Cannon finds out though that you struck water before then and my ass will be in a sling."

"As long as he don't come by, there ain't no way he could know. I won't say a word to him."

"Nor will I," Bash assured as he looked at Colby.

"You're lucky I like you some, Colby, or I'd be telling Cannon that this part of your community service is complete and you'd be harvesting potatoes come morning."

Colby nodded in appreciation.

"For what it is worth, I thank you, Bash. I'd much rather work on this well with Riley than dig up potatoes."

"So it is settled then. I'll get Colby in the morning?" Riley wanted Bash to confirm.

"I suppose so. Yep," Bash responded.

"Good. Thanks, Rick. I guess that'll be it for the day then. Got to let the water clear some before we'll know for certain if it is gonna stick around. I'll gather up some timbers tomorrow and if the water remains, we can start lining it. That'll likely take us the rest of the day tomorrow. Then we'll back fill and build the rest," Riley said as the three men turned and made their way back to the coach.

"Can I interest the two of you in another coffee? Hate to see a pot go to waste."

"I suppose we can have another. Then we'll head back to the station. How does that sound, Colby?"

"I ain't going to c'mplain. The more time I spend outdoors the better I feel when you lock the cage," Colby said as they sat down again.

Riley filled their cups for a second time and they conversed back and forth until their coffees were finished. Then Bash and Colby headed back to the station. Riley watched as they disappeared around the bend.

Walking over to the well again, he looked on and smiled. The water was slowly clearing. Reaching in, he cupped his hands and took a drink. It was good water and he wiped his mouth with satisfaction.

"That is damn good water. I knew we'd find it eventually," he said beneath his breath as he stood up.

He calculated how many timbers he would need to line the hole. He guessed he would need at least fifteen twenty-footers that were twelve by eight. They would cut them at five foot each. It would be enough, he figured, to line the well on all four sides. Then they could back fill and finish it up.

"Yep, a few more days work I reckon," he said to himself as he turned and made his way back to his coach.

Sitting down he dumped out the little bit of coffee that was still in the pot. Looking at his pocket watch, he noted that he still had time to make it to Jefferies lumber yard. Hopefully they would have the timbers he would be needing. Saddling up his horse, he headed in that direction to find out. It took him a few minutes to make the distance. Tying his horse to the horse rail outside, he entered the lumber yard.

"Hello, Mr. Scott. What can we do for you today?"

"Evening, Clarence. Any chance you have fifteen twenty-foot twelve by eights?"

"That is quite a load. Step outside with me and let's go have a look. What are you needing such big timbers for?"

"Hoping to line my well with them."

"Oh, so you did find water on that piece of land, eh?"

"Yep, finally struck it today. We're down about fifteen feet, maybe less."

"Uhuh that be the reason you need them to be at least twelve inches wide, eh?"

"I reckon so," Riley said as Clarence removed a tarp from a pile of timber.

"Here we are. Let's see," Clarence said as he started counting them off. "Yep, looks like we have twenty. They ain't cheap; two and a half dollars each. You still want fifteen?"

"Sure do. Can I get them delivered early tomorrow morning?"

Clarence tossed the tarp back over the pile.

"Yep, we can deliver them in the morning. That'll be an extra two dollars for the delivery. Is that all right?"

"No complaints from me, Clarence. That is fine."

"Okay, let's go ring it up," Clarence said as the two men made their way back inside.

Clarence rang up the cost and wrote out the bill as Riley fished into his pocket for the money. He handed Clarence forty dollars and Clarence handed back his fifty cents in change.

"There we go. Anything else, Mr. Scott?"

"Nope, that'll be all for today. So, I can expect those timbers in the morning?"

"First thing. You bet."

"All right, thanks a lot, Clarence."

"And thank you very much as well, Mr. Scott. We'll see you in the morning," Clarence said as Riley began to leave.

"Yep. Will do. Good night, Clarence."

"Good night, Mr. Scott."

Riley exited and swung onto his horse, then headed over to the Snakebite for a shot of whiskey and a steak dinner. The day had ended.

Chapter 11

Friday morning September 11, 1891. It was a day like any, except for one thing. Not far from where Brady and Tyrell sipped their coffee around their morning fire, a single man approached. It was Black Dog who alerted the two. He looked down the trail beyond anyone's view. It was the scent that told him somebody was approaching. He sat alerted, gazing and ready.

"What do you make of that, Travis? Your dog seems to be interested in something coming our way."

"Yeah, I noticed that. He don't seem concerned. Likely another rider coming this way," Tyrell said as he stood up and strapped his holster on.

"Unless the dog gets riled up, I ain't too worried on what or who might be coming."

Black Dog remained stock still, his eyes never averting from the trail. It was then that they could hear the sound of horse hooves.

"Yep, another rider is coming our way," Brady said as he too now stood and strapped on his own holster.

The two men and Black Dog waited patiently for a few minutes. Finally, they could see the rider. Trailing behind him were two packed and loaded mules.

"Look at that, Brady. Looks like that might be George coming this way."

"I see him. That is George all right. We going to apprehend him, Travis?"

"I don't see no point in that to be honest, Brady. If he decides to make a ruckus, maybe we'll consider it."

Tyrell shrugged his shoulders as he stepped into view.

"Hello, there you old codger. Certainly weren't expecting to see you around this area," Tyrell said as old George slowed his horse down and looked onward.

"Nope, weren't 'xpectin' to see either of yous, either. Don't be going for those pistols," George said as he pulled out his old rifle, "or I'll make quick use of the lead balls loaded in this here rifle."

Tyrell raised his hands to let old George know that they weren't about to do anything of the sort.

"No worries, George. We ain't got no reason anymore to do that. You ain't on our list of things to do today."

Tyrell lowered his hands and invited George over to their fire.

"We have fresh coffee, if you're interested."

"I might need to think on that for a moment."

A quick second went by.

"All right, I'll join yous."

George moved his horse closer, the rifle still pointing at the two men.

"B'fore, I slide off my horse, you sure you ain't here to try and take me in again? It has been a lil' while since you last tried."

"Nope, we ain't got no intent to bring you in. We have someone else we're more interested in."

"Oh, and whom might that be? I'm worth five hundred dollars, don't you know," George said with a slant of humour as he snickered.

"We ain't at liberty to say, but rest assured it ain't you," Brady said as he sat down on his saddle and poured himself another coffee.

"Slide off that horse of yours, George. If you want a coffee."

"Maybe we ought to make amends b'fore I do that. I ain't so sure I can trust yous."

"You can trust us. Like Brady said, we ain't looking for you at this time."

"And what is that s'pposed to mean 'at this time'?"

"I ain't sure I can make it any easier to understand, George. The simple truth is we ain't looking for you anymore."

"And why might that be? There is a bounty on my head and yous is bounty hunters," George questioned, somewhat hurt that he wasn't worth the effort and at the same time grateful that he wasn't.

"If it'll make you feel any better, we can pretend to apprehend you," Brady said jokingly.

"That way you can sit with us a spell and have a coffee."

"Oh, so you are here to try and take me in, eh?"

Tyrell and Brady looked at one another, smiles across their faces and shook their heads.

"Ahh, I was jus' funnin' with you greenhorns," George said as he slid off his horse and put his rifle away and gathered his tin cup from one of the mules' backs.

Walking over to the fire he reached out his hand to shake.

"So, you greenhorns don't want nothin' to do with this old fella, eh?" George mentioned as they shook hands.

"Well, that prob'bly be best. Where is that Tanner fellow that yous was runnin' with when you was chasin' me down?"

"He's back at the Fort. Taking care of business back there."

George handed Brady his tin cup.

"Uhuh, good, good. I'll take my coffee black there, kid shin-kicker. So, yous on the trail of another fellow or is you jus' out and about?"

"A little of both I reckon," Brady said as he handed George his coffee.

"Can't be doin' both kid shin-kicker: can't be doin' both," George repeated as he took the coffee and nodded.

"Thank you kindly, shin-kicker."

He brought the cup to his lips and gently blew on it before taking a swallow.

"Hmm, been a while since I last had a coffee. It sure puts the poop back in yer step, don't it?"

"Or makes you poop. One or the other," Tyrell joked.

The three men chuckled out loud as their feel-good mood was set.

"All jokes aside, why the hell would you be out here yourself, George? I see your mules ain't got no drums over their backs, so you ain't packing whiskey."

"Nope, not this time 'round," George smiled as he took another swig from his coffee.

"This time, I'm headin' north into the Athabasca to settle in for the winter. Hopefully, I'll make the distance before the snow flies."

"Athabasca? You live up that way, George?"

"Sometimes, yep."

"This be one of them times, then?" Brady questioned as he filled their cups again.

"It is too. I have a trap line that keeps me busy throughout the winter and a still that keeps me warm," George answered as he took his second cup of coffee that Brady handed to him.

"Still? You make your own hooch?" Tyrell was curious to know.

"Would cost me an arm and a leg to buy the stuff I sell. Been making moonshine for forty years and sellin' it for fifty," George chuckled.

"Now that you know a lil' bit about my whats, buts, and what have yous, what is it that you twos is doin' two days ride from the Fort?"

"Already told you, George, we ain't at liberty to say," Brady brought his cup to his lips and took a drink.

"Official business then, I reckon. That's okay, no need to say more," George waved his hand through the air.

"Where are you coming from George, if you don't mind me asking?" Tyrell tossed another stick into the fire as he waited for George to respond.

"Westerly," George replied as he brought his cup to his lips for a drink.

"I realise that, any place in particular?"

"None whatsoever, nope."

"How long have you been on this trail? You ain't been on it since we last met have you?" Tyrell chuckled.

"Not since, I don't reckon. Shortly thereafter, though. You fishin' for somethin', greenhorn?" George questioned with uncertainty.

"Not really, just friendly conversation. This trail is pretty lonely. We've been on it three days today and we ain't saw another rider yet, except you. Was curious to know if your experience has been the same."

"In the few days I've been on it, only passed one or two folk. Most don't use this trail much anymore. There are better trails goin' in the four directions north, east, south and west."

George looked into his half empty cup and took the last swallow.

"Well," he began as he stood up, "I reckon I best get on with it. Got quite the distance to make b'fore winter."

"Yeah, all right, George. We should be getting on our way too."

Tyrell and Brady both stood up and shook George's hand goodbye.

"One last thing George. Did one of those two folks you say you passed ride a midnight black horse?" Brady questioned out of the blue.

George put his cup away and walked over to his horse.

"So, yous two is lookin' for a rider on a midnight black horse, eh? I knew you was lookin' for somebody. I can tell you I ain't saw any midnight black horse on this trail."

George swung up onto his horse and looked at Brady with a smile.

"By the way, shin-kicker, when you make it back to the Fort, say 'hi' to that nephew Ed of mine."

With that said he turned his horse and two mule team then headed off.

"What the hell do you mean by that, George," Brady hollered after him, but George carried onward not turning back once to answer. Brady looked over to Tyrell and shook his head.

"Did I hear what he said correctly?"

"Depends on what you heard, Brady. Sounded to me like he said Ed was his nephew."

"I thought that is what I heard too. What the hell," Brady responded confused and taken back.

"Who would have ever guessed that law abiding citizens like the McCoy's would have a wayward uncle?" Tyrell started to laugh.

"It's bullshit! He's got to be lying, don't he?"

Tyrell shrugged still chuckling softly.

"What would be the point to lie about something like that?"

"I don't know; to get my goat maybe. I can't believe he's my old man's uncle. That don't make any sense at all. I would have known that."

"Not so true, Brady. Maybe Ed never wanted anyone to know. He's on the right side of the law and well... George ain't so."

"Shit. Now I'm going to be all disgruntled until I find out. You ain't much help here, Travis."

"There ain't nothing I can do, Brady. Besides, we have other things to worry about. We still got to make the distance to Chase. I say we pack up and get."

Tyrell looked over to Brady who was still gazing down the trail in the direction George headed.

"Brady, snap out of it. C'mon, we got to put on some miles."

"Yeah, yeah, sorry about that, Travis. Was taken off guard by what old George said."

"Forget about that for the time being. Let's get our gear cleaned up so we can get back on the trail. Besides, you ain't going to know nothing about nothing until you talk to Ed. Chances are old George was pulling your leg anyway," Tyrell said in hopes to get Brady moving.

It worked and before long the two men were once more on their way heading west.

"Funny how your dog didn't put up a fuss when George came up the trail."

"I would agree. The two have once met, though, if you recall. Likely Black Dog knows he ain't a threat.

Besides, he knows George's nephew," Tyrell teased with a chuckle as they carried on.

Brady didn't respond. He simply shook his head.

"Awe, c'mon Brady what's a matter? So, George claims to be Ed's uncle. You know what that makes him to you?"

"Yeah, I do, Travis, means he's my great uncle."

Brady grew silent as he thought about that possibility.

"That is right, Brady, your great uncle George. He's a damn legend too, from what Ed and Riley have said about him. Harder than a greased up hog to catch and we know that first hand. Not to mention he's as strong as a railroad tie, like you mentioned once. Not many men could withstand a quiver full of Blackfoot arrows. I ain't sure I'd be all disgruntled knowing I had an uncle like that."

"That is you, Travis, not me. I don't like the fact that that old codger claims to be who he claims to be. Probably a frigging lie, but might not be too. It turns out he is, I'll be having words with the old man. If it is true, he could've told me beforehand. Since he didn't though, kind of upsets me some."

"Oh, so you're upset that Ed may have kept a family secret from you, eh? Hell, a lot of folks have family secrets, Brady."

"Yeah. Does your family?"

"Ain't sure. Never knew any of them, 'cept my old man. He died when I was young. Raised myself from then on," Tyrell lied. "Never knew my mother or any of her kin. So, could be my family has secrets. I wouldn't know for certainty," he added to the lie.

Of course, the biggest lie of all was the fact that he wasn't a Sweet, but a Sloan, and the Sloan's had many secrets, there was no doubt about it.

"Ah, anyway, I'll quit razing you about your good ol' uncle George," Tyrell said with a smile.

"I'd appreciate it if you did so, Travis. I need to work it out in my head before I can see the humour in it."

"Consider it done, Brady."

The joking aside, the two men rode in silence for a distance, each of them reflecting on their own lives, the good, the bad and the reasons why.

Three days ride east, back at Riley's place, the load of timber he had ordered was on the way. Colby and Bash were sitting with Riley when Clarence arrived. They put their coffee cups down and met him as he approached.

"Morning, fellas. Sorry about being a few minutes late; got tied up at the store. I'm here now though. We have seven in this load. The old wagon can't handle more than that at one time. She'd break up like a ship against rocks if we loaded more on her. Once we get her unloaded and I get turned around I'll bring the other eight. So, where do you want them, Riley?" Clarence asked as he looked around.

He gestured toward the pile of dirt where the well had obviously been dug.

"Near over there would be best eh, I reckon?"

"Yeah, if you can get the load close that'd be good, Clarence. If not, anywhere around here is fine."

Riley pointed to an area close to the coach he was living in that was cleared of bramble, small stunted bushes and tree saplings that seemed to grow far and wide on his land, not to mention the rock and ground squirrel burrows that were scattered here and there. They were things he thought might get tangled up in the wagon wheels or even cause a wheel to break.

"Not sure you'd want to try and steer that wagon over to the well. A lot of crap is in the way."

Riley paused for a moment.

"Ah, we'll just unload them in this area, Clarence. It makes things a lot easier. I'd hate to see your horses break a leg in a burrow or bust a wheel axle."

"It does look a little bit ratted that way, don't it?"

"It looks that way, Clarence, because it is. I'll clear it up in time, but not until I get that well done and a proper roof over my head. Fall is coming quick," Riley said as Clarence nodded and steered his horses and wagon over to where Riley suggested.

"Yep, right there is good, Clarence," Riley said as he and Colby made their way over to help unload the timber.

Bash sat back down and watched. It wasn't his job to help Colby. If it had been Riley alone, he'd have offered a hand. It took only a few short minutes to off-load the timber. With the task done, Riley asked Clarence if he wanted a coffee. It was early still and plenty of daylight hours remained in the day.

"I wouldn't say no to a coffee, Riley. Thank you kindly," Clarence responded as he turned his wagon around facing home.

Pulling his horses to a stop, he stepped down and made his way over to the small fire that was perking fresh coffee that Bash took upon himself to make.

"Got fresh coffee brewing here, Clarence. Won't take long and she'll be ready," Bash said as Clarence sat down on a piece of wood.

"Thanks for making a fresh pot, Rick," Riley said as he and Colby made the distance and pulled up their own pieces of wood to sit on.

"So, Clarence, what would you estimate the cost of lumber to add on to this coach with an extra couple of rooms and roof?" Riley questioned as they waited for the coffee to be done.

Clarence stroked his chin as he thought about it.

"Depending on what you want to do Riley, I'd guess near three hundred dollars in lumber alone. Nails and such would be an added expense. And if you wanted to add one of them fancy toilets with sink and stuff, now that you got water coming up that'd be extra too. Have you thought about what it is you could do? Adding a room onto this coach of yours wouldn't be a problem I don't think. If it were me, I'd add another wall around the coach myself; build it in to the rest of it. You'll likely need a good woodstove too, to keep the place nice and toasty. The best thing to do is to think about the size of living quarters you want. Once you got the dimensions and such, we could go from there. I can help you with design if you like."

"That is greatly appreciated, Clarence. My idea was to have a sitting room, a small kitchen, bedroom and now that you mentioned it a toilet and bath too. Thought I could make the coach into the bedroom. It's big enough for that; only take a few simple changes too. The rest of it would be three rooms. The sitting room could be ten foot by ten foot. The kitchen don't really have to be that big I don't think. The bathroom could be even smaller."

Riley stood up and looked at the coach as he contemplated.

"It is a good start, Riley. I can work with those numbers and the description of what it is you want it to be," Clarence said as he nodded. "I can work something out for you over the next couple of days."

"Okay, that works."

Riley turned and faced the fire.

"That coffee ready yet, Bash?"

Riley sat back down and waited for Bash's response.

"As ready as she'll ever be, I guess."

Bash removed the pot and poured each of them a cup.

"Riley has sugar in that box there, Clarence if you want any."

He pointed at the box that was sitting on a piece of wood as he handed Clarence his coffee.

"Thank you, Constable Bash," Clarence nodded his thanks as he added a few spoonfuls of sugar and gave his cup a stir.

"By the way, Riley do you have a bow saw?"

"I got a hand saw, if that's what you mean."

"Nope, it isn't what I meant. You are going to need a three foot bow saw to cut through those timbers. They are good and green. A hand saw will take you all day. I'll bring one along with me on my next trip."

Clarence took a drink from his coffee.

"All right. Anything else you figure I might need? I got shovels and a yard stick."

"You want to cut those timbers at near as five foot as you can get, so I think you're going to need a measuring tape. I'll bring a fifteen-footer along with me as well."

"Sure, I probably could use a few tools around here. That measuring tape and saw will be a good addition to my yardstick and shovels."

Riley chuckled at his meagre tool collection.

"If you're going to start building stuff around here, you are going to need a few more things than that."

"I don't doubt it. Can you throw together a few things for me, Clarence? I'll pay for them once I get this well sorted out."

"Of course I can. No problem, Riley. I'll bring along a few things that'll make setting up a homestead easier. I can't imagine you banging a wall together with all the rocks you have."

Clarence and the others began to chuckle.

"Well, coffee is done. I guess I best get back and load up again. I'll see you folks in a couple of hours."

"Yeah, okay, Clarence. Colby and I will start moving those timbers closer to the well," Riley said as he stood up and walked with Clarence over to his wagon.

"See you in a bit," he said as Clarence and his horses headed back to town.

"See you shortly, Riley."

Riley watched as Clarence made it back to the main wagon trail.

"What do you figure, Colby. Should we get these timbers closer to the well? That flat spot right over there be best I reckon."

Riley pointed to the spot.

"The sawhorses will then sit level. Makes cutting easier."

"Anything is better than sittin' here with Bash," Colby said as he stood up and walked over to give Riley a hand in packing the timbers.

"Bash ain't that bad, Colby. You could be here with Cannon," Riley said as the two of them picked up the first timber.

"I'd rather not be here with either. You, I can tolerate. The law, well, that is a different story," Colby responded as they tossed the first timber to the ground.

Seven trips and thirty minutes later they had completed the task.

Standing on the pile of dirt, Riley scratched his whiskered chin as he looked into the well. The water was getting deep. He used a long branch to check its depth. If it was over six feet they'd have to remove some water and at the same time somehow stop it from continuing to fill.

"You see our dilemma here, Colby?"

"Yep, saw it right from the beginning. How are we to line the banks with timbers if it is full of water?"

"Exactly."

Riley looked on and removed the branch.

"Looks like she is about four foot deep. I reckon we can get four timbers in per side before it rises much more. Once we're above the water, the timbers will be a lot easier to stack. We'll have to work fast though."

"So, which one of us is going to jump in when we get those timbers cut to length? I have to tell you, Riley; I'm a little leery jumping into that mud pit."

Riley nodded his head; he was leery too. He couldn't swim and obviously nor could Colby and that is where the fear lay.

"Humph, well. I guess we're faced with another dilemma. I don't suppose we can convince Bash to get down in there," Riley joked.

"Hell, you get him in there and I'll kick the dirt in."

"Now, now, Colby. No need for that. We're faced with a dilemma and we need to figure out how to tackle it."

"I like the idea of getting Bash down in there."

Riley chuckled, "I bet you do."

"Think about it, Riley. He'd only need to stack the timbers four high. After that we could use a plank or somethin' to go from one side to the other. We could stand on that as we continue to add timbers. We move the plank up with each level of timbers we put in place. Wouldn't even get our boots wet."

"I see what you are saying, Colby. That is a damn good idea. Not sure Bash will see it that way though and it ain't likely he'd agree. Anyway, ain't much we can do here for the time being, not at least until Clarence returns with our second load of timber and a saw that'll cut through them. We might as well go back and join Bash at the fire, have another coffee. I might toss him the question on whether or not he'd like to give us a hand. Although I likely already know his answer. I might have to ask Tanner to give us a hand. Depending of course what Ed might have him doing today," Riley stated as the two men walked back to the fire.

Meanwhile Tyrell and Brady were putting behind them a few miles, ever slowly getting closer to Chase. The road they travelled was barren and empty. They didn't see another rider or for that matter any other tracks except George's and his mule team of two. The day was warm and in the emptiness of it all except for the odd bird that whistled, the forest road was silent. The early fall breeze that tousled their hair was warm and pleasant and the sun glowed yellow in the sky. For mid-September in those Rocky Mountains, it was a spectacular day. For ten miles they rode in silence, not because they had nothing to say, but simply because it was so peaceful. It was serenity at its best. The only sound was made by their own horses as they traipsed onward. Even Black Dog seemed to enjoying the silence. Alert however as he always was, he stopped abruptly not far in front of them.

Brady pointed.

"What do you make of that, Travis?" he questioned as the two riders slowed their horses and looked on. Tyrell knew exactly what it meant and he reached for and grabbed his rifle and before Pony could rear up and dart off, he jumped to the ground. Brady, in awe at this, grabbed his own rifle. His horse, though, stood stock still.

"What the hell is that all about?" Brady asked as Pony bucking and farting danced his way to where Black Dog stood. Together, the two animals darted forward in a heated rush, then crashed over a bank and disappeared into the undergrowth.

"Damn!" Tyrell said as he shook his head.

"What you jus' witnessed there, Brady, is my damn fool horse chasing after a bear. I knew it was too quiet."

Brady began to chuckle.

"Jesus, I know you mentioned that your horse does that on occasion. Seeing it, though, sure puts a new perspective on the story telling."

"Well, now you know it ain't fiction. It has been a while since he's done that. The bear must've been close. Funny Black Dog didn't chase it off on his own."

Tyrell had only finished the sentence when, from the corner of his eye, he spotted a bear cub and he knew then things weren't going to be the same. He couldn't recall another time when Black Dog and Pony chased after a sow bear let alone one with cubs.

"Shit, Brady there is a yearling behind that clump of rock," Tyrell said and he pointed toward it.

"I see it," Brady responded as he and Tyrell watched the cub stand up on its hind legs and look around puzzled and confused.

"I reckon your dog and that horse of yours may have more of a challenge then they can handle. That there, Travis is a grizzly cub. That sow ain't going to be too happy at losing her yearling or, for that matter, being chased. We best go after them. C'mon, swing up."

"Yeah, that might be best," Tyrell said as he approached Brady and his horse.

"Damn shame to maybe have to kill a bear; more of a shame though to lose my horse."

Brady leaned forward and gave Tyrell a hand in swinging up.

"There, let's get."

Brady heeled his horse to follow Black Dog and Pony. Heading off the trail where the dog and horse had gone, they ducked and tucked as they wiggled their way through the bush. By the size of the bear tracks they spotted every now and again, the sow wasn't small.

"I reckon that bear ought to weigh near eight hundred pounds," Brady mentioned as they carried on.

"Yeah, and she's pissed off too! That can't add up to nothing good."

Shortly after that they heard the huffing, puffing, snorting and growls of what sounded like an epic battle.

Adrenaline and unknown fear coursed through their veins as Brady turned his horse in the direction of the sound.

"C'mon, Brady, can't you get this horse to speed up some?"

"Can only go so fast through all this bramble, Travis. It ain't that far ahead."

Finally, they could see the ruckus through the dense bush. The sound of the battle sent chills down their spines as Tyrell swung off from behind Brady and fired a few shots into the air in hopes of breaking up the vicious battle going on. It did nothing, though, but intensified the battle.

Running now in the direction, hooting and hollering, Tyrell did all he could to scare the bear off, but it stood firm and rose on its hind legs swatting in his direction as though it were swatting away black flies. Tyrell had a clear view now and he brought his rifle up. Aiming at the massive sow grizzly, he squeezed the trigger, but the only sound he heard was the 'click' of an empty chamber. He reached for one of his pistols in the blink of an eye, but the grizzly darted off and crashed through the forest then disappeared as though it were never there before Tyrell could even get a shot off. With his pistol still in hand he ran the distance to where the battle had taken place. Lying on the ground, unable to move and sparsely breathing, was Pony. Tyrell's heart jumped into his throat as he approached and it almost stopped when he saw all the blood that scattered the area and even more so when there was no sign of Black Dog.

"No, no, Pony, oh my God!"

Tyrell knelt next to his wounded companion. Nothing else in the world seemed to matter anymore. Pony lay there unable to move, a gash across his throat so deep and jagged there was no chance he would recover.

By now Brady was standing over Tyrell,

"Awe, son-of-a-bitch, Travis. Jesus Christ, I'm sorry to see this."

Brady shook his head. It was saddening to see Pony lying there. Tyrell was speechless and withdrawn. Brady gave him some space and leaned against a tree. He knew what Tyrell had to do and watching a man put a bullet in his own horse's head in itself was disconcerting. He turned his head and looked away as he heard Tyrell pull the hammer back on his .45.

Tears welled up in Tyrell's eyes and he put his hand gently on Pony's side and caressed him one last time before he pulled the trigger. Standing, he wiped his eyes with his shirt sleeve and looking over to where Brady stood, he nodded.

"He was a damn good horse while he lived."

Tyrell grew silent as he looked once more at Pony.

"Now I guess he can pull the good Lord's carriage across the sky. I knew one day this was going to happen, jus' wish it wouldn't have. It has, though, and there ain't a damn thing I can do about it."

"You did the right thing, though, Travis. There is no way he'd have lived through that and if you hadn't done what you did, he'd have suffered more than he already had. I hate to see a man lose his horse."

Brady lowered his head.

"I know what he meant to you," he added to console Tyrell.

"Yeah, he was arrogant, misbehaving, hated bear and grouse for that matter and rarely listened to any commands. But I never once doubted he wouldn't lay his life down to protect mine. And that is how I got to look at this, Brady. Chances are we'd have come around that bend in the trail and that old sow could have very well charged us. Pony though and that damn dog took it upon themselves to make it safe for us."

Tyrell looked around and called for Black Dog, but not even his calling or whistling for him produced the dog.

"I don't know where the dog has got to. I hope like hell he's all right."

Brady though had his doubts. The amount of blood that stained the moss covered ground and young saplings where the fight took place looked like a slaughter.

"I sure hope he is Travis. All this blood though makes me wonder."

Tyrell nodded in agreement, "I know," he said as he looked around and called for Black Dog again and again to no avail. They waited for a few minutes but there was no sign whatsoever of Black Dog. He was either out of earshot or he was lying in the forest somewhere gravely wounded. The forest as thick as it was would certainly make it difficult for them to find Black Dog if he were wounded and dying. And with a pissed off sow grizzly bear running amuck, they decided to head back to the trail. At least, there they had a fighting chance to spot the bear if it were to circle around them and cause grief.

Tyrell and Brady removed the gear, bridle and saddle from Pony and tied them down onto Brady's horse. They didn't bother to cover Pony up with rocks or sticks, although Brady had suggested it. Instead Tyrell covered the horse with his saddle blanket and one of his bedrolls. Then, he nodded one last good bye, turned on his heel and walked away. It was one of the hardest things he had ever done, but he knew Pony would have wanted him to do exactly that.

They led Brady's horse back the way they came until finally making the distance to the trail. Tyrell constantly called for Black Dog, but with each unanswered call, the more he thought that Black Dog had succumbed to any wounds he may have had. It saddened Tyrell and broke his heart all at once. How unkind the world was to take away his horse and possibly his dog all in one day.

"You know what, Brady. Right now I wish I had a shot of whiskey. This day has made me lose faith in a lot of things."

"I bet it has, Travis. One day, though, that faith will come back."

"I ain't so sure, Brady. Pony and Black Dog, they're like my family or at least the closest thing to what I can call family. Of course, I still got my friends and all, but without that dog and horse, I ain't got no kin left."

Tyrell sighed in heart wrenching disappointment.

"I guess, though, it is what it is, eh, Brady?"

Brady didn't respond right away. He too was feeling the loss of Tyrell's companions. He was enlightened on how Tyrell was taking it. A lesser man, he knew, would have been distraught and perhaps even vindictive towards the bear that caused the death or deaths. Brady inhaled deeply as he looked over to Tyrell.

"Yep, I would agree. It is what it is. I am sorry at your loss; there is no doubt about that, but shit happens. It always does."

There wasn't much more he could say about the turn of events. Averting his eyes westerly, he looked on down the trail.

"We still have a few days ride to make it to Chase. The Fort is closer, though, if you want us to head back that way and pick up that other horse of yours that you lent the old man back some time ago."

"Nope. I don't see much point in heading back to the Fort. We'll carry on, Brady. We got a job to do. Between here and Chase there has to be a farm around. Maybe they'll sell me another horse. If the dog is still alive, he'll find me."

Tyrell looked around hoping to see Black Dog pouncing his way, but he saw nothing.

"We could hold up here a while longer if you like, Travis. Maybe that dog of yours is nearer than we know."

Tyrell lowered his head and shook it.

"No point in that either, Brady. I say we carry on. We've jus' been slowed down some now that we only got one horse. I ain't about to leave my saddle behind so that means we ain't going to be able to double. I'll walk, you ride," Tyrell said as he turned west and began to walk.

"C'mon, Brady let's get."

Brady turned his horse and walked alongside Tyrell who was on foot.

"I'll tell you what, Travis, we'll take turns riding and walking."

"That's fine... for now, I'll walk."

Brady took that as Tyrell's need to be left alone for a while and he completely understood, so he slowed his horse down and let Tyrell walk ahead.

The only thing coursing through Tyrell's mind as he walked was Pony, the ups and downs the forthcomings and misgivings. Emptiness greater than an empty whiskey bottle enveloped him as he thought about Pony. The sadness was amplified with the fact that he may have also lost Black Dog. His mind raced with visions of both Black Dog and Pony, the hot sunny days they spent on lonely ridges and the cold winters they had spent together, the way they made him laugh and even at times made him angry. So deep were his thoughts. Now alone without either, he felt beaten and licked. There was nothing he could do to change the way things turned out that day, but deep down he certainly wished he could.

For five miles his mind was blurred. He wanted to holler and scream, but that would never change the outcome nor would it bring back his horse Pony to him. As for Black Dog, without knowing for sure if he too were dead, there was hope. Soon though he knew hope would have to give way to the reality that both were lost to him. Black Dog was resilient, cunning, brave and smart. There was a chance, he knew, although slim as it may seem that the dog did manage an escape and perhaps one day he would find him again. He would have to leave it at that, keep his fingers crossed and hope for the best. In time, a few days or more, if Black Dog didn't track him down then he would have to live with the reason why as bleak as that might seem.

Back at McCoy's, Tanner and Ed were going through some new information that Bob Cannon released to them regarding Miles Ranthorp, the Pinkerton man accused of killing Emery Nelson up north in Hazelton. According to the documents, Miles Ranthorp was an undercover name that he used when providing private security for civilians. Miles' real name was Thomas Lierrp. The only reason it had taken the Pinkerton office in Montana so long to reply to the documents sent to them by the Mountain Police in Fort Macleod was because they needed hard proof that Miles was indeed the Miles Ranthorp from the Pinkerton Company. When it was finally confirmed by the fingerprints and black and white photo of the dead Miles Ranthorp, the Pinkerton office was legally required to send the documents that were now in the hands of McCoy's men. Somehow the two documents sent to the Pinkerton Office got mixed up in the delivery process and the picture and fingerprints did not arrive at the same time as the written documents with Miles name, badge number and description. It mattered little now that the Pinkertons had admitted that, indeed, Miles did work for them.

"These documents don't mean shit, Ed. All it tells us is that Miles was an undercover name that this Thomas fellow used whilst doing undercover private security for civilians," Tanner said as he flipped through the pages and slurped his coffee. "It don't say anywhere in these writs on why he'd be up here in Canada or for that matter up in Hazelton. I just don't get it."

"I know it ain't much help. The writ I'm reading proclaims Miles as an upstanding and well-established Pinkerton agent with some forty solved investigations to his name. That is a lot for a single man, I'd think," Ed responded as he stood up and poured another coffee for himself and looked out the window.

"I don't know, Tanner. We still haven't any conclusive evidence other than what Matt Crawford claimed that Miles is the one that killed Emery. With a record like Ranthorp has, I don't understand why he'd kill a bounty hunter or for that matter, try to kill two more by putting lead in their horses and leaving them on foot out in the middle of nowhere."

Ed inhaled deeply as he turned to face Tanner and leaned against the counter.

"Whether he did or didn't kill Emery, he's still the man like you say that shot both Riley and Brady's horses. Which again don't make much sense. The only thing that I can figure is that Miles wanted that reward for Crawford badly enough to take out Emery so that he alone could track Matt and reap the bounty. It would also then make sense on why he killed Riley's and Brady's horses, 'cause they was getting close to Crawford as well. Take their ability to do so away and you are left to bring Crawford in on your own."

Tanner scratched the side of his face as he thought about it.

"Maybe he had a gambling debt and the ten thousand for Matt Crawford's apprehension would have cleared it up for him. Many a man would kill for ten thousand, even a law abiding Pinkerton."

The room grew silent for a few moments as the two men contemplated the possibility.

Ed rubbed his whiskered chin. What Tanner had said did make viable sense. *But could it be that simple?*

"Hazelton is a bit of a gambling town, ain't it?"

"I wouldn't say it isn't. Vermillion on the other hand certainly was. With it burnt down, though, the gambling could have moved to Hazelton."

Tanner shrugged his shoulders as he continued to read the writ in front of him.

The more Ed thought about what Tanner pointed out, the more sense it made. There was no clear reason on *'why'*, but they did now know *'who'*.

"You know what, Tanner? I think you might be onto something. What we know without a doubt is that Ranthorp did indeed take out two of our horses and left two of our men without rides miles away from any town or establishment. We also know that Matt Crawford claims that Ranthorp is the fellow who killed Emery. That part of the equation, though, is only hearsay. What we don't know is why Ranthorp would kill Emery, if indeed he is the fellow who did it. The ballistics that the Mountain Police reported, claim that Emery was shot with a .45 Colt revolver, which most folks carry, so that don't really help us much. The fact, though, that Ranthorp was on Matt Crawford's tail and had no problem taking out Brady's and Riley's horses, does lead me to think now that he wanted the cash Crawford was worth. Whether it was to clear up a gambling debt, or so the man could retire is something we can't be assured of, unless we look into it."

"Well then, let's look into it," Tanner stated as he pulled out his new badge.

"This badge right here gives us the right to do so. I can be packed and ready to head to Hazelton in the morning, Ed," Tanner said with conviction and sincerity.

Ed chewed the inside of his bottom lip as he thought about it for a moment. Sending Tanner alone up into the north country was never one of Ed's plans. He had thought that the three of them would do it together, that is, Riley, Tanner and he, since both Travis and Brady were on their way to Willow Gate. Ed's plan had always been that he, Riley and Tanner would look into the possibility that Matt Crawford had been in the Fort on or near the date of the Atalmore sentencing which would explain the notebook found in the McCoy's stable. It would also confirm that Matt Crawford was heading west as well to take out Gabe Roy. If it turned out that way, then the plan was to follow behind Brady and Travis to Willow Gate and apprehend Crawford so he could be exonerated for past crimes. If didn't turn out like that then the three of them, Tanner, Riley and he would head north, and investigate Emery's murder together.

Plans often changed, though and there was no reason why this one couldn't. He and Riley could look after the investigation at the Fort while Tanner headed north to put together the pieces on why Ranthorp may or may not have killed Emery Nelson or, for that matter, what a Pinkerton man was doing up in Canada in the first place, if the obvious answer was not to take in Matt Crawford. There was definitely something dirty going on with Ranthorp as well as with the Mounted Police constable who led the investigation into Emery's death up in Hazelton.

Ed nodded his head.

"I suppose me and Riley can look after things down here. I ain't so sure though sending one man up to Hazelton is a good idea."

"Is that doubt I hear in your voice, Ed? Do you doubt that I could handle that investigation?"

Tanner wasn't sure what Ed meant and he wanted to be clear.

"Not at all, Tanner. I was thinking more for safety reasons. Two sets of eyes is always better than one."

"Yeah, no sets is worse. Trust me, Ed. I can handle this. I'm good with cards. Getting in good with a few gamblers and asking questions ain't an issue for me nor is questioning folks about this, that or the other thing. I know what it is we need to find out. One is why was Ranthorp on Matt's ass if not for the obvious reason. The other is why did he kill Emery if it is he who did it. Finally, we need to know why there are so many discrepancies in the police folder we got from the Mounted Police up in Hazelton regarding Emery's death. This ain't wagon wheel building, Ed. It is a cut and dry straight-forward investigation, not much different than taking in a bounty. I'm up for the task and I know I can get us some answers."

"All right, Tanner. You've convinced me. Hazelton is a good three hundred mile ride due north and it is going to get cold before you make the distance. Make sure to pack appropriately."

"No worries there, Ed. I got all I need to assure I won't freeze or die in the elements," Tanner chuckled.

"You are going to need some spending cash too, I reckon. Five hundred dollars ought to be plenty. You think you'll need more than that, Tanner?"

"I have three hundred cash on me right now. You add five hundred to that and I have eight hundred dollars, more than some make in a year in wages. I figure that is more than enough."

"Okay, so five hundred from cash is what I'll get you to sign off on come morning. Now that we got tomorrow planned, what do you say about heading over to Riley's place and checking up on things over there? There ain't no more we need to read up on in these writs we got today from Cannon. Besides, I'd like Riley to have a look through them as well. Chances are he ain't going to be showing up here today, so we'll show up there. What do you figure?"

"You're the boss, Ed. I'll certainly tag along."

Tanner stood up, set his coffee cup on the counter and grabbed his hat from behind his chair.

"I'm ready."

"All right, let's lock up, saddle up and head over," Ed responded as he picked up the two folders and locked the front door.

It took a few minutes to saddle up and soon they were riding over to Riley's.

Meeting up coincidentally with Clarence on their way, they had friendly conversation as they sauntered on.

"You got quite the load there, Clarence. Those timbers for Riley's well?" Ed asked already knowing the answer.

"Yep, these be the last load. Got the first load delivered to him early this mornin'. How are you folks fairin' t'day, Ed?"

"Not much to complain about, Clarence. Sure a nice day out today. A good day for Riley to get that well of his lined, I reckon."

"He's got quite a lot of sawing to do. Not sure he'll get it done t'day. These timbers ain't going to be easy to cut through."

"Well, he's got the help of that young fellow, Colby. They might manage."

"I suppose it's possible, but I wouldn't put a wager on it. I cut through a couple of these not long ago for another order and it took me twenty minutes to saw through one. He's got more than a couple."

"I reckon you might be right, Clarence. They do seem a bit green don't they? The timbers I mean."

"I knew what you meant, Ed. Riley, though; I think is pretty green too. He don't even have a decent saw or tape measure. I have those things packed in this load for him along with a few other things I know he don't have. I kind of chuckle at folks like him, who want to set up a homestead and don't even have the tools to do so. So, I say Riley is about as green as these here timbers. He'll learn though."

Ed and Tanner chuckled.

"Yeah, he'll learn."

By now they were getting close to Riley's place and from the road they could see that he, Colby and constable Bash were sitting around the fire.

"See what I mean, Ed. There is work to be done and Riley and his helper would rather sit around a fire and drink coffee."

"Likely waiting for that saw you got in there, Clarence," Tanner responded with a smile.

"Could be, yep, and likely true."

A few minutes later they pulled up to Riley's coach.

"Hey, Ed, Tanner, what brings you folks here? You here to saw some wood maybe?" Riley asked with hope. A few extra sets of hands to get his well lined would be nice.

"I told you once, Riley, that I'd give you hand. I don't mind sawing a few pieces of wood," Tanner said as he swung off his horse.

"How is the water level in the pit?"

"Glad you asked; that is another reason I could use a hand. She's up about four feet and I ain't sure my heart could take it if I were down in it and it rose more. I can't swim worth a damn nor can Colby."

"What are you trying to ask, Riley? You want me down in that pit?"

"I tried to convince Bash, but he don't want nothing to do with that. Said he'd rather saw wood than get his pretty red uniform all messed up. I was going to leave Colby and Bash here sawing lengths once this load arrived and head over to the office to ask. So yeah, I'd really appreciate it if you would, Tanner."

"Shit, the things I wouldn't do for a friend," Tanner commented as he tethered his horse.

"So, you'll do it then?" Riley questioned.

"It needs to be done, don't it? Obviously you're afraid of a little water, same as with Colby. Bash is a big baby and Ed is too old, so I guess that just leaves me, don't it?"

"Hey now, I ain't that old, Tanner."

"I reckon you and Riley are near the same age, so that makes you old, Ed," Tanner teased. "These timbers are what, twelve by eight? So, we'll need four per side to get to the water level. That comes to, I reckon, sixteen lengths. Yeah, I don't have a problem doing that, as long as I ain't 'xpected to saw wood. I'll contribute my time to do one or the other, but not both," Tanner responded with a smile.

"All right, that works for me, Tanner. Thanks very much too for doin' it."

Tanner waved his hand through the air.

"Ah, no thanks is needed, Riley. I'm happy to give you a hand. C'mon let's get Colby and Bash over here to get this spectacle started. Shouldn't take us more than a couple hours once we get going on it."

"Hey, Colby! Rick! Could use your help over here unloading and stacking these timbers. Tanner said he'll jump in the well," Riley hollered over to the two of them as he and Clarence started to off-load the wagon.

A few minutes later with everyone lending a hand, the timbers were stacked, the tools were laid out and Clarence was on his way back. The sawing began. Tanner drank coffee and watched as Riley, Colby, Bash, and even Ed took turns cutting the sixteen lengths that he would need to start the lining process. Half of the time he chuckled at their bitching on how tough the wood was to actually saw through. It was indeed a spectacle and most times a humorous one at that.

The only one who seemed to have any sense about the process was Colby. He did the measuring, helped with the sawing and pointed out what the others were doing wrong. Ed and Riley were both too old to keep up, and Bash was just stupid about what it was they were trying to accomplish. He had no manual labour sense about him whatsoever. All the while Tanner lounged around, drank coffee and enjoyed the day.

Finally, at 2:00 that afternoon, the last piece of timber fell from the makeshift saw horse and the cutting was done. The four sawyers cheered with elation.

"Jesus, Clarence wasn't kidding when he said these would be tough to saw through," Ed commented as he sat on the stack and wiped his brow.

"Yeah, whew, it weren't as easy as I thought," Riley added as he gestured for Ed to slide over so he could sit too.

Bash and Colby sat down on a pile of rocks to catch their breath as well.

"I'm certainly glad that is over with," Bash said as he pulled up a blade of grass and stuck the stalk in his mouth. "That is only four feet of the total amount you'll need, Riley. There is still a lot of cutting to do."

Riley lowered his head and nodded.

"Yep, I know," he said with weariness.

"Still got a few hours of sunlight left. If you old folk and that man in red weren't so wimpy we might get another sixteen cut," Colby said.

All three looked at him and shook their heads.

"Nope, I think I'm done with the cutting for today. With the saw and all the timbers here now, we get an early start in the morning and we should be able to finish up. I think the next order of business is to get the first sixteen lengths in place. That'll likely take us a couple hours give or take and by then it will almost be dark."

"You figure it is going to take the four of us to help Tanner put those timbers in place?" Colby asked with confusion.

"I ain't sure. Maybe," Riley shrugged his shoulders.

"I don't think you think that, Riley. I think you is wore out from sawin'."

Riley laughed and nodded, Colby was right. He was tired from the sawing and by the look of both Ed and Bash they were too.

"I won't deny that Colby, the damn sawing did lay me out."

"Leastwise you admitted it," Colby smiled. "I figure if we want these timbers in place, we best get at it. I ain't so inclined to want to wander back to the holding cell hotel jus' yet," he said as he rose.

"Hold on a second there, Colby. You don't make those decisions. That is up to me to decide," Bash pointed out.

Colby looked at him with disdain.

"You goin' to decide then or what?"

Riley, seeing that an argument and bickering were about to start, interrupted the conversation.

"Before the two of you ruffle each other's feathers more, I don't think it'll takes us long, Rick, to get those timbers in place. I could still use Colby's help."

"I realize that, Riley, and I was going to allow him to give you a hand in doing so. I only want Colby to know that he isn't the one that makes the decision on whether or not it is time to head back. Community service doesn't work that way."

"Well then, if you're going to allow me to continue on, Bash, then let me continue, would ya? You know and I know that Cannon has allowed Riley here to work me eight to twelve hours a day and I've only put in half of that now."

It was funny how that statement made Bash sit up. Colby was right and Bash knew that what Cannon said is what was expected nothing less and nothing more.

"That's fine, Colby. Riley can have you for few more hours. Just keep in mind who the authority is here."

"Pfft, whatever, Bash, whatever," Colby said as he turned and picked up one of the five foot lengths of timber and walked over to the well.

"All right, well I'm glad that is over with," Tanner said as he rolled his eyes and followed after Colby with a timber in his own arms.

"Yeah, I guess we should grab one of these too, Ed," Riley said as he stood up and picked one out.

"You grab that end, Ed, and I'll grab this end," Riley gestured as he and Ed struggled to handle the piece of wood.

Colby and Tanner seeing this from where they now stood shook their heads.

"Look at that. Two full grown men strugglin' over a little piece of wood," Tanner teased as they made the distance and tossed the timber to the ground.

"We ain't as young as we used to be, Tanner. You said that yourself."

"Shit, Ed," Tanner began as Ed cut him off.

"What's that? Did you call me a shithead?" Ed joked as he and Riley turned quickly and headed back for a second piece.

The two of them together moved more of the timbers than Tanner and Colby did on their own and they did it a lot quicker too. By the time both Colby and Tanner hauled four pieces each, they were as tired as Ed and Riley were after cutting the wood.

"Who is the shithead now, Tanner?" Ed teased as Tanner tossed his last piece to the ground and almost fell over.

"Yeah, yeah, ya old bastard. I see what you two did there. A lot easier having help packing them boards this distance than doing it on one's own. I get it, you win," Tanner responded as he lay down and looked up to the sky as he caught his breath.

Colby followed suit. The two of them lay there, their arms weak and their legs wobbly.

"Don't get too comfortable there, Tanner. You still got to get wet," Riley bantered.

"Like I said earlier, Riley, the things I won't do for a friend."

Tanner sat up and looked on.

"All right, I guess I'll jump in there."

He stood up and walked over to the well.

"You fellows might want to fetch some rope and tie it to the ends of those timbers. It makes lowering them into place a lot less perilous. In the meantime, I'll get comfy and cozy at the bottom."

He looked again into the well.

"You sure that water is only four foot deep, Riley?"

"According to the measuring stick, yep."

"All right, well, here goes nothing," Tanner said as he climbed down the makeshift rope ladder and splashed into the water below.

"Yep, I'd say she's four foot at least. Come on, let's hurry up and get those timbers lowered. The damn water is freezing my nuts," Tanner hollered from the bottom.

It took the rest of the daylight hours to put the sixteen lengths of timbers in place, but finally it was done. Colby and Bash had already headed back to the station and now the three of them stood on the pile of dirt and admired the work they had done.

"Well, Tanner, I certainly appreciate you doing this. It's going to make the rest of the work a lot easier."

"I ain't sure how you and Colby alone are going to be able to finish up. You might be four foot closer to the top, but you have at least double that to go. I reckon you'll be needing at least the help from one more lending hand."

"You going to swing back in the morning then and lend it?"

"Sorry, Riley. I'll be on my way to Hazelton. Didn't Ed tell ya?"

"Tell me what?"

"I'll fill you in around your fire, Riley. I think a fresh pot of coffee is due. I got some things to go over with you."

"All right, well, let's get some brewing. You going to join us as well, Tanner?"

"I wouldn't mind warming up and drying off around a fire. Coffee sounds good too," Tanner responded as the three of them made their way back to Riley's coach.

With a fresh pot of coffee percolating over the low burning embers, Ed told Riley what it was that he and Tanner discussed earlier that day. During the explanation, Riley thumbed through the two writs Ed had received that morning from Bob Cannon.

"I guess that does make sense. You and I, Ed, can certainly handle things here at the Fort. I reckon Tanner can handle the other part of the inquiry. Well then, since I think I'll be needing two lending hands tomorrow, you going to stop by Ed and give me and Colby that extra help?" Riley questioned as he poured each of them a coffee.

"I'll do what I can, Riley. Sure, I'll give the two of you a hand in the morning once I get Tanner sent going north."

247

"Good. I don't know how exactly Colby and I would do that alone. Could always tie the timbers to the ass end of my horse. He knows how to back up and could lower the timbers, but I much prefer your help, Ed."

The three of them conversed for a couple hours until the stars began to flicker in the clear evening sky. Then, Ed headed home and Tanner went back to the office and his back room cot.

At the Mounted Police station, Bash and Colby were unexpectedly greeted by Lieutenant Bob Cannon. He was there to inform Colby that in the morning he was going to be helping the widow Donale again. This time, though, he was to help her with laundry. The reason was that an influential lawyer had taken an interest in Colby for one reason or the other and Colby was due to face another judge and possibly be set free a week early. The court appearance was set for the following Monday, September 14.

"So, jus' because of that I have to help some old lady with her laundry obligations. I'd rather keep on with helpin' Riley, thank you very much," Colby complained after the situation had been explained to him.

"There you go again. Speaking off as though you have a say in the matter," Bash said as he pulled up to his desk.

"The both of you can quiet down right now. I haven't finished talking yet," Lieutenant Cannon voiced with authority. "The reason you'll be helping her, Colby is to also get your own clothes washed up. You look ragged and you stink. So you'll be needing to clean up before you face the judge whoever that might be. I would think you'd be a bit more relieved that chances are come Monday you'll be allowed to leave this here fine establishment."

"So, I help the old lady tomorrow. What do you have planned for me to do on Sunday?"

"Obviously you aren't going to be working in any dirt. You have to look respectful for Monday."

"I guess what you are tryin' to say then is that today was my last day out in the civilised world and now I'll be stuck in that damn cell for the next two days. I never ordered no lawyer and if I don't want his assistance, I don't have to take it, do I?"

"Jesus Christ, Colby. I have never argued with any man regarding a possible earlier release date. What the hell is a matter with you?"

"There ain't nothin' a matter with me, Cannon. I'd just much rather finish up my twenty days and be out in the fresh air for eight hours a day than be sittin' in a barred room for two solid ones. As for this lawyer fellow, I don't know who the hell he is or what interest he has in me. B'sides come Monday, I'll be released four days afterward. Don't see much point in going before a judge with only that many days left."

Lieutenant Cannon shook his head. Colby was in his right to refuse counsel if that is what he insisted. It didn't make much sense, but he *did* have the right to refuse.

"I thought that you would have been a lot more grateful that someone took an interest. It is up to you, though. You can certainly refuse."

Cannon wasn't in any mood to continue to argue so he simply left it at that. Perhaps Colby would change his mind overnight and he would ask him again in the morning. Until then he left Bash in charge of Colby and headed home.

Even Tyrell and Brady were settling in for the evening. Sitting on their saddles around their own fire, they spoke intermittently. Tyrell was still shook up about his loss that day and Brady understood. Their conversations that evening were more of a silent din than anything else. As the evening grew dark the two of them finally rolled out their bedrolls, closed their eyes and hoped for a better day in the morning.

Chapter 12

Saturday, September 12. Tyrell was the first to rise that morning. He tossed a few sticks onto the coals of their past evening fire, rolled up his bedroll and then set the coffee pot on the slow burning flames. The sky to the east was red as the bloodshot eyes of a drunkard, *a red sky in morning is a sailors warning,* he thought to himself as he looked on. Even the early morning air was chilled. They had another mountain range to cross over before they would be heading to lower altitudes and by the look and feel of that morning, it was going to be a cold one. Tyrell rubbed his hands over the fire. He could see his own breath and it hung over his head like a fog. Lonely as he felt without Pony and Black Dog to wake up to, he reminisced until finally Brady began to stir.

"Morning, Travis. Damn chilly ain't it?" Brady said as he crawled out of his bedroll and relieved himself behind a clump of trees.

"Yep. Once we get moving, we'll warm up. Coffee is almost done. Are you interested in some biscuits, maybe?"

"Nah. I'd much rather have a coffee and get going. With only the one horse, we've been slowed down, 'specially since I ain't much of a long distant walker and it is your turn to ride," Brady mentioned as he knelt next to the fire and warmed his own hands.

Tyrell waved his hand through the air.

"Ah, I ain't got no problem walking, Brady. You can ride if you like."

"I don't think I'd like doing that, Travis. It don't seem fair."

"If I had been out here on my own, I'd be packing a saddle and walking anyway. Maybe you could ride ahead. There has to be someone lives around here. Maybe you could gather me another horse. I'll keep walking whilst you go ahead. You find a horse for me, head back my way and I'll meet up with you."

"How far ahead should I go? What if I don't come across a homesteader or such? And even if I did, there ain't no guarantee they'd sell me a horse."

Tyrell opened the map he had and looked at it. If he recalled correctly there was an outpost not far from where they were. It was twenty or so miles west and Brady could do that distance in a day if he stuck to the trail and nothing unforeseen came about. There might even be a chance he could pick up a horse from there, if not before, and head back. If things went well, Tyrell could be riding a horse by early afternoon the following day.

"According to this map, some twenty or so odd miles west there is an outpost. From what I recall it ain't that big, but there were folks milling around at that time. I figure you could make the distance by evening if you ain't slowed along the way. If there ain't no one there that'll sell you a horse head back and we'll carry on as we are. It would for certain speed up this trip having two horses. We walk side by each until making that distance, we'd be a few days behind," Tyrell pointed out as he reached for the coffee pot and poured each of them a cup.

Brady took his cup and brought it to his lips and gently blew.

"That there makes sense. I reckon the horse and I could make that distance by sunset. It is early enough. Still, I ain't so sure I'd feel comfortable leaving you behind, if only for a day. God only knows what could happen to a man alone out here with no horse."

"Shit, anything coming my way will have to pass by you, 'less of course they come from the east. I ain't worried at all about anything happening other than a nice long walk along a decent trail. Nope, you ain't got nothing to worry about in that regard, Brady. I'll be fine."

Brady nodded in agreement.

"All right. I guess I'll finish this coffee and get. You sure you're going to be all right? You got everything you'll need?"

"I got my rifle, my pistols, a bedroll, a sack of beef jerky, a coffee pot and grinds. For one or two days, I don't see any shortcomings," Tyrell assured with a smile.

Brady finished his coffee and saddled up.

"If I don't come across anyone wants to sell me a horse, I'll meet up with you sometime tomorrow. Walking you should make ten miles, eh?" Brady teased as he swung onto his horse.

Tyrell chuckled.

"Ain't sure I'll make ten, but I might make fifteen."

"You make fifteen miles today and I'll buy you a steak dinner in Chase. That mountain range up ahead don't look so easy to go up and over on foot."

"Go on, get out of here, Brady," Tyrell said as he swatted Brady's horse's behind.

"All right. I'll catch up with you some time tomorrow and if we're lucky maybe even later on today."

"Either or, I'll see you when you get back. Stay safe as you carry on and don't lose my saddle that you're packin'. Check on it every now and again to make sure it is strapped down good and tight. In other words don't rush it, Brady. Be careful."

"Is that for my safety or the damn saddle's safety?"

Brady chuckled.

"No worries, I won't lose your saddle, nor will I have the horse do much trotting. See you tomorrow, Travis," Brady said as he and his horse headed west toward the outpost.

Tyrell watched as Brady vanished into the misty September morning. Alone now, he sat back down and poured himself another coffee, his mind still trying to make sense of what had happened the day before. Tears of sadness and mourning gently ran down the side of his face. He wiped them away as he sipped his second cup of coffee and watched as the silent flames from the fire swayed this way and that. His mind drifted easterly from which they came to a lone stand of birch and pine that sat off the main trail by three miles and to the place where his horse Pony now rested for eternity and his companion Black Dog may have been lost. He couldn't get the images out of his mind of what he saw the day before and for some time he sat transfixed. Finally, shaking his head, he inhaled deeply, stood up and poured out his coffee. Swinging his bedroll over his shoulder, he followed behind Brady westerly.

Back at the Fort and McCoy's office, Tanner filled up the woodstove in the staff room and set it alight. He waited a few minutes for the flames to take before making that morning's office coffee. It was early still and it would be a while before Ed showed up. Tanner sat down at the table and went through the gear he would need to travel north and to Hazelton. It was going to be a long ride and he made sure that he had at least one of everything he would need. In some cases he packed two. Satisfied, he poured his first coffee of the day and wandered over to the office's front counter. Leaning against it with his hands wrapped around his coffee cup, he looked east to the rising sun.

The red and pink hues told him what kind of day it was going to be. *Looks like we're goin' to be hit with some cold weather,* he thought to himself as he looked on. Bringing his coffee cup up to his lips he took a drink and sighed.

"Might not make Hazelton before the first snow flies. I best double check that I have my long underwear," he said to himself as he turned and made his way back to the staff room and double checked.

He rummaged through some of his stuff and added a few woollen sweaters and socks to the gear he had already packed. *There, that ought to take me through to Hazelton without freezin',* he thought as he sat back down and finished his coffee.

It was around this time that Ed showed up. He joined Tanner at the small table and the two of them conversed as they drank a second cup of coffee together. Ed had Tanner sign off on his kitty. With the money now in his pocket and his gear packed, Tanner headed north. It would take him at least two weeks or twenty days to make the distance. He was expected to send a telegram back to Ed once he made it to Fairmount in a few days' ride.

With Tanner on his way north, Ed returned to the staff room and poured himself another coffee. In a short while he'd be heading over to Riley's place to help with the well. Once that was out of the way, hopefully by the beginning of the week, he and Riley could then concentrate their efforts in finding out whether or not Matt Crawford had recently been at the Fort. The investigation into his whereabouts, if not on his way to Willow Gate, could begin. Ed swilled back his coffee and removed the pot from the stove. Adding a few more pieces of wood, enough to burn gently throughout the day, he turned down the damper a half turn or so, to slow the flames, but not enough to put them out. He already knew what kind of day it was going to be. His ride into the office was chilly. Locking up, he headed over to Riley's place early enough that he knew he'd have to rouse him out of bed. He lit the outside fire while Riley dressed and came to terms that a new day had started.

"I certainly weren't expecting you so damn early, Ed. Did you have an accident in your sleep," Riley teased as he stepped out of the coach still tucking in his shirt.

"Brrrr, she's cold this morning. Thanks for getting the flames dancing."

"Yep, she is definitely a cold one. She'll warm up, though, by midday, I reckon. What the hell were you doing still sleeping? It is near 7:00 a.m., Riley. What time do you and Colby usually get started?"

"Whenever Bash brings him along, usually around 8:00 or so. They've been gettin' here early lately, since Cannon ain't got anything left for the kid to do. You got a pot of coffee going, Ed?" Riley asked as he made the distance to the fire.

"Ain't had time to round up the fixings. Besides, I don't know where you keep that stuff."

"Look around, Ed. You can see right there on that table what looks like a coffee pot, and oh, look at that, got a container here with a big "C" on it. An educated man such as yourself should have been able to figure the rest out."

"I saw the coffee pot, Riley, but had no clue what the "C" on that container stood for. For all I knew, it was for cookies."

Riley looked at him and frowned.

"Cookies? Now where would a man like me get cookies?"

"I don't know, Riley. I heard a rumour that the widow Donale has taken a shine to you. Maybe you got the cookies from her."

Ed shrugged with a smile as he looked at Riley, who was standing there confused and holding the coffee pot in his hand.

"What? The widow Donale? Shit, Ed, she's near ninety, ain't she?"

He knew as fact that she wasn't and he also knew she wasn't to terribly looking for a woman in her mid to late fifties, likely the same age as himself.

"Well, you do come across as a bit of a mama's boy," Ed teased.

"And when have I ever come across like that?"

Ed started to laugh.

"I'm just teasing you, Riley. Calm down and get that coffee cooking. Your help is going to be along soon and I'd like to get that well of yours lined today."

Riley stumbled around for a few minutes as he gathered his thoughts and put the coffee pot to perk.

"There, should have coffee in a short while. What's this you said about the widow Donale?"

He was curious. He had actually been thinking of her and had a bit of a crush on for her ever since he had asked her about her brother the water dowser.

Ed chuckled.

"It weren't me who heard anything. Beth was over there the other day. They was having a hen party of

258

sorts, I guess. Beth said the widow couldn't stop talking about you. I reckon she has a bit of a shine on for you."

Riley raised an eyebrow and smiled.

"Really? She couldn't stop talking about me, eh?"

"That is what Beth claims, yep."

"Huh, ain't that something. I reckon I best go over there soon and have a bath, maybe get some laundry done."

Riley was, it seemed, quite enthralled.

"Probably wouldn't hurt none. You ain't shaved it looks like to me in a week or so. Your hands is as dirty as the soles of my boots and you smell like a slew."

Ed, once more, began to chuckle.

"Jesus Christ, Ed, I've been digging dirt for a few days, been sawing wood and packing timbers. What do you expect?"

"No worries, Riley. I understand it is hard for a man to take care of himself. When he ain't got a woman in his life, he ain't got much need to."

"I jus' ain't had the time, Ed. That Colby kid works me harder than a mule team."

Riley checked on the coffee.

"Good, the coffee is done. Grab yourself a cup there, Ed, and help yourself. I need to step out back and take a piss."

Ed gathered a couple of clean cups and poured a coffee for Riley and himself. Adding sugar to his own cup he sat back down and waited for Riley to finish his business.

Around this time back at the Fort Mounted Police station, Lieutenant Bob Cannon was bringing Colby his breakfast.

"So, did you sleep on it, Colby? Have you decided on what you want to do?"

Colby sat up on his bunk and rubbed his eyes.

"I already told you, Cannon, I don't want no lawyer. I'll jus' finish up my time and be done with it."

Standing up, he walked over to Cannon who handed him his coffee and breakfast.

"What kind of slop did you bring me t'day?" he asked as he removed the foil that covered his meal.

"Nice," he began, "hot cakes, eggs and salt pork. It don't look so bad, Cannon. Thanks."

Colby sat back down on his bunk and began to eat.

"You know what, Colby; I don't understand your train of thought. Why the hell wouldn't you want to be released sooner?" Cannon responded as he looked on.

"I really don't want to keep explainin' myself, Cannon. I jus' don't. Can we leave it at that?"

"We can and we will. It doesn't make any sense to me."

"It don't have to make sense to you Cannon, only to me. Now, when I get done here with breakfast, you goin' to ride me over to Riley's place so I can continue helpin' him with that well of his? Or what?"

"I can't disobey a judge's order, Colby. So, yes, you'll be heading back to Riley's. I'm not sure it'll be me who takes you, though. It'll likely be constable Bash."

Colby looked up from his plate of food.

"Yippee, another day with the drab Bash."

"Community service was never meant to be exciting, Colby. Be grateful Rick can put up with you. Now finish up your breakfast and coffee. I'll send constable Bash here in a few minutes to get you."

Cannon turned and walked away. Locking the big steel door again, he tossed the key over to Bash.

"He's all yours, Rick. He'll be finished with breakfast soon. Get him over to Riley's. He doesn't want to see that lawyer fellow. Would rather finish his time and be our guest for a few more days."

"I figured as much. No problem, Lieutenant," Bash conceded as he put the paperwork he was working on away.

A few minutes later he rounded up Colby and they headed over to Riley's place.

"Cannon tells me you don't want to be released earlier. Why is that, Colby?"

"You know you lawmen ain't that smart. Say, I went before another judge and say that judge found me guilty of some other crap, would I be released? You already know the answer and it is 'no' I wouldn't be. I'd either be on my way east to join Atalmore or I'd be stuck back in that holding cell for another stint. Once these twenty days is done, I'll be walkin' away. Now if that explanation don't satisfy your curiosity, nothin' ever will, Bash."

The two rode in silence after that. Finally making the distance to Riley's place they joined him and Ed for a coffee before they started on cutting the remaining timbers into lengths.

"You figure we'll get the sawin' done t'day, Riley?"

"Depends I guess on how everything goes. I'd sure like to get the last of them timbers cut to length. Come tomorrow we could finish up lining the well and then start back filling. That is my hope at least."

"Sittin' here like we are ain't going to get it done. You ol' folk ready to get dirty and sore?" Colby teased as he downed the last of his coffee.

"My old bones are as ready as they'll ever be. You ready, Ed?"

"Sure am. Just let me finish this coffee. Only got a couple swallows left."

Ed brought his cup to his lips and took a drink.

"Who is going downstairs into that well when we have the timbers cut?"

"I ain't sure if we even discussed that. Ummm, I dunno. Ah, Colby, you think you can crawl down in there?"

"I knew this was going to be a question for me right from the start since Tanner ain't here, which reminds me, where the hell is he?"

"He's working, Colby," Ed said as he took another drink from his coffee.

"Well, I guess the only one here that has the man parts is me," Colby smiled.

He wasn't so sure he was up to the task, but also knew neither Ed or Riley could be expected to climb down. As for Bash, there was no hope in hell that he'd volunteer.

"I think I'd feel a lot better, Riley, if we had a plank or somethin' to set across those timbers, somethin' for me to stand on like we talked about yesterday. You got anythin' like that 'round here?"

Riley looked over to the stack of uncut timbers.

"I reckon we could use one of the timbers we cut today to go from side to side. We'll jus' make sure to keep one a lil' bit longer than the rest and that'll be the last we'll put in place. You think that would work, Colby?"

"No reason it wouldn't. So then, let's get cuttin' fellas. We have near a dozen that need sawin'."

Colby stood up and made his way over to the sawhorses and measured the first timber into four sections.

"All right, which one of you old timers is gonna stand up and start this first cut? You ol' folk cut 'em and I'll pack 'em to where the work needs doin'. Well? Which one is it goin' be?"

"I'll start off. Ed can cut the next and so on. Maybe in between the cutting those that ain't cutting can give you a hand packing, Colby."

"Nah, wouldn't want to see one of you ol' codgers pull an ass muscle. I'll be all right. Just make sure you cut them on the line. I already marked this first one out for you. Carry on," Colby said with humour.

And so the sawing began for a second and final time.

Tyrell, by now, had walked a few miles. Resting and sitting on a log on the side of the trail, he nibbled on a piece of jerky and instinctively pulled out a couple extra pieces for Black Dog. It saddened him when realised it.

"Damn, where are you, Black Dog?" he questioned the silence as he looked around and drank from his canteen.

Life was certainly going to be different without his two favourite comrades. Rested, he finally stood up and once more trod west. His footprints and rustling of leaves as they fell to the ground with each little breeze that blew were the only sounds in the quiet wood. His mind no clearer than it was that morning often wrestled with memories of his past. Visions of Black Dog as he grew and Pony's constant antics seemed to be highlighted with every thought and memory. Once in a while his mind drifted to Red Rock Canyon to Marissa and the people and places he left behind, but more than not he thought of Pony and Black Dog because they were the freshest memories in his mind. In time, those memories like all others in one's life would be forgotten. New and perhaps better memories would come along.

Tyrell stopped again as he looked west toward the first mountain pass he'd have to ascend. *Yep, she is steep, going be quite the walk,* he thought as he looked on. Looking to the sky he estimated the time.

"A few more hours and it'll be dusk. Ah, I'll walk a ways further, stop at the base of that hill and call it a night," he said quietly to himself as he proceeded.

264

Brady by now was getting close to the outpost. He hadn't passed any other traveller or for that matter any homestead.

"I don't reckon we're gonna get lucky finding Travis a steed by day's end, horse. We'll have to keep slogging onward. The outpost can't be much further," Brady said to himself as much as to the horse.

"Wonder how he's faring. Likely ain't even made the mountains yet. Knowing Travis, he'll stop at the bottom and set up for the evening. Not much point walking in the dark up no mountain, he'd say," Brady chuckled as he carried on.

An hour later the outpost finally came into view.

"There it is, horse and here we are. Don't look like anyone is about, does it?"

Brady slowed his horse to a stop and swung off, tethering him to the horse rail. He approached the small building and tried the door, but it was locked. He knocked a couple of times and was about to saddle up again and find a place to set up his camp for the evening when he heard footsteps inside.

"Hello, who is there?" Brady heard the voice from inside say.

"Name is Brady McCoy. I'm looking to buy a horse for a friend who lost his to a bear."

The footsteps grew closer and finally the door opened up.

"Brady McCoy, you say?" the man asked as he looked at Brady.

Brady reached out his hand to shake.

"That is right. I'm from the Fort."

"I knows where you is from," the man said as he shook Brady's hand.

"You say your friend lost a horse to a bear and you're lookin' at findin' one here?"

"That's right. Any chance you have one or know someone who might want to sell one?" Brady asked as the man gestured for him to come inside.

"I might have an answer come mornin'. There ain't no one here at the moment 'cept me and all I got is my mule, Buffalo Chips. You want a coffee, mister? I got some brewin'."

"Thank you kindly. I wouldn't say no," Brady replied as he removed his hat and looked around.

For an outpost, it was certainly small inside. It boasted a single bunk in one corner, a two stool table sat in the middle of the room and a counter was against the east wall with a couple of chairs. The woodstove was nearest the table and it gently warmed the place. The man gestured Brady to pull up a stool at the table and to sit.

"I'll have a coffee for you in a few short minutes," the man said as Brady sat down.

"You said you knew I was from the Fort. How did you know that?" Brady questioned now that he was seated.

"Your last name. I know of the McCoy's back easterly. You must be Ed's son," the man stated as he poured each of them a coffee.

"I am so. You know my old man then?"

Brady took the cup of coffee the man offered. "Thank you."

"You are welcome. Yes, I know Ed. By the way I'm sorry I never gave you my name. I'm Harvey Wilchuck."

Harvey sat down and added condiments to his coffee.

"Nice to meet you, Harvey. I don't suppose after this coffee you'll have any problem with me camping outside near here, would you?"

Brady took a swig from his coffee.

"Not at all. Heck you could probably lay out your bedroll on the floor if you plan on stayin' 'til mornin'. That'd be your best chance to find someone who'd sell you a horse, I think. Or I could lend you old Buffalo Chips and you could gather your friend. It's up to you."

Brady thought for a moment. It wasn't too late and if he did turn around and headed back to pick up Travis, it'd put the two of them at the outpost by the next day. He wasn't sure, though, how Travis would feel about riding a mule.

"If I don't find a willing horse seller in the morning, would you still lend me your mule? I've rode hard today to get here. Not sure I'd want to turn around. In the morning, though, I'd take you up on that offer."

"By all means, no problem."

The two men conversed pleasantly until their coffee was finished. Then, Brady took Harvey's invite to lay out his bedroll on the floor and spend the night.

Back at the Fort, Ed, Riley, Bash and Colby were finishing up for the evening as well. They had managed to saw all the timbers to length and had added another eight pieces to the well. Come morning they'd finish lining it.

"That's the last piece I want to play with today. Damn that took a long while," Riley said as he sat down and caught his breath.

"Yep, time to call it a day," Ed agreed. "I'm winded and tired myself."

"Tomorrow we'll at least get that water well of yours lined, Riley. If the rest of you weren't so damn eager to call it a day, I bet we could get another four timbers in place," Colby pointed out as he looked on.

"Nope, I'm done for the day. Got to keep something for the morning. How about we head over to the coach and have a splash of coffee?"

Riley stuck his hand out for someone to give him some help in getting up.

"I suppose we could stick around for a while longer. Colby worked his ass off today. I reckon he deserves a coffee," Bash said as he helped Riley get up.

"Good, c'mon then, let's get to making some. Damn back hurts like the dickens," Riley said as the four men walked over to Riley's coach and seated themselves around the low burning embers.

Riley tossed another log onto the coals and a few minutes later the flames began to dance. Adding water and coffee to the pot, Riley set it on the grate. It took a few minutes to perk, but finally it was done. It was good coffee, not too strong and not like tea. A short while later, Bash and Colby headed back to the station. Ed and Riley remained seated around the fire and finished the last of the coffee before Ed, too, headed for home.

"I'll see you some time tomorrow, Riley. I have to make an appearance at the office first, though. Then I'll swing by, likely the same time as today."

"All right, Ed. I guess I'll see you then," Riley responded as Ed swung up onto his horse.

"Yep, see you then, Riley. I know what the "C" stands for now on that can, so if you ain't got coffee going when I turn up, I'll get it started."

Ed turned his horse and headed for home.

Tyrell, too, was adding a few more sticks to his own fire at the base of the mountain road where he decided to set up his evening camp. It was a cool evening and he made the flames grow high as he warmed himself. Finishing up a few sticks of jerky, he laid out his bedroll and curled up next to the flames of his evening fire. Another day had ended.

Chapter 13

Sunday September 13, 1891. Rising before dawn, Tyrell stoked the fire, and set his coffee pot on the flames. His canteen was less than full. From what he recalled as he traveled east when he was making his way to the Fort almost a year earlier, there was a small creek near the summit of the mountain he would soon be traipsing over. It would take a few hours to make the distance on foot and he would certainly not die from thirst before then. The morning, as the morning before, was chilled. A dense fog enveloped the low valley he was in. He could faintly see the sun through the thickness. It was rising and in no time he knew the sun would break through and shine upon him. He had slept well considering things and his dreams as he slept were as he expected; all about Pony and Black Dog.

His coffee ready now, he poured his first. Today he'd have to drink it black as he had no sugar to add. Huddling over his fire, he drank it slowly and absorbed the heat from the flickering flames. He did his best not to think about what had taken place two days earlier, but his thoughts, of course, drifted to that very day. Inhaling deeply he sighed with disappointment and sadness. He tried to convince himself that at least Black Dog may have survived, but that thought was soon taken over with the possible reality that he did not. A new horse he knew was easy to come by. Sure it would never be like

Pony, but horses were a dime a dozen. Dogs weren't, at least none like Black Dog. In time, he knew, he could live with the loss of both, but for now he was finding it hard to do so. What he wished for was some laughter, something to bring him out of the state of mind he was obviously in. Soon he would get what he wished for.

Finishing his coffee, Tyrell kicked dirt onto the fire and rolled up his bedroll. Gathering the minute amount of gear he carried, he headed toward the mountain. Dragging his ass more than usual, he picked up the pace and in two hours of steady walking he finally made the distance to the slow glacial fed creek. Filling his canteen and splashing some of the cold water on his face he wiped away the sweat and dirt that ran down. In the two hours that he had walked, the sun had come out and now it was pleasantly warm, considering it was only near 7:00 a.m. That and the fact that he had been walking non-stop had certainly brought up his body temperature. He sat down on a rock and rested. He still had at least another two maybe three hour hike before he would crest the mountain and begin the descent into the valley below. In time he would get there. He wondered how Brady was doing in finding him a horse. It would sure make life easier if Brady met up with him some time that day towing behind an extra horse. Until then he would keep walking. Rested now, he stood up and continued his hike up the steep mountain trail.

Back at the western trail outpost, Brady and Harvey were beginning to stir. Harvey added some wood to the stove to make coffee while Brady relieved himself in the outhouse. Finishing his business, Brady made his way over to where he tethered his horse and checked up on him. The first visitor to the outpost that day was an old fellow who stopped in on Harvey every day and joined him for coffee. Today was no different. Noting the stranger standing by a horse he questioned if Harvey was awake.

"Morning there, young fella. Is Harvey up and about?" the man asked as he swung off his own saddle and tethered his horse.

"Sure is," Brady said as the man turned and walked inside.

"Morning Gustev. Coffee is brewing," Harvey confirmed as Gustev entered and sat down.

"Good to know. Can't never start my day without a coffee brewed by you, Harvey."

Gustev removed his hat and tossed it on the table as he waited for Harvey to sit.

"I see you got company, met a young fellow out front tending his horse."

"Yep, he pulled in last night. That's Brady McCoy from the Fort. Came here last night looking to buy a horse. Seems his travelling companion's horse was took down by a bear."

"You mean Ed's boy, Brady?" Gustev questioned with surprise.

He hadn't seen Ed McCoy in years. In fact, the last time he recalled seeing him, his son Brady was only a teenager.

"He's all growed up now, but that is Brady."

"I would have never expected in seeing the boy up here. You say his friend lost a horse to a bear?"

"That is right. You wouldn't happen to have any in your stable that you'd be willing to sell would you, Gustev?" Harvey asked as he poured him a coffee.

"Wrong time of year for that, Harvey. Mine have all been auctioned. Won't be getting another bunch 'til early spring. So, nope. I ain't got one to sell."

"I guess there is the Mountain High Ranch. They might have one."

"Wrong again, Harv; Benoit only has those fancy breeds and he ain't about to sell one to a McCoy. He and Ed haven't the slightest compassion for one another ever since Ed brought in that no good brother of his. The only place I reckon young Brady might be able to find a horse is that ranch... what the hell is it called?"

Gustev frowned as he tried to remember the name.

"You know, Harv, the one on the other side of Chase."

"You mean Dublin's Ranch?" Harvey questioned.

"That's it. The Dublin Ranch. They'd likely have one. It is a good four or five day's ride from here, though."

"What about Frank Diamond? You know if he got any for sale?"

"I never even thought about Frank. I know for certain his housemaid don't keep stock on hand when he ain't around. I ain't sure he is even back yet from that

Red Rock venture. Ain't saw any horses feeding in his fields; still has the cows, though."

"He's back. Rolled home, I think, last week. He and that Jake fellow are finished with the Red Rock find. Their contract expired a couple weeks ago. From the few words we shared the other day, the Red Rock find was worth every one of his blisters, he claims. I didn't mention that to you the last couple of times you sat at that table?" Harvey questioned with confusion.

Gustev took a drink from his coffee as he contemplated.

"Nope, I don't recall any such conversation. I should've known he'd be back by now. I knew that Red Rock contract expired this month. If he's back as you say, he might have one. I wouldn't bet on it though. His place is a lot closer, that's for certain. Maybe young Brady could head over there and find out. It's only a couple miles' ride. I'm afraid, though, if Frank ain't got any, then Dublin's Ranch is his only hope."

Brady by now was finished tending to his horse and he came back inside and sat down.

Gustev looked at him and chuckled with admiration.

"Harv here tells me you are Ed McCoy's boy Brady."

Brady, somewhat confused, smiled back.

"Indeed I am. You know my old man too, then, eh?"

"I do. He still running that bounty hunting establishment?"

"He is. Things have changed, though, for us," Brady mentioned as he poured himself a coffee.

"Oh, yeah. I heard about this new Government changing things for those in that business. I thought, though, those changes weren't going to be introduced 'til next year."

"That is true, but if you know Ed, you know how he likes to get on top of things. McCoy's don't retrieve bounties much anymore."

"If he ain't bounty hunting, what's he doing now?"

"We're now listed under the Private Security sector," Brady said as he took a swig from his morning coffee.

"We're full-fledged Private Investigators licensed and all and ruled by police law," Brady said with pride.

"Ain't that something. Congratulations. So you must work for your pa, then?"

"I do so and have been since I was eighteen or there about."

Brady took another drink from his coffee.

"Can I ask how you know Ed?" he questioned as he put his cup down and looked at the man across the table from him.

"Ah, geez, I'm sorry about that. I didn't introduce myself."

Gustev reached his hand out to Brady to shake.

"I'm Gustev Raincoat. I've known Ed for a long time. In fact that last time he and I met up, if I do recall, you were a teenager going on fifteen or sixteen. It's been a long time, Brady."

Brady shook Gustev's hand.

"Uhuh, to be honest, I don't remember you none. Still, it is nice to meet you Gustev. Harvey here knows Ed, too."

Brady looked over to where Harvey sat behind the counter.

"Odd how all these years later, I'm meeting up with two of my old man's acquaintances."

"It is a small world. Yep, I used to drink whiskey and play stud with Ed, Harv and I both."

Gustev now averted his eyes over to Harvey as well.

"Those were some good times, weren't they, Harv?"

"I recall many hangovers without a doubt," Harvey chuckled.

"Yep, we passed a lot of time downing shots of whiskey and dealing out cards, come to think of it."

Harvey paused for a moment as he pulled out an old ammunition box and opened it. He thumbed through a few items and then pulled out a piece of paper.

"As I was saying now that I think about it, Ed owes me twelve dollars. I got his IOU still. God damn."

He began to laugh.

"I forgot about this 'til just now as we spoke about those days gone past."

He walked from behind the counter and showed it to Brady for shits and giggles.

Brady took it from him and looked at it. He smiled as he looked it over.

"That was quite some time ago, Harvey. You ought to add interest to that."

The three of them chuckled.

"I'm sure if I were to go through some of my keepsakes, I might have a couple of those IOUs as well," Gustev responded after the laughter settled.

"Yeah, Ed he wasn't ever that good at five card stud. We always knew when business for him was slow 'cause he always wrote IOUs when they were. Always honoured them too. When times was good, though, he always paid on the spot."

Harvey smiled as he reminisced. It had been years since then and now he wondered where all the time had gone.

"Harv tells me you're looking at buying a horse? I would have been able to help you out a few months back," Gustev said as he noted Harvey's mind twittering.

That was the thing about Harvey. Every now and again his mind drifted and most times he didn't snap out of it for a couple of minutes.

"You have a few options, though. Frank Diamond, a neighbour not far from here might have one. If he don't, though, you'll have to head to the Dublin Ranch, west of Chase, 'bout four days ride," Gustev mentioned as he took a swallow from his coffee.

"Damn. I wasn't counting on that," Brady responded as he contemplated.

He couldn't very well leave Travis wandering aimlessly west for that long a period. That'd be a ten day round trip. They could be in Willow Gate by then.

"How far off does this Diamond fella live?"

"Three miles north, up along the old trail. If you like, I can wander on up there with you. Jus' let me finish my coffee."

"Sure. All right. I guess if I come up dry there, Harvey has offered me the use of his mule. I could then gather my associate and we could leastwise be back here by tomorrow. Ain't sure what we'll do after that," Brady said as he looked over to where Harvey stood for assurance.

"You wanna borrow old Buffalo Chips and that damn sidekick of his?" Gustev questioned with a half chuckle.

"Sidekick?" Brady asked, "Harvey never mentioned any sidekick."

Gustev looked over to Harvey.

"Hey, Harv you were going to lend Brady here that mule of yours to gather up that friend of his that lost his horse to a bear?"

Harvey shook his head as he came back to reality.

"Umm, sure was, yes. What is matter with my mule, Gustev?"

"Ain't nothing wrong with the mule. It's that bloody sidekick of his that he insists on traveling with. I sure hope for Brady's sake Diamond has a horse to sell."

"Come on now, Gustev. Chops and Buffalo Chips have been companions since day one. That is why I never butchered that damn hog."

Brady had a confused look on his face as the two old codgers bantered back and forth.

"Hold on a minute. That mule of yours travels with a pig, a real life pork roast pig?"

Brady wanted to be clear. If that were the case, it was the damndest thing that he ever heard.

Gustev looked at him and smiled.

"He sure does. Quite the thing to imagine, ain't it?"

Brady was at a loss for words and all he could manage was a simple 'indeed'.

Harvey poured each of them another coffee.

"Chops and Buffalo Chips ain't ever been separated. Bought them both at the same time six or seven years ago, I think. They've slept together; they eat together and most times seem to crap at the same time, too. Chops don't get in anyone's way. He tags behind and every now and again might take the lead. You'll hardly even know he is about."

Harvey pulled up behind the counter once again and sat down.

Brady was having second thoughts, however, thinking it might be an insult to Travis to show up towing a mule and godforsaken hog. At the same time, though, he thought it to be quite humorous in the event that it turned out that way. For now, he hoped that the Diamond fellow did have a horse to sell. Otherwise he had only a few other options. One was to head back east and take turns with Travis in riding his horse. Another was to head west to the Dublin Ranch that Gustev mentioned. The last but not least option was to take Harvey up on his offer to use his mule. One way or another it was going to be an interesting day. The only off thing about using Harvey's mule to gather Travis was that once they made it back to the outpost in a day or two, they'd still be without a second horse.

"There ain't no stagecoach that travels between here and Chase is there?" Brady asked.

If there were, he and Travis had one more option.

"Not 'til early spring. The last coach to leave this outpost was at the end of August. Most folks ain't traveling about this time of year. The coach can't make any profit during September through 'til May on this trail," Harvey responded with clarification.

"The odd horse traveller as yourself, though, comes by every once in a while. Other than on those rare occasions, this trail heading west to Chase and beyond ain't that well-travelled," Harvey added as he took out a plug of tobacco and pinched up a chew.

"Either of yous want a pinch?" he offered.

"None for me, Harv. No thanks."

"I don't chew none neither, Harvey, but thanks for asking," Brady said with a nod.

"To each his own, I guess, all right."

Harvey put the tobacco back in his shirt pocket.

"How about another coffee?"

"I reckon I'll finish this one up, Harv and take Brady here over to Diamond's place. When we get back, though, I'll sit again with you for a spell. Ain't got much on my plate today," Gustev responded as he finished his second coffee and set his cup down.

"You almost done there, Brady? Old Frank should be awake by the time we make the distance, depending, of course, on how much whiskey he drank last night."

"Ready as I'll ever be. I'm ready if you are."

Brady stood up and slid his stool back under the table.

"All right, then, let's get."

Gustev stood up.

"Keep the coffee warm, Harv. I'll be back shortly."

"I'll have a fresh pot ready. You'll be joining us too, won't you, Brady?"

"I will. You make damn good coffee, Harvey and I wouldn't pass up another."

The two men turned heel and began to exit.

"I wish you luck in finding your friend a horse. If luck ain't with ya, my offer to borrow my mule still stands," Harvey said before Brady made the door.

"Sure thing, Harvey. Thanks. I'll see you when we get back."

Harvey nodded as the two men exited.

The first thing Gustev noticed now that there was a little more daylight than when he first met Brady outside by his horse, was the extra saddle strapped to its rump. He stopped to take a second glance. He knew the work.

"Jesus, is that a Horst Voycanin saddle?"

"A what?" Brady questioned.

"A Horst Voycanin saddle."

Gustev looked closer. Sure enough, he saw the initials 'H.V. 1889'.

Brady was still confused.

"Say again," he asked.

"Horst Voycanin is an old fellow used to make saddles and boots and sell them out of his livery stable. Made the best damn saddles around."

"Really?" Brady questioned as he looked to where Gustev was looking.

"Yep, mine is made by him as well. It is a lot more dated then this one, though. Damn that is some fine work," Gustev replied as he continued to admire the saddle.

"This is your friend's saddle, I take it?"

"It is uhuh."

"Well, he certainly knows good quality. Horst don't make saddles no more."

"Why is that?" Brady asked showing interest.

"Can't make saddles pushing up daisies. He died a year or so ago. The date on this saddle is 1889, likely the last work he ever did. Your friend has quite the treasure there."

"I guess I now know why he was so adamant that I don't lose it and why he didn't want to leave it behind. We could've doubled here, but no way did Travis want to leave that saddle behind even though we could've stuck it up in a tree or something to keep the critters away and gathered it at a later date. Hell, he would have probably packed it if he had been alone. Really seems to like that saddle."

"I'd have done the same thing. Yes sir, this saddle will outlive him and is likely worth a lot more now then what he paid for it. You said your friend's name is Travis?"

"I did," Brady confirmed.

"His last name wouldn't happen to be Sweet would it?" Gustev asked with the same interest Brady had shown regarding the maker of the saddle.

"It might be. Why?"

"Curious is all. If it is he, he certainly has a reputation in these parts. I won't pry, though. It makes no never mind."

Gustev walked over to his horse and swung up onto the saddle, deciding to leave the questioning alone. Brady too swung up onto his horse and the two headed north toward old man Diamond's place and, he hoped, a new horse for Travis. They conversed as they travelled about this, that, and the other thing and sometimes about nothing at all. Brady came clean about Travis' last name being Sweet. There was no reason not to admit it as far as he was concerned and he was proud to call Travis his friend and associate.

"I'll tell you one thing, folks in these parts sleep better at night since he put to rest that Brubaker fella. He was a damn menace 'round here," Gustev said with conviction and truth.

"Earl, you mean?" Brady questioned already knowing the answer.

"The one and only. He was rotten to the core, that son-of-a-bitch. Pure evil he was."

"I knew he was a hired gun and those types live by their own rules. Ain't so sure he was evil."

"Oh, he was. I can tell you that. He had no problem belting around women, beating up drunks and taking advantage of anyone who saw him as a threat. He may have been a hired gun, but he was also a cold-blooded killer."

"What is the conclusion there, Gustev? What makes you think he was a cold-blooded killer?" Brady wanted to know.

He knew Earl had a reputation, but he never really did know why.

"I know of a dozen incidents and none less where he simply shot someone in the back. One of those he killed was my kid brother, five years ago up north near Vermillion. One day he got to playin' cards with my brother or so the story goes, lost a thousand dollars to Kitt. That was my brother's name. Kitt won it fair and square, but Earl saw to it that Kitt would never have a chance to use it. He waited outside the Vermillion saloon and the first chance he got to put lead into Kitt's back he took and ripped the thousand cash right out of his pockets.

No one in Vermillion wanted to get involved. They all knew Earl was quick with his pistol, so most was scared. Kitt got a good look at Earl when he took back the money. He lived a few minutes before dying, long enough to tell the lawman that was keeping law and order in the area who his killer was. The lawman, though, did nothing to bring justice to Earl. That is how the story goes, leastwise, and from a few that saw it took place later on admitted it was Earl that shot down Kitt. I never got an opportunity to avenge my brother's death. If I had, I would have shot Earl in the back the same as he did to Kitt. Your friend Travis did the world a favour when he killed Brubaker."

"I'm sorry to hear all that, Gustev, and my belated condolences on your brother's death. Travis, though, don't look at it as though he did anyone any favours. Most times he'd rather not talk about that. It bothers him some I think that he has that reputation. Obviously, on that day when he met up with Earl, he proved to be the quicker. A few months back he was approached by Alex Brubaker. Alex thought he might try his hand at killing both Travis and my old man. Travis, though, blew off a couple of Alex's fingers instead. The old man told me he never saw a man draw his gun so quick. Said Travis' speed was like that of the fluttering wings of a hummingbird."

"A man would have to be to beat Earl. Many tried and none of them walk the earth today. I hope your friend is aware that every hoodwink and gunslinger on this side of the Rocky Mountains is waiting for the day that they meet up with Travis Sweet."

"He's aware of it all right and half expects to be coerced into a few gunfights. I don't think he has much to worry about though," Brady said as he shrugged his shoulders, knowing full well that Travis would more than likely always come out on top.

A rickety old fence finally came into view and behind it some distance away was a matching house.

"That there is Diamond's place," Gustev said as he pointed at the house.

"Don't be fooled by the look of the place, Frank Diamond is a wealthy man. Owns most of the land 'round here and a few ore mining outfits too. Smoke is coming from the chimney so he must be home and awake."

The two men rode in silence as they approached the house. The yard was scattered with a bunch of mining equipment. Behind the house was a barn that seemed to be in better shape than the house and from it emitted the smell of horse and cow manure.

"You might get lucky, Brady. Smells like the barn is full of horses."

"Yeah, I got a whiff of that too. I sure hope so and if there are a few, I hope he's willing to sell one."

"He'll sell you one if he's got any. I can assure you of that. He does a lot of horse dealing with folks around here and keeps the stagecoach company stocked with fresh ones."

They pulled their horses up to the horse pole and tethered them.

"C'mon I'll introduce you," Gustev said as they made their way to the door and knocked.

There was no reply so Gustev knocked a second and third time. Still no reply came. He shrugged his shoulders and shook his head.

"Must be out at the barn. Let's go have a look see. He can't be far."

The two of them headed toward the barn when they heard an upstairs window open.

"Hello, who is that?" they heard a man ask as they looked up.

"It's me Gus. Got a fellow here whose interested in buying a horse if you got any, Frank."

"Shit. Gustev Raincoat? I ain't heard from you in a while. Come on back. I'll meet you folks at the door," Frank said as he closed the window and made his way downstairs to the front door.

Opening it, he reached out his hand to shake Gus's.

"You're looking good, Gus. Nice to see you. And this must be the fellow looking to buy a horse?" Frank guessed as Gustev introduced the two.

"Yep, this is Ed McCoy's boy Brady from the Fort."

Frank smiled and nodded as they shook hands.

"Nice to meet you. Brady, was it?"

"Yep," Brady responded.

"Your Pa is that bounty hunter from back at the Fort, ain't he?"

Frank knew the name McCoy. Most folks in the area did.

"That's us. Yep," Brady confirmed.

"Won't you folks come in? I can get Sarah my housemaid to make us coffee."

"I ain't sure we have the time, Frank. Brady here needs a horse. Has a friend back easterly some that lost his to a bear and at the present time is on foot."

"Ah, I see. A quick coffee ain't going to change that fact."

"No, it ain't, but we was heading west and need to make the distance as quickly as we can," Brady said.

"On business, then are yous?" Frank questioned somewhat disappointed that they were in a rush.

"In a roundabout way," Brady responded. "So, do you have any horses to sell, Frank?"

"Unfortunately, Brady, not today. I'm sorry. We got some coming in by week's end, so this Friday, if you'd like to come back. You can try Dublin's Ranch. He's always got horses."

"Yeah, Harvey and Gus here both mentioned that. Well, I guess that is it, then."

Brady sighed as he thought about his other option.

"Since that is out of the way, you sure the two of you can't join me for a coffee? It won't take long for Sarah to make it."

Gustev looked over to Brady.

"What do you say, Brady. You want to join Frank for coffee?"

"I hate to be rude, Gus, Frank, but I really ain't got the time. I need to head back and pick up my associate, one way or the other. And it looks like it is going to be the other," Brady said referring to borrowing Harvey's mule.

"All right, Brady. Like I said, I'll have horses here in a week and I never turn down a sale. You come back Friday; I'll make sure you get a good bred steed."

"I might take you up on that offer, or rather, Travis might. It depends I guess on how long it is going to take us to get back to the outpost and if we don't get lucky in finding a horse between now and then."

"Your friend's name is Travis?" Frank questioned with curiosity.

"Yes sir, and if your next question is if his last name is Sweet, the answer to that is also yes. Gus here asked the same. And yes he is the same Travis Sweet that took out Earl Brubaker," Brady summed it all up rather than answering a bunch of questions.

"Goddamn! I'd sure like to meet him," Frank said with sincerity and hope.

Brady half-smiled. He was beginning to understand how Travis always felt when folks put two and two together.

"You might get that chance, Frank, if we decide to come back around on Friday. Waitin' that long to pick up a second horse, puts us way behind schedule, though. Still, it might happen. Depends I guess on other events that might take place."

"Well, I hope things work out for the two of yous, if not..."

Brady cut him off there.

"I know, I know. You'll have horses by Friday. I'll tell you what, Frank; I'll talk it over with Travis. He might see the logic or he might decide to keep walking to the Dublin Ranch. Each day that we continue west puts us a day closer to our destination. A few days behind schedule is better than a week," Brady pointed out.

Frank waved his hand through the air.

"I guess you are right in that aspect. Okay, well, you know when and where to get a second horse if the two of you are so inclined to do so."

"That I do, Frank. Thanks again for the offer of coffee. Who knows, we might have a chance to sit down together come Friday."

Brady decided to leave it at that.

"Gustev, you going to head back to the outpost with me or are you going to stick around here a while longer, maybe get reacquainted with Frank," Brady asked as he turned and made his way back to his horse.

"I think I'll join Frank here for a coffee, that is, if the offer still stands."

"Of course it does, Gus. I'd love to catch up. Like I said, it's been a while since we sat down," Frank smiled.

He was glad to have the company, even if it was only for a quick cup of coffee.

Brady swung up onto his horse.

"All right, Gus, Frank. I might see you both in a day or so."

"Yeah. Okay, Brady. Let Harv know I'll be around soon."

"I will," Brady assured as he turned his horse and headed back toward the outpost.

It took him a few minutes to get there and after tethering his horse, he went inside. Harvey was cooking hotcakes on the wood stove and in a pot was a can of beans. The coffee pot bubbled and perked as well while the stove snapped and crackled.

Harvey looked over to Brady as he walked in.

"Made her back, eh? Any luck with a horse?"

"Frank won't have any available until Friday," Brady said as he found his cup and poured a coffee.

"I guess I'll be needing the loan of that mule of yours, Harv."

Brady made his way over to the table and sat down.

Harvey stirred the beans and flipped a couple of hotcakes.

"That is no problem, Brady. Care for some breakfast? Beans is done and I have four hotcakes ready to be ate?"

"I wouldn't say no. They do smell good."

Brady took a drink from his coffee as Harvey found him a plate and put a scoop of beans on it and the four hotcakes.

"Here you go, Brady. I'll get ya some butter and sweet Canadian maple syrup to go along with those if you like?"

"Ain't sure I'll need any of that. I'll mop up my beans with the hotcakes."

Brady dug in. The hotcakes certainly worked well with the beans.

"Forgot to mention," Brady began as he put a spoonful of beans on his pancakes and took a mouthful. He finished chewing before he continued.

"Harvey says he'll be by later. He and Frank I guess wanted to catch up."

"Ah, I don't suppose then I'll be seeing him today. He and Frank will get into the whiskey before too long. Frank has been away for a couple years, only came back last week."

Harvey continued to cook the hotcakes and once in a while gave the pot of beans a stir.

A short time later he joined Brady at the table and ate his own serving of beans and hotcakes. Brady, by then, had finished his and sat satisfied at the table with another cup of coffee.

"You have a time piece Harvey? I'm curious to know what time it is getting on to be."

"Sure do."

Harvey reached into his pocket and took out his pocket watch.

"Says near 9:00 a.m. according to my watch."

He put the watch back and continued to finish his breakfast.

"9:00 a.m., eh? I reckon once you get those beans done, but don't rush none, Harvey, once you get done there we should gather that mule of yours and I should head off. Ain't sure how far along Travis may be, but I don't reckon he's within walking distance yet," Brady slurped his coffee as he waited for Harvey to finish.

"Yep, we'll get to that soon," Harvey said as he too took a drink from his coffee.

"How far along do you suppose your friend is by now?"

"Knowing Travis, it is hard to say. He was a little off center yesterday morning when I left him. I could make a fair assumption he might be ten miles closer. I don't think we'll make the distance back here today. Might make it here by Monday, though, depending, of course, how things go from here."

"What are your plans once ya get back, since ya ain't got a second horse?" Harvey asked as he scooped up his last mouthful of breakfast.

"I ain't come to a decision on that jus' yet. I have a bit of an assumption we might carry on from here without a second horse. I know Travis ain't going to want to stick around too long. He'd rather walk, I'm certain, than wait for Friday to roll around. Going to have to play it by ear, I guess."

Brady shrugged his shoulders.

"Hell, you wouldn't even make the distance to the Dublin Ranch by Friday on foot," Harvey said as he stood up and set his and Brady's plates down on the back counter.

"I know it is a distance away. Gus mentioned that. Logic tells me we should stick around 'til Friday, get a horse from Frank and then carry on. Ain't sure Travis will see it that way."

"It turns out you folks decide to stay, my floor is free for yous to use. There ain't much to do around here, though, you'd still be welcomed."

"Thank you kindly, Harvey. It may turn out that way. As for not much to do, I'm sure we'd come up with something."

"There is always stud," Harvey smiled. "Anyway, if you're ready to meet Buffalo Chips I'm ready to introduce yous."

Brady stood up from the table.

"Lead the way, Harvey. That mule take a saddle by any chance?"

"You could slap one on him, yep, he don't mind. C'mon, follow me, Brady."

"Right behind you, Harvey," Brady responded as he followed Harvey out the backdoor and over to a small barn and corral. Harvey opened the gate and the two of them walked over to the barn. They hadn't even stepped inside when a loud squealing and huffing took over the sounds of morning. It startled Brady some.

"Jesus Christ! What the hell was that, Harv?" Brady asked with surprise and concern.

Harvey didn't need to answer as Chops came running to the opened door as though charging the intruders. Brady's eyes got big and he jumped to the side as Chops went darting by and began running circles in the barnyard. Brady, frightened somewhat, had lost his hat in the onslaught and by now Chops had it in his tusked jawed mouth.

"He's got my hat, Harvey. How the hell am I gonna get that back?" Brady asked with worry.

"Look at those damn teeth of his. You sure that is a pig, Harv?"

Brady had never seen such a big boar his entire life. Chops was as black as night, tall as the third rail of a fence and from what Brady guessed to be, near six foot long. Chops wasn't your everyday hog.

Harvey began to chuckle.

"Jus' walk up to him and take it back. He won't hurt ya none."

"No damn way, Harvey. I ain't going near that thing. What the hell? He's like a monster or something."

Brady continued to gaze at Chops. No way was he going to take his eyes off the pig. Harvey moved closer to Brady and stood beside him. The two watched as Chops sauntered around the corral with a mouthful of hat.

"You ain't afraid of him, are you, Brady? That pig is the gentlest and most protective critter I've ever ran across. He ain't no ordinary hog. He's a cross breed of a Hylochoeus and a Sus Crofa, leastwise that's what was told to me when I bought him and the mule."

Brady didn't avert his eyes once.

"That don't mean a damn thing to me, Harvey. What I see is the biggest, ugliest pig I've ever laid eyes on. Look at the size of them damn teeth."

"Nope, they ain't called teeth, Brady, them's tusks."

"Whatever they are, the damn thing looks like he could eat a man whole."

Harvey noting Brady's concerns and fears decided himself to play on it a while longer.

"He's near seven hundred pounds of solid muscle and fat. He could eat more than one man."

Harvey began to chuckle as Brady darted a look at him his eyes as big as saucers.

"Goddamn it, Harv, that ain't even funny. I don't doubt he could eat a man or two, but you didn't have to go ahead and confirm it."

"Ah, c'mon, Brady, let's go get your hat back," Harvey said as he began to walk away and toward Chops.

"Ya coming? I'll introduce yous. He ain't going to hurt ya none, Brady."

"I don't know, Harvey. He's staring at me right now like he wants to eat me."

Brady took a few steps forward.

"He comes charging me, Harv, I'll put lead in him," Brady said as he walked closer.

Harvey shook his head and laughed.

"Trust me; he ain't going to eat you, Brady. Might snot on ya, but that be it."

"Ain't sure I want any pig snot on me either."

Brady caught up with Harvey.

"The closer I get the uglier he looks."

"Oh, don't say that too loud. He don't like to be called that," Harvey said with sincerity.

He was, of course, only joking, but Brady bought it as truth.

"What do you mean? He can't understand words can he?"

"Like all domesticated animals, they learn a few and understand a couple more. Just don't call him ugly to his face."

"Hell, I'll never be close enough to his face, I hope."

Finally, making the distance to where Chops stood, Harvey reached out his hand and took back Brady's hat and handed it to him.

"See, that's all you'd have had to do, Brady. He ain't mean. No sir, are ya, Chops?"

Brady looked his hat over then put it back on his head.

"Never even put a hole in the brim with those damn tusks of his."

"Oh no, he'd never wreck a man's hat, nor would he ever hurt one. C'mon closer, Brady, let him get a good sniff of ya," Harvey coaxed.

Brady reluctantly stepped closer and Chops spun around and stared at him. Again, because of the pig's sudden movements, Brady jolted back and again his hat fell off. He didn't even have time to pick it up before it was in Chops' jaws once more.

"Damn, he's got my hat again, Harv."

"Walk over to him and take it back, Brady. Go on. I ain't getting it for you this time," Harvey said with a snicker.

"Come to think about it, Harvey, he can keep the damn hat. He seems to want it more than I do."

297

"So be it. C'mon then, let's go see the mule. I reckon Chops got your scent now anyway," Harvey said as he turned and started to walk back to the barn.

"Are you serious, Harvey? You ain't going to get my hat for me?" Brady asked as he trailed behind.

"Said you didn't want your hat no more."

"Come on, Harvey, you know damn well I was hoping you'd get it for me."

"Nope, not this time. You get it."

Brady stopped mid-stride and looked again at Chops and the hat dangling out of his jaws.

"All right, I've decided... he can keep it."

Brady turned and followed Harvey into the barn. Three stalls in, Buffalo Chips began to bray and kick at the boards of his stall. Brady shook his head, *what have I got myself into here,* he thought to himself as they made the distance to Buffalo Chips' stall.

"Here he is, Brady, this here is Buffalo Chips."

Harvey swatted the mules behind as he opened the stall gate.

"He's a good mule, both for riding and for packing."

"Leastwise he looks like an ordinary mule, not like that other thing that is supposed to be a pig."

Brady ran his hand up and down on the mules face as he got acquainted with him.

"So, he'll take a saddle, eh?" Brady questioned again to be sure.

"Yep, a saddle, no saddle, Buffalo Chips don't care either way. Let's get him out and about. C'mon Buffalo

Chips, Brady here is going need ya for a day or two," Harvey said as he led the mule outside and slipped the halter and reins on.

"There you go, Brady, he's ready. You want another coffee before setting off?"

"Nah, I best get on the trail. Don't want to get too late of a start. Going to be slowed down some towing a mule and pig. Likely won't meet up with Travis until sometime tomorrow," Brady said as he walked over to the outpost and gathered his gear and saddled up his horse.

A few minutes later he, Buffalo Chips and the ugly pig Chops, who still had Brady's hat in his mouth, were ready to leave.

"So, the pig is jus' going to follow. There ain't no special lead for it or anything?" Brady asked.

"Nope. He follows. Don't worry too much if you don't see him all the time. He'll be near even if you can't see him."

"All right, Harvey, I'll take you word on that. So I don't need to feed it or nothing."

"He'll eat the grass and twigs along the way if he gets hungry. He don't mind a bowl of coffee, black and strong first thing in the morning or at night. You give him more than two bowls, he might get a bit unruly."

"Hold on a second. He drinks coffee?"

Brady wasn't sure that is what Harvey meant.

"He does. You don't have to give him any if you don't want to. It keeps him happy though. He don't mind a handful of old grinds, either," Harvey smiled.

"Shit, all right. Is there anything else I might need to know before we start off?"

"Nope, that be it. Oh, one more thing. Buffalo Chips kind of fusses when being led by a man with no hat. It might take him a day to notice you ain't wearing one, so you might be okay."

Brady looked at him and shook his head.

"Damn you, Harvey. If the mule leads until I meet up with Travis I won't care."

"I hope he does. You could always get yours back from Chops."

Brady waved his hand through the air and turned east.

"We'll see you in a couple days, Harvey."

By 3:00 p.m. that afternoon, Tyrell had crested the first mountain range and was now faced with the next. It looked steeper than the first from where he stood. He rested as he looked on. His feet hurt and he knew he had blisters on both of his heels. He took a drink from his canteen and nibbled on a piece of jerky as he tried to decide if he were up to walking a few more miles or if he simply wanted to set up for the evening where he now sat. He was in a bit of a clearing and had a good view of the mountain and both east and west along the trail. He'd be able to see anyone approaching from either direction. *Yeah, I reckon best thing to do, is set up here for the night,* he thought as he removed one of his boots to look at the blister that was on his heel. His bloodied sock told him the story.

He poured water over the wound and washed away the dried blood.

"Damn," he said beneath his breath, "that hurt like a son-of-a-bitch."

He sucked on an eyetooth as he removed his other boot and did the same with the blister on that foot. Once the stinging subsided he put his socks and boots back on as gently as he could and then gathered wood for his fire. It was early he knew, but he was undoubtedly tired. By his estimation had walked steadily for seven maybe eight hours, four hours of which was up and over the first mountain and the second, as he noted earlier, was a lot steeper. His hope was that Brady would meet him near the top or on this side of it sometime the following day.

Back at Riley's place, Riley, Ed, Bash and Colby worked together the entire day to get the last few timbers in place for Riley's well. They were finished now and the four men admired their work.

"I'm sure glad we got that finished as early as we did. The sun still shines and is warm and wonderful," Riley said as he sat down on the pile of dirt.

"It was a cold evening last night and a cold start this morning. I reckon, though, the cold spell is gone for a while. Look at the western sky; red as the dirt I'm sitting on."

"I'm glad we got her done t'day as well. Being Sunday and all and early as it is, I might get my weekly bath," Colby hinted as he looked over to Bash.

"I could probably use one of them myself. I'm sure the widow Donale has a couple of warm baths still. I'd tag along with you folks if you're going to be heading that way," Riley said as he slowly rose.

"Well, it is Sunday and Colby does need a cleanup. Yeah, we can head over that way, Colby. You're going to have to wear those dirty clothes, though. I don't think the widow could have them washed and dried by the time you get cleaned up," Bash pointed out.

"It makes no never mind to me if the clothes is dirty. I'd jus' like to get all this damn sweat and stink off," Colby made clear.

"All right, well, if you folks are heading over to the widow's for baths, I reckon I'll head home myself," Ed said as the four men walked back toward Riley's coach and over to Ed's horse.

"I appreciate your help today, Ed. Thank you for lending a hand."

"No problem, Riley. Was kind of nice staying away from the office today. I hope to see you there tomorrow." Ed swung on to his horse.

"Yeah, I guess I should swing by. It is the beginning of a new week after all. I'll see you at the office in the morning," Riley nodded.

"Yep, we'll see you then, Riley. Good night, fellows," Ed said as he turned his horse homeward.

"What about the back fillin'?" Colby asked.

"I think I need to make an appearance at the office tomorrow, Colby. Depending on what I need doing there, we might still be able to start the back filling."

"You don't have to be here, Riley. I'll bring Colby by, no problem. He can slog dirt."

"That I can, Bash. Yep, a lot better than sittin' on a steel bunk all day."

"Okay, if that is all right by you, Bash, I'd appreciate it. Thanks," Riley said as he stepped inside his coach and grabbed a handful of clothes, soap and shaving razor.

"All right, I'm all set. Off to the widow's we go, I guess."

Chapter **14**

Monday, September 14, 1891. Tyrell stirred the coals of his past evening fire, and added a few sticks. Warming his hands above the flames he looked westerly down the trail. He didn't know how close Brady might be or for that matter if he was close at all. It didn't matter really. He'd keep walking regardless. Eventually they'd meet up, and with luck Brady would be leading a horse. Tyrell set his coffee pot on the flames and waited for it to perk. It didn't take long and soon he was having his first cup of the day. Wrapping his hands around the warm tin cup he looked east to the rising sun. Soon it would be out full and, by the look of it, it was going to be bringing heat. *Good. Looks like today is gonna be warm,* he thought as he continued his gaze of the eastern horizon.

He watched as the first few rays of sun peaked above the Rocky Mountains. When it came out fully he rolled up his bedroll and gathered the little amount of gear he carried. Kicking dirt into the flames and emptying his coffee pot, he once more headed west toward the next mountain pass. Forced to stop more than usual due to his blistered feet, it was taking him longer than he expected. He could see parts of the mountain trail from where he now stood as it snaked its way up. What he couldn't see was obscured by the patches of forest that scantily hid parts of the trail. Close as he was, the illusion seemed he wasn't making any distance. He sauntered on.

By this time, Brady was on the other side of the mountain and slowly making his way up and over. So far, the mule and pig hadn't been unruly and in fact Brady himself was almost used to the pig's presence. Even though the damn thing still had his hat between its jaws and he still hadn't attempted to get it back, he was slowly growing used to the fact that the pig was there for the long run. Deciding to rest, Brady slowed his horse down to a stop and slid off the saddle. Removing his canteen, he sat on a rock shaded somewhat. He looked easterly toward the mountain summit. When he had descended it two days earlier it didn't seem as steep as it now looked.

Mopping the sweat away from his brow with his shirt sleeve, Brady took a long swallow from his canteen. He looked over to Chops who, as usual, was staring back.

"I wouldn't be sweating like this if I had my hat, you damn pig."

Chops took a few steps forward, making Brady feel uneasy, then turned and carried on up the trail. Brady shook his head.

"I guess this is when the pig leads. Damn thing, anyway," he muttered as he brought his canteen to his mouth for one last drink before following Chops.

Swinging onto his horse he followed behind. It didn't take long before the pig vanished from sight; he was that much further ahead. Two hours later, Brady made the summit. Standing in the shade nibbling on clover was Chops. Brady smiled. Perhaps now that Chops was eating, he'd finally get his hat back. He looked around the grassy hill as he sat on his horse hoping to spot the hat. He did.

Trying not to seem conspicuous, he reined his horse in that direction and slowly rode toward it. He was about to swing off and grab it when he heard the ground rumble and the pig squeal. Before he could reach his hat, Chops once more had it between his jaws and stood there as if daring Brady to take it. Brady remained on his saddle and crossed his arms. Shaking his head he looked on.

"There is no damn way, pig, that I'm gonna fight you for that hat. No sir. You are big, ugly and quite frankly put a bit of a scare into me. Besides, it's all full of your snot and slobber; I ain't so sure I want it anymore," he said for the third or fourth time since the pig had got it from him.

Chops, satisfied that he still had the hat, turned and walked away back to his patch of clover.

Brady sighed in derision.

"Well horse, mule, I guess we'll rest up a bit here. Ain't much further and we'll be heading down. Somewhere between here and the other mountain range, we're likely to come across Travis," Brady said as though it mattered to his horse and the mule.

Swinging off the saddle, he sat on a log and drank from his canteen as the animals nibbled on the plush green mountain grass and clover. The sun was at its highest now and it beat down warm and pleasant. Brady enjoyed the serenity as he sat there listening to the sounds of fall. High alpine birds chirped, whistled, and fluttered by. Squirrels chattered in the distance and the warm gentle breeze that could only be the beginning of an Indian summer, caressed the tall mountain grass, making it sway this way and that.

It wasn't long before Brady once more set off with the mule and pig in tow and began his final ascent of the mountain. Making the distance to the top a short while later, he rested briefly before starting the descent into the valley below. Tyrell, by now, wasn't too far away. In fact, he thought he had spotted Brady on the mountain trail. He stopped and squinted as he looked to the distance. From where he was, though, whatever it was that he was looking at was just a blur. Cautiously, he carried on, never removing his eyes from the object that grew closer with each passing minute as he walked. Finally, he could make out a rider and indeed the rider was leading what looked like a horse. Tyrell's spirits lifted and he sped up his pace.

"Brady!" he yelled when he could finally make out that indeed it was him.

Brady looked up the trail.

"Hey, Travis," he said as he waved and began trotting toward him.

It wasn't until he grew closer did Tyrell see that what he was leading wasn't, in fact, a horse, but a mule. Anything, though, as far as he was concerned, was better than walking. Brady drew closer and was about to say something when all of a sudden, Chops came darting out of the bush and ran toward Tyrell hell bent for leather. Tyrell needed a second glance before he realised what it was that was running toward him. Dropping his bedroll he pulled a pistol from his holster and was about to pull the trigger when Brady began to yell.

"Travis, no, no, don't shoot! That pig ain't going to hurt you!"

Tyrell looked at Brady puzzled, his pistol still drawn.

"What the hell, Brady?"

Finally, Brady made the distance to where Tyrell stood. Chops just stood there in the middle of the trail, Brady's hat still in his mouth.

"Jesus, am I glad you didn't shoot."

"Why are you glad about that? What is that thing?" Tyrell asked with trepidation.

"Give me a minute to explain," Brady said as he slowed his horse down and swung off the saddle.

"You can put that pistol away, Travis. That pig ain't going to hurt you."

"That ain't no pig, Brady, no damn way," Tyrell said as a mater-of-fact.

"Yeah, it is. It's friends with the mule."

"What?" Tyrell was more confused now than he was beforehand.

"There weren't no horses for sale at the outpost nor did I find anyone that had any. Harvey, the fellow who works at the outpost, this mule and pig belong to him.

He was kind enough to lend the mule to me, but the pig travels with the mule. So, you see I couldn't borrow one without having to travel with the other."

"That is an odd relationship don't you think, Brady?"

Tyrell put his pistol back now that he knew the what and who.

"Why does that damn thing have your hat in its mouth?" Tyrell questioned as he continued to stare at the thing in the middle of the trail.

"Ah, he took it from me yesterday morning; I ain't been able to get it back from him since."

"Why not just take it back? You said he's harmless."

"Well, I don't know, Travis. To be honest, he kind of puts a bit of a scare into me, he's so damn big and ugly. Look at them damn things growing out of his face. Harvey says they're tusks."

"Yep, that is what they are all right and he is big and ugly, ain't he?" Tyrell agreed.

"Yeah, but don't say it too loud. Harvey says he don't like that. And he ain't had no coffee today neither."

"What? Coffee. That damn pig drinks coffee?" Tyrell shook his head and half chuckled.

"So I've been told; eats the leftover grinds, too."

The two men stood watching Chops. Every now and again he'd take a few steps closer and Tyrell and Brady stepped back a few.

"You know, he keeps stepping forward like that and we keep stepping back, we're going to end up back at the Fort," Tyrell pointed out with a slant of humour.

"We should probably ignore him and get on our rides."

"That brings up another question, who gets the mule?" Tyrell asked with a smile.

"I'm just teasing you, Brady, you can ride him," Tyrell joked as he stepped closer to Brady's horse as though he was expecting Brady to hand him the reins.

The mule he knew was for him, but a little bit of humour never hurt anyone.

"What, no... The, the mule is for you. I have a horse," Brady said with distraction and confusion.

"All right, I'll take the mule," Tyrell laughed.

Anything was better than walking in his damn boots. He had blisters on both of his heels and big toes. Tyrell walked over to the mule.

"These critters got names by any chance, Brady?"

"Yeah, the mule is Buffalo Chips, the pig, Chops."

Brady swung onto his horse.

"Buffalo Chips and Chops eh? Now ain't them unique names for a mule and pig," Tyrell chuckled.

"You know if the mule can take a saddle?"

"Harv says so. You gonna strap yours on?"

"If he can take a saddle, I ain't riding him without one. You ever ride a mule, Brady? They're a real pain in the ass literally to ride without a saddle."

Tyrell moved over to Brady's horse and untied his saddle.

"You need a hand with that, Travis?"

"Nope, I think I got it."

Tyrell cinched the saddle up and climbed on.

"Well, Brady, let's get. I reckon we still have a few hours of daylight. Should be able to get on the other side of the mountain before dusk."

"Yep," Brady said as he turned his horse back the way they came.

"So, you said no one near the outpost has any horses for sale?"

"There is one fellow that will have some come Friday. Other than that, nope. Was told, though, there is ranch west of Chase, the Dublin Ranch, four or five days ride from the outpost that'll have some. 'Less of course you want to stick around the outpost for a couple days and get one from that Frank Diamond fellow."

"Frank Diamond? Is that what you said?"

Tyrell knew that name, that is, of course, if it were the same Frank Diamond who worked for the Wake Up Jake mining outfit he had hired before he left Red Rock. Diamond knew his true identity. He had to avoid that introduction. The last thing he needed was for Frank to blurt out his name.

"Yep, Frank Diamond, he's some kind of miner or something that also sells horses. Sounds like you know him, Travis. Do you?"

"Nope," Tyrell lied. "I just wasn't sure I heard the name right."

"He'd sure like to meet the fellow that took down Brubaker, same as with Gus and Harv."

311

"Human nature, Brady, for folks who want to meet folks that killed others. Ain't a human trait I care much for. By the way, who is Gus?"

"Just another fellow I met at the outpost. He and Harv and that Diamond fellow are friends of some sort. They, well, Gus and Harv also know my old man."

"They know Ed?" Tyrell asked with surprise.

"That's what they said. They used to play cards and drink whiskey with him back in the day."

"Small world, eh, Brady."

"It is too, Travis. Small indeed. So, what do you think? Think we should stick around the outpost 'til Friday?"

"I ain't sure I want to do that. We're already a few days behind schedule due to all that has taken place."

"I'm aware of that, Travis. We ain't going to make the distance to the outpost until tomorrow. That leaves only three days until Friday."

"I need to think on it some, Brady. Gabe is expecting me."

"He ain't expecting you for another eight to ten days."

"True as that might be the longer it takes us to make the distance to Willow Gate, the greater the chance that if Crawford is heading that way that he'll take out Gabe before we get there. That is, of course, if he ain't already done it. Like I said, Brady, I need to think on it some."

"All right. We have another option," Brady mentioned as they continued onward.

"What might that be Brady?" Tyrell questioned.

"I kind of figured you wouldn't want to stick around, so I got to thinking today as I travelled that you could just take my horse and I'd stay behind 'til Friday, buy another and meet up with you in Willow Gate or down the trail some, whichever came first."

Tyrell nodded.

"That'd certainly work. I'd be three four days ahead of you, but that don't matter none. Gabe is only expecting me at this time. That's a good idea you bring up there, Brady."

"I figured you'd like that, since I know how you don't like to sit idle."

"Nope, you got that right," Tyrell stated with sincerity.

The truth was he didn't want all the attention it sounded like he'd be getting at the outpost when they finally made the distance nor did he want to meet up with Frank, not yet at least.

"How far along until your last evening camp, Brady?" Tyrell questioned, trying to estimate the time it might take them to make the distance.

"I'd say four or five hours; should get there by early evening. Might even be light out still," Brady answered as the two rode on.

"If it is still light out, you figure your horse could continue on? Or should we expect to stay at your last camp tonight?"

"The hill we're about to climb will be the depending factor, I reckon. The horse has already been up the one side and down and it won't be long before we're going up again and down the other. I take it you'd like to keep going 'til it gets dark?"

"Wouldn't want to push your horse none, but yeah, I would."

"Can't make no promises, but let's see how it goes. If the horse ain't too tired, I don't think he'd mind."

"All right. I sure hope we can make a few miles past your camp. It would put us closer to the outpost and the closer we are the less traveling we'll need to do come morning."

The two men conversed back and forth as they carried on. Every now and again they'd look around and made sure Chops was in the vicinity, although he wasn't always spotted. When they did spot him, he still carried Brady's hat in his mouth. It was an odd sight, seeing that big hog traipsing along with the hat in his mouth, not to mention the oddity of travelling with a hog in the first place. For Tyrell, it seemed peculiar that here he was riding a mule and the mule's best friend was a damn hog. It was reminisced of Pony and Black Dog. He felt the loss for a brief moment and it saddened him. Still, he put on a smile just *because*.

There was another man at the outpost that day. Around his waist he wore no holster, but in his right hand he carried a .45-70 long barrel rifle, U.S Ranger issued. Harvey knew right away that the man was not a local; *it wasn't like the rifle he carried didn't give that away.* He was dressed in casual garb, a mountain shirt and vest, denim pants and high top boots. His hat had seen better days and it looked tattered and worn. Harvey guessed him to be in his late thirties or early forties, his sandy hair was shoulder length and whiskers hid his weathered face. His eyes where grey blue and he stood about six foot, not over weight and not underweight, just simply fit. Whoever the man was and whatever he was doing there, Harvey couldn't turn him a way. The outpost had always been a refuge for many travellers seeking a warm meal and shelter for an evening or two and Harvey wasn't about to change that. He was cordial as the man approached the counter.

"Good afternoon, sir. Pleasant out today, isn't it?" Harvey questioned the man as he drew near.

"It is, I suppose," the man replied as he looked around.

"Any chance a man can find a whiskey around here?"

"Sorry, there ain't no saloon in these parts and the outpost don't sell it."

"Uhuh."

The man looked at Harvey, his grey blue eyes sharp and clear.

"Would a man such as yourself object to me grabbing a bottle from my saddle bags and sit a while?"

"I don't see any problem with that. I ain't got no complaints about a man bringing his own whiskey bottle inside. We do have coffee and I cook up quite a meal when inspired. Is there anything I can get for you, to eat that is?"

"I'll think on it."

The man turned heel and exited. Returning a short time later, he pulled up to the table and sat down. Cracking open his bottle of whiskey, he sat in silence as he poured himself a swallow. Harvey feeling the need that the man for whatever reason wanted to be left alone obliged and sat quietly himself behind the counter playing solitaire. The man hearing the shuffling of cards looked over to Harvey.

"You play?" he asked as he poured himself another whiskey and kicked it back in one shot.

Harvey knew exactly what the man was asking.

"I wouldn't say I'm a stranger to it," Harvey made clear.

"Well, I got a bottle of whiskey here; you have a deck of cards. If you're interested, grab yourself a glass and let's play a friendly hand or two. I've been on the trail a long while and ain't felt cards in my hands for quite some time."

"You're a gambler?" Harvey asked as he stood up and made his way over to the table and sat down.

"Nope, only play when the mood hits me," the man responded as he looked at Harvey and slid his bottle of whiskey over to him.

Harvey poured a glass and nodded his thanks.

"So, are you on your way to somewhere particular?"

"In time I hope to make it to Willow Gate; you know how far that is from here?"

"Sure do. It's a ten-day ride give or take."

Harvey shuffled the cards.

"You want to have a couple hands of stud, one or two card draw?"

"I'm all right with one draw," the man said as he poured himself another whiskey.

"You ain't afraid that these cards might be marked?"

"Not at all. Besides, we ain't wagering nothing. Go ahead deal them out."

"All right, by the way, before we get started, I'm Harvey and what did you say your name was?" Harvey asked as he cut the deck and gave them a good shuffle then dealt them out.

"Never said," the man responded as though he didn't want to mention his name.

Picking up his hand of cards he went through them and tossed two down.

"You can call me Ron," the man said as waited for Harvey to deal him two fresh cards.

"Nice to meet you, Ron."

Harvey looked through his cards and tossed two to the table as well. Dealing out two new cards each, he looked at his hand once more and waited for Ron to make his play.

"Got two queens," said Ron as he laid his hand out for Harvey.

"Shit. That beats my ace high. Your turn to deal."

Harvey sipped from his whiskey as he handed Ron the cards. And so his day went, playing five card stud with Ron. It didn't take long for the whiskey to be gone and by that time both men were slurring their words.

317

Ron won most of the hands that day and Harvey lost. Now as the evening grew dark, Harvey made coffee to sober up.

"I'm gonna make coffee, Ron; you gonna want some?" Harvey asked as he stumbled his way through the task.

"You make it and I'll drink it. I ain't gone through a bottle of whiskey like that in one sitting in a long time. It was a big bottle too. So I'm drunk and I need to sober up if'n I'm gonna head west tonight."

"Not much point heading out at this hour, Ron. Stay the night, sober up. I'll toss us together some food too. I jus' don't see any point in traveling whilst one is drunk. You might end up going in the wrong direction."

"Point. All right, I'll stick around. I likely wouldn't make much distance in this state anyway. How is that coffee coming, Harvey?"

"Not much longer."

Tyrell and Brady were also getting their evening coffee ready. They passed Brady's previous camp a few hours earlier and were likely only ten miles east of the west trail outpost. The horse, though, needed to stop. He had worked hard that day, up and over the same mountain twice with Brady on its back.

"We did good today, Brady. Made quite the distance. That is a mighty fine horse you got there; most would've wanted to quit hours ago," Tyrell said as he stirred the fire with a nearby stick.

"I'm surprised actually that the horse never gave up sooner. I figure we're ten miles, give or take a few, east of the outpost. If we'd stayed at my last camp it would be more like fifteen or so. I'm glad we carried on. Makes the trip tomorrow less miles to cover and easier on the animals, my horse in particular."

Tyrell nodded in agreement as he reached for the coffee pot. Now that the coffee was ready, he poured each of them a cup. Chops, sensing it was coffee time sauntered over so silently that neither Tyrell or Brady saw him approach and it wasn't until Tyrell finally sat back down did he notice how close the pig was. It startled him and he stood up in reckless surprise spilling his coffee.

"Jesus Christ, pig! Couldn't you have at least made a snort or something before sneaking up on me like that," Tyrell said as he looked at Chops, who simply continued to stare back.

"I think he may want a coffee there, Travis. I'll grab a cooking pot from my gear. Harv says he likes it in a bowl. I ain't got a bowl so a pot will have to do."

Brady stood up and retrieved his bean cooking pot and handed it to Tyrell who continued the staring contest with Chops.

"Why don't you give it to him, Brady? Why do I have to?"

"Nope," Brady said evasively, "I already told you, Travis, that damn thing puts a bit of scare into me. I don't know why, he jus' does."

319

"How do you suppose he's going to drink coffee with that damn hat of yours still clenched in his mouth?"

"He'll set it down. Maybe then you could grab it for me, Travis," Brady said with hope.

"No way. I ain't going to grab your hat, Brady. I'll put some coffee into this pot and set it down over yonder some, but I ain't grabbing your hat."

Tyrell slowly moved closer to the fire and poured coffee into the pot, never once taking his eyes off the pig. Setting it down a few paces away he made his way back to the fire and Chops made his way over to the pot.

"That is a strange hog, you know that, Brady? A hog drinking coffee; what a thing that is," Tyrell said as he refilled his own cup and watched as Chops slurped from Brady's bean pot.

The evening passed by and before too long the two men laid out their bedrolls. Tomorrow was another day. Tomorrow they would make the distance to the west trail outpost.

Chapter 15

Tuesday morning as Tyrell and Brady drank their coffee before heading off, Ron was saddling up his horse back at the outpost getting ready to head west. Harvey stood nearby and watched as Ron prepared to leave.

"It was nice meeting you, Ron. You ever come back this way don't forget to stop in."

"You can bet on it, Harvey. It was a pleasure meeting you too, and thanks for your hospitality, coffee and food."

Ron swung up onto his saddle and tilted his hat.

"I'll be seeing you, Harv. Take care," he said as he and the midnight black stallion he rode headed west.

Harvey watched as Ron disappeared down the trail his back to the rising sun. A short time later Gustev showed up for his coffee. Opening the door, he walked in and slumped down at the table. Tossing his hat on the floor, he put his elbows up and head into his hands. It pounded relentlessly.

"Morning, Gus. Looks like you have a hangover."

"Been at Frank's the last couple of days. Drank a drum of whiskey, I swear. My insides are pickled, Harv. How about some of that coffee of yours. Hell, bring the whole pot over and set 'er down."

Harvey chuckled as he brought the fresh coffee over and set it down.

"You want a cup or are you gonna drink it from the pot?" Harvey joked as he went to retrieve a clean cup.

"Cup, no cup, it don't matter any, as long as it is hot and strong."

Harvey returned with a cup and set it down.

"Best drink it from a cup, Gus. The pot might burn your lips."

"It might take the pounding in my head away."

Gus poured himself a cup and sighed.

"I tell ya', Harv, that Frank can sure put back the whiskey. I don't care if I ever see another bottle."

Gus brought the coffee to his lips and took a long welcoming swallow.

"Ahh, damn. That is good coffee."

"I had a visitor here last night myself, a fellow by the name of Ron. He weren't from around here I don't think, leastwise I ain't ever saw him. Played some cards and got into the whiskey ourselves. He left only a short while ago," Harvey mentioned as to make conversation.

"Look at us, Harv, two old folk with nothing better to do than to rot our guts with whiskey," Gus replied as he yawned.

"This time of year around here, there ain't much to do, Gus, so we got into the whiskey. Big deal; the hangover will pass."

Harvey poured himself another coffee.

"True as that might be, it's living through it that'll kill ya."

Harvey chuckled, "Well if we live through it, we didn't die from it."

322

"Yeah and if it don't kill us, it'll make us stronger. Ain't that what they say? But I tell ya, Harvey, I'm done with the whiskey for a while."

"I hear you, Gus. Me too, I reckon."

Harvey took a drink from his coffee.

"You feel like any food, Gus? I can make us something; I got salt pork and the fixing for biscuits."

"Some hot food jus' might cure my current health. Thank you, Harvey. I wouldn't say no."

"All right, let me finish up this coffee and I'll get to it."

It took Harvey a few minutes to finish his coffee and few more to cook up the biscuits and salt pork. The whole time, Gustev sat with his head in his hands, moaning about how badly he was feeling due to all the whiskey he had drunk. Finally the food was done and Harvey set a couple of plates out and tossed salt pork and a couple of biscuits onto each plate.

"Here you go, Gus," he said as he set the plates down.

"Hot and greasy, should fix us right up."

"Sure smells good, Harvey. Thanks a lot."

The two men ate the food and finished off a second pot of coffee as they sat and conversed. It was near 10:00 a.m. before either one actually began to feel better. Gus decided then to head home and sleep for the rest of the day.

"I might have a nap myself, Gus. I reckon Brady and that friend of his should be getting here sometime today. You going to swing by later?"

"Depends if I wake up before dawn or not. I'm god awful tired, Harv. I'll certainly be back in the morning, though."

"All right. If I don't see you later, I'll expect you in the morn," Harvey said as he walked with Gus outside to his horse.

The yellow sun was high in the sky and the two men squinted as they stepped out.

"Nice weather like this don't come around too often this time of year. Sure feels nice."

Gus swung up onto his horse.

"Yep, I reckon we might be having an Indian summer. I'd much rather have the sun than the frost. Anyway, Harvey, I'm off. I'll catch up with you in the morning."

"We'll see you then, Gus."

Harvey turned and went back inside deciding he didn't want a nap after all. It was too nice a day to pass up. He left the front door open and cleaned the outpost up some, swept the floor, did the dishes and generally made it look respectful again.

Brady and Tyrell were well on their way back to the outpost by then and around 2:00 p.m. they could finally see the small building come into view.

"There it is, Travis, the outpost," Brady said as he slowed his horse down and waited for Tyrell to pull up beside him.

"It don't look like much, does it?" Tyrell pointed out as he finally caught up to Brady and looked on.

"Nope, it ain't what one might expect of an outpost. There ain't much to it," Brady agreed as the two of them continued on.

Making the distance, the two men swung off their rides and tethered them to the horse rail. Brady looked around.

"You ain't saw Chops lately have you?"

"Come to think of it, no I haven't," Tyrell answered as he too looked around.

"There he is," Tyrell said as he pointed. "Looks like he still has your damn hat, too."

"That's all right. I'm jus' glad we didn't lose him. I guess he'll be along shortly. Let's get inside and let Harvey know we're back."

"Lead the way, Brady. I'm right behind you," Tyrell said as he followed Brady inside.

Harvey was standing behind the counter when they walked in.

"Hey, Brady. Was expecting yous today. How did the mule and pig fare?" Harvey asked as he came out from behind the counter and met the two men.

"Both are fine. Never gave us any trouble whatsoever."

"That's not unusual. Never expected them to give you any trouble. I see you still ain't got your hat."

"Nah, I decided along the way that Chops could keep it. It's pretty much ruined now anyway," Brady chuckled sheepishly, not wanting to tell Harvey that in fact the damn pig still made him uneasy.

"Oh, come on now, Brady, tell the man the truth," Tyrell teased as he sat down.

"The truth is that Brady is still afraid of that pig."

"I wouldn't say so much afraid, jus' leery is all," Brady stated.

"Anyway, Harvey, this here is Travis."

Harvey walked over to where Tyrell sat and reached out his hand.

"Nice to meet you, Travis," Harvey said as Tyrell stood up to show respect.

Tyrell shook Harvey's hand.

"The pleasure is all mine, Harvey. If it weren't for your hospitality to lend Brady that mule of yours, we wouldn't be standing here now. I appreciate that."

"Ah, it was no problem. I'm glad I was able to help. Not sure what the two of you are going do now with only one horse, but at least you're here and you're both welcome to stay until Frank gets his horses in on Friday. Brady did mention that, didn't he?"

"Yes, he did," Tyrell said as he sat down again.

"We've decided though that I'll carry on from here with his horse and he's going to stick around to pick one up from that Frank fellow."

"That is fine. You folks want a coffee?" Harvey asked as he turned to get the pot and a couple of cups.

"We'd love some, Harvey. Thank you very much," Brady said as he too now sat down.

Tyrell looked around at the inside of the small outpost. Brady was right there wasn't much to it.

"It must get lonely around here; not much business at this time of year, I don't reckon, eh Harvey?" Tyrell questioned.

"We only passed one other traveller as we proceeded here. Never saw another rider, horse, buggy or wagon after that."

Harvey made his way over to the table with the pot of coffee and three cups.

"Had a visitor here last night, a fella by the name of Ron happened by. He spent the night, actually. He had whiskey and I had cards. The rest of the story tells itself I suppose."

Brady and Tyrell looked at one another.

"This Ron fellow wouldn't happen to have been riding a coal black horse would he have?" Brady asked as he poured himself a coffee.

"As a mater-of-fact he did, yep. Why you ask Brady, do you know Ron?"

"In a roundabout way, you could say that, Harv."

Brady looked back to Tyrell.

"What are you thinkin', Travis?"

"I ain't sure what to think. How long ago did Ron leave here?"

"Early morning. I'd guess it were around 7:00 a.m. or thereabout. What is the interest the two of you have regarding Ron?" Harvey asked as he grabbed a stool from the counter and pulled up to the table.

He was curious now.

"We'll get to that shortly. You notice if he was packing a pistol or not?" Tyrell asked as he took a swallow from his coffee.

If it was the same Ron, aka Matt Crawford, he was only a half-day's ride ahead which meant it wouldn't take long for him and Brady to catch up.

"Nope, he had no holster. Carried a long barrel rifle, US government issue type."

"Sounds like that might be our man, Brady. What do you think?" Tyrell looked at him and raised an eyebrow.

"It could be. What else can you tell us, Harv?"

"Not much, I don't reckon. He was a nice fella. Played a mean hand of stud. Said he'd been on the trail a long while," Harvey shrugged.

"You going to tell me your interest now that yous have in Ron?"

"His real name is Matt Crawford. He's an ex-Rebel Ranger wanted for crimes in the U.S.A. and possibly a murder here in Canada," Tyrell said referring to the death of Miles Ranthorp, the Pinkerton man.

Harvey's eyes got big and his mouth dropped open.

"No way. It can't be the same fella. This fella never portrayed to me he was a murderer."

"Criminals don't go around bragging about their misdeeds, Harv," Brady pointed out.

"I jus' can't see him being that way. I do admit I had reservations when he first showed up. After spending the day playing cards and drinking whiskey with him those reservations became clear, that he was jus' a passerby in need of shelter and conversation which I gave to him."

Harvey shook his head.

"I still don't think he's the fella you two claim."

"We got a poster of his likeness. I'll get it for you," Brady said as he stood up and exited.

It took a few minutes for him to return and he set the poster down in front of Harvey.

"Did that fellow Ron look like this man?" Brady questioned as he sat down again.

Harvey looked at the poster and swallowed deeply.

"That does look like him. Jesus, so I was host to a murderer?"

"Yep, but you ain't got nothing to worry about, Harv. He ain't the type of murderer that goes around blasting folks for the fun of it. He has a list of names that he's going through and, trust me, your name ain't on the list," Brady confirmed.

"That don't make me feel any better, Brady. I can't believe I sat with him, but like I said he didn't come across to me as that man yous are portraying. No sir. He was quite cordial and friendly."

Harvey took a drink from his coffee.

"If it'll make you feel any better, Harvey, McCoy's ain't looking to bring him to justice by the noose. We want to get him exonerated for said crimes. There is more to it than we can speak of, but our interest ain't to prove his guilt, rather to prove the guilt of those he's killed and to prevent the killing of another," Tyrell explained.

"That does make me feel a wee bit better. Still I can't believe I sat with a killer."

Harvey shook his head, still not sure if it made any sense.

"Did he say where he was heading by any chance, Harv?" Brady asked.

"Sure did, yep. Said he was headin' west to Willow Gate."

"It is exactly what we suspected. What do you say, Brady? Should we double up and go after him; he can't be too far away."

"Doubling will only slow the horse down, Travis. He's saw me and Riley. He doesn't know you. You might get an upper hand in convincing him of our intent. I figure he'll recognise me and that'll only put him on the defensive."

Tyrell sat there and lowering his head he nodded at Brady's logic.

"That does make sense, I suppose. I guess if I'm going on alone, I best get. I might catch up to him this evening 'round his fire," Tyrell said as he stood up.

"Think your horse will be okay to travel some?"

"The ten or so miles we managed today ain't going to make him any less willing. I reckon he'll be fine as long as you don't run him."

"No worries there. I ain't about to go running toward what could be a gunfight. I'll go easy," Tyrell assured as he picked his cup off of the table and finished his last mouthful of coffee.

"That's done; I guess I'll head off. Your horse ain't going to mind me switching saddles is he?"

Brady stood up.

"Nah, I don't think he'll mind. Let's get them switched over. I know how you don't like that saddle of mine. Harv, I'll be back in a few minutes," Brady mentioned as he and Tyrell headed out and switched over the saddles.

"The old fellow Gus sure took a shine to this saddle of yours, Travis. He's got one made by the same hand."

"Is that right? Interesting indeed," Tyrell said not wanting to bring any more attention to the saddle and who it was made by simply because at that time it mattered little.

Tyrell swung up onto Brady's horse.

"If things go well, Brady, I hope to be back here early morn or later this evening. Hopefully, I'll have Matt with me. If I don't see you by tomorrow, you can assume things didn't go well. I'll be sure to leave behind a mark on the trail somewhere, a pile of rocks or something, once I get close to Crawford. Leastwise then you'll have something to go by if I don't make it back."

"Shit, Travis, quit talking like that. You know what you need to do and how to do it. It turns out you need to put lead in him, don't hesitate. A wounded or dead Matt Crawford ain't going to bring any less of a reward nor would it mean that we can't exonerate his name after death, if it turns out that way. Stay alert and ready, Travis."

"No worries there either, Brady. I know how I need to play this hand," Tyrell assured.

"Today could be our lucky day, Brady. I bring in Crawford, your trip to Willow Gate won't be necessary and you'll have to turn around and head back to the Fort with our prize. Gabe, I'm sure, will still be expecting me. He's the next apple we need to throw into the sack."

Tyrell tilted his hat and smiled.

"I'll see you later, Brady," he said as he turned Brady's horse west and headed after Matt Crawford.

"Be careful, Travis," Brady hollered after him as he headed down the trail.

Tyrell looked back and waved. "I'll get 'er done, Brady," he responded as he went on his way.

For three hours he headed west and by early evening he knew he was getting close because up the trail some he could see smoke rising in the sky, a telltale sign that not too far ahead was another traveller. *Was it Matt though?* That was the question and only time would give up the answer. At that point, Tyrell swung off Brady's horse and piled a stack of rocks on the side of the trail and with the heel of his boot he drew an arrow. *There, that ought to work should things go awry in the next while,* he thought as he once more swung up onto his saddle and carried on.

Anxious and somewhat nervous, Tyrell could sense that something wasn't right. He didn't know if what he felt was a good thing or a bad thing, but he certainly felt something. He scoured both sides of the trail as he

332

sauntered on, but saw nothing. Eventually the feeling he had subsided and he once more felt alone. The truth was Black Dog, who by now was healing up nicely from the vicious bear attack, wasn't too far away. He had picked up both Tyrell and Brady's scents the day before and he was now making the distance to the outpost. Only thing was, he wasn't following a trail. He cut through the bush using his sense of smell to locate the man he missed so dearly and in the process was soon followed by a small pack of rogue wolves, four to be exact.

They trailed behind him now like soldiers following their commanding officer. Black Dog had already proven to them that he was the alpha, the leader, and so the wolves' instincts were to follow the leader of the pack. Black Dog ignored them most of the time and only on occasion did he even acknowledge that they were indeed following him. The scent of Tyrell became stronger with each passing mile that the dog and his pack trudged. It was growing dark when his senses finally revealed to him that his master wasn't too far ahead. For a brief moment he sat down and stared in the direction from which Tyrell's scent wafted on the gentle breeze. With it came the scent of another man, one he did not know.

The four wolves also stopped and from the undergrowth they watched their leader as he scented the air. To them what they smelled was man. It confused them somewhat. *Why would their leader be interested in any man?* The wolves became uneasy. The largest of the four stepped out of the bush as though he were going to confront Black Dog. Black Dog, however, cared little about the wolves' intent and instead he turned around and faced the approaching wolf. With a low growl and curled up lip, Black Dog made his point.

For a short while the two animals stared at one another, neither one making any move toward the other. It was as though they were simply communicating, making a plan. Finally, the wolf turned tail and joined the others hidden in the bush. The wolf was clear on what it was their leader was doing or so it seemed. With a few growls of his own he communicated to the others. Now it would seem they all understood. Black Dog, rested now, was convinced that Tyrell was in need of help. He carried on at a running trot, the wolves following closely behind.

Tyrell was getting closer to what he suspected to be Matt Crawford's evening camp. It wasn't too far ahead, a mile or two at the most. Tyrell took this time to confirm that his rifle and pistols were loaded for bear. He wanted nothing more than a casual confrontation and an easy apprehension. His plan was to approach as though he were only a traveller himself, ease his way into conversation and when the time was right, make his move. It seemed simple enough. Matt, though, was no dummy and one slip of the lip, Tyrell knew, could be disastrous and perhaps even deadly for either him or Matt. The only advantage Tyrell knew he had was having the pistols around his waist and knowing the speed with which he could draw them. Matt's advantage, however, was the distance from which he could send lead into a man's heart.

Tyrell inhaled deeply as he thought about that. For all he knew Matt was already sighting in on him. That thought in itself caused a shiver to go up his back.

"Although I walk through the valley of death, I shall fear no evil," Tyrell said beneath his breath as he turned the last bend in the trail and saw the low burning flames of a small fire off to the side.

He sauntered on. The only sound he heard was that of his own heartbeat and the clip-clop of Brady's horse.

"Hello there," he blurted out as he drew closer. He couldn't see anyone standing or sitting near the fire and this concerned him. Removing the hammer ties that kept his pistols from falling out of his holster, he slowed the horse down and with caution proceeded forward.

Matt Crawford stood in the bush a short distance away from the gentle glow of his evening fire, his horse tethered only a few paces behind. He had heard the traveller coming and now waited for him to approach his fire. From where he stood he would get a clear view of the passerby once the traveller made the distance to his fire. He sat in silence, his breathing low and steady, his rifle across his knees as he crouched there watching. Tyrell slowly approached. He could confirm now that no one was near, not even a horse. More uneasy now than ever, he once again called out.

"Hello, is there anyone here?"

He looked in all directions, but due to darkness he saw nothing.

Matt brought his rifle up to his eye and looked through the scope at the man now standing at his fire. From the way the man was dressed and the manner in which he seemed to be looking around, Matt didn't even need to second guess. The man he was looking at was either the law or bounty hunter. Sighting in now at the lone man's horse, Matt confirmed what he already knew. The horse he was looking at he had seen at the Fort in McCoy's corral. Not sure what it was he wanted to do at that point, Matt lowered his rifle and looked back to his own horse. He could simply swing back on the saddle and hightail it. That, of course he knew, would only make the man pursue him and eventually others would follow too. His other option was to simply shoo*t. Damn,* he thought to himself. He wasn't a killer and killing the man at his fire would make him so; and running would only bring more heat. For a few more minutes, Matt contemplated and finally decided that killing the man was his only viable option if he didn't want to swing from a rope or spend the rest of his life in prison.

Inhaling deeply he once more brought his rifle up to his eye and sighted in on the man who now seemed to be looking directly at him. It was the reflection from the fire that showed the glint of Matt's scope. Noticing this, Tyrell knew he had only one chance to dodge what was coming his way. As Matt pulled back the hammer of his rifle, Tyrell ducked and rolled into the shadows and over the bank. With a pistol drawn, he looked back to where he had seen the glint, but saw nothing. Matt, though, could see Tyrell's silhouette and sighting in on it with steady hands he pulled the trigger.

The big .45-70 echoed with a loud clap in the silence of early evening. Dirt and rock scattered in all directions as the projectile ricochet off the hard surface of the ground only inches from where Tyrell looked on. Rolling again to his side, he quickly slid along the bank until the small fire that continued to burn, giving off some light, was directly in his view. The forest grew deathly silent as he waited for more rifle reports. He could see nothing move nor hear any sound. He continued his gaze of the forest on the other side of the trail, hoping for some clue as to where Matt was.

Matt, unsure if he had made a clean shot, concentrated on the area where he saw the man's silhouette. Nothing moved. He used the scope to look closer. The crater in the ground on the other side where he sent his bullet told him the story. *He had missed.* Although he had missed by only a fraction, a miss was a miss.

"Won't make that mistake twice," he said to himself in a low voice.

Looking now along the bank, he tried to decipher any anomalies, any out-of-place shadow or a silhouette, anything that could possibly be the man he was trying to kill. Finally, there he was. He had a clear view and once again he pulled back the hammer and sighted in. Before he could pull the trigger, however, Tyrell slid down the bank some. He, too, had seen Matt in the nick of time. He knew now the general area. Removing his hat as to not make himself an easy target, he cautiously crawled up the bank a short distance away and looked back to where he had seen Matt. To his surprise, he now had the upper hand. Matt was still crouching in the same spot. Obviously, he hadn't noticed that Tyrell had spotted him a few seconds earlier. Matt simply assumed that the man was going to pop up his head anytime in the same spot. He waited.

Tyrell without his own rifle had only his two .45 pistols, neither of which he knew would be as accurate as his rifle.

"Shit, should've grabbed my rifle," Tyrell said beneath his breath as he watched to see if Matt was going to move closer.

Matt, though, lay stock still. Tyrell continued his gaze as he contemplated how he was going to pull off the charade, and live to tell about it. He was over-gunned and under-powered. He had to use his wits.

Looking back toward the fire that was slowly growing dimmer as the flames slowly died, he thought about perhaps crossing the trail. The forest, though, as dense as it was, would never give him the clear view of Matt that he had now and his pistols at that distance weren't going to be much help. There were too many rocks and shrubs in the way that could easily deflect a pistol's bullet. As for his horse, he had no idea in which direction it might have darted off when Matt fired the rifle. Tyrell knew he had only one shot, that was all. If he missed, Matt would know exactly where to look and the gunfight would be on. In the darkness of evening it would be anyone's win.

For one reason or another, after a few more minutes of stalemate, Matt called out.

"Mister, if you ain't hit, I'll give you one chance to get." Matt tried baiting the man to respond.

If he did, he'd know where to send his next bullet. Tyrell was no dummy either and he knew what Matt's ploy was. He shook his head.

I could I suppose answer back, then like a madman crawl back to where I first was. That might throw him off some; give me that extra second to get the drop on him. He fires once, it'll take a second or two to reload that rifle of his, Tyrell thought. Then he decided to play.

"I ain't hit, Matt and I ain't here to cause grief. I'm here to help," Tyrell responded as he headed back to where he once was.

He was actually surprised that Matt didn't fire. It also ruined his plan. Matt decided to keep the man talking. If he talked once he'd talk again and eventually he might get that fatal shot off.

"Help me? How the hell are you going to help me and what makes you think I need any help?" Matt hollered back.

"Shit," Tyrell said beneath his breath.

Matt obviously knew what he was up to.

"I'd say there are ten thousand reasons why you need my help."

"You talking about that stupid monetary reward there is for me?"

Matt now looked in the direction the man's voice came from and he sighted his rifle in, but he saw nothing and once again the evening grew silent. The whole time that Matt talked, Tyrell moved again. This time he managed to cross the trail. Speaking now, he knew, would certainly be his downfall. Matt, on high alert because the man didn't respond, looked around in all directions and listened for any sound.

Tyrell crossed again to the other side of the trail and responded. His hope was it would keep Matt interested in that particular area and maybe give him some time to circle around before Matt replied.

"That is what I'm talking about, Matt. That and a certain letter you once wrote to your sister Anne, some time ago. My name is Travis Sweet. I work for McCoy's out of the Fort," Tyrell responded as he stayed behind the cover of a few boulders.

Matt hearing this looked on, puzzled at what he had heard. Tyrell realising that he may have hit onto something remained where he was as he waited for Matt to respond. Minutes passed by, then a few more. Neither man moved. Finally Matt hollered back.

"Letter? What do you know about any letter I sent my sister and how the hell do you even know I have sister?"

Matt, still sighting in on where Tyrell's voice was coming from, now waited for Tyrell's response.

"Two men, three or four years ago, were hired by your sister's husband to keep their eye on her while she was running for office. They intercepted a letter you sent her, regarding what you knew about the way things was being run down there in the U.S., the crooked government and all. Any of that sound familiar, Matt?"

"Who signed the letter?" Matt questioned back.

If the response was Ron Reginal, then he'd know that this Travis fellow wasn't lying. Still, he had grown cold since all that took place and there was one more man that needed to pay. He wasn't convinced that he wouldn't kill the bounty hunter on the other side of the trail regardless. Getting taken in at this stage wouldn't serve Gabe Roy any justice or so Matt thought.

"If I give you the name of who signed the letter, would you agree to a cordial talk regarding such? No guns involved?"

Tyrell knew that Matt wouldn't likely agree to those terms, but it was worth a try.

"Nope. I wouldn't agree to that at all. My business ain't done yet. There is still dirt that needs to be swept away. I will, however, allow you to walk away to live another day."

Tyrell sighed. The more they talked the more it seemed it wasn't going to end well for either of them. He decided to try another tactic.

"Is that dirt you talking about, a fella by the name of Gabe Roy?"

Matt slowly lowered the hammer of his rifle back into a non-firing position and bowed his head as he contemplated. His mind racing.

"I ain't going to answer that until you give me the name of who signed that letter."

341

"It was signed Ron Reginal," Tyrell responded.

Matt shook his head as he thought about that letter. It could, he always knew, in the least, prove his innocence of certain crimes that played their role in his losing everything he once had and falsely naming him as the killer of a few certain men. The only thing was, and the only reason he hadn't turned himself in yet was due to the fact that for all these years, he thought the letter to be lost. If it were lost, he could never prove his innocence or his coherent mindset at the time it was written or, for that matter, his reasons for killing those he had.

Although he felt a sense of relief that the letter still existed, he was sceptical on what the outcome would be if he were to set his rifle down for the final time and admit his wrongdoings and his reasons for his actions. As far as he was concerned, the men he admittedly killed deserved nothing less. In a court of law, the law, he would hope, would see it the same. Still, he wasn't sure it would ever end like that.

Matt looked across the trail.

"So, you have a letter and a name. I still don't see how you can help. I'm in it deep, mister bounty hunter."

"Yep. Some might see it that way, Matt. Others don't. McCoy's is one of the *'others'*. We also heard tale and have a witness who says you saved a town full of folk up in Vermillion when Talbot Hunter came a calling. And as you know, you're the same man who killed a Pinkerton named Miles Ranthorp after he killed two of McCoy's men's horses and left the two men stranded out in the middle of nowhere. I believe that alone proves you ain't a cold-blooded killer that the U.S. law has made you out to be. This is Canada, Matt. Things is different."

Tyrell inhaled deeply. How he wished he was making headway.

"I ain't so sure things are different. The moment the U.S. Marshals found out that I've been brought in they'd come a running. I don't want to take that risk. I was once a Ranger myself. I know how they think."

"I know you was a Ranger once, Matt. I also know you we're a damn fine one too, decorated and all."

"Yeah, well, that don't matter much anymore, does it?" Matt said as he brought his rifle up to his shoulder and pulled back the hammer again, now that he had a good idea on where Travis was.

"You see, mister bounty hunter, I ain't got much left. I may have been decorated once, might have even had a pension coming to me. It's all gone now though; I don't suppose my own extended damn family, including my sister, want me in their presence. I'm likely a bad apple in their eyes by now."

"What makes you think that? You spoke to any of them since?"

"Nope. No need too. I also know how they think."

Matt now had a partial visual on Travis. He kept the rifle tucked into his shoulder waiting for the opportunity to send lead into him as he waited for Travis to respond or to move in one direction or the other. Travis, unaware that he was once more in Matt's line of sight continued to talk.

"That is all hearsay, Matt. If you ain't spoke to them, you're making plain assumptions. That's all."

"Well, sometimes assumptions is all we have."

"I can't deny that. Right now I'm assuming one of us ain't going to see tomorrow," Tyrell tossed back.

"That is a pretty good assumption I think, mister bounty hunter. 'Less of course you turn around and walk away."

"You know I can't do that, Matt. We can sit here for the rest of the night until dawn bantering back and forth, but the *'fact'* that you are either going to kill me or me you or the other option which I prefer which is to take you in alive and well, so that you can at least face a fair trial and be exonerated, ain't going to change."

"The fact is, mister bounty hunter, I'm not going to submit to you. Nope, I think I'd much rather have it out here. So, we're back to square one, I think."

"Come on, Matt. You don't want to kill me any more than I you. I'm telling you we can help. What do you have to lose except a few more days of running free after you kill me before you're faced by another man who might not be so interested in seeing you get a fair and just trial? I ain't the only one on your trail at this moment, Matt. I can assure you of that."

"That don't mean nothing to me. I've had men tracking me for years now and guess what? They still do, otherwise you and I wouldn't be yelling back and forth across this trail."

"Again, Matt, I can't argue that point. Sooner or later though, you'll mess up and somebody will be there with the cold steel of a pistol against your head."

"Until that time, I prefer to finish up what it is I started," Matt responded.

Neither man saw or heard as the four wolves and Black Dog surrounded Matt. It was the snap of a twig behind him that Matt even noticed the predicament he was now in as all four wolves showed themselves. Matt spun around and was about to fire at one of them when from out of the darkness he was overtaken by Black Dog. Tyrell hearing the snarls and ruckus stood up quickly, his pistol ready to fire. His first thought was, of course, that Matt was indeed being attacked by wolves. He ran across the trail in the direction of the noise and fired a few rounds into the air hoping to scare the intruders away and save Matt all at the same time.

Making his way through the bush he sprinted up the embankment stumbling as he went. Gathering his composure as adrenalin coursed through his veins, he broke through the bush to where Matt now lay, Black Dog standing on his chest. Tyrell's heart sped up and he shook his head in disbelieve and awe, thinking that maybe he had been shot by Matt and this was his death dream. No dream though he knew could ever be so real.

"Black Dog!" he exclaimed as he dropped to his knees. Tears welled up in his eyes and for a brief moment he cared little about Matt Crawford.

"This is your dog?" Matt asked as he looked over to Tyrell.

Tyrell looked at Matt and smiled.

"Damn right he is," he admitted as he kicked Matt's rifle out of reach and secured him with a set of handcuffs.

"Did he hurt you any?" Tyrell asked as he looked Matt over for any gouging wounds. Not seeing any, he averted his attention to Black Dog who proudly stood by.

"Jesus, Black Dog, am I ever glad to see you, you ol' son-of-a-gun," he said as he wrapped his arms around the dogs chest and hugged him gently.

"You never mentioned you had a dog," Matt said as he looked on and shook his head knowing he had been beat.

"Up until this point, I wasn't so sure I still had. Thought he'd met his maker, same as my horse did some miles east of here a few days ago."

Tyrell reached over to Black Dog and scratched him behind the ear.

"Where did the rest of them go?"

"The rest of who?" Tyrell questioned, not sure what Matt was alluding too.

"The wolves. Must've been at least three or four of them," Matt said as he looked around dazed and confused.

Tyrell shook his head.

"Never saw any 'cept my dog sitting on your chest when I got here."

"I could've swore I saw wolves."

"You just might have, Matt. I fired into the air a couple of times whilst I ran over. That likely scared them off."

Tyrell helped Matt stand up.

"You ain't hurt any are you?"

"Nah, not really. My pride more than anything," Matt responded, as Tyrell guided him back to the trail and the coals of Matt's fire, Black Dog trailing close behind.

"I bet you weren't expecting things to turn out like they did eh, Matt?" Tyrell questioned as he now helped Matt sit.

"Nor did I. I thought one of was going to die tonight. Thanks to Black Dog, we'll both see tomorrow."

Tyrell looked over to Black Dog who now lay at the base of the fire and he smiled. His life was once more half-full. Tossing a few sticks onto the low burning embers, Tyrell, Matt, and Black Dog watched in silence as the flames came to life. Once they did, giving light to the lonely trail, Tyrell finally stood and looked around for Brady's horse.

Finding the horse's tracks heading west, he knelt next to the fire.

"Looks like my horse took off down the trail some. Yours is jus' up yonder. I'm going to leave Black Dog here in charge and gather them. Trust me, Matt, don't try anything stupid. The dog don't take too kindly to that. I should have the horses rounded up in no time. We'll talk then."

Tyrell stood up.

"You stay here, Black Dog, keep an eye on Matt," Tyrell said with confidence as he went about rounding up their horses.

It didn't take long to complete the task and soon afterwards he was once more sitting near the fire. The horses were tethered nearby. Matt was secured, but most importantly for Tyrell, Black Dog had come home.

"Sitting here with my hands in cuffs knowing I'll be facing the law soon sure makes a man think," Matt said as he looked into the flames of the fire.

"I imagine so. You have a lot going for you though, Matt."

Matt looked up to Travis.

"Like what?"

"Well, you saved all those folks up in Vermillion for one. Two, you gave up a dead man's horse to two of McCoy's men. Three, you cleaned up some dirt that walked the earth, including Talbot Hunter. Four, Ed McCoy has that letter you wrote your sister. And five, you used to be a U.S.A. Ranger and was well decorated. There ain't nothing about you, Matt, that is off center. You ain't crazy and you ain't a cold blooded killer either. Any law man and or circuit judge that is worth his salt will see that," Tyrell pointed out.

"Could be all that is true. Could also be ain't no one going to care. Every man I killed had a family. They may have been dirt, but they were still men. To be honest, Travis, in a sense I kind of feel relieved that it is all over. It was a lot of weight on my shoulders. Feels good to lose that weight now, even if it means I'll be hung."

Tyrell shook his head.

"I don't think you'll be hung, Matt. I think the worst case is you'll spend a few years behind bars; might not even spend any. Once the truth about the who, what and why comes to light and we get you a good lawyer my hope, as well as the rest of us that work for McCoy's, is that you'll be exonerated. A free man."

"A free man with no prospects might as well be a hung man."

Matt looked into the flames of the fire once more as his mind and memories drifted to a better time in life when he served justice and upheld the law.

"I wouldn't say you ain't got no prospects, Matt. I think you have plenty once we get this mess all cleaned up."

"You seem to have a lot of faith in that, Travis. Why is that?"

"I like to think you'll get a fair and just trial. I have to have some faith in the law and what is right and wrong. There are others, too, Matt. They're going to see it for what it is, not what folks have made it up to be."

"You think so? I guess in five or six days we'll know."

Matt looked into the flames of the fire again.

"By the way, I was going to ask earlier while we was screaming back and forth, you said your last name is Sweet, are you the..."

Tyrell cut him off there.

"The same Travis Sweet that took down Earl Brubaker? That I am, Matt. All the attention that has brought to me doesn't make me feel any better about the fact. I regret that life event. It is what it is, though."

"There aren't many men that don't have some kind of regret in their lives. Why should two folks like you and me be any different," Matt pointed out.

"My regret is that I won't get my chance to clean up one more lead deserving man."

Tyrell looked across the flames and to Matt.

"You mean Gabe Roy, don't you?"

"He stole one hundred thousand dollars from Anne and took away from many others their means to support themselves. What I mean about that is he took their land in shoddy land deals and bullying. He was also a player in the assassination plot to kill Anne. I ain't sure what part he played and I'll never know now, but he played a part all right. I would bet my last dying breath on that."

"I should let you know, Matt, that McCoy's is onto Gabe Roy. In fact, I'm on my way to Willow Gate to be personal protection for him or so he thinks.

In all actuality, I have a deeper reason than that. With what you only now said to me, I think it would be in your interest to fill Ed McCoy in on what Gabe did to your sister. When McCoy's unmask his corrupt ways, you could be one of our witnesses."

Tyrell looked deeply into Matt's eyes.

"Before you go off on the fact you don't want to do that, you should know that being our witness, will protect you from the reaches of Canadian law until such time that we complete our investigation and bring law justice to him."

"You're talking about statement and such, ain't ya?"

"Yep. Give Ed your statement on anything and everything you know about Gabe Roy. Ed will declare you as a provincial witness needed by McCoy's firm. The Mounties won't have any say on what happens to you after that, leastwise not until we finish up with our investigation. Don't get me wrong, Matt. It doesn't mean you won't eventually face a judge for your past crimes, but you'll be under McCoy's care and direction until such time. Plus your cooperation will undoubtedly be noted by Federal and Provincial judges. I'd think on it before I said *'no'*. It will benefit your trial if there ever is one."

"Of course, there'll be a trial. Why wouldn't there be?" Matt asked.

Either way as far as he was concerned, he was going to hang.

"The only crime the law knows about that you committed here in Canada was shooting that Pinkerton - Ranthorp and for what he did to Brady and Riley by killing their horses, I can almost guarantee the law will frown more on what he did. When McCoy's can prove that Ranthorp also murdered Emery Nelson in Hazelton, an employee of McCoy's no less, a murder that you claimed to witness as well according to what both Brady and Riley have already stated, no federal or provincial law will see what you did to Ranthorp as murder."

Tyrell threw his hands up in the air.

"The rest of your crimes were all down south. I have a good feeling once you shed light on all that has taken place, Canada law ain't going to care about what happened down south. There'd be no extraditing you south. In other words, you'll be free up here in Canada. You might not ever be able to go back to the states, but Canada is a big place. Lots of room for a man to start anew."

"Why wouldn't there be no extradition? The marshals would jus' come up from the south and take me back on their own accord."

"That is a possibility, but you'll have gone before a judge already by then and if said judge declares you innocent of those crimes as well as the killing of Ranthorp, you'll have no criminal record up here. After that, you can work on your Canadian citizenship, take an oath and be done with the U.S.A. With that taken place and as long as you don't go south, U.S. law would have a lot of red tape to cut through. Yeah, there are a few steps to take and a few barriers to get over, but I know it can be done."

Tyrell was certain of that and he was right in every respect. It all boiled down to Matt's willingness to cooperate with both investigations: *Gabe Roy's corruption and Miles Ranthorp's cold-blooded killing of Emery Nelson.*

"What I know as fact is that Ranthorp is the very man I saw leaving that bounty hunter's room. I heard every shot. Some were muffled and I reckon that would be due to both the wall thickness and perhaps a pillow also being used to help hide the sound... but I heard it."

Matt grew silent for a moment as he relived what he saw that night when Emery was killed.

"It was Ranthorp who stepped out of that room. I got a good look at his face as well as the gun in his hand and the clothes he was wearin'. It was indeed that Pinkerton man. Then, he ran down the backstairs. Of course, I left directly afterwards, knowing without a doubt the lawman up there would have accused me and I would have been accused of another murder that I did not commit," Matt said with sincerity and conviction.

As an ex-U.S.A. Ranger, he knew he was an invaluable witness for the McCoy's and Travis did talk sense. Matt looked over the flames.

"I'll be McCoy's witness. If I can't put lead in Gabe Roy, the least I can do is help prove his guilt."

Tyrell smiled and nodded his head.

"You are making the right decision, Matt."

"Let's hope," Matt responded as he thought about the commitment he just made.

"I told you at the beginning, Matt, that I was here to help, more than to simply bring you in. Now you know there is more of a reason. McCoy's don't see you as a man guilty of murder, but a man forced to act; one we want to see get exonerated. By helping us, you have already helped yourself in that process."

"I guess I ought to tell you something, too."

"What's that?"

"Seconds before the wolves or your dog pounced on me, I had a clear shot of your head and I was going to pull the trigger. I'm glad now things were interrupted."

Tyrell's eyes got big.

"You ain't nearly as glad as me, Matt. Whew, I had no idea you had a visual."

He shook his head at his own lack of alertness and fault for not paying attention and what the results could have been.

"I did," Matt nodded with seriousness.

"Your dog, though, like you said earlier, saved us both tonight, you from death and me from the guilt I would have had to carry around knowing I killed a man without providence."

There was nothing else that needed to be said. The two men grew silent as they thought about what the outcome of their confrontation could have been that night had it not been for Black Dog and the grace of God's hand.

Chapter 16

It was 10:00 a.m. on Wednesday morning when Tyrell and the wanted fugitive, Matt Crawford, arrived at the west trail outpost. Sliding off Brady's horse, Tyrell tethered him to the horse rail. Then, he helped Matt get down from his horse and tethered his horse as well. By now, Brady and Harv were both standing on the porch looking on.

"Morning, Brady, Harv. I'd like to introduce you to Matt Crawford. Harv, you know him as Ron."

Tyrell and Matt stopped short of the steps.

"Got some other interesting news as well. Brady, you might like this."

Tyrell looked around and whistled a couple of times and finally Brady saw the news Tyrell was talking about. Prancing toward the outpost trotted Black Dog. Brady's eyes lit up and he smiled.

"Now that right there, Travis, is a sight long awaited. He found you did he? Damn, that is impressive," Brady said as Black Dog made the distance.

Brady knelt down and scratched him behind the ear.

"Good to see you back with the living, dog. Travis has certainly had a run of good luck, hasn't he?"

"Yep, I sure have. It all started last night. C'mon let's get inside and I'll tell you all about it," Tyrell said as he led Matt indoors and got him seated.

355

Harvey perked a fresh pot of coffee as Tyrell told the tale on what had taken place the night before, right down to the detail about almost being shot.

"So, if the dog hadn't jumped in when he did, chances are you'd be dead or gravely wounded and Matt would have been on the run again, eh? Well, I'm certainly happy for the way it turned out," Brady commented as he now looked over to Matt.

"We've been huntin' you a long while, Matt, and since Travis here has explained our intent and you have agreed to being our witness regarding a couple of investigations, I'd say you pretty much proved your innocence to me. Ain't even sure I see much point in keeping those handcuffs on ya. What do you say, Travis. Think we can trust Matt not to run?"

Tyrell took a swig from his coffee as he contemplated the question.

"The truth is, Brady, until we get him into McCoy's holding cells, he's a fugitive and a risk. Even though I might agree about what you're asking, I think it is best to keep him under guard, if only for his own protection. Sorry, that's the way I feel about it."

Matt sat in the corner. He knew Tyrell was right and he understood his reasoning.

"It's okay, Brady. Travis is right. I'm a fugitive. It ain't that far from here to the Fort anyways, is it? I don't mind keepin' the cuffs on. I'd more appreciate them up front though," Matt shrugged and smiled.

"That, I don't have trouble with," Tyrell said as he stood up and undid Matt's left hand from the handcuff and snapped it back on once Matt brought his hands up front.

"There you go, Matt. That probably feels better leastwise. I am sorry about the formalities and all."

"Don't sweat it, Travis. I understand," Matt said as he made himself comfortable.

Tyrell made his way back to the table and sat back down.

"Brady, now that we have Matt, I think I'd like to carry on west to Willow Gate. Of course, that will leave you with only one horse, but that is what we had anyway. You reckon I could carry on west with yours while you and Matt wait 'til Friday. It's only a couple days away and I'm certain Matt ain't going to be no trouble. He's got too much to lose at risk."

Brady nodded, "I can't deny we still have Willow Gate as a priority, Travis, but damn, holding up here for a couple of days with Matt as my prisoner and with the odd passerby that comes around every now and again, are you sure that'd be a wise thing to do?"

"Hmmm, ya. I see your point. Him being cuffed and all would certainly make folks talk."

Tyrell looked over to Matt and then back again to Brady.

"I guess then this relates back to your first question, Brady. Can we trust him un-cuffed? The two of you would then seem to any passerby that you were the same, simply travellers waitin' for a second horse. I know we could trust Harvey not to mention it. Can't be sure that no one else might recognize Matt, though. Damn, complications."

Tyrell took another drink from his coffee as he tried to come up with a viable solution.

"The barn is warm. No one goes to the barn but me. Matt here and Brady could leave through the backdoor if anyone shows up between now and Friday. It ain't nothin' for me to lock the front up and open it when someone knocks or hollers. Most folks know I close the front during the stagecoaches off season. It wouldn't seem no different than any other day here at the outpost," Harvey pointed out.

Brady contemplated the idea for a brief moment. It wasn't something he'd have hoped the solution would have been, but there really wasn't an option. It was indeed important for Tyrell to carry on to Willow Gate. They had Matt and the plan had always been if they apprehended him before making Willow Gate, it would be Brady who took him back to the Fort.

"All right, then. I guess we got a solution to the problem, Travis. You don't mind Harv if we put Matt's horse in the corral do you? It would be less conspicuous that you have company that way. We can't very well leave him tethered out front," suggested Brady.

"By all means. I ain't got no problem with that. In the meantime while no one is here, Brady, you and Matt can make yourselves comfortable. You'll only need to slip out back if'n someone shows up. Simple," Harvey shrugged.

Tyrell inhaled deeply. He was glad there was a solution and that Brady agreed to it. Now he and Black Dog could make their way to Willow Gate with one less distraction. Matt was in their custody, Black Dog was back, he had a horse to use, one he kind of liked. It wasn't Pony that was for sure, but it wasn't Buffalo Chips either, Tyrell smiled to himself. Although Pony would never be in his life again, he was content knowing that he had been. With the return of Black Dog, the pain of Pony's loss was somewhat lessoned and with the apprehension of Matt Crawford, he had one less worry to grapple with regarding Gabe Roy. Things were far from perfect, but at least now they were far less perilous.

Eight days ride north-west of the outpost, Tanner McBride was on the outskirts of Fairmount as he coursed his way to Hazelton and hopefully to some answers regarding the murder of Emery Nelson, McCoy's man. As well, he hoped to get any information he could dig up on Miles Ranthorp - the Pinkerton man witnessed by Matt Crawford to have been the possible killer or any other information he could discern on the correlation between both incidents. He had travelled hard and steady for four days. Tired, dirty and wanting a hot meal and bath, he slowly rode into town. Tethering his horse, he made his way to the front desk of the hotel and paid for an overnight stay. To his surprise, the saloon seemed to be hopping with patrons for that time of day. At a table in a scantily lit corner, four men were shuffling cards and playing poker. Tanner's curiosity now piqued, he ordered a draft beer and made his way to a table a short distance away.

For now he'd watch the men, and perhaps in time he would ask to join. *There is no time like the present to build up a reputation as a gambler as I travel north, a damn good cover for a man looking for answers,* Tanner thought as he sipped his draft and reminisced about days gone past when gambling and women were his *forte*. He questioned himself as he sat there if he even still had the moves. It had been so long since he delved into such activity, leastwise at the professional level. A smile crossed his face as he recalled how much fun it had actually been. The money, the booze, the beautiful women and the feeling one got when winning, the adrenalin that coursed through his veins when faced with a sore loser. Tanner shook his head at the memories. He wasn't that person anymore, but he could certainly play the part to a lesser extent and at the same time dig for answers among the ring of men that gambling brought to every town. Perhaps he should have rethought that decision, but for now that is what he decided and so began his efforts into that investigation.

Back at the outpost, Tyrell was checking over his gear, getting ready to head west to Willow Gate. He and Brady had talked over all that needed talking about and the sooner he headed out the better. Chase and Willow Gate were still miles away. The afternoon sun still shone and he and the horse had rested long enough.

"All right, Brady, I guess I'm set. Regardless of the time it'll take me to make Chase and a telegraph office, I'll make sure to send a telegram to Ed and fill him in on what has transpired. Remember this too, Brady. Colby is likely going to already be sent on his way by the time you and Matt begin heading back to the Fort. You'll need to keep that in mind as you travel. We ain't sure what he and Alex might have up their sleeves, if anything. Jus' something to keep in mind, I guess."

Tyrell wanted to make clear and to remind Brady that anything was possible.

"I know. I ain't worried. Matt is in our custody now and I'll be damned to give him up if that is what you might be referring too, Travis," Brady replied with assurance.

Tyrell nodded, "Good. I guess if things do turn sour you can arm Matt. That'd even up any odds," Tyrell pointed out as he smiled and swung onto Brady's horse.

"Matt's rifle is in its scabbard, it's emptied and his bullets is in one of his saddlebags. Make sure you secure them, Brady."

Brady chuckled.

"You know I will. Now go on, get. You have a lot of miles to go, ten days' ride at the least. Me and Matt, well, we only got four. Make that six since we ain't likely going to be riding out of here before Friday. Still it is less than you. Once we get Matt all squared away, I just might turn around and follow behind you, Travis, if not to give you a helping hand in whatever it is you may need help with, then to leastwise gather my horse,"

Brady smiled. "This thing in Willow Gate just might take longer than any of us anticipate. Good luck with it, though, Travis, and keep sharp."

"Like you, Brady, I ain't too worried on what might be down the trail some. Not now. Matt is with you, Black Dog is with me, hell, what could go wrong?"

Tyrell waved, turned Brady's horse west, heeled his flanks and set off for Willow Gate and the trials and tribulations that lay ahead. That was September 16, 1891.

Other Books by Brian T. Seifrit

A Bloodstained Hammer (with Alison Townsend
MacNicol)
The Coalition of Purgatory
Voracity
Red Rock Canyon
Return to Red Rock
The Missing Years Part I
The Missing Years Part II

Forth Coming- Matt Crawford's Exoneration
Followed by: Willow Gate Justice
Followed by: A Wayward Uncle

William Jenkins, Publisher

This publishing activity was started in 2014 for the purpose of self-publishing mystery-adventure stories that are supplementary reading for elementary school students (about Grade 5). The titles as follows:

The Case of the Ancient American
The Case of the Brainy Birds
The Case of the Cannabis Cat
The Case of the Diligent Detectives
The Case of the Electrified Envoy
The Case of the Forgotten Fort
The Case of the Greedy Goat
The Case of the Hidden Hound

Mr. Jenkins edits and publishes stories submitted to him. See http://williamjenkins.ca for details on this free service.

Mr. Jenkins can be contacted at:

williamhenryjenkins@gmail.com

67530700R00207

Made in the USA
Charleston, SC
15 February 2017